W9-AGP-268

Praise for the Paige Turner Mysteries

MURDER ON A HOT TIN ROOF

"Paige is a delightful, irresistible, funny, and charming sleuth. She is witty and observant and Abby makes the perfect Watson to assist her. I found Amanda Matetsky's knowledge of life in the 1950s interesting and informative . . . I enjoyed this book for its wit and likable characters. A good read with some good laughs." —*Gumshoe Review*

"It is refreshing to be back in a time where good, old-fashioned gumshoeing got the work done. Paige is a believable heroine whose teeth-gritting in the light of being a working girl in a man's world will make the blood of any woman boil, while her antics with her free-spirited neighbor will have you laughing! This is a delightful book and every mystery reader will love to read on." —*Roundtable Reviews*

"Lively characters, loads of offbeat charm, and spirited hijinks . . . What makes this book fun is Paige's saucy narrative voice . . . Amanda Matetsky invests her heroine with enough pluck, sincerity, and charm to make this an entertaining ride." —*Habitual Reader*

"[The] banter is delightful and quick and moves the story along at a fast clip . . . From the first line to the last, the action never stops . . . The tale is pert and funny. I enjoyed the characters for their freshness and enthusiasm." —*MyShelf.com*

HOW TO MARRY A MURDERER

"The author has successfully evoked the spirit of the people and the times of the 1950s and New York. The characters are delightful, especially Paige, who is hardworking, energetic, clever, and funny." —*MyShelf.com*

continued . . .

Berkley Prime Crime titles by Amanda Matetsky

MURDERERS PREFER BLONDES
MURDER IS A GIRL'S BEST FRIEND
HOW TO MARRY A MURDERER
MURDER ON A HOT TIN ROOF
DIAL ME FOR MURDER

Dial Me for Murder

Amanda Matetsky

BERKLEY PRIME CRIME, NEW YORK

THE BERKLEY PUBLISHING GROUP
Published by the Penguin Group
Penguin Group (USA) Inc.
375 Hudson Street, New York, New York 10014, USA
Penguin Group (Canada), 90 Eglinton Avenue East, Suite 700, Toronto, Ontario M4P 2Y3, Canada
(a division of Pearson Penguin Canada Inc.)
Penguin Books Ltd., 80 Strand, London WC2R 0RL, England
Penguin Group Ireland, 25 St. Stephen's Green, Dublin 2, Ireland (a division of Penguin Books Ltd.)
Penguin Group (Australia), 250 Camberwell Road, Camberwell, Victoria 3124, Australia
(a division of Pearson Australia Group Pty. Ltd.)
Penguin Books India Pvt. Ltd., 11 Community Centre, Panchsheel Park, New Delhi—110 017, India
Penguin Group (NZ), 67 Apollo Drive, Rosedale, North Shore 0632, New Zealand
(a division of Pearson New Zealand Ltd.)
Penguin Books (South Africa) (Pty.) Ltd., 24 Sturdee Avenue, Rosebank, Johannesburg 2196,
South Africa

Penguin Books Ltd., Registered Offices: 80 Strand, London WC2R 0RL, England

This is a work of fiction. Names, characters, places, and incidents either are the product of the author's imagination or are used fictitiously, and any resemblance to actual persons, living or dead, business establishments, events, or locales is entirely coincidental. The publisher does not have any control over and does not assume any responsibility for author or third-party websites or their content.

DIAL ME FOR MURDER

A Berkley Prime Crime Book / published by arrangement with the author

PRINTING HISTORY
Berkley Prime Crime mass-market edition / September 2008

Copyright © 2008 by Amanda Matetsky.
Cover illustration by Kim Johnson.
Cover design by Rita Frangie.
Interior text design by Kristin del Rosario.

ISBN: 978-0-425-22050-4

BERKLEY® PRIME CRIME
Berkley Prime Crime Books are published by The Berkley Publishing Group,
a division of Penguin Group (USA) Inc.,
375 Hudson Street, New York, New York 10014.
The name BERKLEY PRIME CRIME and the BERKLEY PRIME CRIME design are trademarks belonging to Penguin Group (USA) Inc.

PRINTED IN THE UNITED STATES OF AMERICA

10 9 8 7 6 5 4 3 2 1

For the readers who've stuck with me
from the first Paige to the last

Acknowledgments

I am infinitely grateful for the support (and tolerance) of my family and friends—especially Harry Matetsky*, Molly Murrah, Liza, Tim, Tara, and Kate Clancy, Ira Matetsky, Matthew Greitzer, Rae and Joel Frank, Sylvia Cohen, Mary Lou and Dick Clancy, Susan Frank, Ann Waldron, Nelson DeMille, Dianne Francis, Art Scott, Betsy Thornton, Santa and Tom De Haven, Nikki and Bert Miller, Herta Puleo, Esther and Harold Schoenhorn, Marte Cameron, Sandra Thompson and Chris Sherman, Cameron Joy, Donna and Michael Steinhorn, Stephanie and Burt Klein, Lois and Eric Rosenthal, Mark Voger, Gayle Rawlings and Debbie Marshall, Judy Capriglione, Martha Cevasco, Judy Dini, Betty Fitzsimmons, Nancy Francese, Jane Gudapati, Carleen Kierce, April Margolin, Doris Schweitzer, Carol Smith, Roberta Waugh, and her right-hand man, St. Joe.

The Lovely/Lively Literacy Ladies—Julia Berkowitz, Anne DuPrey, Carole Edwards, Demetria Muldaur, and Marilyn Tinter—are the most literate (and amusing) friends a writer could ask for. And my co-agents, Annelise Robey and Meg Ruley of the Jane Rotrosen Agency, and my new editor at Berkley, Kate Seaver, are the skillful, cheerful (and patient!) ones who make it all happen. Many thanks to one and all.

---

*Hats off to my husband, Harry, who slogged through a bad case of writer's block to pen the poems of Jimmy Birmingham. It was hard work, but somebody had to do it.

Prologue

LIFE IS JUST A DREAM, THEY SAY, BUT LATELY mine has been more like a nightmare. Shocking, sweaty, and horrifying—filled with visions and demons so ugly and evil they'd cause even the bravest soul to wake up screaming. You may think I'm exaggerating, but let me assure you I'm not. I've experienced things in the past few days no woman should ever have to endure . . . or even know about.

But don't worry—I'm going to tell you about it anyway.

That is, after all, what I do. For a living, I mean. I tell stories. True stories. And unfortunately for me (and most of the other pitiful, or in some cases abominable, characters you'll soon meet if you keep on reading), the tale I'm about to tell is as factual as it is frightful.

But first, a few facts about me. . . .

(Sorry, but I have to give you some background information, you know! I need to explain a few things about my peculiar life—and some of the peculiar people who populate my peculiar life—so that you can understand how I got caught up in the aforementioned nightmare, and why I'm compelled to tell you all about it now. Please bear with me. The following introductory details will lay the groundwork for the disturbing story to come, and help you separate the good guys from the bad guys . . . well, sort of, anyway.)

My name is Paige Turner (no laughing or groaning or rolling eyes, please!), and I'm an investigative reporter for a popular true crime magazine, *Daring Detective*. At this particular point in time—Wednesday, October 19, 1955—I'm the only female crime reporter in all of Manhattan . . . probably even the whole country. And you can take it from me, that's a darn scary place for a woman to be (even when she's *not* in the process of probing into and writing about the most abhorrent murder scandal she's ever encountered in her short but stressful career).

I'm not complaining, mind you. I really love my job. I've wanted to be a crime and mystery writer since the age of fourteen, when I discovered that reading Erle Stanley Gardner and Rex Stout was a lot more fun than studying Shakespeare. And now, at the ripe old age of twenty-nine, I'm really proud that I've finally broken through the gender barrier to become a *Daring Detective* staff writer, and that I've managed to develop and expand a couple of my true *DD* stories into twenty-five-cent paperback novels (like the one you're reading now).

It hasn't been easy, though. And as hard as it was for me to break into the "manly" world of crime periodicals and paperbacks, that's how tough it's been to maintain my position.

Did I say tough? Ha! That's an understatement if ever I wrote one. Being the only woman on the six-member staff of a testosterone-driven magazine like *Daring Detective* is downright treacherous. Except for Lenny Zimmerman—the skinny, smart, bespectacled art assistant who's my only friend in the office—all of my male coworkers would like nothing better than to see me stripped naked, tarred and feathered, and run out of the publishing business on a rail. They simply can't handle having a determined, ambitious, and reasonably attractive young woman running alongside (and in some cases ahead) of them in the nine-to-five rat race. It threatens their supremacy and makes them turn beastly.

Brandon Pomeroy—the tall, dark, and somewhat handsome editorial director of the magazine—is the most beastly one of all. Not in a brash, masculine, animalistic kind of way (I could deal with that), but in a cold, slithery, reptilian way that makes your skin crawl. If Brandon Pomeroy—or *Mister* Pomeroy, as he insists on being called, even though he's only six years older than me—ever had a soft, warm, friendly feeling for any female in his life, I'd eat my favorite hat (and those of you who know me know I wouldn't part with my beloved red beret without a fight).

Pomeroy comes from a very rich and powerful family. In fact, his older second cousin is none other than Oliver Rice Harrington—the superwealthy publishing mogul who owns half the country's newspapers and magazines, *Daring Detective* included. That's the only way Pomeroy ever landed his job at *DD,* you should know—by being born into the right family. He certainly isn't qualified to be an editorial director! Not unless acting like an effete snob, drinking gin for breakfast, and snoozing at one's desk are the main requirements for that lofty position.

Fortunately for the lowlier members of the staff (of which, by virtue of being female, I am the lowliest), Pomeroy isn't *DD*'s first in command. That distinction belongs to Harvey Crockett, the big-bellied, white-haired, cigar-chewing ex-newspaperman who's been editor in chief since the magazine's inception. Crockett is gruff, grouchy, and impatient—a lifelong bachelor and proud of it. The only reason he ever brought a woman (i.e., me) onto the staff was to make and serve the coffee. (All the typing, filing, phone-answering, letter-taking, news-clipping, invoicing, and proofreading chores were, I'm convinced, an afterthought.) And the only reason I was ever assigned to write any stories for the magazine was because the exclusive, in-depth, first-person reports I investigated in secret and wrote on my own time—and finally prevailed upon Crockett to publish—increased *DD* sales by more than 30 percent.

So, guess what. I'm being "allowed" to write lots of *DD* stories now.

Mike Davidson, the magazine's near-illiterate yet ultracocky head staff writer, isn't too happy about that. And neither is Mario Caruso, the touchy-feely art director who thinks he has a right to touch and feel me whenever (and wherever) he likes. Mike and Mario are both married and in their early thirties, and they each have two little kids. That explains, I suppose, why they're so grudging and possessive of the *Daring Detective* payroll. They have families to feed, and they don't want some "flighty female upstart" (their words, not mine) laying claim to any portion of the magazine's extra assets—even when she's generating those assets herself!

But Mike and Mario don't know me very well. I'm not the

least bit flighty (except when I'm swooping around the city, flapping my investigative wings), and I don't have an upstart bone in my body. I've been working for the magazine for almost four years now, and I'm still making just seventy-five dollars a week. (The guys all make a hundred or more—and in the case of Crockett and Pomeroy it's *much* more.) And though I *do* try a lot harder, and take many more risks, and work many more hours than any of my male coworkers do, that doesn't mean I'm an upstart. What it means is that I'm a single working woman—a struggling Korean War widow, if you want to get specific—striving to pay my bills and cough up the fifty-dollar-a-month rent on my tiny, rundown, cockroach-infested Greenwich Village apartment.

Paige Turner isn't my given name, you should know. (What decent, self-respecting parents would burden a daughter with a ridiculous moniker like that?) And it isn't my pen name, either. (I've had some stupid ideas in my life, but that wasn't one of them.) What it is, is my married name, and I have only my late husband, Bob Turner, to thank—or should I say blame?—for it.

My best friend, Abby Moscowitz—the gorgeous, oversexed, opinionated beatnik artist who lives right across the hall from me—says I should change my name altogether. "It's a joke!" she keeps insisting. "When people hear it, they laugh, you dig? You'll never be taken seriously—especially in the publishing industry. You need a smart and sassy name. Something that will grab people's attention without giving them the giggles."

Abby's right, I know—but I don't care. Paige Turner I am, and Paige Turner I'm going to stay (unless my divorced, thirty-eight-year-old boyfriend, Detective Sergeant Dan Street, ever offers me *his* last name—which at this point in our troubled relationship seems a distinct impossibility). I was very much in love with Bob Turner, you see, and—though we were married for only one blissful month before he was sent off to die in a blast of machine gun bullets in a dirt trench in North Korea—I will always keep him safe in my heart. And I will always honor his name . . . no matter how silly mine became because of it.

Dan isn't jealous about this, in case you're wondering. Quite the opposite. As the staunchest, most resolute homicide detective in the entire NYPD, he's really proud of me for sticking to my guns. Dan values loyalty and stamina above all other character traits, and openly praises me for keeping my married name in the face of constant ridicule (Mike and Mario waste more energy cracking Paige Turner jokes than they do watching for the hands of the office clock to land on lunchtime). It's lucky for me that Dan is seduced by my small reserve of faithfulness and fortitude, because when it comes to his next most highly valued character trait, I come up shorter than bobby socks on a giraffe.

I'm talking about honesty now, and according to Dan, that's the one area of my moral makeup that needs improvement. A whole *lot* of improvement. You know what Dan says? He says I can't be trusted—that I don't even know *how* to be honest. He insists I wouldn't know the truth if it walked right in the door and kicked me on the shin. He claims I've told him more lies during the one and a half years of our stormy relationship than Lucy ever dreamed of telling Ricky.

But that's not true! I swear it isn't! Honest to God!

Okay, forget I said that. The truth is, I *have* told Dan a few fibs in the past—but not so very many, I promise! And the pitiful, self-defensive expression of a few little white falsehoods doesn't make me a dishonest person! Not in the *true* sense of the word. Not in the devious, unscrupulous, mean-spirited sense. No way, Doris Day! I can honestly say that I'm a *very* sincere, conscientious, and steadfast individual, and I've never, ever, ever told Dan a lie unless I had to.

If Dan would just accept the fact that I work for a detective magazine and stop carrying on about how much danger I'm always putting myself in, we wouldn't have a problem in the world. No lie. If he hadn't forbidden me to work on any more unsolved murder stories and threatened to end our relationship if I did . . . well, then I wouldn't have had to keep my more dangerous story investigations secret from him or create a single coverup to hide my activities.

You see what I'm saying? Dan *makes* me lie. And it's all because I'm searching for the truth! How ironic is that? Jeez! Doesn't Dan realize that we're both working for the same thing? Can't he see that the triumph of justice matters just as much to me as it does to him? If only he would stop worrying about me so much! If only he would support me in my undercover quest for the facts instead of demanding that I stop "meddling" in police business and putting myself in peril.

But Dan's never going to change his position on this point,

and I know it. He didn't get to be the most renowned and respected homicide detective in the whole darn city by questioning his own beliefs or backing down from confrontations. He's as strong and solid as a hardwood tree trunk—the most loyal, courageous, and, yes, honest man I've ever known—and when he takes a stand on something, you can bet it's for real.

But I'm pretty stubborn, too. And I didn't get to be Manhattan's only female crime reporter by caving in to opposition or running away from danger. And if there's anything in the world I hate, it's an either/or ultimatum. Either I leave the job I love . . . or I lose the man I love. I ask you, what kind of choice is that?

I'll tell you what kind it is. It's the kind I can't—and *won't*—make!

Which is why I'm now sitting alone at midnight in my dreary Bleecker Street apartment, smoking one L&M filter tip after another, listening to Nat "King" Cole on the radio, wondering if Dan will ever forgive me for my latest transgressions, praying that nothing too dreadful will happen to me tonight, and typing away on my trusty baby blue Royal, trying to wrap up this self-pitying prologue and get on with the story.

It's a shocking and scary story, and I've had to risk my life—as well as my relationship with Dan—to get it. (I've told more lies and gotten into more trouble during the last few days than ever before.) It's all been for a good cause, however, and—though I'm still working to conclude my investigation and am not a hundred percent sure how the story's going to end—this much is certain: If, or rather, *when* I get to the bottom of this sensational murder scandal, all of Manhattan is going to benefit. In a big, sensational way.

Okay, I realize that's a pretty bold statement, and—considering my admitted frailties in the honesty department—you may choose not to believe it. And you may not believe (or even read!) the horrific, behind-the-scenes tale I'm going to start putting down on paper right now. I sincerely hope you will, though. It's a very important story, and—as astonishing and incredible as my exclusive, first-person version may be—I've got my right hand in the air and my left hand on the Bible when I say it's the truth, the whole truth, and nothing but the truth.

Chapter 1

FOR ME, THE NIGHTMARE BEGAN IN THE MORNing. It was 8:35 AM on Wednesday, October 5, 1955. I was sitting alone in the *Daring Detective* office—at my desk in the front of the large communal workroom—waiting for the vat of coffee I'd just made to finish brewing, and combing the pages of the *Herald Tribune* for fresh, hot-off-the-press murder reports. I hadn't worked on a major story in over two months, and I was getting antsy.

Hey, don't get me wrong. I certainly wasn't hoping that somebody had been killed! Heaven forbid! I just wanted to make sure that if there *had* been a headline-making murder in the last twenty-four hours or so, I would be well versed on all the reported facts, and prepared to swing into action if Crockett or Pomeroy decided to give the story assignment to me.

The first four pages of the *Tribune* were, however, devoted to milestones other than murder. The Brooklyn Dodgers had just won their first World Series, four games to three over the New York Yankees, in a 2–0 shutout pitched by southpaw Johnny Podres. Roy Campanella scored in the fourth and Pee Wee Reese in the sixth. President Eisenhower was still in the hospital, recovering (slowly) from the massive heart attack he'd suffered in Denver last month, and the stock market was continuing to fluctuate (wildly) according to reports of his health.

The country was also still reeling over the tragic death of actor James Dean, who had crashed his beloved Porsche Spyder into a tree in California just five days ago. A lengthy article about this shocking event appeared on page 3 of the *Tribune*, complete with a rehashed accident report and numerous mournful statements by the young star's grieving fans. (I didn't read the article all the way through, I must admit. My friend Abby had been supplying more than enough tearful reminders of Dean's sudden demise while staggering back and forth between her apartment and mine, extra-strong highball in hand, wailing about the "atomic loss" of her "fave new screen boy" and vowing to wear black for the rest of her life.)

Finding nothing homicidal—or even very interesting—on page 4, I turned my attention to page 5. Much to my horror, there it was—the new murder story I had been searching for. It was printed in a short, slim column under a big, bold headline: NUDE BODY OF SLAIN SECRETARY UNCOVERED IN CENTRAL PARK. No photo accompanied the article. I sucked in a chestful of air, let out an audible moan, lowered my nose to the newsprint, and read every appalling word.

A young, unmarried secretary named Virginia Pratt had been killed Monday night, and her bound and gagged nude body was found wrapped in a bedsheet and buried under a mound of leaves in Central Park yesterday afternoon. Cause of death: suffocation—determined by the fact that the victim's nose and mouth were packed with turpentine-soaked wads of cotton and tightly sealed with adhesive tape. Police believed the young woman was murdered in an unknown location and then dumped in the park. Her blue satin cocktail dress, mink jacket, lacy underwear, diamond jewelry, high heels, purse, and identification were found wrapped in the bedsheet along with her body. Anyone with information about the crime should contact Detective Sergeant Casey O'Connor at the Midtown North Precinct.

Several alarms went off in my brain at once. And my head was jangling with questions. Since the victim was found nude, tied up, and gagged, I took for granted she had been raped. But if she had been, why had all her clothes been left with the body? And why had she been dolled up in a fancy cocktail dress on a Monday night? Monday was usually the quietest, least dressy night of the week. Had Virginia gone to a private party before she was murdered, I wondered, or had she been on her way to a formal function?

And what about the mink jacket and diamond jewelry? How many single young secretaries could afford such luxurious accessories? (I knew I couldn't!) And why hadn't the killer snatched those expensive items to sell or pawn? Was he so well off he didn't need the extra cash?

Most puzzling of all was the fact that Virginia's purse and identification had been stashed in her bedsheet shroud with her asphyxiated body. What could have been the motive for this unusual act? Most killers, I knew, tried to hide the identity of their victims. They figured the longer it took the cops to identify the corpse, the colder their own trail would become. And they were right! So what was the deal with *this* murderer? Was he stealthy or stupid? Had he simply acted in haste, or did he *want* the police to identify Virginia immediately?

(You see how my mind works? Questions, questions, questions. I'm so curious, sometimes I can barely breathe. Give me a puzzle to solve, and I won't sleep until the answer is clear . . . or at least a little less murky.)

I didn't scan the rest of the *Tribune* for further murder reports. Why bother? I was already hooked on the Virginia Pratt homicide and determined to grab that story assignment for myself. Dying to cut out the article for my personal story file, I grabbed a pair of scissors from my drawer. But then I came to my senses and put them away. Mr. Crockett would be arriving at the office any minute now. He'd want to read the morning news while he was having his coffee, and he'd blow his top if I didn't bring him the papers while they were still intact (i.e., before I'd performed my daily duty of clipping out all the crime reports). I reluctantly slapped the paper closed, shoved it to one side of my desk, and started flipping through the *Daily Mirror,* looking for another article about the Pratt murder.

I found it immediately, up front on page 2. Either the *Mirror* editors placed more importance on the brutal murder of a young secretary than they did on the accidental death of James Dean, or they were more eager to appeal to their readers' prurient interests. Judging from the headline of their piece—BLONDE BOMBSHELL FOUND NAKED, BOUND, AND DEAD UNDER HEAP OF LEAVES—I suspected it was the latter.

The *Mirror* article dished out most of the same details that had appeared in the *Tribune,* along with several tantalizing additions. Virginia Pratt, the tabloid noted, had been a beautiful, well-built champagne blonde, an aspiring folksinger, a resident of Peter Cooper Village on the Lower East Side, and a secretary at the 23rd Street accounting offices of Gilbert, Mosher, Pechter & Slom.

I was committing these new facts to memory when the office entry bell jingled and Harvey Crockett walked in.

"Good morning, Mr. Crockett," I said, cocking my head to one side and drawing my words out in a long, dry line. "How's tricks?" If I had to be subservient and submissive (as all female office workers are—at all times—required to be), I could at least do it with a flip, droll Eve Arden attitude.

"Hummph!" Mr. Crockett replied, squinching his bushy white brows and trudging over to the coat tree. He hung up his hat and coat, then headed down the center aisle of the main workroom toward his private office in the back. As he passed my desk he gave me a quick nod and a snort. "Coffee ready?"

"Yes, sir!" I croaked, resisting the urge to salute.

"Then bring me some," he growled, maneuvering his wide body down the narrow aisle. "And the papers, too," he said over his shoulder, as if I hadn't heard those very same words every morning of every single day I'd worked at *Daring Detective.* Did he really think I wouldn't remember? Or was he still refusing to admit to himself that a woman—any woman—might actually have a brain?

I rolled my eyes at the ceiling, rose to my full height (five feet seven without heels, five feet ten with), and sadly scooped up the newspapers. My search for more information about the Virginia Pratt murder would have to be put on hold. I knew better than to mention my interest in the story to Mr. Crockett. He would just tell Brandon Pomeroy about it, and then Pomeroy would make it a point to give the assignment to Mike Davidson— just for the pleasure of watching me squirm.

Doing my best Lauren Bacall (i.e., acting as cool and indifferent as possible), I carried all four morning editions into Crockett's office and plunked them down on his desk. Then I went back into the workroom to fetch his coffee. (God forbid he should ever have to get his own!)

"Here you go, Mr. Crockett," I said, returning to his office, walking around the front of his desk, and setting his coffee down next to his phone and ashtray—right where he liked it. The *Daily News* was open in front of him. (Having once been a staff reporter for the *News*, Crockett always read that paper first.) I leaned over the desk, tucked my shoulder-length brown hair behind my ears, stared down at the spread of newsprint, and madly scanned the upside-down headlines. Luckily, there was no story about the murder on either page, or I might have snatched the paper right out from under Mr. Crockett's nose. (As hard as I try to contain myself, I can get a little carried away sometimes.)

"Will that be all, Mr. Crockett?" I asked, stalling, hovering, hoping he would turn the page so I could check out the next batch of headlines.

"Yeah," he said, "except for lunch. Make a reservation for two at the Quill for twelve thirty. I gotta take the distributor out for a steak." He didn't look up from the *News*, but he didn't turn the page, either.

"Yes, sir," I said, giving up and walking back to my desk. Further stalling or snooping was pointless. I'd just have to keep my curiosity under control until Crockett finished the morning papers and gave them to me to clip—hopefully before Brandon Pomeroy came in.

As I sat down and reached for a galley to proofread, Lenny Zimmerman made his usual wheezing, gasping, red-faced entrance. (Lenny is deathly afraid of elevators and always climbs the full nine flights of stairs to the office.) Actually, he was more red-faced and wheezy than usual. Rivulets of sweat were trickling down his florid cheeks, and he was panting so hard his glasses were all steamed up.

Knowing it would take a full minute or two for my friend to recover from his arduous climb, I corrected all the typos in the first few paragraphs of the article I was reading. Then, as soon as Lenny's breathing returned to normal, I grinned and gave him a hearty "Good morning."

"Morning," he mumbled, still standing just inside the door. He removed his black-rimmed glasses, wiped the lenses with his muffler, then returned the spectacles to their off-kilter perch on his large, distinctive nose. "God, Paige!" he said, aiming his bloodshot eyes at me. "It's as hot as a steam bath in here. Do you have the radiator turned up too high?" His feet were firmly planted on the floor, but the rest of his thin body was swaying like a willow in the wind.

"Nope. I set the knob in its usual position. But you know what, Lenny? I think *you're* turned up too high. Your face is still flaming. Do you feel all right?"

"Uh, yeah, I guess so," he said, slowly stumbling across the room and looping his hat, muffler, and jacket on the coat tree. "I'm just a little tired, that's all."

"Late night?"

"Hardly. My mother thought I looked sickly and made me go to bed at nine o'clock."

I smiled. Lenny was twenty-three years old but still lived at home with his parents. He probably wouldn't move out until the day of his wedding—if that day ever came. His mother was a tad possessive . . . and a really good cook.

"Hey, wait a minute!" I said, as Lenny walked up to my desk and turned to head for his drawing table in the rear. "Your mother was right. You *do* look kind of sickly. Stand still for a second." I jumped to my feet and put my palm on his forehead. "Gosh, Lenny! You're burning up. You should have gone to the hospital instead of coming to the office!" I was exaggerating, but not by much.

"You're worse than my mother," Lenny said. "She just wanted me to stay home."

"You should have listened to her."

"I couldn't," he said. "The cover paste-up and all the boards have to be finished and sent to the printer today. If I didn't come in, Pomeroy would have me arrested and sent straight to the electric chair."

"That would be funny if it weren't true."

"Tell me about it." He looked so feverish I thought he might faint.

"What can I do for you, Len?" I asked. "Do you want a cup of coffee?"

"God, no. That would make me throw up."

"A glass of water? Some aspirin?"

"Nothing, Paige. I just want to go sit down."

Giving me a sad excuse for a smile, Lenny turned away and slunk down the aisle to the deepest recesses of the workroom. As he passed the open door to Mr. Crockett's office, he muttered a quick hello, then sat down at his drawing table. Propping his elbows on the table and resting his head in his hands, he let out a moan that could have been heard in Hoboken. Poor Lenny. He was sick as a dog, with a major deadline looming—like the blade of a guillotine—over him. He knew he had a long, hard, harrowing day ahead.

I was in for a harrowing day myself, but—unlike Lenny—I didn't know it yet.

Chapter 2

MIKE AND MARIO ARRIVED TWO MINUTES LATER. I don't know how they do it. They live on opposite sides of town, but they always get to work at the same time and burst into the office together. I think it's some kind of conspiracy.

"*Buon giorno!*" Mario bellowed, removing his hat and coat and hanging them on the coat tree. He straightened his tie, drew a comb from his breast pocket, and swiped it through both sides of his slick, black (and ridiculously juvenile) ducktail. Then, the minute his hands were free, he scooted over to my desk and put them on me. "How are you feeling today, Paige?" he said, standing behind my chair and squeezing my shoulders.

"Since you're the one doing the feeling," I said, "why don't you tell me?" I tried to shrug him off, but he just laughed and kept on squeezing—pressing the fleshy parts of my upper arms as if testing them for ripeness.

"Well, you feel pretty good so far," Mario sniggered, "but I think I need to do some more research."

"Cut it out!" I sputtered, vaulting out of my chair and around the side of my desk before his stubby fingers could find something else to fondle. "I'm not a piece of fruit!"

"No, but I bet you're a good piece of . . . pie," he murmured, substituting one three-letter word for the one he really wanted to say. He gave me a lecherous grin to make sure I got his meaning.

Oh, brother! I muttered to myself. *Is this joker ever going to grow up?*

Mike waltzed over to join in the fun. "Now you've done it, pal," he said to Mario. "You've turned one too many of Paige Turner's pages. If you're not careful, she's gonna close the book on you." Snickering at his own vapid wordplay, Mike skimmed one hand over the roof of his straw-colored flattop, lit up a Lucky Strikes, and sat down at his desk—the one right next to mine. "Bring me some java, doll," he said, blowing smoke in my direction. "I need a jump start."

"Yeah, me, too," Mario chimed in, reluctantly ditching the groping game and propelling his short, stocky body toward his desk in the rear of the workroom. "And make it snappy, will ya? It's deadline day."

There was a time when Mike and Mario wouldn't have let me off so easy. They would have teased and taunted me till the cows came home (or until Mr. Crockett poked his head out of his office and told them to pipe down). But that was before I'd proved myself as a writer . . . before I'd increased *DD*'s circulation by a third . . . before I'd earned the respect of the magazine's profit-loving (but by no means profit-*sharing*) owner, Oliver Rice Harrington . . . before Mike and Mario had lost the power to have me fired.

Everything was different now that I was a bona fide staff writer. Well, not *everything*. I still had to kowtow to my male "superiors" (i.e., suffer fools gladly), and I still had to serve the damn coffee.

IT WAS 9:55 AM WHEN THE APOCALYPTIC PHONE call came in. I had just finished my morning coffee chores, checked up on Lenny (who was near death, but working like a slave on the next issue's paste-ups), retrieved the *Daily News* and the *New York Times* from Mr. Crockett, and sat down at my desk to casually (okay, frantically) search for more articles about the murder of Virginia Pratt.

So when the phone rang, I was more than a little upset. I wasn't in the mood for any more interruptions.

"*Daring Detective*," I snapped into the receiver. "Can I help you?" What I really meant was *Please leave me alone! Can't you tell I'm busy?!*

"I'd like to speak with Paige Turner, please." The voice was smooth, composed, and female. I was certain I'd never heard it before.

"May I tell her who's calling?" I asked. (In my line of work it pays to be cautious.)

"Yes, of course," the woman said. "My name is Sabrina Stanhope. This is a personal call."

Oh, really? Then how come I've never heard of you in my whole entire life?

I nabbed a cigarette out of the pack sitting on my desk, lit it, and inhaled deeply. "Mrs. Turner isn't here right now," I said, exhaling slowly. "May I take a message?" I really hate having to be the *DD* receptionist—except when I like it.

There was a long pause, and then a curt reply. "But you just said you wanted to tell her who was calling. How could you do that if she isn't there?"

Smart cookie.

"I'm sorry, but Mrs. Turner just stepped out of the office. If you'll leave your name and number and the reason for your call, I'll make sure she calls you back." (I like to think I'm a member of the smart cookie club myself.)

There was another long pause. "I already gave you my name. It's Sabrina Stanhope."

"And your phone number is . . . ?"

"Never mind. I'll call Mrs. Turner back at a more convenient time. When is she expected to return?" She sounded anxious now—as though my whereabouts really mattered to her.

"Well, I'm not sure, but I'll—"

"Look, if you'll just tell me when Mrs. Turner is expected, I'll call her back at the appropriate—"

"Okay, okay!" I surrendered, mentally throwing both hands in the air. (My curiosity always gets the best of me. Every single time.) "This is Paige Turner," I confessed—so breathless I was bug-eyed. "How can I help you?"

"*You're* Paige Turner?" I could almost hear her smiling.

"Yes," I said, with a defensive sniff.

"Are you quite sure?" At first I thought she had an English accent, but then I decided she was just putting on a high-class act.

"As sure as I am that you're Sabrina Stanhope," I said, puffing on my ciggie, ear suctioned to the receiver.

She laughed (rather nervously, I thought) and tossed me a flip "Touché."

"Okay, now that we think we know each other's names," I said, "what's next on the agenda? Are you going to tell me why you're calling, or do we have to engage in a round of Twenty Questions?" I was playing it as tough and cool as I could—trying to make my white flag colorful.

"I called to invite you to lunch today, Mrs. Turner." Her tone was challenging and apprehensive at the same time. The flag she was waving was red.

"Lunch?!" That was the last thing I expected her to say. I was thoroughly discombobulated, and—to make my composure even more difficult to maintain—I was hungry.

"Yes," she politely replied. "I'd like you to join me for lunch at twelve thirty this afternoon, at my place on Gramercy Park. There's a very important matter I need to discuss with you."

The last time a woman needed to discuss an important matter with me, I almost got killed for my trouble. "You'll have to do better than that," I said, crushing my cigarette in the ashtray. "For me to give up my feast at Horn and Hardart and come all the way down to Gramercy Park to eat, you'll have to tell me what you're serving."

She laughed again, but instead of nervous, she sounded relieved. "Poached salmon," she said, "with onion soup, asparagus vinaigrette, and a freshly baked baguette."

"Anything for dessert?"

"Chocolate mousse."

My mouth was watering so much that my next words sailed out on the tide. "Sounds good," I said, with a slurp that I dearly hoped was silent. "But I'm still not satisfied. You left something off the menu."

"What do you mean?"

"The topic of the conversation. I want to know what the 'very important matter' is."

She heaved a loud sigh. "That's impossible. The subject is too sensitive and complicated to discuss over the phone."

"Then can you at least give me a clue? I've got a lot of work on my plate today, and I can't leave the office without good reason."

"Oh, all right!" she said, annoyed. "It has to do with the death of a friend of mine. You may have read about it in the paper this morning. Her name was Virginia Pratt."

I almost swallowed my tongue. I was so stunned—so close to speechlessness—I barely managed to ask for Sabrina Stanhope's address and confirm that I'd be there at twelve thirty sharp.

I SPENT THE REST OF THE MORNING CLIPPING the newspapers, reading and rereading all four articles about Virginia Pratt (no photos or new information in the *News* or the *Times*), making Mr. Crockett's restaurant reservation, filing stock shots, approving invoices, correcting all the grammatical mistakes in Mike's latest story, and begging the hands of the office clock to move faster. I was itching to make my lunch hour getaway before Brandon Pomeroy came in . . . which was not an impossible dream, you should know. Pomeroy often shunned the office until later in the day, after his own lunch (his customary repast of olives, peanuts, and at least three very dry martinis) had been consumed.

But my booze-loving boss must not have been very thirsty that morning. He strolled into the office at eleven forty-five—a good fifteen minutes before my lunch hour was due to begin— and he was stone-cold sober.

My heart was sinking, but I managed to keep my sprightly tone afloat. "Good morning, Mr. Pomeroy," I chirped, watching him remove his gray felt fedora and custom-tailored overcoat and carefully arrange them on the coat tree.

"Good morning," he replied, but you could tell he didn't mean it. Not the "good" part, anyway. There was a deep black frown on his pale, funereal face. "Are there any messages for me?"

"No, sir," I said, wondering why he thought there would be. Pomeroy rarely received any calls at the office because (a) he was hardly ever there, and (b) he was so impersonal—and did so little actual work—that he seldom dealt directly with any of the magazine's contributors or suppliers.

"Expecting an important phone call, sir?" I asked, thinking that might be the reason he came to work so early (and letting my naturally snoopy self come out to play).

"That's none of your concern, Mrs. Turner," he said, still scowling. "You're required to write down every message I receive, whether I'm expecting it or not." Holding his spine erect and his snotty nose in the air, Pomeroy strode deeper into the workroom and sat down at his desk. He took one of his precious Dunhill pipes out of the top drawer and filled it with Cuban tobacco ("the finest money can buy," he liked to boast), then leaned back in his cushy leather chair.

"Bring me some coffee," he said. "Black."

I was shocked out of my seamed silk stockings. Pomeroy never (and I do mean *never*) drank the office coffee. He had declared it to be substandard (I believe the actual word he used was "putrid"), and he'd sworn a public oath that the distasteful stuff would never pass his lips. That didn't bother me one bit, I admit—the less coffee consumed, the less I had to make and serve. Besides, I had always suspected that Pomeroy's aversion had nothing to do with taste, and everything to do with caffeine (which diminishes the intoxicating effects of gin, don't ya know).

"Black coffee coming up, sir," I said, rising to get him a cup and wondering what had brought about the dramatic change in Pomeroy's behavior. *Is he sick?* I questioned myself. *Is he nursing a bad hangover? Has his doctor told him to stay off the sauce? Or does he have some special reason for wanting to stay alert?*

I knew he hadn't renounced his martinis and rushed to the office just because of the art department's deadline. That wasn't his style. Pomeroy was strictly a get-soused-now, crack-the-whip-at-the-last-minute kind of guy. Besides, he hadn't even said hello to Mario or Lenny, much less gone back to their desks to check on their progress.

Something else, I sensed, was afoot. Something unusual, or downright weird, or maybe even sinister. For a moment I wondered if he had skipped his so-called lunch just so he could come in early and force me to skip mine! (That sounds a little paranoid, I know, but I wouldn't have put it past him.)

"Here you are, sir," I said, setting the coffee on his desk and lingering there for a second, studying his sullen face for clues. He was well-groomed as always—cheeks and chin clean shaven, mustache perfectly trimmed, brown hair neatly styled and combed—but the dark circles under his eyes were almost as blue as bruises.

"What are you staring at?" Pomeroy asked, shooting me a menacing glare.

"Oh, uh, er—"

"Don't just stand there," he barked. "Bring me the new crime clips. Now."

To avoid any further discord, I stepped over to my desk, picked up the labeled and dated manila folder containing the articles I'd cut from the morning newspapers (including those about the Virginia Pratt murder), and handed the file over to Pomeroy.

"That will be all, Mrs. Turner," he snorted. "You may take your lunch hour now."

"Excuse me?" I stammered, struck nearly speechless for the second time that day. In all the three years and nine months I'd worked at *Daring Detective,* Pomeroy had never once deliberately given me leave to go out for lunch. In fact, if he happened to be in the office at noon—the official beginning of my lunch hour—he generally found a way to delay my departure, thereby shaving a few minutes off my allotted time.

"What did you say, Mr. Pomeroy?" I asked again, thinking my ears must be playing tricks on me.

"I said take your lunch hour now!" he growled, glancing up at the clock and chewing on the tip of his pipe stem.

"Yes, sir," I said, secretly rejoicing over my prompt dismissal, but still shocked to the core to receive it. I snatched my purse off my desk, plucked my camel's hair jacket and red wool beret off the coat tree, and hurriedly let myself out into the hall, before he could change his mind.

What the hell is going on? I wondered, making a wobbly, high-heeled dash for the elevator. *What on earth is Pomeroy up to? Why does he look so worn-out and worried? And why was he so eager to get rid of me?*

I couldn't answer any of those questions, of course, and by the time the elevator arrived, I'd stopped trying. Pomeroy's shady schemes and mysterious problems had faded—like a weak radio signal—from my mind. All I cared about now was Virginia Pratt and Sabrina Stanhope; they had taken complete control of my thoughts.

And before my lunch hour was over, they'd be controlling my actions, too.

Chapter 3

AT NOON, THE SIDEWALKS OF MANHATTAN ARE like rows of cages in a zoo—full of hungry animals darting this way and that, scrambling toward their appointed feeding stations, hoping to get a good place at their favorite trough. I exited my building at 43rd and Third and merged with the herd, hurrying past the Automat (one of my favorite troughs), crossing under the recently closed Third Avenue el, and forging my way to the IRT subway station at 42nd and Lex.

Once seated and lurching southward on the downtown local, I slipped my feet halfway out of my shoes (my new red suede pumps were killing me!) and removed my white cotton gloves (I didn't want to get them dirty). Then I began studying the advertisements on the placards overhead, hoping the goofy pictures and silly slogans would take my mind off murder and have a soothing effect on my rattled nerves.

No such luck. The ad for Blatz beer—featuring Liberace in white tie and tails, wearing a piano keyboard smile, lifting his frosty glass up to the heavens and proclaiming Blatz to be the finest beer in his hometown of Milwaukee—just made me violently thirsty. And the even more absurd ad showing a baby boy in a party hat, with a *very* happy look on his face, saying (in a cartoon balloon) to his smiling, smoking mother, "Gee, Mommy, you sure enjoy your Marlboro!" just made me desperate for a cigarette (naturally, I was all out). And the ad for the new Decorator Refrigerator by International Harvester, picturing a red plaid refrigerator designed to match a set of red plaid kitchen curtains, just made me groan out loud. (I've never had the slightest desire to own a plaid refrigerator, and I can promise you I never will.)

Especially annoying was the message posted by the Pan-American Coffee Bureau, urging subway riders to "Think better! Give yourself a Coffee-break!" The ad showed Edward R. Murrow and several other men from CBS-TV's *See It Now* staff, sitting amid the studio spotlights, cameras, and video control boards, enjoying the coffee that had just been served to them by a pretty brunette. *Jeezmaneez!* I grouched to myself. *Is there a man alive who knows how to pour coffee into a cup?*

As the train was pulling into the 23rd Street station, I forced my feet back into my shoes and hobbled over to the exit, holding on to a dangling leather strap until the doors snapped open. I was the first one to leave the train, and the first one to climb the steps into the sunlight. Steeling myself for the painful two-block walk to Gramercy Park, I pulled on my gloves, straightened my beret (or, rather, set it at what I hoped was a confident, jaunty angle), and hurried onward.

I soon reached Gramercy Park North and turned left, marching—like a tightly wound tin soldier—toward the Gramercy Park East address Sabrina Stanhope had given me. I was so mobilized and so driven (and so fixated on the hideous murder of Virginia Pratt) that I barely noticed the bright blue sky, or the colorful leaves on the trees and grounds of the private gated park, or the crisp, clean autumn air that was filling my lungs and lending a spring to my step (in spite of my torturous stilettos).

Finally, as I turned the corner onto Gramercy Park East, walked down the block to number 36, and gazed up at Sabrina Stanhope's building, I became more aware of—and thoroughly surprised by—the physical details of my surroundings.

Where the heck was I? England? France? Italy during the Renaissance? What was this crazy, mixed-up, churchy white stone structure rising twelve stories above me? A palace built for Louis XIV or some medieval Teutonic king? Where did all those finials and shields and cherubs and gargoyles come from? And why, pray tell, were those two helmeted, silver metal knights (statues in shining armor, for god's sake!) standing guard at the entrance? Were they welcoming me in, or warning me to stay out?

I'd never seen such an edifice in all my life. And I wasn't sure I ever wanted to again. As I climbed the white stone steps to the wide, ornate entryway, I felt a deep sense of dread. And as the short, skinny uniformed doorman ushered me in, asked me who I had come to see, and then led me across the gleaming veined marble lobby to the elevator, I felt as though I were walking into an elegant but oh-so-deadly trap. My high-heeled footsteps echoed loudly, mimicking the beat of the opening theme of *Dragnet* . . .

Dum da dum dum!

The elevator boy was wearing a maroon suit with gold buttons and gold braid. With his round, freckled face and twinkly eyes, he reminded me of Huckleberry Finn (or Mickey Rooney, take your pick).

"Eighth floor," the doorman said to him, quickly motioning both me and the young operator inside the modern, wood-paneled elevator. "Our guest is joining Miss Stanhope for lunch."

"Yes, sir!" the elevator boy replied, all but clicking his heels in compliance. He pulled the door shut, eased the big brass dial to the right, and—giving me a toothy grin and a playful wink—took me on a slow, smooth, sure ascent to the point of no return.

A TALL, BEAUTIFUL, DISTINGUISHED-LOOKING Negro woman in a trim navy dress and a white organza apron answered the door to Sabrina Stanhope's apartment.

"My name is Paige Turner," I told her. "I'm here to see—"

"Yes, I know, miss," she said, pulling the door wide and stepping to one side. "Won't you come in? Miss Stanhope is waiting for you in the library. I'll take your jacket if I may, and then show you the way." Her ink-black hair was swept back in a stylish French twist, and her lipstick was the color of ripe strawberries. The top of her head was at least two inches higher than mine, and she wasn't wearing heels, so I guessed her to be about six feet tall. Her age, I estimated, was around twenty-five.

"Thank you," I said, allowing her to help me out of my jacket. I removed my beret and gloves and handed them over to her as well. While she was putting my stuff in a nearby closet, I hastily

combed my fingers through my unruly hair, twisted my black
wool pencil skirt into position (kick pleat in the back, not
halfway around to the side, as it had been), and adjusted the
hem and the sleeves of my gray angora sweater. I thought I
should at least *try* to look tidy.

The maid backed out of the closet, closed the door, and then
gave me a strawberry smile. "Come with me, please," she said,
beckoning, gliding across the green-and-gold-tiled foyer floor
like a swan. (Pardon the cliché, but the woman's long neck and
fluid movements were so utterly swanlike I couldn't help making the comparison.)

I followed her down a short hall and up to a partially closed
hand-carved wood door. She tapped on the door twice and waited
for an answer. When a muted response wafted out from the
other side, the maid opened the door a bit wider and announced
my arrival.

"Mrs. Turner is here, mum," she said, sounding like a British
parlor maid instead of the African princess I was convinced she
must be.

"Please bring her in," Sabrina Stanhope replied, in the same
cool, composed voice I remembered from our phone conversation. I peered through the opening, hoping to get a glimpse of
my hostess before she saw me, but all I could see was a wide
swath of Oriental carpet and a backdrop of floor-to-ceiling
bookshelves.

The maid opened the door all the way and gestured for me to
enter the room. Feeling like Alice tumbling down the rabbit
hole into Wonderland, I took a deep breath, stepped over the
threshold, and ventured inside.

The woman rising from behind the large ebony desk on the
far side of the room was an attractive, fortyish, slim-figured
blonde of average height. She was wearing a belted, scoop-
necked, full-skirted black dress and a double string of pearls.
As she edged around the desk and crossed the carpet to greet
me, I saw that she walked with a slight limp.

"Mrs. Turner," she said, flashing her perfect teeth in a frosty
Grace Kelly smile. "It was nice of you to come."

"It was nice of you to invite me," I said, although I wasn't
sure it was.

"Won't you sit down?" she asked, leading me to a cream-
colored leather couch with orange accent pillows. "I thought

we'd have a little talk here in the library before lunch. Will you join me in having a cocktail?" she added. "A whiskey sour? A vodka gimlet? Or a glass of sherry, perhaps?"

(I never, ever drink at lunch, you should know. None of my noonday haunts—the lobby coffee shop, or Horn & Hardart's, or Chock Full o' Nuts—serves alcohol. But there's another thing I also never, ever do: turn down a free cocktail.)

"A whiskey sour would be great!" I exclaimed, trying—but failing—to keep the excitement out of my voice. Then, feeling embarrassed by my girlish show of enthusiasm, I sat down on the couch, crossed one leg over the other, and made a decided effort to act like Veronica instead of Betty. "This is a very unusual building," I said, with a haughty air. "Have you lived here long, Miss—or should I say Mrs.—Stanhope?" (I was fishing for facts, you understand. Both the doorman and the maid had called her "Miss," but considering the woman's age, good looks, and obvious wealth, I felt I needed more information on that score.)

"Please call me Sabrina," she snapped, providing no clues to her marital status or length of residency. She gave me another chilly smile, then turned her attention to the maid. "Bring us two whiskey sours, please, Charlotte. We'll have lunch in the dining room in twenty minutes."

Charlotte? I croaked to myself. *That's a strange name for an African princess. Pretty weird for a Negro maid, too.* I was jumping to conclusions, I knew, but I'd have bet my life savings that the beautiful, dark-skinned domestic was using an alias. (When your savings account totals twenty-eight dollars, you can afford to risk it.)

Charlotte smiled, nodded to her employer, and made a graceful exit.

Sabrina watched Charlotte leave with the kind of gaze a teacher trains on her favorite student. Then she sat down in one of the black leather club chairs facing the couch and focused her gaze on me.

"Thank you for coming, Mrs. Turner. I appreciate your—"

"Please call me Paige," I cut in, figuring one first name deserved another.

"Yes, let's dispense with the formalities, shall we?" she said. "That'll make things so much easier."

Things? What things? I was burning to ask about Virginia

Pratt, but I clenched my teeth and zipped my lips. Sabrina was the type who liked to be in control; her stiff demeanor and decisive tone made that quite clear. So, in the interest of not ruffling her very fine feathers, I decided to wait until she brought the subject up herself.

I didn't have to wait long.

"I know you're wondering why I invited you here today," she said, leaning slightly forward in her chair, "so I'll come straight to the point. I want you to do some undercover work for me. I want you to conduct a secret, aggressive, in-depth probe into the murder of Virginia Pratt."

"Holy smoke!" I blurted out. (Bye-bye, Veronica—welcome back, Betty.) I was truly astonished by her request. Was this a crazy coincidence, or what? Was Sabrina actually asking me to investigate the very crime I was already determined to explore?

Yep.

"Virginia was one of my closest, most intimate colleagues," Sabrina went on. "Her death has left me both desolate and, for reasons I will clarify later, quite desperate. It's *extremely* important to me that the vicious brute who killed her be apprehended and imprisoned immediately. And you, my dear Paige, are the only one I can trust to make that happen."

"Me?!" I sputtered. "Why me?" Those were the only three words I managed to get out. I wanted to ask why she didn't go to the police, but I couldn't utter another syllable. (It's hard to talk when your tongue is dangling out of your gaping mouth.)

"I read about you in the papers a couple of months ago," Sabrina explained, "after you tracked down the killer of a young Broadway actor. They said you were a relentless investigator and the only female crime reporter in the city. And that's exactly what I need—a tireless, tenacious sleuth who's also a *woman*. No man will ever sympathize with my concerns. Only a woman can understand the nature of my relationship with Virginia and the special problems it—" She stopped herself mid-sentence and gave me an anxious look. "Are you feeling all right, Paige?" she asked. "You seem upset. I suppose you're startled by my proposition. Here, have a cigarette," she said, opening the lid of a small silver box on the glass-topped coffee table between us. "It'll settle your nerves."

I gave her a grateful nod and snatched a cigarette out of the box, then quickly lit it with the large silver table lighter. After a couple of deep, tranquilizing drags, I found my tongue. "Okay, so I'm a woman," I said, "but why is that so important? And what are the 'special problems' you feel no man could understand?"

"I will explain everything in a moment," she said, "but it's a rather delicate situation. May I rely on your discretion?"

"Of course," I said, without thinking. "Discretion is my middle name. If there's one thing I know, it's how to keep a—"

I clammed up when Charlotte reentered the library with our drinks. Who knew how much *she* knew about Virginia Pratt? Or how much Sabrina wanted her to know? I sat in silence as Charlotte set our whiskey sours on the table in front of us and informed Sabrina that lunch was ready to be served.

"Have the asparagus spears been properly chilled?" Sabrina asked her.

"Yes, mum," she said.

"And the dressing for the salmon has been prepared?"

"Yes, it has."

"The soup is hot and the bread is quite warm?"

"Oh, yes, mum."

Sabrina tilted her head back, slowly raised her soft gray eyes, and gave her towering maid an approving smile. "Thank you, Charlotte," she said. "Mrs. Turner and I have an important matter to discuss. We'll be in as soon as we've finished our cocktails."

Apparently she hadn't noticed that I'd finished mine already.

Chapter 4

HAVE YOU EVER HAD THE SENSATION THAT you've been plucked off the Earth and plunked down on another planet? That you're twirling around on a foreign globe in an entirely different galaxy? Then you know how I felt that Wednesday afternoon as I sat on the cream-colored couch in Sabrina Stanhope's luxurious library, listening to a tale so aberrant and unexpected it was almost beyond my comprehension. My head was swimming and my stomach was churning (and it had nothing to do with the chugalugged cocktail—I swear!).

Sabrina was sitting calmly in her black leather chair, smoking a cigarette, sipping her whiskey sour, and revealing the shocking truth about her private life and her personal affiliation with Virginia Pratt as if there were nothing the least bit unusual about either. She had been talking for just a few minutes, but I'd experienced so many different emotions during her brief monologue, it felt more like a month to me. And in spite of Sabrina's ordinary tone, and the casual, offhand way she concluded her confession, I still found her disclosure astounding, practically impossible to accept.

"I don't believe it!" I said to her. "You're making the whole thing up!"

"I promise you I'm not," she insisted, thin lips curling in an enigmatic smile. "My situation is exactly as I have described it."

"But how can that be?" I blustered. "You're not the type to get involved in anything sordid or disreputable! You're refined and sophisticated. You live in a posh apartment overlooking Gramercy Park. You have elegant clothes and jewelry, and a devoted maid. Jeez! You even have a library!" I sounded more Bettylike than ever.

Sabrina smiled again. "It's really very simple, Paige, but since you're so skeptical and confused, I'll spell it out for you one more time. Please listen carefully. I don't want to have to go over this again." She paused for a moment, cleared her throat, then gave me a curt, matter-of-fact, but nonetheless mind-boggling summation.

"I was born into a wealthy and prestigious family," she said, "raised by governesses and educated in Switzerland. I used to be a fashionable, celebrated socialite—a true lady of leisure—but my circumstances have changed. Now I have to earn my own living. Now I own and operate my own business—a very professional, very *successful* escort service. I am, in fact, what you would call a 'madam,' and I manage an exclusive salon of the smartest, loveliest, highest-priced call girls in the city. Virginia Pratt was one of my girls—the most desirable and high-priced of them all."

"But the newspapers said she was a secretary!" I protested. "For a 23rd Street accounting firm!"

"And so she was. But only during the day. At night she was a luminous temptress who was wined, dined, and adored by some of the richest, most powerful men in Manhattan."

"Men *you* procured for her, I suppose." It was a statement, not a question, pronounced with a hint of sarcasm. The truth was finally sinking in.

"Yes, of course," Sabrina agreed, straightening her shoulders and brushing a wave of ash-blonde hair off her forehead. "My upper-crust background is finally being put to good use. During my debutante days I became friends with many wealthy young men who were on their way to becoming important. Now they *are* important, and even wealthier than before, and some are clients as well as friends. They're very eager to enjoy—and more than happy to pay for—the company of the beautiful, exciting, accommodating young women I provide."

"Do your clients ever give your . . . er, girls expensive gifts?" I was thinking about the mink jacket, satin dress, diamond jewelry, and lacy lingerie found wrapped in the bedsheet with Virginia's body.

"Some do and some don't. And sometimes it depends on the girl. Virginia, for instance, received many such offerings."

I gave Sabrina a steady, penetrating look. "Was Virginia on an arranged date with one of your rich, important friends the night she was killed?"

She sighed and nodded sadly. "Yes she was, and I'm anxious to talk to you about that. But let's go into the dining room now, shall we? We can continue our conversation over lunch."

MINUTES LATER WE WERE SEATED AT ONE END of the long mahogany table in Sabrina's formal dining room, savoring our freshly baked bread and French onion soup, and having a genteel dialogue about prostitution and murder.

"Virginia was a wonderful person," Sabrina said, dabbing at her mouth with a white linen napkin. "She was as bright and talented and kind as she was beautiful. All the other girls loved her—and so did I."

The proverbial heart of gold, I thought, wondering if every hooker had one. "You said she was your most desirable and—how shall I say?—*expensive* girl, so I guess your clients loved her, too."

"They did indeed. She was the fair-haired favorite. Only my top clients could afford her, though, and I had a hard time arranging her schedule to satisfy their frequent, often overlapping demands."

I swallowed the last mouthful of my soup, set the spoon on the plate, and politely inquired, "Which one of your clients was having his demands satisfied the night of the murder?" (I wasn't being sarcastic now; I was just being curious. Insanely, obsessively, about-to-lose-my-cool curious. Could the name of that one client be the only clue needed to crack the case?)

Sabrina returned her napkin to her lap and gave me a penetrating gaze. "Before I answer your questions, Paige, I must ask you to answer mine."

"Oh?" I said. "What questions are you referring to?" I didn't recall being asked anything other than what kind of cocktail I wanted.

"There are several things I need to know before we can proceed," she said. "First on the list is how much you will charge to undertake this private investigation for me. Don't be shy. I intend to compensate you handsomely for your time, and if you succeed in identifying the murderer, I will give you a generous bonus."

"You don't have to pay me one dime, Sabrina. I was determined to investigate this story before I ever talked to you. Virginia died a horrendous death, and I'd like nothing better than to see the creep who killed her behind bars. I'm sure my editor will feel the same way, and I expect he'll assign this story to me as soon as I get back to the office. So, you see, I'll be delving into this homicide for *Daring Detective* magazine, and couldn't possibly accept any money from you. I will, however, be very grateful for any information you can give me."

Her penetrating gaze turned into an ugly grimace. "But that's impossible!" she shrieked, emotions erupting like a volcano. "I can't allow you to *write* about Virginia's murder! That would be the worst thing that could happen."

Hey, wait a minute! She can't allow *me? When did Sabrina Stanhope become my boss—or should I say my madam?*

"Sorry, Sabrina, but I have a job to do. And writing about murder *is* my job. If that disturbs you, I—"

Charlotte entered the dining room with a large tray in her hands and walked over to the table to collect our soup bowls and plates. "Shall I bring in the main course now, mum?" she asked, voice soft as a spring shower.

"Yes, of course," Sabrina snapped, so distraught she forgot to say please.

When Charlotte disappeared into the kitchen, I turned to Sabrina and said, "What's your problem? Why are you so upset? I thought you'd be glad to hear I'll be working on this case at no cost to you. What difference does it make who pays me? All that matters is finding the monster who killed Virginia."

Sabrina gave me the kind of look that said, *You are, without a doubt, the stupidest woman I ever met in my life.* Then she composed herself and vocalized a more civil version of that thought:

"Are you out of your mind?" she cried. "I told you about my business—and Virginia's leading role in my business—in the strictest confidence! If I had thought for one moment that you would expose us both in a national magazine, I never would have breathed a word about our profession. Prostitution is illegal, in case you haven't heard." She shot me another ferocious glance. "If news about my private enterprise gets out, I'll lose my entire livelihood. And I'll probably be sent to jail! And what about Virginia's grieving family? If it's revealed that she was a call girl, they will suffer even *more* grief, plus an intolerable amount of public shame."

Oh, I muttered to myself, embarrassed by my unthinking reaction. *Is being a dope the same as being stupid?*

"And that's not all," Sabrina went on. "If the police find out that Virginia was a call girl, they will feel little or no sympathy for her. And they won't work very hard to catch her killer. And then the psychotic beast who tied her up and stuffed turpentine-soaked cotton into her poor nose and mouth may get away with murder! Such things happen more often than you can imagine, Paige. When a prostitute is killed, the police like to think she asked for it—that she got what she deserved for being a whore—and they simply don't bother to carry out a thorough investigation."

"But that's not true!" I objected. "My boyfriend is a NYPD homicide detective, and he's the most honorable, most compassionate, most determined seeker of justice you could ever hope to—"

I stifled myself when Charlotte returned to the dining room and glided over to the table, wheeling a small chrome and glass serving cart in front of her. She put a platter of poached salmon, a bowl of mayonnaise-caper dressing, and a dish of asparagus vinaigrette on the table, then placed two silver-rimmed china plates in front of Sabrina and me. After refilling our water glasses and checking to see that we had enough bread, Charlotte asked Sabrina, "Will there be anything else, mum? Tea? Coffee?"

"No, thank you, Charlotte. We'll have coffee with dessert. I'll let you know when we're ready."

The minute Charlotte left the dining room, Sabrina resumed her rant against the police. "I hate to burst your bubble, Paige, but if your detective boyfriend is as noble as you say he is, he's an out-and-out oddity." She sat up straight as a stick and poked her chin out in defiance. "Every officer of the law *I've* ever known has been arrogant, dogmatic, misogynistic, and unbearably cocky—*including* those who are my clients. They are, after all—in spite of their big, shiny badges and guns—merely men. And like most men, they think a woman who *sells* her body is more of a criminal than the man who *buys* her body—and if bad things happen to her body in the bargain, she has only herself to blame. Believe me, I follow these kinds of cases carefully, and I know what I'm talking about."

Okay, she had a point. I'd run across enough sexist, racist, and otherwise prejudiced police in my line of work to know that Sabrina's words carried some weight. The last story I'd worked on, in fact, involved a hateful, hotheaded detective who wanted to convict an innocent man of murder just because he was homosexual. But that was an uncommon case, I believed, and by no means indicative that *all* homicide dicks were bigoted or chauvinistic. Not on your life! I'd met a lot of fine, upstanding cops in my day, and one was so fine I'd fallen in love with him.

Trying to think of a way to defend the NYPD without provoking another argument, I squared my shoulders, took a drink of water, and fished around in my muddled brain for a few convincing but noncombative points to raise.

I could have saved myself the trouble.

"That's enough about the police!" Sabrina sputtered. "I can't bear to talk about them anymore. It disgusts me just to *think* about them!" With an angry toss of her head, she thrust out her hand and gripped the rim of the silver salmon platter, steering it across the crisp white linen tablecloth and mooring it, like a yacht, in front of me. "Please help yourself." It sounded more like an order than an offer.

"Thank you," I said, although I wasn't very hungry anymore. I took a small portion of the perfectly poached fish and placed it on my plate. *Maybe Charlotte will give me a doggie bag,* I mused.

Watching me like a hawk, Sabrina kept talking. "*Now* do you understand why I can't let you write about Virginia's murder?" Her fierce gray eyes were staring into my soul. "So many people would be hurt! And I don't mean just myself and Virginia's family. I'm worried sick about the rest of my girls. If my business is shut down, they'll lose most, if not all, of their income. And many of them are raising young children and supporting needy relatives. And don't think they can just go to work for another agency. I'm the only madam in the city, and I manage the only *decent* escort service in town. The others are run by men who abuse their girls and pay them next to nothing."

"I'm very sorry to hear that," I said in all sincerity, "but it still doesn't change my position. I'm a writer, for heaven's sake! And you knew that when you called me. Whatever made you think I would investigate this murder without writing a story about it?"

Suddenly breaking eye contact, Sabrina reached for the asparagus and put three spears on her plate. She cut them into bite-size pieces, forked one segment into her mouth, and chewed it slowly. Very slowly. Then finally, after she'd stopped her merciless chewing and swallowed what was left of the mutilated morsel, she turned her attention back to me.

"You're a widow," she said, "so I thought you'd be more understanding. The papers said your husband was killed in Korea—that you had to turn to crime writing to support yourself—so I hoped you'd grasp the seriousness of my situation and take pity on my single working girls. You know what it's like to be a woman alone, and how hard it is to make your own way in a man's world."

"Yes, but the *way* I make my own way is by *writing*." Would she ever get my drift?

"But that is *not* a problem in this case!" she argued. "I will pay you *much* more just to investigate the murder than you would ever make by writing the story."

I released a tired sigh. "I'm not a detective, I'm a writer." How many times would I have to say it?

Sabrina sat up straight, took careful aim, and shot her next question—like an arrow—straight into my conscience. "What's more important to you, Paige—helping to bring a savage killer to justice, or writing a sleazy story about him?"

Aaargh! I groaned to myself as the arrow hit home. Justice was—and always had been—my primary objective, of course, but I couldn't tell Sabrina that! The knowledge would give her too much power. She'd have me pinned to the wall (and signing on the dotted line) in no time.

"Both," I said, refusing to fall into her trap.

She shrugged and gave me a crooked grin (or was it a smirk?). "Well, I've got news for you, Paige Turner," she said, sounding far less polite and refined than she had earlier. "You won't be able to accomplish either of those goals without me."

And she called the police cocky!

"I don't need your permission, you know."

"No, but you *do* need my cooperation," she said. "You'll never get anywhere without it."

I hated to admit it, but Sabrina was right. I simply *had* to have the name of that client—the one Virginia was supposed to have been with the night she was murdered. And I needed the names of Virginia's other regulars, too—plus those of her closest girlfriends. I might never get to the truth without those specifics, and Sabrina was the only one who could supply them. She had me right where she wanted me—and we both knew it.

"Let me get this straight," I said. "You won't give me any further information unless I swear not to write the story?" I already knew the answer to that question, but I asked it anyway.

"That's right," she confirmed, forking another tiny asparagus segment into her mouth and chewing it to a pulp. Then she swallowed and said, "But you mustn't condemn me for that, Paige. I have to protect myself and my girls and Virginia's family. And I'm obligated to protect my clients, too. Some of them hold very important positions in government, business, and society. If their lecherous, philandering, and *illegal* activities were exposed to the world, it would mean the end of their careers. Perhaps their marriages as well."

"But one of them could be a cold-blooded murderer!" I screeched. "How do you feel about protecting *him?*"

"Awful," she said, with a cunning smile. "That's why I called you."

Chapter 5

ABOUT FIVE MINUTES LATER—AFTER I'D CAVED in and vowed that I wouldn't write the story; after I'd sworn on my great-grandmother's grave that I'd never breathe a word about my secret investigation to the police (Dan included)—Sabrina rang for dessert and coffee. (That's right—she rang. She actually picked up the little silver bell next to her plate, gave it a jingle, and—presto!—Charlotte appeared with the goodies. I'd never seen anything like it, except in the movies.)

I remained silent while Charlotte served the chocolate mousse and poured the coffee, but became vocal as soon as she returned to the kitchen. "Tell me about the client who was scheduled to . . . er, see Virginia the night of the murder," I said to Sabrina. "He's one of your rich, important friends from the past, right? What's his name? What kind of business is he in? Is he married? Does he have any kids? Have you spoken to him since the murder took place?" To say that I was eager for answers would be like calling the Three Stooges just a wee bit wacky.

"Before we get into that," Sabrina said, stalling, spooning sugar into her cup, "I need to know that you understand the urgency of this operation. You must begin your investigation at once, and you must pursue every clue with the utmost intensity. There can be no delay or letup in your search. It is *imperative* that the killer be identified and apprehended immediately." She sounded like Senator Joe McCarthy calling his Commie-hunting cronies to arms.

"Well, I wasn't planning to go on vacation, you know." I was getting annoyed with Sabrina's cautionary, controlling tactics. Besides, *she* was the one who was dragging her heels, not me. How was I supposed to "pursue every clue with the utmost intensity" when she hadn't given me any clues to pursue? How could I spring into action and check out the prime suspect if she couldn't bring herself to tell me who he was? I scooped up a spoonful of mousse, shoveled it into my mouth, and downed the rich creamy goo in one gulp.

"And what's the big fat hurry, anyway?" I asked, head reeling. "Sometimes it doesn't pay to move too fast. That's how mistakes get made and entire inquiries go awry. Haven't you ever heard that haste makes waste?"

"In this case the opposite is true," she insisted. "A slow-paced approach could be *terminally* wasteful."

"Why do you say that?"

"Because the longer it takes to find the killer, the more chances he'll have to kill again."

Okay, *that* was a pretty disturbing thought. And I was an idiot for not considering it before. (After my own close calls with homicidal madmen, you'd think it would've been the first thing on my mind!) But idiot that I was, I happened to be focused on a different worry at the moment—and it had as much to do with Sabrina as it did with the man who killed Virginia.

"What's going on here, Sabrina?" I said, a warning signal beeping in the back of my brain. "Have you been keeping something from me? Do you have reason to believe that the killer intends to strike again?"

"Uh, no," she said, "not really. It's just a feeling. And I'm so worried about my girls! What if the murderer is on some kind of sick crusade to rid the world of prostitutes? And what if he's using *me* to accomplish his hideous goal?" She gave me a desperate, wild-eyed look. "I couldn't stand it, Paige. I couldn't live with myself if I sent another one of my girls on a date with death."

Her words were a bit melodramatic, I thought, but heartfelt. And very effective. "I get the message, Sabrina," I said, "and I promise you I will work just as hard and fast as I can. I do have a nine-to-five job, though, and I have to get at least four hours of sleep a night, so you can't expect miracles."

"Couldn't you take some time off from work?" she pleaded.

"No way, Doris Day. I have two *very* demanding bosses. One of them is always looking for an excuse to fire me and the other one will have a stroke if I'm not there to make the coffee. I might be able to grab some extra time on my lunch hours, or call in sick one day or something, but I can't guarantee anything. I'll just have to play it by ear."

"What about this weekend? Can you give the case your undivided attention then?" She looked kind of panicky now.

"All except for Sunday afternoon," I told her. "I go out to lunch and the movies with my boyfriend and his daughter, Katy, every Sunday. It's a sacred ritual."

"Break the date," she said, giving me orders again. She leaned forward and took a sip of her coffee, glaring at me over the rim of the white china cup.

"I can't, Sabrina. Dan would get very suspicious. He'd jump to the conclusion that I'm working on a new murder story, and then he'd start investigating *me*. And, trust me, you don't want *that* to happen. Dan Street is the smartest detective alive. He would uncover the truth about you and Virginia in no time. You're just lucky that Virginia's body wasn't found in *his* precinct. Otherwise, he'd be in charge of this case and you and your prestigious clients would already be under surveillance— or under lock and key."

I was laying it on pretty thick, but I believed every word I said.

"Oh, all right!" Sabrina slammed her cup down in its saucer. "Go ahead! Search for the killer in your own sweet time. But if you know what's good for you, Paige Turner, your own sweet time will be goddamn quick!"

Her threatening tone was offensive, to say the least. And it sent me into a tailspin of anxious misgivings. Who was this woman—this madam!—I was now in cahoots with, and what evil, irresistible force had convinced me to agree to her unorthodox proposal? More to the point, who was *I*, and how did I ever let myself get mixed up in this murderous mess? Was I a courageous, brave-hearted, truth-seeking heroine, or just a snoopy, bullheaded, trouble-seeking fool? (Don't answer that!)

"You shouldn't speak to me that way, Sabrina," I said, stiffening my spine and looking her straight in the eye. "I don't react very well to threats. Sometimes they upset me and make me do something threatening in return." I felt it went without saying that if I told my detective boyfriend about her escort service, she could find herself in deep doo-doo.

"We seem to have each other over a barrel," she said, smiling.

"Yes, but you have a bit more to lose than I do. You could lose your fortune and your freedom. All I stand to lose is a story."

"Or your life," she said.

She wasn't smiling anymore. But she wasn't threatening me, either. The soft tone of concern in her voice and the anxious expression on her face made the motive for her dreadful warning clear: She was simply urging me to find the murderer as fast as I could, and cautioning me to be careful while I was at it.

I didn't know whether to laugh or cry. Our dirty deal was done, and Sabrina was now as protective of me as she was of her other employees. I had—in a crazy, roundabout kind of way—become one of her girls.

"OKAY, TIME'S UP, SABRINA!" I SAID, AFTER devouring two more mouthfuls of mousse. "If you want me to turn on the speed, you've got to do the same. I want the name of the man you sent Virginia to meet last Monday night, plus the names of the other clients you regularly fixed her up with. I need to know which of your girls were her closest friends, and I want a list of their addresses and phone numbers. And you'd better make it fast," I added, giving her a taste of her own aggressive medicine. "I've got to get back to the office." (That, by the way, was a gross understatement. My lunch hour had ended more than an hour ago. I was so late it was ludicrous.)

Sabrina stood up and tossed her napkin on the table. "I've already made you a list," she said. (Would she always be one step ahead of me?) "It's in the library. Come with me and I'll give it to you." She turned and headed for the door, obviously expecting me to follow.

I was on my feet in a flash. I hadn't finished my dessert, but I was hungry for proof, not pudding. Scrambling to catch up, I trailed Sabrina out of the dining room, across the large tiled entry, down the hall to the library, and across the plush Oriental rug to her desk. Her pace was fast, her posture was perfect, and her limp was barely noticeable.

Sabrina took two sheets of lavender stationery from the top

drawer of her desk and held them close to her chest. "You must guard this list with your life, Paige. Don't let anyone else see it. If it should get into the wrong hands—"

"Don't worry!" I broke in, panting like an overheated poodle. "I promise you nobody will handle it but me!" It was all I could do not to pounce onto the top of her desk and tear the list away with my teeth.

"Okay, then," Sabrina said, folding the list up like a letter and sticking it into a lavender envelope. She licked the flap of the envelope and sealed it tight. "Virginia's three primary patrons are listed on the first page, and her two closest girlfriends on the other. I've given you their names, addresses, phone numbers, occupations, and any other biographical facts I have on file. I've written down Virginia's information, too. That should be more than enough to get you started."

I shot a crazed glance at the sealed envelope, then aimed a frantic gaze at Sabrina's face. "But which one of these men was Virginia with the night of the murder?" I begged. *If she doesn't give me the answer this minute, I'll have to kill myself!*

Sabrina cast her eyes down to the floor. "I don't know," she said, with a sad shrug of her shoulders.

"What do you mean?" I shrieked. "Didn't you make the appointment for her?"

"Yes, but I made *two* appointments for her that night. One at eight, and another one at eleven. The papers didn't say what time she was killed, so I don't know which—if either—client she was with."

Aaargh! There went my hopes for cracking the case with one blow. I should have known it wouldn't be that easy.

"Okay," I said, quickly pulling myself together. (I didn't have time to kill myself.) "So which one was scheduled for eight, and which one for eleven?"

"They're listed in order," she explained. "The first man was Virginia's first client, and the second, as you might surmise, was her second. The last man on the list also called for a date with her that evening, but I had to put him off. I never ask any of my girls to accept more than two engagements in one night." Sabrina struck a staunch pose and held her head high, obviously proud of her strong personal principles.

Jeez Louise! Is she ever going to give me the damn list?

"Hand it over, Sabrina!" I demanded, stretching my arm and

open palm in her direction. "Give me the envelope. I've got to get back to the office right now."

With a deep frown and loud sigh of surrender, she relinquished the list to my feverish grasp. "Don't forget, Paige. You have given me your solemn promise. You will not share this information with anybody."

"I get the message already!" I fumed. "How many times do you have to say it?"

"As many times as it takes for the message to sink in. All three of the clients on this list are very important, well-respected men. And that's why I have to be so careful—why I have to do everything in my power to protect them. Do you understand?"

"Well, yeah, but—"

"But what? You believe they deserve to have their lives and reputations destroyed? You think all three should be punished for their sins whether one of them turns out to be a murderer or not?"

"Well, no, I just—"

"And what if one of them *is* the killer?" she barreled on. "How much do you think *my* life would be worth if he thought I wouldn't keep his relationship with Virginia confidential?"

My head was spinning with the awful magnitude of it all. So many secrets to keep. So many reputations and careers and families in jeopardy. So many lies to tell. So many lives at stake—including, perhaps, my own. I could lose my job, too, if I didn't get my tail back to the office!

"I've got to go, Sabrina!" I sputtered, staggered by the time shown on her silver desk clock. I spun around and headed for the door, grabbing my purse off the couch en route. "But I still have to talk to you about this!" I cried, pulling to a stop near the door and thrusting the lavender envelope in the air. "Can I call you tonight when I get home, after I've had a chance to read and study your notes?" *And after I've had about six glasses of Chianti?*

"Call me anytime—night or day. My private number is Gramercy 5-6003. I've written it down for you on the second page. Right under the information about Melody."

"Melody?" I croaked, folding the envelope and stuffing it down into the bottom of my purse. "Who is that? One of Virginia's girlfriends?"

"Melody was Virginia's professional name," Sabrina said, "the one she used when she was working for me. Her clients

knew her *only* as Melody. They were never told her real name.
That's one of my strictest, most important measures of protection. *All* of my girls have pseudonyms."

"Do you have one, too?"

"Of course."

"What is it?" I asked.

"Sabrina Stanhope," she said, smiling again.

Chapter 6

CHARLOTTE WAS WAITING FOR ME IN THE ENtrance hall. (How the heck did she know I was leaving? Did Sabrina ring a hidden buzzer, or something?) She helped me into my jacket, returned my hat, and gracefully opened the front door.

"Thank you, Charlotte," I said, slapping my beret on my head and charging into the hallway. I wanted to stop and talk to her for a few minutes (i.e., ask her a few probing questions), but I didn't have time. It was 2:45! I wouldn't get back to the office until after three. If Mr. Crockett didn't give me the axe, Crown Prince Pomeroy surely would.

The uptown subway was abnormally crowded (was B. Altman's having its annual girdle and corset sale?), so I didn't take a seat. I just clung to a strap near the door, clutching my purse (and the crucial list it carried) so tight to my breast you'd have thought it was full of money (my purse, not my breast). When the doors snapped open at my stop, I was off the train, up the stairs, down the block, and around the corner in a wink. And just a couple of minutes after that, I was bursting into the *Daring Detective* office, feeling like Brenda Starr on a life-or-death mission, but probably looking like Imogene Coca on a bug-eyed bender.

To my great astonishment and relief, Pomeroy wasn't there.

Mike said he'd gone out about 12:30 and wouldn't be back until 4:30—in time to make sure that Mario and Lenny met the art deadline.

"Mr. Crockett isn't here, either," Mike grumbled, leaning back in his chair, lighting a Lucky, and spewing the smoke straight up at the ceiling. "He went from lunch to the typesetter, or the distributor, or someplace like that. Won't be back today. Said he'd see us at nine sharp in the morning." He plunked one penny-loafered foot on top of his desk. "And where the hell have you been, sweetheart?" he asked, taking another drag on his weed. "Sticking your snoot in the sewer again?"

Mike was a coward, you should know, and he deeply resented the fact that I wasn't. Like almost all crime writers in the detective magazine field, he wrote only clip stories—long, florid, trumped-up accounts of the grisliest, most sensational murders, pieced together from previous reports and composed totally inhouse. He had never been to a real murder scene in person, or investigated a killing on his own, and you could bet your bottom dollar he never would. All Mike had the courage to do was razz and belittle me.

"You look kind of ragged, doll," he said, with a smirk. "What's the scoop? All that digging in the garbage dump got you down?"

"Not likely," I said, giving him an ugly smirk in return. "In fact, I'm flying sky-high! I'm working on something really, really big," I added, just to upset him (and to try out my Ed Sullivan impression). "It's a *very* juicy and important story, but please don't ask me any questions about it. I can't discuss it with anybody. It's top-secret."

Mike's jaw dropped (as I'd known it would), and then he quickly dropped the conversation, too. He didn't want to hear about my important exploits. Enjoying Mike's shamefaced silence to the hilt, I hung up my beret and jacket, hid my purse under some papers in the bottom drawer of my desk, and then ventured to the back of the workroom to see how Lenny was doing.

Mario didn't even look up when I passed his desk. He was so focused on finishing the cover paste-up, he was barely aware of his surroundings. *He's in a real panic,* I told myself, chuckling under my breath, glad that the crushing art deadline had kept him from noticing my late return from lunch. I'd never seen Mario work so hard before.

Lenny was working hard, too—just to stay conscious.

"You look awful, Len," I said, feeling his forehead. His fever was raging and his skin was clammy to the touch. "You shouldn't be here. You should be in bed."

"Er, ah . . . yeah . . ." he mumbled, struggling to straighten the caption under a photo of a bloody, bullet-ridden corpse. His fingers were shaking, his eyes were bulging, and his nose was swollen and red. There was a huge glob of rubber cement stuck in his hair. "I, ah . . . can't leave, though," he said. "The boards . . . aren't done."

"Who cares about the stupid boards?!" I cried, overcome with concern for my friend. "I only care about you." I picked up his scissors, snipped the gummy ball of glue out of his hair, chucked it in the wastebasket, and then screwed his rubber cement jar closed. "C'mon, let's get your stuff together," I said. "You're going home." I felt I had to get Lenny out of there before Pomeroy came back and forced him to work late, making him even sicker than he already was.

As I helped Lenny to his feet and began guiding him to the front of the workroom for his hat, muffler, and jacket, Mario snapped out of his trance. I'm talking *far* out! He jumped up from his desk and followed us down the aisle, screaming his head off and yanking on the back of my sweater like a two-year-old in the throes of a three-alarm tantrum.

"Where do you think you're going?" he wailed, grabbing a handful of gray angora and pulling so hard I stumbled two steps backward. "Lenny can't leave! He hasn't finished pasting up the boards! And the messenger's coming to pick them up at five!"

I tore away from Mario's grasp and spun around to face him head-on. "Shut up, Mario! And keep your grubby hands off my clothes. Lenny's too sick to work. He shouldn't have come in today at all. I'm going to help him downstairs now and hail a cab to take him home. You'll just have to finish the damn boards yourself." I turned back to Lenny, took him by the arm, and continued steering him toward the coat tree.

Mario and Mike didn't make a move or say a word. They were shocked by my forceful behavior, and—to tell you the truth—so was I! As the only woman on the staff, I was accustomed to being submissive and servile—*not* strong. And I certainly wasn't used to calling the shots. I realized my newfound power had a lot (okay, *everything*) to do with the the the fact that Crockett and Pomeroy weren't there, but it felt really good to be assertive, and I decided to savor the sensation as long as I could.

After getting Lenny into his cap and jacket and wrapping his muffler around his skinny neck, I put on my own jacket and grabbed my purse out of the drawer. (I couldn't take the chance of leaving it—or, rather, the *list*—unattended, plus I needed money for the taxi.) Then I escorted Lenny out of the office and down the hall to the elevator.

He protested all the way, of course (Lenny's fear of elevators was all-consuming), but I knew he was too weak to walk down nine steep flights of steps. When the elevator doors opened, I pushed him inside, pinned him to the wall with my shoulder, punched the DOWN button, and held his hand tightly until we reached the ground floor and he stopped whimpering. Then I piloted him across the lobby, maneuvered him through the revolving glass doors to the street, bundled him into a cab, and gave the driver my last two dollars.

It was while I was standing there on the sidewalk—waving good-bye to Lenny and sticking my empty wallet back in my purse—that I saw Brandon Pomeroy hurrying up the block. *Poof!* My new sense of power disappeared in a cloud of smoke. I ducked back in the lobby and snagged the first available elevator, hoping I could make it back to the office, hang up my jacket, hide my handbag, and be safely seated behind my desk before the feces hit the fan.

FOUR THIRTY CAME AND WENT, AND THERE was still no sign of Pomeroy. I couldn't imagine what had happened to him. After all, I had *seen* him marching up the block toward our building and, by all appearances, he'd been determined to get here in a hurry. And that was over half an hour ago! So where the heck did he go? Did he have another appointment? If so, it must have been *extremely* important, because Pomeroy would never, under normal circumstances, let an art or editorial deadline slip by without seizing the opportunity to whip the slaves.

Mario didn't finish all the paste-ups on time, but after he realized that Pomeroy wouldn't be coming in to harass him, he didn't care anymore. He just plopped the boards that *were* complete on my desk, telling me to check to see that all the titles, blurbs, captions, copy blocks, and photos were in position, then package the stuff for the messenger and call the printer to arrange for another pickup tomorrow. Then he snapped his fingers at Mike—who jumped to attention like Sergeant Bilko—and the two of them swiped their coats off the tree, waved bye-bye, and left.

Ten seconds later the messenger waltzed in. Slouching in front of my desk and whistling the tune to "Dance with Me, Henry," the young man waited for me to write a quick note to the printer and seal it, along with the stack of completed boards and marked-up photos, in a large manila envelope. Ten seconds after that, he and the package were gone.

I shouted a silent *hooray*. I was alone. I could finally do the one thing I'd been aching to do all afternoon: look at Sabrina's list. Whisking my purse from the bottom drawer, I removed the lavender envelope, ripped it apart, took out the folded sheets of lavender stationery, and smoothed them open on my desk. Then, starting with the first name on the first page of the list— Virginia's (I mean, Melody's) eight o'clock date the night she was killed—I took a deep breath and read Sabrina's notes about suspect number one:

SAMUEL F. HOGARTH—Manhattan District Attorney. Age 49; married to Winifred; two teenage children, Shirley and Christopher. Graduate of Harvard Law School; son of cosmetics baron Gregory Hogarth; elected DA five years ago; resides on Central Park West. Office address and phone: 100 Centre Street, HAnover 2-4000.

Sam Hogarth?!!! I screeched to myself, shock waves shooting down my spine. *Our esteemed district attorney? It can't possibly be true!*

The way I saw it, Sam Hogarth was the least likely man in the whole darn city to use an escort service. He was the brightest, handsomest, most popular DA in Manhattan history, and everybody said he was destined to become a dynamic and respected figure in national politics. Word had it he was going to run for the Senate in '58. His younger wife, Winifred, was gorgeous (all the gossip photogs loved her), and some thought she'd make a lovely First Lady someday. Had Hogarth really risked his good name, career, and marriage—not to mention his brilliant future—for a few hours of illicit sex?

And could the fear that his indiscretions would be discovered have led the lustful law enforcer to commit murder?

It was a burning question that was much too hot to handle. And when I considered the fact that finding the answer had now become *my* responsibility, I broke out in a serious sweat. I felt sick. I was dizzy. I had to have a cigarette! Why hadn't I bought a pack when I was downstairs? *Because you didn't have enough money, you numskull!* I vaulted out of my chair, scooted over to Mike's desk, and started rummaging through the drawers, praying he had a spare pack of Lucky Strikes stashed somewhere.

Bingo. I found a familiar white package with a big red bull's-eye in the middle right-hand drawer, on top of a Webster's dictionary I'd never seen Mike use. I ripped the pack open, took out one cigarette, tossed the Luckies back in the drawer, and slammed it closed. Then I tore back to my desk, lit up, inhaled deeply, and—fastening my eyes on the lavender list again—moved on to suspect number two:

TONY CORONA—Singer/Movie Star. Age 37; divorced three times; no children. Engaged to actress Eva Lavonne. Has many hit songs on the charts, including "The Tender Kiss," "Love on the Rocks," and "Hearts on Fire," and two new movies in theaters: *Young and Foolish* and *The Man with the Naked Blonde*. Maintains offices and residences in Hollywood, Las Vegas, and in New York at the Plaza Hotel. Phone: PLaza 5-6655.

This name didn't surprise me nearly as much as the first one, but I still found it hard to believe. Tony Corona was as well-known for being a ladies' man as he was for his astoundingly successful recording and acting career. His three former wives had been gorgeous young actresses, and his current bride-to-be was the sexiest new starlet on the screen. Corona was fairly good-looking (average height and weight, enormous brown eyes, large head topped with wavy dark brown hair), and he was so rich and famous he could have any woman in the world he wanted.

So why did he need to hire a prostitute? Did he like it better when he paid for it, or was Melody more desirable to him because she was costly? Was he just showing off his wealth—proving to his peers that he could buy and control the most expensive call girl in the city—or was he an insatiable womanizer, so addicted to sex he always had to have an extra bedmate waiting in the wings? Could it be that his lady-killer libido had raged out of control and turned him into a *real* killer?

There were lots of homicidal possibilities, and it was up to *me* to sort them all out. But how the hell was I supposed to do *that?* How was I, a lowly writer for a two-bit detective magazine, ever going to get in to see—much less observe and interrogate!—two such mighty men?

I was in over my head this time. *Way* over my head. And if the first two names on Sabrina's list hadn't totally convinced me of this fact, then the third one made it downright official. Throat so constricted I couldn't breathe (or even smoke!), I stared at the final entry in utter awe and bewilderment.

OLIVER RICE HARRINGTON—Publishing Magnate. Age 52; married to Katherine; three sons, Clayton, Edgar, and Zachary. Owns over half the country's newspapers and magazines, plus largest book company in the world. Works out of his New York offices: Harrington House Publishers at Madison and 45th. Private line: MUrrayhill 5-7001.

Get the picture? One of the clients who frequently "met" with Melody—and may even have *murdered* her—was the man who paid my salary!

Oliver Rice Harrington, if you'll recall, was the owner of *Daring Detective* magazine, and also a blood relative of my immediate "superior," Brandon Pomeroy. So I was in *double* trouble now. I'd never met Mr. Harrington in person, but I knew from the office grapevine that he knew who I was, and that he'd seen my picture in some of his own newspapers. So how the devil was I going to sniff out the truth about his involvement in the case without attracting both his *and* Pomeroy's attention? And without getting myself fired?

I thought I was going to throw up. There were too many shocking details to absorb. Too many questions and crazy complications to consider. My stomach was tied in knots of confusion, fear, curiosity, disgust, and self-doubt.

I needed a stiff drink, and I needed it fast. And I knew right where to get the strongest and (by necessity) cheapest highball in the city. Without even glancing at the second page of the list, or dialing a single phone number on the first, I refolded the two sheets of stationery and jammed them back in my purse. Then I grabbed my hat and coat and took off for Abby's.

Chapter 7

STRETCHING FROM EIGHTH AVENUE ON THE west side to the Bowery on the east, Bleecker Street cut a narrow, busy, smile-shaped path through the hub of Greenwich Village. Abby Moskowitz and I lived on Bleecker between Sixth and Seventh Avenues, in the very heart of the hub, in a tiny, rundown three-story building that had probably been built before the turn of the century (which one, I couldn't say).

There were two apartments in our building, each perched above a small ground-level storefront. Abby's pad sat atop Angelo's fruit and vegetable store, and my humble abode was planted over Luigi's fish market. Due to the particular placement of our respective apartments—or, rather, the distinct aromas rising from the two shops underneath—Abby and I usually got together at her place instead of mine. Even rotten fruit smelled better than fish.

"Well, look who's here!" Abby chirped, sticking her head out into the hall and watching me climb the creaky flight of stairs from the street to the landing between our front doors. "It's the illustrious Paige Turner, and she looks thirsty."

Abby wasn't clairvoyant, you should know. I arrived home around this time most evenings, and I was *always* thirsty. Luckily for me, Abby was both a cheerful hostess and a very accommodating bartender. (I think she invented the term "happy hour.")

"What have you got?" I begged, staggering into her apartment, tossing my beret and jacket on a chair, and plopping myself down at the round oak kitchen table just inside the door. "Vodka? Gin? Bourbon? Cat pee? Whatever you're serving, I'll take two."

Abby didn't skip a beat. "A double Scotch and soda comin' right up!" She pulled her thick, waist-length black ponytail over one shoulder and stepped across the linoleum to the kitchen counter. Cracking open a fresh tray of ice, she plunked a pile of cubes in a tumbler and covered them with J&B. A twist of lemon and a splash of club soda completed the concoction.

"Bottoms up," she said, handing the drink to me. Her gorgeous Ava Gardner face was glowing. Next to painting sexy pictures (Abby was one of the best men's magazine illustrators in the city) and eagerly indulging in the forbidden practice of free love, Abby's most passionate pastime was the preparation and distribution of intoxicating beverages. She believed all the world's problems could be solved by a healthy combination of booze and sex.

"Cheers," I replied, throwing my head back and pouring half the highball down my throat.

"Hey, take it easy!" Abby cried, startled by my hasty alcohol intake. " 'Bottoms up' is just an expression, you dig? I didn't mean it literally! That's almost straight Scotch in your glass, kiddo. You gotta take it slow. Keep on slugging, and you'll knock yourself out."

"That's not a bad idea," I said, taking another sip (okay, gulp).

Abby cocked her head and studied my face for a second or two. Then she frowned, smoothed out the sleeves of her tight black turtleneck, and sat down at the table. "Okay, what gives, Paige? What's with the heavy chugalug action? Are you feeling all right? You look really meshuga to me . . . like a *Beat the Clock* contestant who has four seconds to balance a vat of hot grease on her nose."

"That's one way to describe it," I said, scouting the tabletop for a pack of Pall Malls, Abby's favorite brand. I found one behind the sugar bowl. "Can I bum a cigarette?" I asked, snatching one out of the open pack and lighting up before she could answer. "I'm all out. Out of money, too, so I couldn't buy any on the way home. All I had was a dime for the subway."

"Take the whole pack. I've got a carton upstairs." She swept a stray lock of ebony hair off her cheek and twisted her uncommonly beautiful features into another worried frown. "So what's the dope, Hope?" (Abby liked to end a sentence with a rhyming name, whether it fit the person she was talking to or not.) "Why are you so wigged-out? No, wait! Don't tell me. Let me guess. You're hot on the trail of a vile, bloodthirsty murderer, and you're setting yourself up to be his next victim."

She wasn't being clairvoyant now, either. Abby knew me—and all the morbid milestones of my hazardous crime-writing career—like a book. She had helped me investigate a few murder stories in the past, and she'd been a witness to more than one of my almost fatal run-ins with homicidal maniacs. (Did I say *witness?* Ha! You can strike that gutless, passive word right now. Abby had been a fearless *participant* in some of my most dangerous escapades, and she'd nearly been killed herself. Twice.)

"Am I right?" she barreled on. "Are you working on another story?" She was breathless with excitement. Her big brown eyes were dancing a jig, and her glossy red smile was stretched to the limit. Abby liked solving mysteries (and sticking it to the bad guys) as much as I did.

"Nope," I said, telling the God's honest truth, but feeling deceitful just the same. I wasn't working on a story, but I *was* about to plunge into another dangerous murder investigation, and I knew Abby would want to hear all the dirty details.

"Oh, come on, Paige!" she wailed, angrily flipping her long ponytail over the opposite shoulder. "You're not leveling with me. Something's up, Buttercup, and you'd better tell me what it is!"

I took another big swig of Scotch. "Okeydokey," I said, grinning like an idiot and surrendering on the spot. My resolve to keep Sabrina's secrets had disappeared faster than the liquor in my glass.

(Don't look at me that way! Yes, I *had* made numerous cross-my-heart-and-hope-to-die promises to Sabrina, but keeping the truth from my best friend, Abby, had *not* been one of them! And besides, the booze had suddenly kicked in, and knocked me for a loop, and—like every lonely drunk at every corner bar—I was desperate to tell my troubles to somebody.)

"I'm not working on a story," I began, pausing to take another drink, "but I *am* on assignment. And you know what, Ab? It has nothing to do with *Daring Detective!* The assignment, I mean, not the story—which I'm *not* going to write, and which has plenty to do with *Daring Detective* since the owner is— *hic!*—one of Sabrina's clients, and could turn out to be the slimy creep who killed Mirginia. Oops! I mean Velody. Either him or the district attorney. Our big fine Daddy-O DA! Can you believe that? Or maybe Corona the crooner, who has no earthly reason to hire a hooker, and if you ask me—"

"Hold it right there!" Abby cried, jumping to her feet and pushing her palm out like a traffic cop. "You're not making any sense, Spence! You drank too much too fast." She snatched my near-empty glass off the table and put it on the kitchen counter, out of my reach. "You've got to pull yourself together now, you dig? Slow down before you fall down."

"Whaddaya mean? I am *too* making spence!"

"Not to me," she said, propping both hands on her hips and raising one eyebrow to a peak. "I don't know who or what you're talking about!"

"Then you must be drunk or somethin'. It's perfeckly clear that—"

"No, Paige, it's *not* clear. You're babbling like a goddamn brook. Everything you said is just a crazy muddle to me."

"Muddle, muddle, deep mud puddle."

"Is that all you have to say for yourself?"

"Inky dinky parlay vooooo!"

"Okay, that's enough. You're bombed. I'm taking you home now." She extracted the burned-out cigarette stub from my tightly clenched fingers and tossed it in the ashtray. "C'mon. Stand up. I'll help you walk across the hall."

"Don't wanna go home! Wanna talk about the lavender list and—"

"I don't have time now, Paige. It's getting late and I've got a hot date. We'll talk tomorrow, when you're sober." She took hold of my hands and pulled me to my feet.

"Late, late, for a very important date. . . ."

"That's right, sweetie," she said, scooping my stuff off the chair and steering me into the hall. Then she dug my keys out of my purse, unlocked my apartment, and ushered me inside. What happened after that, I wouldn't know. My consciousness got lost somewhere along the way.

WHEN I CAME TO, I WAS FLAT ON MY BACK ON the couch in my dark living room, arms and legs flopped out in all directions. My shoes were missing, my skirt was hiked up to my hips, and my sweater was twisted so tight around my rib cage I could barely breathe. One of my stockings had popped free from my garter belt and was now wadded in a wreath around my ankle. My crusty eyes were seeing double, my gaping mouth was dry as cotton, my entire body was paralyzed in pain, and my buzzer was ringing repeatedly.

Great.

If I could have moved, I would have gotten up to answer the door. As it was, though, I could only lie there like a slab of cement, hoping whoever was standing out on the street and ringing my buzzer over and over again like a crazy fool would go away and leave me alone. I wanted to suffer and die in private.

My buzzer finally stopped ringing, but my caller didn't go away. Instead, he let himself into the building, climbed the squeaky flight of stairs to the landing, and then opened the door to my apartment, using the key I'd had made specially for him.

"Paige?" Dan called out, stepping inside and closing the door behind him. "Are you here?"

"*Mmmmph*," I replied, horribly ashamed of my dazed, disheveled, prostrate position, but unable to do anything about it. My only hope was that he wouldn't turn on the light.

Click! My only hope vanished with one flip of the switch on the wall by the door.

(Look, I really hate to break into the action here and interrupt the flow of my tale, but it's for your own good. Seriously. I need to describe the layout of my apartment so you can properly visualize this and other forthcoming scenes. I know it's annoying, but keep your shirt on! It'll only take a second:

When you enter my modest domain, you're standing in one small, narrow room, smack between the kitchen area and the living area. There's no wall separating these two zones, but you can tell them apart because the stove, sink, Frigidaire, and second-hand yellow Formica dinette set are all to the left of the entrance, and the armchair, bookcase, rented Sylvania floor model TV, telephone table, and makeshift couch—which I constructed myself from an old door, six screw-on legs, a single mattress and lots of Woolworth's throw pillows—are all to the right.

The windows in the living area look down on Bleecker Street, and the windowed door at the opposite end of the room—the rear of the kitchen—leads out to a rusty metal balcony-cum-fire escape, whose metal stairs lead down to the weed-choked, rat-infested courtyard below. And there's another staircase inside my apartment. This one is extra-extra-narrow, with a wooden handrail and banisters, and it rises from the hind corner of the kitchen to the second level, where my tiny bedroom, tinier bathroom, and closet-size office are located.)

Do you get the picture now? When Dan stepped into my apartment and flipped on the overhead light, the whole first floor was illuminated. And so, therefore, was I! In all my slovenly, hungover, spread-eagled glory.

"Well, well, well," Dan said, walking over to the couch and aiming his coal-black eyes down at me. "What have we here? Little Nell tied to a railroad track? Sleeping Beauty waking up from a ten-year nap?" He leaned over and gave me an overtly sexy smile. "You know, at first glance I thought you were offering your body to me, but now that I've had a closer look, I think somebody else beat me to it."

That did it! Stifling a howl of pain and squeezing my eyes shut against the light (and the glare of Dan's smile), I pushed myself up on my elbows, swung my legs around till my feet hit the floor, and then forced my stricken spine into a sitting position. The effort left me weak and dizzy. And so embarrassed I wanted to crawl under the rug.

"Very funny," I groaned, rubbing my face with my hands and raking my fingers through my tangled hair. "It's a comfort to know you find my agony so amusing."

"What do you expect?" he said, still grinning. "I'm an officer of the law. It makes me happy when the punishment fits the crime."

"Crime? What do you mean? What crime have *I* committed?" As the memory of my pact with Sabrina leapt back into my addled brain, a wave of guilt and panic swept over me. Had Dan found out about our furtive conspiracy? Did he know that

I'd agreed to search for a brutal killer, and that I'd sworn to keep it a secret from him?

"You obviously drank too much tonight," Dan answered, removing his gray felt fedora and trench coat and laying them on the armchair, "and now you're suffering the consequences of your misconduct. That's what I call *justice*." He gave me an amicable wink, loosened his tie, and unbuttoned his shirt collar. Then he took off his suit jacket and leather shoulder holster and carefully draped them over the back of the chair.

As many times as I'd watched Dan perform this hat-coat-and-gun-removing ritual, it never ceased to excite me. He looked incredibly sexy in his open-collared white shirt, and I loved the way his dark, wavy hair fell over his hatless forehead. And since Dan had once revealed that he felt naked without his gun, I found the absence of his shoulder holster particularly provocative. Even in my deranged, dehydrated condition.

"I need a drink," I said, slowly struggling to my feet and staggering into the kitchen, one nylon flopping around my ankle.

"Don't you think you've had enough?" I could hear him chuckling behind my back.

"I meant *water,* and you know it!" I croaked, grabbing a clean glass out of the dish drainer and filling it from the tap. After guzzling two glassfuls and thoroughly rinsing out my mouth, I splashed some water on my face and wiped it off with the dishtowel. "What time is it?" I asked.

"Eleven thirty," he said.

Aaargh! I had been asleep (okay, passed out) for almost five hours. I hadn't thought—or even dreamed—about the Virginia/Melody case at all. I hadn't studied the second page of the lavender list or dialed any of the phone numbers on either page. Jeez, I hadn't even followed through on my intention to call Sabrina to get more scuttlebutt on the suspects!

Some detective I was panning out to be. Slow and stupid as a slug. And now Dan was here, and I was a total wreck, and it was too late at night to do anything.

Well, maybe not *anything*.

Dan walked up behind me, took hold of my shoulders, and turned me around to face him. "Feel better now?" he asked, gazing down at me with his hot black eyes, pressing his warm, resilient body so close to mine I felt weak in the knees.

"I . . . I think so," I said, doing my best not to wobble.

He brushed my hair back from my face, then traced his fingers around my ear and down the side of my neck. "Better make up your mind, babe, because if you haven't fully recovered, I think I should go home and let you get some rest."

"Oh, no, I'm fine!" I lied, hastening to reassure him (i.e., convince him to stay). "I feel pretty darn good, if you want to know the—"

I was about to say the word "truth" when Dan's open mouth descended and enveloped mine, making further fabrication unnecessary.

Chapter 8

ABOUT FORTY-FIVE MINUTES LATER, AFTER DAN
had carried me back to the couch and had his way with me
(well, sort of, anyway—explanation to follow), we rebuttoned
and rezipped our rumpled clothes, and returned to the kitchen.

This was our usual routine when Dan stopped by to see me
after he got off work. First would come the banter—friendly or
otherwise, depending on the situation; next would come the
groping—Dan and I were so wildly attracted to each other it was
shameful; next would come the coffee or Chianti (whichever
seemed more appropriate) plus an ardent tête-à-tête at the kitchen
table; and last would come a long, lingering, loving good-night
kiss, or—if Dan had discovered that I was involved in another
dangerous murder story investigation—a hideous fight.

Having reached the coffee stage of the evening (Chianti was
out of the question!), Dan sat down at the kitchen table while I
prepared the pot and put it on the stove to perk. (I didn't mind
making coffee for Dan at all. In fact, I liked it.) "So how was
your day?" I inquired, placing cups, spoons, cream, and sugar
on the table. I was dying to know if he'd heard anything about
the Virginia Pratt murder, but I didn't dare ask.

"*You're* the one who needs to answer that question," he
replied with a knowing snort. "I'd say your day was a hell of a
lot more stressful than mine."

"Why?" I blurted, getting nervous again. Had Dan really learned what kind of day I'd had? "What on earth makes you say that?"

"Gee, I don't know," he teased, "but it probably has something to do with the fact that I found you flat on your back in a stupor with all your clothes bunched up under your chin . . . except for one stocking—which, by the way, is still hanging around your ankle like a soggy donut."

"Oh!" I exclaimed, finally remembering my sagging nylon. I bent over, lifted my skirt, pulled the stocking all the way up my outstretched leg, and refastened it in the snaps of my black garter belt.

Dan let out a goofy wolf whistle and gave me an exaggerated wink. But then suddenly—in the literal blink of an eye—he turned serious. Real serious. "Okay, Paige," he said. "That's enough foreplay. It's confession time now. Are you ready to tell me what's going on?"

"What do you mean?" I cried, widening my own eyes to innocent Little Orphan Annie proportions. "I don't know what you're talking about."

(Okay, so I was being a tad deceitful at this point. But before you pass judgment on me, I hope you'll reconsider my predicament: If I confessed the truth to Honest Dan, he'd be furious at me for getting involved, and we'd have a big fight, and he might walk out on me for good. And then he'd definitely take everything I told him straight to the homicide detective in charge of the case, who would then haul Sabrina in for questioning, bust up her entire operation, and surely put her in jail. And then all of her girls and some of her most important clients would be busted, too—even if they had nothing whatsoever to do with Virginia's murder.)

But that wasn't the worst part.

Not by a long shot.

Something *else* had occurred to me that made it even more imperative that I keep my deal with Sabrina concealed from Dan: All three of the prime suspects were profoundly rich and powerful, if you'll recall. So rich and powerful they could easily have some control over the police! District Attorney Sam Hogarth certainly fit that bill, and publishing giant Oliver Rice Harrington carried enough weight in this town to sink it. Even Tony Corona, who was believed to have close ties to the mob, was in a position to pull some very significant strings.

So, what if the killer *was* one of these three ultrapowerful men? And what would happen to Dan if he tried to investigate or expose them in any way? He could be kicked off the force, or destroyed by the press, or dumped into the East River with an anvil tied around his neck. And then the city would lose the smartest, staunchest, most honorable protector she's ever had, and I could lose the man I love more than life itself, and the demon who bound, gagged, and asphyxiated poor Virginia Pratt might get away with murder.

Dan pierced me with his sharp, insightful, and suddenly distrustful gaze. "Are you hiding something from me, Paige?" (I *told* you he was a good detective.)

"Of course not!" I said, changing my tone from innocent to indignant and stamping one foot on the floor. "Why are you always so suspicious of me?"

Dan laughed out loud. "Stop playacting, Paige! We both know the answer to *that* question."

"Okay, okay!" I huffed, waving both hands in the air. "Maybe I have been a little cagey on occasion. But that was in the past, and it was always for a very good cause, so that's no reason for you to distrust me now!" I spun away, whipped back to the stove, snatched the coffeepot off the burner, and stomped over to the table to fill our cups. I wasn't playacting anymore. Now I was really annoyed. And scared. And desperate to make Dan believe me.

"Calm down, baby," Dan soothed, lighting up a Camel. "I wasn't accusing you of anything. I was merely concerned. I just wanted to know what got you so upset today—why you felt the need to get so drunk."

Whew! "Then why didn't you just ask me about my day," I whined, "instead of suggesting that I was hiding something and demanding that I confess?"

He laughed again. "That's just the way I talk, Paige. It's the language of my profession. You should be used to it by now." He paused and took a sip of his coffee, keeping his eyes fixed, like flashlights, on my face. "Well . . . ?" he continued, stretching the word out in a long slow growl and emphasizing the question mark.

"Well what?" I snapped. I was getting tired of his stupid cat-and-mouse game.

"Quit stalling," he said. "I'm waiting to hear why you drank yourself into a coma, and I haven't got all night." It was obvious from his tone that Dan was getting a trifle testy, too.

The jig was up. I plunked the pot on the stove, stumbled back to the table, and sat down to face the music, stirring cream and sugar into my coffee and racking my brain for something persuasive to say.

"There really isn't that much to tell," I began, deciding to stick to the truth, but not the *whole* truth. "It was deadline day at the office, so everybody was feeling extra tense. Pomeroy was acting really weird, and Mario was so frantic to get the boards done on time, he was totally out of control. To make matters worse, Lenny was so sick he couldn't see straight."

I took a fast swig of my coffee, burning my tongue in the process. "Lenny never should have come in to work at all," I continued, "and when I realized how deathly ill he was, I. . . ." Blah, blah, blah, I went on, making the afternoon's office events sound as dreadful as possible, spouting extradramatic descriptions of the violent, sweater-wrenching abuse I'd taken from Mario before hustling Lenny downstairs and thrusting him into a cab to go home.

"And after I paid for Lenny's taxi," I blabbered on, "I didn't have any money left. I couldn't even buy cigarettes! If I hadn't found a dime in the bottom of my purse for the subway, I'd have had to walk all the way home! I tell you, Dan, by the time I got to Abby's, I was a mess. And by the time I finished the enormous Scotch and soda she made for me, I was dead drunk. I don't know why it hit me so hard, but it did. One minute I was sitting at Abby's kitchen table talking about my rotten afternoon, and the next minute I was passed out on the couch in my own apartment."

"I figured it was something like that," Dan said.

"You did?" I said, pulse quickening in surprise. "How come?" I was delighted that he'd accepted my evasive explanation, but astonished that he'd bought it so quickly.

"The first clue was the Pall Malls," he said, pointing to the red pack of cigarettes sitting in plain sight on the table. "You don't smoke this brand and Abby does, so it was obvious to me that your naughty neighbor had something—maybe everything— to do with the course of the evening's events, not to mention your inebriated condition."

I snatched a Pall Mall out of the pack and quickly lit it with

Dan's Zippo, thanking Christ, Yahweh, and Allah—but especially *Abby*—for the heavenly cigarettes and the proof they provided.

"Then, when I noticed your open purse sitting here on the table," Dan went on, "and saw three dollar bills stuck partly *under* the bag instead of inside it, I reasoned Abby had left the money for you, in a place where you couldn't possibly miss it. *If*," he added, with an irritating grin, "you ever came out of your coma."

"Hardeeharhar," I said, giving Dan a dirty look, then shooting a glance at the bills that were, indeed, prominently displayed on the kitchen table and anchored under one corner of my red suede clutch.

My first reaction was a huge rush of gratitude to my most generous and thoughtful best friend. Abby had left me enough money for a breakfast muffin, a soup-and-sandwich lunch, and transportation to and from work—all I'd need to get through the day tomorrow. My second reaction was a jolt of extreme shock and dismay, because partially hidden under the three dollar bills and the edge of my purse—but still visible to the naked eye— were two folded sheets of lavender stationery.

Sabrina's list! I shrieked to myself, wondering why the hell Abby had taken it out of my purse, and how the hell I was going to get it back in (without arousing Dan's suspicion, I mean).

"There's a note here, too," Dan continued, showing off his superior skills of detection, "and judging from the purple paper, I'd say it's from Abby. She's probably apologizing for getting you swacked tonight, and inviting you over for cocktails tomorrow."

Taking advantage of the sudden opportunity, I yanked the list out from under the money and opened it in front of my face, acting like it *was* a note from Abby, and pretending to read both pages.

"You're one hundred percent right, Detective!" I said, mentally crossing my fingers behind my back. "Abby says she's sorry she put so much Scotch in my glass and swears she'll double the soda next time." I quickly refolded the list and stuffed it, along with the money, into the depths of my open purse. Then I snapped the bag closed and put it on the seat of the chair next to mine, out of Dan's sight. "She says she hated to leave me alone in such a weakened state, but she had a hot date and figured I'd be sleeping for hours."

"Weakened?" Dan chided. "Sleeping? I'd call it drugged and senseless." He crushed his cigarette in the ashtray, downed the rest of his coffee, leaned back in his chair, and stretched his long legs out in front of him. Then he raised his arms and crossed them behind his head, breathing deeply and broadening his chest. His warm, wide, wonderful, welcoming chest.

He looked so adorable (and so seductive) I forgot all about Virginia and Sabrina and the three all-powerful men on the lavender list. I stubbed out my cigarette, leapt out of my chair, scrambled around the table, threw myself down in Dan's lap, and wrapped my arms around his strong, steady (and sometimes overly stiff) neck. Then I relaxed for the first time that night, moaning softly, burrowing my head into his shoulder, and letting my crazed, anxious, and exhausted body collapse—like a rag doll—on top of his.

Dan chuckled and pulled me close, cradling me like a baby in his virile, protective warmth. "You're pretty wiped out, aren't you, kid?"

"*Mmm-hmm,*" I reluctantly admitted. I didn't want him to leave. I wanted to stay coiled up on his lap forever.

"Then I'd better go home and let you get to bed."

"*Unnnph,*" I protested.

"It's late," he said.

"Not really," I whimpered, snuggling closer and holding on for dear life.

"C'mon, Paige, get up. If you keep on this way, you'll get me excited again and I won't go home at all."

"Would that be so bad?"

"No, it would be great. But you'd hate yourself in the morning."

Rats! Dan was right, as usual. As much as I adored him, and as much as I was longing to consummate our relationship (i.e., make mad, passionate love with him), I still believed that breaking our society's strict edict against extramarital intercourse would lead to nothing but heartbreak and ruin.

What would I do if I got pregnant? I'd asked myself a thousand times. Would I coerce Dan into marrying me, then spend the rest of my life wondering if he'd taken me as his wife out of duty instead of love? Or would I be courageous enough to have the baby on my own? Would I try to raise it without a father—in total disgrace and greatly impoverished circumstances—or give it up for adoption to utter strangers? Most unthinkable of all, would I have a dirty, dangerous, illegal abortion that could mark the end of my life as well as my baby's?

None of the choices were good ones, it seemed to me.

I had gone to the Margaret Sanger clinic on 16th Street to be fitted for a diaphragm (just in case), but I hadn't yet used the contraband contraption. It wasn't foolproof, I knew, and I didn't want to take any chances. So I was determined to remain celibate (though not a virgin, since my late husband had already relieved me of that label) until I was happily remarried. That didn't mean I wouldn't engage in plenty of hot, convulsive (i.e., mutually satisfying) fun with Dan on the couch (as you may have noticed at the beginning of this chapter). It just meant I wouldn't go to bed with him, or—as the Village bohemians were fond of saying—go all the way.

Not if I could help it, at any rate.

But my determination was dwindling fast.

Luckily, Dan was totally supportive of my wed-before-bed decision. As a rigorous law-abiding—not to mention law-*enforcing*—citizen, he was inclined to follow society's rules as well as those of our criminal justice system. And after the pain and shame he'd suffered during the process of divorcing his unfaithful ex-wife, he was truly glad that I was the virtuous type. (All right, I admit it: I was a lot more cautious than virtuous. Sorry if I misled you, but what do you want from me? I had to try the halo on before I could tell it didn't fit.)

"Cut it out, Paige!" Dan sputtered, twisting his head and yanking his earlobe out of the reach of my tongue. "You're asking for trouble, and if I don't get out of here quick, you're going to get it." He shifted his weight forward and began to stand up, forcing me out of his lap. Fortunately, my feet hit the floor before my bottom. "I'm going home before we both do something we're sorry for," he said, walking over to the armchair and strapping his holster back on his shoulder.

"Will I see you tomorrow night?" I asked, wanting to know his after-dark crime-fighting plans so I could safely make my own.

"Not likely," he said, putting on his jacket and trench coat, then setting his hat at a slanted, sexy angle on his head. "I'm looking into a string of Mafia hits right now. There's a mob war going on. I have to track down and question some of Frank

Costello's boys, and they never come out to play until after midnight. By the time I knock off, you'll be drifting in dreamland."

I wished.

Dan walked over to the door and opened it. Then he turned around and opened his arms to me. "Come say good night, Gracie," he grunted, doing a really dopey imitation of George Burns.

I flew into his embrace, rose to my tiptoes, and lifted my lips to meet his, swooning with relief that our evening was ending with a kiss instead of a fight—and that my top-secret pact with Sabrina was still a big secret from Dan.

Chapter 9

I HADN'T HAD ANY DINNER, BUT I DIDN'T care. Food was the last thing on my mind. My coffee was stone-cold, but I didn't care about that, either. All I wanted was to unravel the murder of Virginia Pratt—fast!—before Dan could discover what I was up to, forbid me to become further involved, get himself assigned to the case, and then find himself in serious (perhaps deadly) trouble with one (or all!) of Sabrina's suspect clients.

I poured my coffee down the drain and quickly cleared the kitchen table. Then I grabbed my purse off the chair and pulled out the list. Unfolding it to the second page—which was crammed with much more information than the first—I began pacing from one end of my apartment to the other, reading and analyzing every word Sabrina had written about Brigitte and Candy, Virginia's two best friends at the agency.

Brigitte's real name was Ethel Maguire. She was a married nineteen-year-old nursing student, and she lived in Hell's Kitchen with her husband, Ralph, who was twenty years her senior and so crippled from polio he was confined to a wheelchair. Ethel bathed and fed her husband every morning and then left him in the care of the elderly woman next door while—in noble pursuit of her chosen career—she attended classes at the Hunter College School of Nursing on East 68th Street. At night—after she'd given her husband his dinner, helped him get undressed, and tucked him safely into bed—Ethel transformed herself into Brigitte (so named by Sabrina because of her resemblance to screen sex kitten Brigitte Bardot). She slipped into a slinky dress, put on a pouty face, let down her long blonde hair, and went to work. Clever Brigitte. She had found a way to satisfy her deep personal desires and her demanding creditors at the same time.

Candy's real name was Jocelyn Fritz. She was twenty-four years old, single, an assistant designer in the hat salon at Saks Fifth Avenue, and a confirmed gold digger. All she wanted out of life was to marry a millionaire and curl up in the lap of luxury and leisure. Jocelyn had become one of Sabrina's girls in 1952, when she first moved to New York from Idaho and discovered that living in Manhattan cost a heck of a lot more than living in Boise. And then—even after landing her respectable, fairly well-paying job at Saks—she remained with the agency. She felt an ongoing need to (a) meet and mingle with Sabrina's wealthy clients, (b) acquire and maintain a dazzling, millionaire-worthy wardrobe, and (c) pay the sky-high weekly rental on her private suite at the Barbizon Hotel for Women. According to Sabrina, Jocelyn liked coming home after a hard night's work to a clean, roomy residence where no men were allowed.

Grabbing a Dr. Pepper from the fridge and a Pall Mall from Abby's pack, I went into the living room and switched on the radio. Dean Martin was singing "Memories Are Made of This." His voice was sort of soothing (and God knows I *needed* soothing), so I left the dial set where it was and sat down on the end of the couch closer to the phone. Then I took a swig of the soda pop, fired up the cigarette, and—steeling myself against the disturbing, sorrowful details to come—read the lengthy profile Sabrina had written about Virginia.

Virginia Pratt had been incredibly beautiful and incredibly young (twenty, by Sabrina's account), unmarried, and a secretary at the accounting firm of Gilbert, Mosher, Pechter & Slom, just as the newspapers had reported. She had worked at this firm *not* because she needed the money (her earnings as a call girl easily quadrupled her meager salary as a secretary), but because the head of the firm, Paul Gilbert, was her uncle, and if she'd ever tried to quit the job, he—as well as her strict, controlling parents in Vermont—would have become suspicious, and asked a lot of questions, and begun monitoring her every move. And if they'd ever found out what she *really* did for a living, they'd have had her spirited away, fitted for a straitjacket, and locked up in a sanitarium.

In order to keep her secret life as secret as possible, Virginia had lived alone—in a fairly new, but quite reasonable, apartment in Peter Cooper Village on the Lower East Side. Though the Peter Cooper apartments had been built as affordable housing for World War II veterans and their families, Sabrina had called in a favor from one of her big real estate clients and seen to it that Virginia's name was put at the top of the three-to-five-year waiting list. Six days later a shell-shocked vet and his wife moved out, and Virginia—aka Melody—moved in.

She never got to spend much time in her new apartment, however—working night and day the way she did—but whenever Virginia *was* at home, and not grabbing some much-needed sleep, she had rehearsed her music. She practiced scales on the guitar, exercised her perfect soprano voice, and stayed up into the wee hours of the morning playing and singing the lovely folk songs she composed. To hear Sabrina tell it, Virginia wanted one thing, and one thing only: to become a successful singer/songwriter—and her talents were so exceptional she was sure to hit that target someday.

I could see why Sabrina had given Virginia the name Melody, but I couldn't understand why Virginia had gone to work for Sabrina in the first place. She must have needed a lot of money—but what had she needed it *for?* She didn't have Candy's overly expensive tastes, or an invalid husband like Brigitte's to support. With her simple, unassuming, unfettered lifestyle, Virginia could have gotten by on the salary her uncle paid her. And she would have come *much* closer to achieving her singing and songwriting goals if—instead of working nights as a call girl—she had spent the time performing in the Village coffeehouses and clubs, building an audience and making a name for herself. The *Billboard* charts were studded with songbirds who'd flown to the top in just that way.

So the burning question was: Why had Virginia taken the low road?

Sabrina surely knew the answer, but she hadn't revealed it in her notes—a conspicuous omission which led me to wonder what *else* she had neglected to tell me.

I looked at my watch. It was 2:30 AM. I glanced down at the phone number written at the bottom of the list: GRamercy 5-6003—Sabrina's private line. She had said I could call her anytime, night or day. Without a moment's hesitation (except for the split second it took me to down another dose of Dr. Pepper), I picked up the phone and dialed.

SABRINA ANSWERED AFTER TWO RINGS. "HELLO?" Her voice was alert and clear, with an edge as sharp as a switchblade.

"It's Paige, Sabrina. I hope I didn't wake you up." I said this even though she didn't sound the least bit sleepy.

"You didn't," she said. "I never go to bed before three."

"Why so late?"

"I stay up until all of my girls have phoned in to report they're home safe."

"Oh," I said, thinking that was a nice thing for her to do. More motherly than madamly (unless she had also been tracking how much money she'd made for the evening). "How many, er, girls do you have in all?"

"Twenty-two," she said. "No . . . wait. That's wrong. That was the number before. Now that Melody's gone, it's just twenty-one." Her voice had lost its edge and turned as doleful as a dirge.

"I see," I mumbled, sorry that I'd brought Sabrina down. I wanted to get her talking about Melody/Virginia, but in a confessional rather than a mournful manner. "Where's Charlotte?" I blurted, hastening to change the sad subject (and simultaneously probing for info on the mysterious dark-skinned domestic).

"What?" Sabrina was shocked by the question. "Why in the world do you want to know where Charlotte is?"

"Well, I don't, really," I lied. "It's just that I thought she was a live-in maid, and I expected her to answer the phone."

"This is my private line. No one answers it but me."

So much for Charlotte. Better stick with Virginia.

"I guess you're wondering why I called," I said.

"No, I knew you would."

"Huh?"

"I knew once you'd studied my list and given it some serious thought, you'd lose your nerve and try to back out of our deal."

"I have *not* lost my nerve!" I sputtered, hoping that saying the words aloud would make them true. "And I'm not backing out of anything." (That much *was* true. I've never been a quitter in my life, and I didn't intend to become one now—no matter how much I wanted to turn tail and head for the hills.)

"I'm glad to hear that," Sabrina said, with a haughty sniff. "Because you're my only hope. You're the only one I can trust."

"Yes, but can I trust *you?*"

A long, tense silence ticked by before Sabrina spoke. "What, exactly, do you mean by that? Are you questioning my integrity?" She sounded mad.

"Not really. It's just that I feel you're holding something back—that you're not telling me everything I need to know."

Another heavy silence.

"And I don't like being kept in the dark, Sabrina. It makes me jumpy. I don't do my best work when I'm jumpy." I was shocked by my stern, commanding tone. Was that really *me* speaking? When did I become so authoritative?

"I don't know what you're talking about," Sabrina insisted. "I've been very open with you. I've given you all the pertinent facts—even those which could be most harmful to me."

"No, I'm quite sure you haven't," I said, standing my ground. "You haven't told me, for instance, how a beautiful, overprotected, unencumbered young woman from Vermont—a very sweet soul with outstanding musical talents, a decent job, and a supportive uncle—happened to become a high-priced call girl."

I waited for a response, but Sabrina didn't say a word.

"And I need to have a full and immediate explanation, Sabrina," I barreled on. "Without it, my hands are tied. I need *all* the bread crumbs to follow the trail. I feel certain that the reason Virginia became a prostitute is directly and conclusively linked to the reason she was murdered." (I wasn't *certain* of anything, of course. I just used the word for dramatic purposes—to get a rise out of Sabrina.)

"You couldn't be more wrong," Sabrina said. Her tone was angry and adamant. "Virginia joined my agency for very private, very personal reasons which had nothing at all to do with her death. Nothing whatsoever. You have my word on that."

"I'd rather have the facts."

Sabrina heaved a loud sigh. "I won't say anything more on

this point, Paige. Seriously. I promised Melody—or Virginia, as you seem to prefer—that I would never, under any circumstances, reveal her true motives to anyone. And I swear to God I never will."

"Even though it could help me catch her killer?"

"But it won't!" Sabrina shrieked, losing the last shred of her icy composure. "How can I get that into your stubborn head? Melody's motive for becoming an escort had absolutely nothing to do with her murder. Nothing, nothing, *nothing*! I know this for a fact because *I'm* the only one who knows the whole story. Melody never confided in anyone but *me*."

"Oh, really?" I said, temper and suspicions rising. "Then I guess *your* name will have to be added to the prime suspect list."

This time the silence was deafening. I mashed the receiver tight to my ear, straining to pick up any word or sound, but all I could hear was a slight, almost imperceptible click, then the whooshing in and out of my own breath.

Sabrina had hung up.

Chapter 10

FOUR HOURS OF FITFUL SLEEP, A LONG, HOT shower, and a forty-five-minute subway ride later, I was back at the office brewing coffee, eating a buttered English muffin at my desk, and combing the pages of the morning newspapers for more articles about Virginia. There were new write-ups about the murder in every paper (including the ones owned by Oliver Rice Harrington) but not a single photo of the victim or scrap of new information. The reports were just sensationalized recaps— yesterday's news rehashed with an emphasis on the more lurid aspects of the crime; they could have come straight out of *Daring Detective.*

As I was refolding the papers and arranging them in a neat stack for Mr. Crockett (*Daily News* on top, the way he liked it), the phone rang. Thinking it might be Sabrina calling to apologize for her rude behavior and divulge all her fiercely guarded secrets about Virginia, I snatched up the receiver in a hurry.

"*Daring Detective,*" I croaked, dispensing with my usual spiel.

"Hellohh? Hellohhhh?" The voice—not Sabrina's—was female, nervous, and reminiscent of Gertrude Berg's (the actress who used to play Molly Goldberg on the radio, and still does on TV).

"Yes, hello," I said, speaking softly, trying to put the caller at ease. "This is *Daring Detective* magazine. How may I help you?"

"Don't be meshuga. A magazine can't talk."

"You're right, of course," I said, smiling. "I meant to say this is the *office* of *Daring Detective* magazine."

"*Oy!* Are you trying to trick me? I know what's an office, and it can't talk, either."

"Yes, well . . ." I was at a sudden loss for words.

"Enough already!" the woman exclaimed, mood swinging from nervous to nervy. "A big secret you're keeping? I'm *plotzing* here! Why don't you tell me who you *really* are?"

I usually don't give my name out over the phone until I know who's on the other end, but this time it seemed like a good idea. "My name is Paige Turner," I said, wondering what I was letting myself in for.

"*Oy, vey iz mir!* Why didn't you just say it? Paige Turner is the lady I want!"

"Well, here I am," I said, "at your disposal. Is there something I can do for you?"

"You bet your life!" she said, adding nothing.

I was starting to feel dizzy. And more than a little curious. "May I ask who's calling, please, and what this call is in reference to?"

"Reference, shmeference! I'm Sadie Zimmerman, and I'm calling about my son."

Zimmerman? . . . son? . . . "Oh!" I blurted, "you're Lenny's mother!"

"Who else would I be?"

I didn't have an answer for that one.

"I'm so glad you called, Mrs. Zimmerman," I said. "I've been worried about Lenny. He was very sick yesterday. How is he feeling today?"

"*Nisht git.* Not good. That's why I'm standing in the hall in my housedress talking on this *farshtinkener* phone."

I didn't quite get the connection. "You mean you called to tell me Lenny won't be coming in to work today?"

"Work, shmerk. He has to stay in bed. I'm making soup."

"Good," I said. "That's what Lenny needs. Please tell him I'll take care of everything, and that he shouldn't come back to work until—"

My words were cut short when the office entry bell jingled and Mr. Crockett tromped in. Seeing that I was on the phone, he didn't say anything. He just looped his hat and coat on the tree, scooped the stack of newspapers up off my desk, and—snorting like a rhino and pointing urgently at the coffeepot—waddled off to his office.

"Hellohh? Hellohhhh?" Lenny's mom repeated, sounding even more like Molly Goldberg than before. "Who's there? Am I talking to my own ear?"

"I'm still here, Mrs. Zimmerman. Tell Lenny not to worry. Tell him that you spoke to me, and I said he should stay home until he feels better."

"Better, shmetter. I'm keeping him home till he's perfect."

"Good idea," I said, smiling again. "Tell Lenny I said to eat all his soup and get perfect soon."

THE REST OF THE MORNING WENT AS SMOOTHLY (i.e., shakily) as my phone conversation with Sadie Zimmerman. Mike and Mario came in shortly after I hung up, making their usual stupid, sexually suggestive jokes, demanding that I serve them coffee, and generally acting like total boobs.

When Mario found out that Lenny wasn't coming in, he went insane. His face turned purple, he broke out in a profuse sweat, and he started cursing like a sailor. Most of those curses were aimed, as you might expect, at poor little defenseless me.

I didn't pay much attention, though. It wasn't *my* fault that Mario hadn't done his job. Only *he* could be held responsible for slacking off every chance he got, making Lenny do all the work, and looking at girlie magazines all day. And I certainly couldn't be blamed for the fact that he was going crazy right now, knowing the art deadline had been missed yesterday, and that—without Lenny—there wasn't a chance in hell it would be met today.

(Okay, so maybe I could have been blamed a little. I was the one who made Lenny leave early and put him in a cab to go home. And I also told his mother he could take the day off today. But be that as it may, I absolutely refused to take one ounce of responsibility for the fact that Lenny had gotten sick!)

"Yelling at me is just a waste of time," I told Mario. "You'd better focus on finishing the paste-ups instead. Since Mr. Pomeroy wasn't here yesterday afternoon to see that the boards went out on time, he's sure to come in early today. And when he finds out that you missed your deadline, he's going to be really mad. And if you don't get the completed boards out to the printer today, he's going to be even madder.

"And don't think you can talk your way out of it, either," I added for good measure. "Pomeroy shoots first and asks questions later. By the time the sun goes down this evening, you could be out of a job." In the interest of promoting good office relations, I resisted the urge to grin.

Mario gave me a nasty look and scratched his head. It took a few moments for the truth of my statement to sink in, but when it finally did, he let out a petulant grumble, slunk back to his desk, sat down to work, and left me alone for the rest of the morning.

Mike didn't mess with me either—not until later, around eleven, after I'd retrieved the stack of morning newspapers from Mr. Crockett's desk and sat down at my desk to clip them.

"If there's any new reports on the Virginia Pratt murder in there," Mike said, snickering, "you can cut 'em out and give 'em to me."

I wasn't sure I had heard him correctly. "The Virginia Pratt murder?"

"Yeah, you know. That hot blonde secretary who was tied up naked and choked dead with turpentine. Mr. Pomeroy gave the story to me." Mike fastened his eyes on my face and bared his small yellow teeth in a gloating smile.

I was truly shocked by this revelation. I'd been so sure that Pomeroy would want an exclusive, in-depth, first-person account of such a sensational (i.e., salesworthy) crime, I had taken for granted he'd assign the story to me. I was, after all, the only one who would do the job right. Mike would deliver a dull, poorly written, bare-bones report that would disappoint readers and hurt *DD* sales—a story so bad it would have to be buried in the back of the magazine instead of splashed on the cover. And Pomeroy knew it.

So why the devil had he given the assignment to Mike? Was he trying to get even with me for something, or show me who's boss, or deflate my blossoming ego and knock me down in the eyes of my publishing peers?

Or maybe he didn't *want* the job done right, I thought, looking at the puzzle from a different angle. And maybe that was the reason he sent me to lunch early yesterday—so that he could give the story to Mike without me knowing and kicking up a fuss; so that later—if Mr. Crockett or any other *DD* higher-ups caught on and questioned his lousy judgment—he could say that Mike got the job because he was in the office the day the story broke and I wasn't (thereby casting aspersions on me instead of himself).

The more I thought about this particular scenario, the more believable it became. Yet my brain kept concocting new questions. What did Pomeroy have to gain by keeping me off the case and suppressing the story? Was he personally involved in some way? Was he shielding himself or someone else? Was he acting alone or just following orders? Maybe he'd learned the truth about Virginia/Melody and was now striving to protect his boss and family benefactor (Oliver Rice Harrington, in case you've forgotten) from a scathing sex scandal and possible murder charges.

When this last hypothesis occurred to me, I felt a little queasy.

But as troubled and confused as I was by Pomeroy's inexplicable behavior, I was also enormously relieved. Thank God he *hadn't* assigned the story to me! How on earth would I have kept my promise to Sabrina and turned the story down? What in the world could I have said? *Sorry, Mr. Pomeroy, but I'll be washing my hair every night for the rest of the month?* Or *I'm too tired to take on any more work right now?* or *No can do, pal. I'm up to my eyeballs in research for a pressing retrospective on John Dillinger?*

Call me a cockeyed pessimist, but I didn't think any of those excuses (or any other on-the-spot pretexts I might have dreamed up) would have worked.

Head swirling with mixed emotions (surprise, gratitude, fear, relief, concern, outrage, suspicion—you name it, I was feeling it), I cut all the articles about the Virginia Pratt homicide out of the papers and handed them over to Mike. Then I hunched over my desk and began correcting the next issue's page proofs, waiting—make that *praying*—for Pomeroy to come in. I wanted to monitor his every move. I wanted to examine every detail of his conduct and demeanor. I wanted to ask him some sneaky questions and study his reactions like a hawk.

I must have sent my prayers to the wrong address, though, because they were never answered. My lunchtime rolled around before Pomeroy rolled in. I considered delaying my departure until after he arrived, but quickly ditched that dumb idea. What if he pulled another stunt like yesterday's and didn't show up at all? Or what if he *did* come in and wouldn't let me go out?

I couldn't risk either occurrence. Both the clock and my pulse were ticking fast. I had places to go and people to see, and I had to get going while the going was good.

Chapter 11

I HAD BEEN INSIDE THE SEVENTEEN-STORY white limestone Criminal Courts Building at 100 Centre Street before, but I had never set foot in the Manhattan district attorney's office. I didn't even know what floor it was on. Standing under the hanging clock in the middle of the two-story-high marble lobby, I looked around at the polished Art Deco lighting fixtures, the gleaming metal doors, the two grand staircases with ornamental railings, and wondered—for the sixty-eighth time in sixty-eight seconds—what the hell I was doing there.

The lobby was swarming with people—determined, fast-walking people who seemed to know exactly where they were going. They whipped past me like stampeding steers. (Had the courts just been dismissed for lunch?) The crowd was mostly male—men wearing suits, overcoats, and fedoras, and carrying leather briefcases—but there were a few females, too. The women wore dresses, coats, white gloves, and hats trimmed with fur and feathers; their high heels tapped noisily across the marble floor as they tried to keep up with their hustling husbands, bosses, lovers, or lawyers.

Spotting a uniformed guard on the far side of the lobby, I cut through the herd and went to ask him for directions. He told me to exit the courthouse, walk around the corner to a different entrance, reenter the building, and take the elevator to the eighth floor.

The eighth-floor hallway was almost as busy as the court-house lobby. People were scurrying every which way—up, down, and across the hall, out one door and in another. The corridor was lined with offices, and most of them were furnished with more than one desk—a fact I observed as I slowly made my way down the crowded passageway, peeping through all the open doors and reading the names on all the others, looking for the hallowed portal marked SAMUEL F. HOGARTH, DISTRICT AT-TORNEY.

I found it at the end of the hall. The stately double doors were closed, but they opened right up when I filled my chest with air, threw back my shoulders, and—doing my best Wonder Woman impression—thrust my way inside.

(Okay, that's a slight exaggeration. What really happened was that I slowly twisted the knob on one of the doors, carefully edged it open a couple of inches, and peered through the crack. Then, when I saw a middle-aged woman with a long, skinny neck and a bun of brown hair sitting at a wooden desk in the center of a small reception area, I ventured into the room.)

The receptionist was talking on the phone, so I just stood there for a second or two, glancing around at the worn dark blue carpeting, empty wood chairs, and leather couches, feeling as nervous as a lamb in a lion's den. I was glad that nobody else was waiting to see the DA, but—since I didn't have a clue what I was going to say to the man—I wasn't the least bit happy that I *was*. Madly trying to think up a good fake reason for being there, and a stealthy but productive way to launch my investigation, I took a seat on the old brown leather couch closest to the door and lit up one of Abby's Pall Malls.

"Oh, yes, indeed, sir!" the receptionist was saying, blushing and batting her lashes like a bobby-soxer. "I have you down on the calendar for this Friday night. Mr. Hogarth confirmed the date just this morning. He said he and his wife are looking forward to it very much. They will meet you at the Copacabana at eight o'clock sharp."

She paused for a moment (during which time, I assumed, the other party was speaking), then she let out a girlish giggle. "Oh, no, sir!" she exclaimed, fluttering her lashes so fast I thought they'd fly off her face. "I couldn't possibly do anything as bold as that!" Her scrawny cheeks looked as if they'd be hot to the touch. She giggled again and cupped her hand over her mouth, conducting the rest of her conversation in a voice so soft her words were indecipherable. When the hushed dialogue was over, she dropped the receiver back in the cradle, tucked a few loose strands of hair back in her bun, straightened the collar of her prim white blouse, and reluctantly turned her attention to me.

"May I help you?" she asked, face still flaming. "Do you have an appointment with the district attorney?

"Uh, no, I don't," I replied, stubbing my cigarette in a nearby ashtray and hastily rising to my feet. "I should have called for one, I know, but I was afraid he wouldn't want to see me."

She sat up straight as a broomstick and narrowed her eyes into menacing slits. The rosy warmth drained out of her cheeks in an instant. "And why, may I ask, do *you* want to see *him*? Please state your name and your business." The blushing bobby-soxer had turned into the Wicked Witch of the East. (Or was it the West? I never could remember.)

"My name is Paige Turner," I said, "and I'm a staff writer for *Daring Detective* magazine." (I didn't dare use an alias or make up a fraudulent occupation on the off chance that Sam Hogarth had seen my picture in the paper and read about my recent crime-busting exploits.) "I'm working on a story about the shockingly high new murder statistics in Manhattan," I continued, "and I was hoping to get the DA's personal views on the subject." (That sounded pretty good, don't you think?)

The woman arched one eyebrow and gave me a look that was dripping with distrust. "Paige Turner, you say?"

"Yes, ma'am," I replied, stepping closer to her desk, flashing my most genuine and sincere Loretta Young smile.

She wasn't buying it. "Humph!" she sputtered. "You expect me to believe that?"

"Well, yes, I—"

"Ha! You must think I'm a total cabbagehead!" She rose from her chair and craned her skinny neck forward. "I know a phony name when I hear one—and Paige Turner is the phoniest one I've *ever* heard!"

See what happens when you tell the truth?

"I know it *sounds* phony," I hurried to explain, "but it really isn't. My parents gave me the name Paige, and my husband gave me the name Turner, and the absurd combination has been giving me grief ever since my wedding day. Whenever I'm introduced to someone, they crack up laughing. Believe you me, if I had it to do all over again I'd marry a man named Smith. Or Jones. Or even Wartbottom. *Anything* but Turner!"

She scowled at me for a couple more seconds, then relaxed her witchy features into something that almost resembled a smile. "Sorry, Mrs. Turner, but I'm sure you can understand my position. It's my job to screen all visitors to this office and to protect the district attorney from kooks, pests, and charlatans."

I chose not to confess that, in the eyes of some people, I belonged in all three categories.

"Don't worry about it," I told her. "With a preposterous name like mine, I'm used to having my identity questioned." I stood quietly for a second, giving us both the chance to compose ourselves, then (in deference to my shrinking lunch hour) I quickly forged ahead. "Mr. Hogarth may have heard of me, however," I said. "My name pops up in the newspapers every once in a while. Would you please tell him that I'm here, and that I'd like to *interview* him for a special *article* I'm working on? I promise I won't take up too much of his time."

(I stressed the words "interview" and "article" because of their irresistible appeal to elected officials. Particularly those who were planning to run for the Senate in three years—and maybe the presidency someday.)

"Yes, I'll tell him," the receptionist said, sitting back down at her desk and reaching for the phone. "But don't be surprised if he refuses to meet with you. He never sees anybody without an appointment, and he has a very important lunch date in twenty minutes."

TWO AND A HALF MINUTES LATER I WAS SEATED in a guest chair across the desk from Manhattan's exceptionally handsome DA, taking note of his thick, wavy, prematurely gray hair, intense blue eyes, strong jawline, broad shoulders, expensive Italian suit, and deep, resonant speaking voice.

"I'm familiar with your work, Mrs. Turner," he said, a slight smile tugging at the corners of his mouth, "and I applaud your admirable courage and persistence. You've solved some complicated homicides in the past, and performed a great service for the city."

"Thank you, sir," I said, caught completely off guard by his good humor and generous praise. (It isn't often that I'm commended by a prominent public official sitting in a thronelike leather chair, flanked by an impressive wall-mounted shield and a gold eagle--topped United States of America flag stand!)

"But I'm the one who should be thanking *you*, Mrs. Turner," he replied. "Your efforts have been nothing short of heroic. I think you should get a medal. The NYPD doesn't agree with me, of course," he added, his smile growing as bright as the midday sun pouring through his office windows.

I laughed. "That's putting it mildly. The police think I'm nothing but a nuisance."

"No, you're wrong about that," he argued. "You're much more than a nuisance to them. You're a profound embarrassment. You've outwitted them on several occasions, and they'll never forgive you for it. They can't handle being upstaged—especially by a woman."

Watch out! I cautioned myself. *Sam Hogarth is as smart as he is charming.*

"I didn't mean to embarrass anybody. I was just doing my job."

"And you did it very well," he said, suddenly dispensing with the smile, taking a pointed look at his watch, and then aiming his eyes directly into mine. "I don't have much time, Mrs. Turner, but my secretary said you wanted to interview me for a special article. What's the article about?"

I decided to keep it simple. "Murder," I answered, saying nothing more, staring deep into his royal blue irises, watching for his reaction.

His pupils contracted into pinpoints, then he quickly shifted his gaze toward the windows. "Murder's a mighty broad subject," he said, staring out at the pigeons on the sill, twisting his wedding band around his finger. "You want to narrow that down for me a little?"

I wanted to narrow it down a lot. I wanted to come right out and ask if he was the monster who murdered Virginia Pratt—but of course I didn't. (Contrary to what you may have heard about me, I'm not *that* stupid.)

"The latest report on crime in Manhattan," I said, "shows that murder is up thirty percent. That's an alarming increase. A lot of the people I talk to—especially young single women—say they're shocked by the new statistics and are now scared to be out on the street after dark. They're literally afraid for their lives. Can you offer any insight into what's causing this sudden surge in homicidal violence? And is there anything that can be done about it?"

Hogarth turned his eyes back to me. "I'm glad you asked that question," he said, sitting taller in his chair, assuming the warm, welcoming, paternal posture of the skilled politician. (If there had been one hundred babies in the room, he'd have begun kissing two hundred cheeks.) "It's true, as you say, that the murder statistics have escalated sharply in recent months," he said, "but those figures are—in some respects—deceiving."

"Oh, really?" I jumped in, hoping to divert a long, evasive speech about the unreliability of certain charts, numbers, and calculations. "Can you be more specific, please? Which respects are you referring to?"

A flicker of annoyance crossed his handsome face. He didn't appreciate the interruption—or my insolent inquiry. He promptly recovered, however, and resumed control of the conversation. "I'm referring to the fact that the rise in the city's homicide rate is due to a rise in *Mafia* murder," he declared, "*not* murder in general."

"Mafia murder? Are you suggesting that—?"

"I'm not *suggesting* anything," he cut in, giving me a taste of my own intrusive medicine. "I'm stating a hard-and-fast fact. An unusually large number of recent homicides have been mob-related. Perhaps you're not aware of it, Mrs. Turner, but a Mafia territorial war has been going on for some time now, and a good many thugs, thieves, goons, and gangsters—as well as a few innocent bystanders—have managed to get themselves killed. The figures are well documented."

"Yes, I know about that, but—"

"And that's why I'm conducting a citywide crackdown on organized crime," he barreled on, ignoring my attempt to ask another question. "I've got my entire staff working on the problem. We're determined to put a stop to this outbreak of violence and bring the crime bosses to their knees. Frank Costello is under investigation, and Albert Anastasia is next in line. And that's only the beginning. Take my word for it, Mrs. Turner, next year's murder statistics will be much lower than the worst grade you ever got on a high school algebra test."

Not likely, I croaked to myself, remembering my nonexistent mathematical skills and admiring the DA's incisive (need I say murderous?) wit and mental agility.

"So you can tell your single girlfriends to relax," he continued, straightening his collar and his royal blue tie (which just happened to be a perfect match for his eyes). "The excessive murder statistics will have no measurable effect on the lives *or* deaths of Manhattan's young, unmarried women. Believe me, they have no more reason to be afraid now than they did before. They are as safe on the streets of the city—morning, noon, *and* after dark—as they ever were."

"That's a very pretty statement," I said, "but I don't think Virginia Pratt would agree." (Okay, so I really *am* that stupid.)

"Who?" He gave me a puzzled look.

"Virginia Pratt," I repeated. "The beautiful young secretary who was murdered last Monday night, and whose bound, gagged, and asphyxiated nude body was found buried in a pile of leaves in Central Park on Tuesday. Surely *she* wasn't as safe in this city as ever before."

"No, of course not," Hogarth said, as quick to respond as a lizard snapping its tongue at a fly. "But that's an isolated case, and it happened just this week, and all signs indicate that the unfortunate young woman was killed by someone she knew. Her murder wasn't a random street crime, and it wasn't mob-related, and it hasn't yet been added to the city's homicide stats. Therefore, Miss Pratt's death, though tragic and *very* disturbing, has absolutely no relevance to this conversation—*or* to the article you're writing. I'm surprised you even brought it up."

Curses! Hoisted by my own petard (whatever that is). I was so annoyed I couldn't think of anything to say.

Words came quickly, however, to Manhattan's nimble-minded DA. "And now, if you'll excuse me, Mrs. Turner," he said, rising from his throne and walking around his desk toward me, "I must bring this interview to an end. I have an important lunch date uptown, and I'm already five minutes late." He hovered by the side of my chair until I stood up, relinquished my elbow to his manly grasp, and allowed him to guide (okay, *prod*) me toward the exit.

"Thank you for your time, Mr. District Attorney," I said, as he opened his office door and nudged me over the threshold. "May I meet with you again soon? I have a few more questions to ask, and this article is scheduled to run in our next issue. My deadline is approaching fast."

"You're out of luck, Mrs. Turner. I'm booked solid for the next couple of weeks. But if anything opens up," he said, hitting me with another radiant vote-getting smile, "I'll have my secretary call you. Leave your number with her on your way out."

Chapter 12

I DIDN'T GET BACK TO THE OFFICE UNTIL TWO
fifteen. Pomeroy hadn't shown up yet, and Mr. Crockett was
still out to lunch. Only Mike and Mario were there, sitting like
dual Dagwoods at their desks, working on tasks they should
have finished days ago and looking very put out about it.

"There's no more coffee left!" Mario whined as soon as I
walked in. "Where the hell have you been? I can't work without
my java!"

"Yeah!" Mike chimed in. "I want some, too. Better make another pot right now."

"Comin' right up!" I chirped, glad they were carping about
coffee instead of my extra-long lunch hour. If I could be
cheerful and helpful, I thought, maybe they'd leave me alone
for the rest of the afternoon and forget to mention my lateness
to Mr. Crockett—or Pomeroy, if he ever decided to make an
appearance.

I lugged the large Coffeemaster down the hall and into the
ladies' room to wash it out and fill it with fresh water, then returned to the office with the heavy, sloshing contraption propped
on one hip. The minute I opened the office door and began
jostling my way inside, I knew that Pomeroy had arrived. The
air was filled with the sweet fumes of his Cuban pipe tobacco
and the decidedly *un*sweet fumes of his rotten temper.

"Shut up!" he shouted at the top of his lungs. "Shut your ugly, fat face!" Pomeroy was standing in the back of the work-room, leaning over Mario's desk, aiming his roar directly into the embarrassed art director's left ear. "Don't give me any more of your lame excuses! There's no justification for missing a deadline. Why wasn't I told about this?"

"You weren't here, sir," Mario sputtered, staring down at the unfinished layout on his desk in shame. "And Lenny was sick all day and didn't get anything done and left early. And then he didn't come in today at all. And it's not my fault!" he cried, bang-ing his fist on the desk to emphasize his point. "*Paige* was the one who made Lenny go home. And she gave him permission to take the day off today. *She's* the one who made us miss the deadline!"

(In case you haven't noticed, in the office I'm like the city of Rome. All roads lead to me.)

Pomeroy rose to full height and turned his angry eyes in my direction, staring daggers as I set the coffeemaker on the table, filled it with Maxwell House and plugged it in. "Is this true, Mrs. Turner?" he demanded, voice cold and sharp as an ice pick. "Have you appointed yourself office manager now? How dare you send Lenny home on the day of a major art deadline?!"

"Lenny has the *flu*," I said, crossing my arms over my chest, refusing to buckle under Pomeroy's tyrannical gaze. (Where my newfound strength came from, I'll never know.) "His tem-perature was raging, and he was on the verge of passing out. People can *die* from the flu, you know. I thought it wise to get him out of here before we all became infected. Better to be shy one art assistant than the whole darn staff, wouldn't you say?"

"You had no right!" Pomeroy shouted, walking toward me with intent to kill. And I believe he would have accomplished his goal if the office entry bell hadn't jangled, announcing Mr. Crockett's return to the office.

"Good afternoon, Mr. Crockett!" I yelped, hastening to snag the boss's attention (and, as a result, his unwitting protection). "Did you have a nice lunch?"

"*Hummph,*" Crockett grunted, declining to answer yes or no. He hung up his hat and coat, scooped the afternoon newspapers off my desk, and—without a single glance in my direction—headed toward the back of the workroom. Pomeroy shot me a demonic grin, then spun around, followed Crockett into his pri-vate office, and slammed the door.

Aargh! I was in trouble so deep it was dismal.

Acting as cool and unperturbed as Grace Kelly in *To Catch a Thief,* I strolled across the room and sat down at my desk, turning my back on my gloating coworkers and burying my nose in a stack of invoices. I was freaked out about what was going on in Mr. Crockett's office, but I'd have swallowed a live slug before letting Mike and Mario know the extent of my discomfort.

Pomeroy came out a few minutes later and marched up the aisle to my desk. "Mr. Crockett wants to see you in his office," he growled. *"Now."*

"Yes, sir," I said, keeping a dozen curse words in my head and off my tongue. Rising to my feet and walking to the rear of the room, I felt like Marie Antoinette on the way to her execution. Would this moment mark the end of my hard-won *Daring Detective* career? Mike and Mario were both staring at me with barely disguised expressions of glee. They were lusting to see my head roll.

"You wanted to see me, Mr. Crockett?" I said, coming to a stop in his open doorway.

"Yeah," he snorted, taking a soggy cigar stub from his ashtray and relighting it. "Come in. Shut the door. Sit."

I followed his instructions like a good little girl.

Crockett got straight to the point. "Pomeroy says you told Lenny to go home early yesterday."

"That's right," I admitted. "He was very sick."

"You knew it was deadline day?" One of his bushy white eyebrows was cocked to the hilt.

"Yes, I did, sir, but—"

"And you told him to take today off, too?" Crockett interrupted.

"Yes, sir. I spoke to his mother, and she said he was still sick, and—"

"You did the right thing," he interrupted again.

"What?!" Were my ears deceiving me?

"I was gonna send Lenny home early myself, as soon as I got back from lunch, but I got detoured by our distributor and never made it back to the office."

"So you're not mad at me for what I did?"

"Nope. I'm glad. Lenny was in bad shape. He couldn't work for beans. And I didn't want the whole office getting sick." He leaned back in his chair, chewing on his stinky cigar. "Pomeroy doesn't feel the same way, though," he added. "He wants me to fire you for insubordinate behavior. Said cousin Oliver wants it, too."

"Oh," I said, steeling myself for the worst. There was no point in arguing. If Pomeroy wanted me out because Harrington wanted me out, I was as good as gone.

"I'm not doin' it, though," Crockett croaked. "Not yet. I want to talk to Harrington first, see if that's really what he wants. You're the only real reporter we've got, and he's been happy with your work in the past, so I'm not sure Pomeroy's tellin' the truth. How could Harrington even know about the Lenny thing when Pomeroy just found out about it himself?"

"Good question," I said, adding nothing, keeping the *real* reason Harrington might want me fired closely under wraps. (Well, what was I supposed to do? Tell Crockett that *Daring Detective's* distinguished owner and publisher might have murdered a prostitute? That he might want me given the axe just to keep me off the story? An allegation like that could cost me a hell of a lot more than my job!)

"So here's what I want you to do," Crockett said, squashing his cigar butt in the ashtray and lowering his voice to a conspiratorial grumble. "I want you to go back out there and *pretend* I gave you the boot. Act upset. Cry a little if you can. Pack up all your stuff, say your good-byes, and get out of here quick.

"Then you can take the rest of today and tomorrow off," he went on. "That'll make it *look* like I followed Harrington's orders, and it'll give me time to find out if the orders really came from *him*. I've got a hunch only Pomeroy's to blame. Harrington knows you're a good writer, and that you sell magazines, and I don't believe he wants me to give you the sack. If it turns out I'm right, you can come back to work on Monday."

"How will I know if you're right?"

"I've got your number. I'll give you a call over the weekend." He sat back in his chair and shoved his stubby fingers through his thick white hair. "Go on, now. Get outta here. Act hurt and turn on the tears. Give the boys a good show."

THE CRYING PART WAS EASY. I FELT SURE THAT I really *would* be fired, so I was truly distraught. The tears poured freely down my hot, humiliated cheeks. The saying good-bye part was hard, though. As much as I disliked (okay, detested) Pomeroy, Mike, and Mario, I knew I was going to miss them.

(In my case, familiarity always breeds as much fondness as contempt. Don't ask me why. That's just the way I am. And you want to know something else? I could tell from the sagging, less-than-satisfied smirks on my contemptible coworkers' faces that they were going to miss me, too.)

It wasn't until a little while later—after I'd dried my eyes, blown my nose, stuffed my few office belongings in a bag, and taken the elevator down to the lobby—that I realized how perfect the timing of my "firing" was. I was free as a bird for the rest of the day, and the whole day tomorrow, and the Saturday and Sunday after that. Except for the time I'd be spending with Dan (however much and whenever *that* turned out to be), I could devote all the rest of my waking hours to hunting down the sick creep who killed Virginia.

Lucky me.

Deciding to launch the next phase of my investigation immediately (i.e., before the thought of losing my job could set me adrift in a sea of self-pity), I darted over to the bank of pay phones on the far side of the lobby and dialed Sabrina. She answered after the first ring.

"Hi, Sabrina," I said. "It's me, Paige."

"Yes, I know," she stiffly replied. "I'd recognize that accusatorial tone anywhere.

"No, I'm calling to *apologize*," I declared. "I'm really sorry about what I said on the phone last night. Please forgive me; I didn't mean it. I was upset that you wouldn't tell me why Virginia became a call girl, but I never once considered you a suspect in her murder." (That was a little fib, you should know. I was still at the stage of suspecting *everybody*.)

"Thank you for your trust." Her words were dripping with sarcasm.

Hoping to deflect her icy hostility, I quickly changed the subject. "I have some news for you," I said. "My boss just gave me the rest of the afternoon and tomorrow off. Now I can focus all my energy on the case. For the next few days, anyway."

"Good. There really is no time to spare." She let out an

elongated sigh. (Relief? Exhaustion? Annoyance? Boredom? I couldn't tell.) "What progress have you made so far?"

Jeezmaneez! She'd given me her list just yesterday afternoon! Was she impatient, or what?

"I met with the district attorney today," I said, big chip balanced on my shoulder. "I asked him a few questions about murder. And about Virginia."

That got her attention. "What? I don't believe it! You actually mentioned her name?"

"Yep. Twice."

"What was his reaction?"

"The first time he acted dumb—like he didn't know who I was talking about. The second time he gave a whole speech about Virginia's murder that revealed he knew exactly who she was."

"What do you mean by *exactly?* Did he mention the name Melody or discuss the fact that she was a call girl?"

"No. He recounted the exact details of her death, but didn't say anything about her life."

"Well, that doesn't prove a thing!" she hissed. "Sam Hogarth *is* the DA, after all. It's his *job* to know the particulars of current crimes. Especially homicides. It's possible he hasn't yet realized that Virginia and Melody were one and the same."

"I'm well aware of that," I said, ticked off by her scornful tone. "I was merely reporting what happened, not jumping to hasty conclusions." I made a cross-eyed face at the receiver but managed not to groan out loud.

"So what's next on your agenda?" she inquired, relentlessly pushing ahead. "Who will you interview this afternoon?"

In spite of her nosy aggression, I was glad she asked that question.

"I'm hoping to talk to Virginia's best friends at the agency," I said, "and I'd like to start with Jocelyn Fritz—aka Candy. But I thought I should check with you first. I need to know if you've told her about me. I mean, is she expecting me to make contact, or do I have to introduce myself and explain what I'm doing?"

Sabrina heaved another long-suffering sigh. "Of course I've told Candy about you! I've told Brigitte, too. They know you're investigating the murder for me, and they will both give you their full cooperation, whenever you decide to get in touch with them."

"Okay, then I'm set to go. Sit tight, Sabrina—you'll be hearing from me soon."

This time I was the first to hang up.

Chapter 13

I FOUND IT FITTING THAT SAKS FIFTH AVENUE, Manhattan's most luxurious and celebrated department store, sits right next door to St. Patrick's Cathedral, the city's most luxurious and celebrated church. Both establishments offer opulent refuge from the seedy outside world, and both give their worshippers plenty to pray for. And if your prayers aren't answered in one place, they may be in the other (as long as you have an open spirit and an open wallet).

Praying that Jocelyn Fritz would be at work, I walked through the main entrance of Saks Fifth Avenue and headed for the gleaming wood-and-glass altar—I mean counter!—closest to the door. I had never been in Saks before (due to time and salary restrictions, I'm more of a Sears Roebuck girl), so I needed to ask for directions.

"May I help you?" said the tall, thin, elegantly dressed saleswoman standing behind the counter. Perfectly coiffed and made-up, she was smiling at me in the same way Sylvester smiles at Tweety—all teeth. "We have some lovely calfskin gloves on sale today," she purred. "Or perhaps you'd like to see our new line of monogrammed coin purses? They're fashioned from the finest Italian leather."

"No, thank you," I said. "I'm looking for the hat department. Can you tell me where it's located?"

Her smile vanished in an instant. "We have two millinery departments," she said with a sniff. "The custom-made hats can be found in the Salon Moderne on the third floor, and the factory-made hats—such as the red beret you're wearing—are on display at the rear of the main floor." She turned and pointed toward the back of the store, certain that I would be heading in that direction.

"Thank you," I said, giving her a quick nod and making a beeline for the elevators.

Sabrina's notes had said Jocelyn was an assistant hat *designer*, so I figured she would be in the Salon Moderne. Following two pearl-laden, sable-coated matrons, I pranced into the wood-paneled self-service elevator and pushed the button for 3. The furry ladies got off on 2 and the car resumed its climb. When it reached the third floor, an ethereal bell sounded and the doors whooshed open. Then I stepped out of the elevator and entered Never-Never Land.

I had read about the ritzy Salon Moderne in Dorothy Kilgallen's gossip column, so I knew that "everybody who *was* anybody" liked to shop there. Marlene Dietrich, Edith Piaf, Claudette Colbert, Irene Dunne, Estée Lauder, Mrs. E. F. Hutton, Betsy Bloomingdale, Mrs. Pierre Du Pont, Mrs. Darryl Zanuck—they were all, according to Dorothy, Salon Moderne regulars.

Nobody who was anybody was here now, though. I was, in fact, the only person (okay, nobody) in the place. Straightening the collar of my camel's hair jacket and hugging my bag of office belongings close to my chest, I ventured deeper into the salon.

The receiving room, or reception area, or showroom (or whatever you want to call it) of the Salon Moderne looked as though it had been transplanted from the Palace of Versailles. The doors, floor, shelves, and ceiling were edged with intricately carved wood moldings, and the walls were covered with pale blue damask that seemed to be hand-embroidered (but what would *I* know about that?). The silvery blue carpet was so thick I felt like I was walking on a cloud.

Four headless, armless mannequins were prominently positioned around the room, each modeling a fancy designer dress. Their heads had been placed on separate pedestals and topped with flamboyant custom-made hats. I wondered what they'd done with the arms.

"Welcome to the Salon Moderne," said a throaty female voice behind me.

Startled, I turned to face a tall, willowy blonde who had managed to enter the room and walk over to me without making a sound. Wearing a pale blue suit, a ruffled white silk blouse, and an enormous sapphire brooch, she looked to be in her late thirties.

"My name is Sophia. I'm the director here. How may I help you?" she asked, making a quick study of my somewhat-less-than-elegant (okay, cheesy) appearance. I could tell she thought I'd wandered into the salon by mistake. "Do you have an appointment with one of our designers?"

"No appointment," I said. "I came to see Jocelyn Fritz, an assistant designer in your hat department. Would it be possible for me to speak with her for a few minutes? I'm her cousin Paige from Idaho. I just got into town today."

Sophia bought my story on the spot. (She probably thought the brown paper bag I was clutching to my breast was full of potatoes.) "I'll see if Miss Fritz is in," she said, turning and walking toward one of the ornate doors leading to the inner sanctum. "Please wait here."

A GOOD TEN MINUTES LATER—AFTER I'D WORN tracks in the carpet and studied every flower, bow, tuft of tulle, and bird wing on every silly hat in the place—another tall, willowy woman appeared. This one was younger, prettier, and more sophisticated-looking. Her long, light brown hair was styled in a sleek pageboy, and she wore a simple, formfitting black wool sheath.

"Come with me, Paige," she said, as she whisked right by me and strode toward the exit. "They gave me only a fifteen-minute break." The scent of Chanel No. 5 wafted in her wake.

I spun around and dashed after her. "I guess you're Jocelyn," I said, catching up at the elevator.

"Good guess." She gave me a quick glance, then pushed the UP button. "Let's go to the café and have a cup of something."

"Okay," I said, as the elevator doors opened and we stepped in.

The car was full of well-dressed shoppers, so we remained silent until we reached the eighth floor. Jocelyn led the way to the café and asked the hostess for a table for two near the window.

The minute we were seated and alone, Jocelyn craned her neck toward me and snapped, "You aren't too smart, are you? Why did you come to see me at work?" She brushed a wave of beige hair off her cheek and fixed her intense green eyes on my face. "Surely it occurred to you that I couldn't talk openly at my place of employment."

"Yes, that thought did cross my mind," I admitted, "but I had to ignore it. My time isn't my own, and I have to make every free minute count." I pulled Abby's Pall Malls out of my purse and offered her one as a peace offering. She took it, and we both lit up.

"Well, you'd better get cracking," she said, spewing smoke toward the ceiling. "My free minutes are dwindling fast."

Glad for the excuse to skip the small talk, I took a deep breath and dived right in: "Okay, how long had you and Virginia been friends?"

She gave me a puzzled look. "Who's Vir—? Oh! You mean Melody!"

"Right."

"She was the best friend I ever had. We were tight for two years. As close as sisters. I miss her desperately." Her demeanor was cool and her words were curt, but I believed she meant what she said.

"Did you tell each other everything?"

"God, no!" She tossed her head and laughed. "That would have been the end of our friendship for sure."

"Did she ever tell you why she became a call girl?"

"No. I asked her about it once, and she pulled the clam act on me. I didn't bring the subject up again. Melody was a very private person, and so am I. We respected each other's boundaries. We never even told—"

Jocelyn cut her sentence short when the waitress arrived to take our order. "Just a cup of coffee for me," she said, without looking at the menu. "What do you want, Paige?"

"I'll have coffee and the soup of the day." I really wanted the turkey and stuffing special (well, I hadn't eaten since breakfast, you know!), but I thought I'd better conserve my (I mean, Abby's) money. Who knew what expenses the rest of the day would bring?

"Where were we?" I asked as soon as the waitress disappeared. "You were saying . . . ?"

Jocelyn patted her pageboy and took another drag on her cigarette. "I was saying that, as close as Melody and I were, we never told each other our real names. She knew me only as Candy, and I knew her only as Melody. That's one of Sabrina's strictest rules, and we both honored it."

"Did you ever discuss your clients with each other, or does Sabrina have rules about that, too?"

"Sabrina is a very smart woman," Jocelyn declared. "She knows we have to talk about our johns with *somebody,* so she allows us to gossip, complain, give tips, and share information among ourselves. We are, however, strictly forbidden to discuss the clientele with anybody *else.* That's a crime punishable by death."

"Death?" I croaked, wondering if I'd dug up my first real clue. I could feel my eyes popping out of their sockets.

"Oh, for crying out loud!" Jocelyn said with a derisive smirk. "Don't be such a dope! That's just a figure of speech. I didn't mean anything by it."

The waitress returned and saved me from further embarrassment. While she served our coffee, I smoked and stared out the window at the heavenly view. Soaring and glistening in the late afternoon sun, the spires of St. Patrick's seemed close enough to touch.

"I'll be right back with your soup," the waitress said, yanking me back down to earth. She tucked her tray under her arm and plodded off toward the kitchen.

Jocelyn sighed and snuffed her cigarette in the ashtray. "I can't stay while you eat. I'm expected back in four minutes." She poured enough cream in her coffee to cool it, then began gulping it down.

"So I'll ask the big question now," I said, putting my cigarette out, too. "Do you have any idea who killed Vir—I mean, Melody?"

"I have my suspicions," she said, clapping her empty cup back in its saucer. "*Strong* suspicions." Her pretty face turned stormy and her eyes flashed like lightning. "It was either Sam or Tony. I'd stake my life on it."

"You mean Sam Hogarth and Tony Corona?" I asked, taking note that she'd used their first names.

"They're both devils in disguise!" she spat. "I know it's

shocking—Sam being the DA, and Tony being such a big star—but from all the dirt I've heard, either one is capable of murder."

"What dirt?" I spluttered. "What have you heard? Who did you hear it from? Did Melody say anything? Do you or any of the other girls have any incriminating information? And what about Oliver Rice Harrington? He was one of Melody's regulars. Did you ever hear anything about him?" My tongue was having convulsions.

"I can't go into all of that now!" Jocelyn slapped her hand on the tabletop. "Too many questions and too little time. I have to get back to work!" She jumped to her feet, opened her purse, and tossed some change on the table. "It's your own fault, you know. You shouldn't have come to see me here. I have my job, my reputation, and my employee discount to protect."

"Then can I meet you later, after you get off work? I could come to the Barbizon," I said, naming the women's hotel where she lived.

"Not tonight," she said. "I've got an early dinner date."

"Anybody I know?" I probed, wondering if Candy had inherited one (or all) of Melody's top three clients.

She nodded, winked, and gave me a cryptic smile.

"Who?" I begged. "Who is it?" My curiosity was killing me. But more than that, I was panicked about her safety. "Have you lost your mind?" I cried. "Do you have a psychotic death wish? How could you accept a date with a man who may have murdered your best friend?"

"Oh, keep your shorts on, Sherlock," she teased, taking pleasure in my crazed discomfort. "I'm not meeting a john. I'm dining with Sabrina."

Chapter 14

IF I'D HAD MY WITS ABOUT ME, I WOULD HAVE chased Jocelyn to the elevator and wangled an invitation to join her and Sabrina for dinner. I might have learned a lot from such a cozy confab. As it was, though, I *didn't* have my wits about me (or anywhere else, for that matter). All I could see or think about was the lovely bowl of corn chowder the waitress had put down in front of me. It was hot, creamy, fragrant, and hearty—and it came with a basket of rolls and three pats of butter.

Five minutes later every corn kernel, bread crumb, and butter pat was gone.

And five minutes after that, *I* was gone—busting out of Saks, dashing down Fifth Avenue to 45th Street, then heading west toward Ninth Avenue and the Hell's Kitchen tenement where Ethel Maguire—otherwise known as Brigitte—lived. It was a quarter to six. With any luck, Ethel's classes at the nursing school would be over for the day, and she'd be at home taking care of her crippled husband.

I climbed the cracked and worn cement steps to the front door of Ethel's building and, seeing that the lock was broken, let myself in. The hallway mailbox for apartment 3B was labeled MAGUIRE, so I darted across the dingy foyer and scrambled up the creaky wooden stairs to the third floor. The odor of boiled cabbage was strong, and a baby was crying somewhere overhead.

I shifted my unwieldy bag of office effects to my other arm, took a deep breath (which was a big mistake, since the smell of cooked cabbage makes me gag), and knocked on the door of 3B.

"Just a minute!" cried a female voice from the other side of the battered wooden door. "I'll be right there!"

Suddenly overcome with exhaustion from the many physical and emotional ordeals of the day, I whined out loud, leaned my back and shoulders against the wall, and waited. . . .

A short while later a young woman opened the door. I knew it was Ethel: She was wearing her uniform, and—even with little to no makeup and her blonde hair pinned up under her student nurse's cap—she was a dead ringer for European sex goddess Brigitte Bardot. "Yes?" she said, brown eyes widening as she wondered who I was and why I was there.

"Hi, Ethel," I said. "I'm Paige Turner. I believe Sabrina told you I'd be coming by. I have a few questions I'd like to—"

"Shhhhh!" she hissed, holding one finger up to her lips and hurriedly stepping into the hall. She pulled the door partially closed behind her. "My husband's sitting in the living room! He'll hear every word you say!"

"I'm sorry," I whispered, "but Sabrina said I could—"

"Who is it, Ethel?" a man called out. "Who are you talking to?" His voice was rough and booming—like Broderick Crawford's in *Born Yesterday*.

A stormy cloud fell over Ethel's striking face. "We can't talk here!" she said to me. "Quick! Go downstairs and wait for me on the stoop. I'll be down as soon as I can." She ducked back inside her apartment and firmly closed the door.

I TRUDGED DOWN TO THE FIRST FLOOR AND WENT outside. It was beginning to get dark. The sun was sinking fast below the Hudson River horizon, and there was a distinct chill in the air. The people on the sidewalks, presumably making their way home from work, were hunching their shoulders and tucking their chins inside their coat collars. Wobbly with fatigue, I propped my bag against the metal railing and collapsed on the top step of the cement stoop. So what if the seat of my skirt got dirty? I was too tired to care. And I couldn't bear the agony of my sadistic stilettos for one more second.

When Ethel finally came downstairs and out on the stoop, I

didn't even try to get up. I just sat there like a stump until she ventured over and sat down beside me.

"Sorry to keep you waiting," she said, putting her purse in her lap and tucking the hem of her navy blue coat tight around her knees. "He's always so suspicious. It took me all this time to convince him that you came to see somebody else in the building and knocked on our door by mistake."

"What excuse did you give him for coming downstairs?"

Ethel sighed. "I said I had to pick up some chops at the butcher. For our dinner. When the subject turns to food, he's always more agreeable."

I laughed. "So the fastest way to a man's heart really *is* through his stomach."

"I wouldn't say that," she sniffed. "Most of the other men I know prefer a more southern route." Her expression was so grim, I knew she wasn't trying to be witty.

"Speaking of other men," I said, leaping into the opening but keeping my voice as soft and supportive as possible, "do you have any dates tonight?"

She gave me a puzzled look. "Just one. At ten. Why?"

"I need to know if the man you're meeting was ever one of Melody's clients," I said, switching to a firmer tone. "Because if he *was,* he may be a prime suspect in her murder. And if that's the case, I don't want you to go out with him." I was challenging Sabrina's authority, I knew, but I didn't give a good goddamn.

Ethel shook her head. "Oh, you don't have to worry about that, Paige. The man I'm seeing tonight is one of my regulars, not Melody's. And you shouldn't be concerned about me, anyway. Sabrina is very protective of me; she loves me like a daughter. She would *never* fix me up with a violent man."

"Are you sure about that?" I asked, thinking poor Melody had probably felt the same way.

"I'm positive," she said. Her expression was adamant, and her jaw was set in stone.

I took my cue and moved on. "Does your husband know how you spend your nights?" (I don't know why I asked that question—it had nothing to do with the murder. I guess pure nosiness was to blame.)

"Of course not!" she gasped. "His legs are crippled, but his arms are strong. If he ever finds out what I've been doing, he'll tear me limb from limb."

"But how have you kept him in the dark? He must see you get all dolled up and go out. Where does he think you're going?"

"He thinks I'm a hostess at a fancy nightclub—that I'm paying all our bills and putting myself through school with my salary. Ha! He's so out of touch he doesn't realize that a hostess makes even less than a busboy—no matter how fancy the nightclub is. It's a man's world."

"Tell me about it," I said, thinking how all the guys at *DD* made much more than I did, and how—if I really had been fired—I'd soon be making *nothing*.

Ethel turned up her collar and buttoned it tight around her neck. "It's getting cold, Paige," she said. "And I have to go to the butcher before I hurry back upstairs. If you have any more questions for me, you'd better ask them fast. I can't sit here much longer."

"Okay," I said, "I'll make it quick. First question: Why did Melody become a call girl? I realize she must have needed money, but do you know what she needed it *for*?"

"No, and I always wondered about that. She certainly didn't spend much on herself. And her job at the accounting office paid enough to take care of her rent and expenses. She wanted to be a successful singer and songwriter, but that's not something you can buy. Maybe she was saving up for something special—a house or a car or something like that."

"A mink jacket was found with her body," I said, "and also some diamond jewelry. Do you know if she bought those items herself?"

"I doubt it," Ethel replied. "Melody didn't care about things like that. They were probably gifts from her clients."

"Anyone in particular?"

"I wouldn't know," she said with a shrug. "She went out with a number of wealthy men. It could have been anybody."

"Sam Hogarth or Tony Corona, for instance? Or Oliver Rice Harrington?"

"She went out with all three of them, but she never mentioned any presents."

I was nearing the end of my investigative rope. "Okay, here's my final and obviously most important question," I said. "Do you have any idea who murdered your friend, or why anyone would want her dead? Please think carefully before you answer."

Ethel turned and gave me the saddest look imaginable. "I've

thought of nothing else for two days," she said, "but I still don't have an inkling. Melody was the kindest, sweetest person in the world. Yes, she was a prostitute, but that didn't diminish her goodness in any way. Her beauty was astonishing, and her heart was as big as the sky." Ethel's body began to shake and her eyes filled with tears. "Oh, God!" she cried, dropping her head in her hands and grasping her face with her fingers. "She suffered such a horrible death. Why would anybody want to kill her? Who could have done this terrible thing?"

I leaned closer and put my arm around her trembling shoulders. "I don't know, Ethel," I said, a jolt of fresh energy shooting up my spine, "but I intend to find out."

Chapter 15

BY THE TIME I LIMPED BACK TO SEVENTH AV-
enue and made my way down to Times Square, my energy had
evaporated. Just putting one foot in front of the other was a
strain. My bag of office stuff felt as heavy as a bag of bricks. I
tried to jump-start my engine at Nedicks—rapidly consuming a
chili dog and an Orange Crush at the sidewalk counter—but the
food (if you could call it that) just made me feel queasy. And the
blinking neon lights of the movie and peep show marquees—
coupled with the loud pops, whizzes, bings, and bangs of the
surrounding penny arcades and rifle ranges—did nothing to
soothe my frazzled soul.

On the verge of another crying jag (were my days at *Daring
Detective* really over?), and too weary to seek out Tony Corona
at the Plaza Hotel as I'd planned, I staggered down the steps to
the 42nd Street subway station and caught a downtown local for
home.

Emerging from the subway at Sheridan Square and walking
the few blocks down Seventh to Bleecker, I was praying to God
(and Jesus and Allah and Vishnu and Buddha, et al.) that Abby
would be home. I needed a good friend to talk to. I needed to sit
down, take my shoes off, and unbosom my dreadful new troubles and secrets. I needed a drink.

When I reached our building and saw that the lights in Abby's living room–cum–art studio were on, I yelped with joy and darted up the stairs to the landing between our apartments. My prayers had been answered! Relief was at hand!

Oops. Not so fast.

Abby's door was wide open, and she was standing at her kitchen counter mixing up a batch of cocktails as usual—but she was not alone. A lean, dark, outrageously handsome young man stood right behind her, pressing his body close to hers, pulling her long, thick black hair to one side and planting a string of steamy kisses on the exposed nape of her neck.

Rats! It was Jimmy Birmingham, Abby's sometime lover—a wildly popular Village poet whose work, I thought, was downright dopey. Likewise, his personality.

"Cut it out, Jimmy!" Abby said, giggling. "You're getting me hot. If you don't stop, we'll have to strip down and do it right here on the floor."

"Ahem!" I croaked, hastening to announce my arrival before the strip show started. "I hate to interrupt, but the door was open and I—"

"Oh, hi, Paige!" Abby butted Jimmy off her back and turned her smiling face toward me. "What's tickin', chicken? I was wondering what happened to you. I'm making a pitcher of martinis. Do you want one, or are you still drunk from last night?"

"Ha, ha," I said, setting my bag of belongings on the floor near the door and taking a seat at the kitchen table. (Had my boozy breakdown been just last night? It seemed more like a month ago. No wonder I was so tired!) "I'd love a martini," I confessed, ignoring the possible consequences. "Make it a big one." I slipped my arms out of my jacket and tucked it over the back of the chair. "Hi, Jimmy," I said. "What's new?"

"A lot!" he replied, stroking his dark, neatly trimmed Vandyke and politely hiding the fact that he wasn't any happier to see me than I was to see him. He sat down across the table from me, took an Old Gold out of the pack in his shirt pocket, and lit up. "I just finished a far-out new poem and came over to read it to Abby."

Uh-oh!

"Did she like it?" I asked, hoping against hope that the reading had already taken place. I was *not* in a poetic mood.

"I haven't heard it yet," Abby said, setting a martini—complete with olive—in front of me. "Ain't that swell, Nell?

Now you can dig it with me." Her emphatic ear-to-ear grin made it clear that she expected me to sit tight for the recitation. (Misery loves company, they say, but Abby *demands* it.)

Stifling a groan and rolling my eyes at the ceiling, I took a big gulp of my drink. "Hey, where's Otto?" I asked, looking around for Jimmy's little dog—the miniature dachshund who was always at his master's side, or tucked under his arm, or curled up like a sausage in his lap.

At the sound of his name, Otto poked his sleepy head up over the arm of Abby's red velvet loveseat (which sits smack between her kitchen and art studio) and started whimpering. Then, when he saw me, he let out a happy yip. He jumped off the loveseat and ran over to me, toenails tapping across the linoleum, skinny tail twirling out of control.

"Hello, sweetie!" I cooed, picking up the little dog and giving him a big hug. Otto and I were old friends. We'd endured many poetry readings together. I helped the friendly pup get settled on my lap, then began stroking his soft brown back— from his wet, pointy nose to his wagging tail.

"So let me tell you about my new poem," Jimmy said, getting excited. His eyes were shining, his beard was glistening, and his young movie-star-handsome face (Tony Curtis with a hint of Gregory Peck) was glowing. If he'd had a tail, it would have been wagging like Otto's. "It's the most important opus I ever wrote!" he proclaimed. "It's so way out, it's gone! I created it special for the big Dylan Thomas blowout they're gonna have at the White Horse next month."

"Blowout?" Abby asked, becoming more interested. (She loves wild parties.)

"White Horse?" I inquired, just to be polite.

"Yeah, that's where Dylan Thomas died!" Jimmy exclaimed. "At the White Horse Tavern right here in the Village! So that's where we're gonna celebrate. Isn't that cool?"

Not to my mind, it wasn't. "In the first place," I said, "Dylan Thomas died at St. Vincent's hospital, *not* at the White Horse. He just *drank* himself to death at the White Horse. And in the second place, Thomas was—like a lot of other Welsh poets—a very serious and solemn person. And he was deathly afraid of dying. So, do you really think it's cool to *celebrate* his demise?"

"Well, it wasn't my idea," Jimmy yowled. His normally mellow baritone had risen to a high-pitched whine. "The Downtown

Poets Society planned the whole thing. And they asked me to write a special poem for the occasion. What's wrong with that? It's a real honor, you know!"

"It sure is, baby," Abby cut in, swooping to Jimmy's defense. She handed him a martini, then sat down next to him with her own. "I'm so proud of you I could *plotz*." Grabbing hold of his whiskered chin and pulling his face toward hers, she planted a whopping open-mouthed kiss on his pouting lips. (Abby, if you haven't already guessed, was a tad more attracted to Jimmy's idyllic body than to his poetic soul.)

Averting my eyes from the sloppy spectacle, I stared down at Otto and fondled his soft, warm ears. He snuffled loudly, laid his head on my knees, and went back to sleep.

"So can I read it now, Ab?" Jimmy pleaded, as soon as she let him up for air. "I'm dyin' to know what you think. I mean, *I* think it's a masterpiece, but if you don't dig it, I'll write another one—and another one, and another one, and another one—until you tell me I've got it right. You're my muse, you know!"

Abby shot me an apologetic look, then said to Jimmy, "Sure, babe. You can read it now. Finish your cigarette, and then stand over there in the light, where we can get the full effect. (Translation: *get a better look at your fine young physique.*)

"All right!" Jimmy crowed, stubbing out his cigarette and bounding to his feet. He took a fast slug of his martini, strutted over to the exact spot Abby had indicated (under the hanging paper lantern she'd bought last week in Chinatown), and pulled a folded cocktail napkin out of his back pocket. Then he cleared his throat and announced to Abby and me—or, rather, to the worshipful, cheering, standing-room-only crowd in his mind— that his name was Jimmy Birmingham and he was here to read his latest poem, a special tribute to Dylan Thomas titled "The Doomer." He stood silent in the spotlight for a few seconds and then, when the imaginary applause died down, he unfolded his napkin and began:

> It may come your way
> By twist or turn
> A case of free samples to all.
> Bedlam's brethren all swallow in the greed!
> If you want to get beat,
> Hang around Sucker Street.

That dank drunky poet's D.T.'s
Gives me the doomer . . .
Mops and brooms together
Make me swoon.
Hot fires and cold night tomorrows
New beats to the jive
Further to oblivion.

Whew! I said to myself, as soon as it was over, *that was mer-cifully short. And not as painful as I thought it would be. Is Jimmy getting better, or am I just getting soft in the head?*

"Oh, baby!" Abby said, rising from her chair and joining Jimmy in the spotlight. She grabbed him by the sideburns, kissed him on both cheeks, and pronounced that "The Doomer" was, indeed, a masterpiece. "It's powerful and it's *perfect*," she declared, laying stress on the last word. "It's atomic! It's going to shoot you into the stratosphere."

But Abby didn't fool me. I knew what she was doing. She was praising Jimmy's poem to the hilt because if she didn't, he'd go back to his apartment and write another one. And then another one. And maybe another one after that. And Abby thought all of that time would be much better spent in her bed-room.

"You really mean it, Ab?" Jimmy asked, looking more like a bashful little boy than the bearded twenty-two-year-old grown-up he really was. Well, sort of was.

"Of course I mean it, you kook! It's the most! I really dig it." Abby led Jimmy back over to the table and put his martini in his hand. Then, still standing, she picked up her own glass and raised it high in the air. "I propose a toast," she said, "to Jimmy Birmingham, a brave and brilliant new artist whose understand-ing of the human condition is beyond compare!"

She could say that again (except for the brilliant part).

"I'll toast to that!" Jimmy said, lifting his glass and clinking it against hers.

"Me, too," I mumbled, raising my martini in the air for a second, then taking a drink. (Well, I couldn't stand up! Otto was still sleeping in my lap.)

"Hey, thanks a lot, ladies," Jimmy said, plunking his glass down on the table. He squeezed one arm around Abby's neck, planted another sloppy kiss on her lips, then released her like a hot potato. "Wake up, Otto," he commanded, snapping his fingers and strutting over to retrieve his peacoat off the back of the loveseat. "Let's make like a tree and leave."

Otto popped to attention, jumped off my lap and skittered over to stand at Jimmy's feet.

"Where do you think you're going?!" Abby cried. (Now *she* was the one who was whining.) "I thought you'd want to stay for a while! Aren't you even going to finish your drink?" (Translation: *Aren't you going to take me upstairs and ravish me?*)

"Don't have time," Jimmy said. "I'm meeting some cats down at the Houston Street pool hall. We've got a hot bet going." He put on his peacoat and scooped Otto up in his arms. "I might swing by the San Remo later. Wanna come?"

"No, thanks," Abby replied, in a huff. "I think I'll go to bed early—with a book of Shakespeare's sonnets. They *really* turn me on."

If Jimmy felt the sting of her snide remark, he didn't let it show. Hugging Otto tight under one elbow, he swaggered over to the open door, bade us both a good-natured good night, then scrambled down the stairs to the street.

Chapter 16

ABBY WAS FUMING, BUT I WAS TICKLED PINK. "Thank God Jimmy's gone!" I blurted, unable to disguise my delight. "I have so much to tell you, Ab, I'm bursting at the seams."

"Oh, yeah?" she said, pacing around the kitchen, cartoon steam coming out of her ears. "Well, I'm bursting, too, but for a different reason. Do you believe the nerve of that *putz*? How could he run out on me that way?" (Abby was so gorgeous and sexy and desirable to men, she wasn't used to being rejected—by Jimmy Birmingham or any other *putz*.) "We listened to his stupid damn poem, didn't we?" she shrieked. "I even praised the silly thing and raised a toast to Jimmy's brilliance! Would it have been so hard for him to show me a little respect in return?" (Translation: *shtup me before he left?*)

My reply wasn't very sympathetic, but I simply couldn't resist: "If you want to get beat," I quoted, "hang around Sucker Street."

"Oh, shut up!" She pulled her wild black hair into a ponytail and tied it with the blue silk scarf she yanked out of a kitchen drawer. Then, shoving up the sleeves of her tight, black scoop-neck sweater, she grabbed the martini pitcher off the kitchen counter and refilled our glasses. "So, what did you want to tell me?" she said sulkily, plopping down at the table and lighting up a cigarette. "This better be good, or I'm gonna hit the sack with Shakespeare."

"Oh, it's good, all right. It's top, top secret, and incredibly shocking, and I couldn't breathe a word of it in front of Jimmy. Or anybody else, for that matter."

"So, how do *I* rate, Kate?" She was getting interested in spite of herself. (Abby's sense of curiosity is as well developed—okay, *overly* developed—as my own.)

"You're my best friend," I said, "and I need somebody to talk to. And you're the only one I can trust to keep all the secrets."

"*All* the secrets?" She was growing perkier by the second. "How many are there?"

"Too many to count. But I'll tell you everything I know."

"Then start blabbing, babe!" she urged, eyes sparkling with excitement. "And don't leave anything out. I've got all night!"

"Okay, but hold on just a second." I jumped to my feet and quickly gathered all my things together. "I'm gonna drop this stuff off in my apartment and pick up something I want to show you. And I want to leave my door open so I can hear the phone if Dan calls."

Abby shot me a dirty look. "Well, you'd better make it quick, Slick. I haven't got all night, you know!" If she had any notion that she'd just contradicted herself, she didn't let on. Fretfully tapping one foot on the floor, she took a drag on her cigarette and blew an irritable whoosh of smoke in my direction.

Not wanting to lose Abby's attention (she has the patience of a gnat), I darted next door, let myself in, tossed all my stuff on the living room chair, kicked off my high heels, snatched Sabrina's list from its hiding place in the bookcase (inside my beat-up paperback copy of Dashiell Hammett's *The Maltese Falcon*), and scooted back to Abby's in a flash.

"You are *not* going to believe everything that's happened to me in the last two days," I blustered, out of breath. "I don't believe it myself." Sitting down at the table, I put the lavender list on my lap and took a big gulp of my martini. "I'm working on a new assignment, Ab, and it's the most atrocious, sinister, and scandalous murder case I've ever been involved in."

She flipped her ponytail over one shoulder and—trying to look bored even though she clearly wasn't—took another puff on her ciggie. "Is this the assignment that has nothing to do with *Daring Detective*—the story you're *not* going to write?"

"Well, yes, but how did you——?"

"And does it have something to do with a woman named Sabrina?"

"Er, yeah, but——"

"And are Oliver Rice Harrington, Sam Hogarth, and Tony Corona somehow connected?"

"Jeez, Abby!" I screeched. "How the hell——?"

"And what about the three girls who each have two names? Lemme see now . . . there's Jocelyn/Candy, Ethel/Brigitte, and Virginia/Melody. I'm figuring they're either models, actresses, strippers, or whores. Am I right?"

I groaned out loud and downed the rest of my drink, including the gin-soaked olive. "I get it," I said, annoyed. "I spilled the beans when I was drunk last night, and then you read my notes after I passed out. I wondered how they got out of my purse and onto the table. Very tricky. But now, since you know the whole story already," I added, deciding to play the game her way, "I might as well go home. I'll catch up on my sleep and let you catch up on your Shakespeare." I rose to my feet, held the folded lavender list high overhead, and——guiding it through the air like a paper airplane——headed for the door.

That got her. I knew it would.

"Stop!" she cried. "I give up! Get your stupid damn tushy back in here and tell me what's going on!"

I didn't need any further persuading. I bounced back to my place at the table and spilled the beans again. All of them this time.

ONE HOUR, FOUR CIGARETTES, AND TWO MARTINIS (each) later, I had disclosed all the details of the whole shocking saga to date——from the moment I first read about Virginia's murder in the paper, to my lunch at Sabrina's Gramercy Park apartment, to my visit to the DA's office, to Pomeroy's strange behavior and my getting fired from my job, to my forays into Saks Fifth Avenue and Hell's Kitchen to interview Jocelyn and Ethel (aka Candy and Brigitte).

"See what I mean, Ab? This is the most complicated, evil, and dangerous murder case I've ever even *thought* of trying to solve."

"Yeah, but it's also the most interesting." She was practically licking her chops.

"Interesting?!" I squawked. "What a mean and thoughtless thing to say! Aren't you the least bit worried about me? I'm playing with fire here, and I could get burned to a crisp! I've already lost my job. What's going to happen to me next?"

"Oh, can the rage, Paige. Your getting fired may have nothing to do with the case, you dig? Maybe the only reason you got axed is because you decided to play boss and let Lenny go home early."

"No. I'm certain there's more to it than that. I've never seen Pomeroy so upset. His cousin has to be putting the heat on him for some reason. And since Harrington was one of Virginia's major clients. . . ."

"Oh, don't waste your time worrying about *him*," Abby said. "He's the least likely suspect of all." She lit another cigarette and blew a perfect smoke ring toward the ceiling. "Virginia was obviously murdered in the heat of passion, and Harrington's too old for that."

"Are you nuts? He's only fifty-two. And if he's too old for passion, why would he hire a call girl?"

"To have her stroke his male ego and make him feel young again."

I wasn't buying her reasoning (if you could call it that), but I didn't want to argue. "What about Sam Hogarth?" I probed. "Don't you find it a teensy bit hard to believe that the Manhattan district attorney could be a murderer?"

"No way, Doris Day! In fact, I'd lay you ten to one right now that he's the one who did it." (Abby's a charter member of the National Jump to Conclusions Club.)

"How on earth can you make a rash statement like that?" I sputtered.

"I have a strong hunch," she blithely replied.

"Based on what, exactly?"

"On the fact that the man is fiercely attracted to the world of crime. Why else would he want the job of DA? And from what I've seen, the act of *fighting* crime is just a few steps away from *committing* it. Look at Joe McCarthy. He's so bent on catching Commies that he's become a traitor himself. He's done more to destroy American liberty than J. Edgar Hoover and his FBI spies! And a heck of a lot of firemen commit arson, you know. And some creeps become cops just so they can carry a gun."

On the one hand, I agreed with her.

On the other hand, I was so hurt and offended I was almost speechless.

Almost, but not quite.

"Are you telling me that *Dan* is just steps away from committing murder?" I screeched at the top of my lungs. "Do you think *I* write about crooks and killers because I'm lusting to lead a life of crime? Jesus, Abby! There *is* such a thing as justice, you know. And, whether you believe it or not, there are *some* people who are working to uphold it."

"Yeah, but I doubt if Sam Hogarth is one of them," she said, totally unfazed by my noisy outburst. "He looks like a real schemer to me. I see his picture in the paper all the time—schmoozing with assorted big shots and celebrities at one ritzy nightclub after another—and he pops up on the radio at least twice a day to brag about his 'tireless and fearless' campaign against organized crime. I kid you not, Dot. Whenever Hammy Sammy spots a camera or a microphone, he steps in front of it. He strikes me as the worst kind of do-gooder—the kind who's just doing good for himself."

Having recently been exposed to Sam Hogarth's self-serving charm, I couldn't argue with that.

"So, how do you feel about Tony Corona?" I asked, moving on to the final suspect on Sabrina's list. "Do you believe he's capable of murder?"

"Of course he is."

"For God's sake, Abby! Couldn't you at least *think* about the question for a second or two before pronouncing your verdict?"

"Why should I think when I already know?"

See what I was up against?

"Then please tell me what you *think* you know," I said, raising my empty martini glass to my lips, throwing my head back, and taking a great big slug of nothing.

Abby put out her cigarette and fired up another one. "I know what everybody knows," she said. "Tony Corona is a terrific singer, a pretty good actor, a big drinker and gambler, a notorious playboy, and the most popular and successful entertainer since Bing Crosby. The ladies all love him."

"So . . . ?"

"So, he's also the biggest snake in show business."

"Snake? What makes you say that?"

"Oh, come on, Paige!" she snapped. "Stop playing dumb.

You've read the gossip columns and heard the rumors! He lies to his friends and screws his business associates; he cheats on all his wives. He climbed to the top by stomping on everybody in his path, and he stays on top by playing footsie with the mob. He's a rattlesnake, and you know it."

"Well, since you put it that way. . . ."

"And that's not all!" she barreled on. "He has the hottest temper in town. He beat a porter at the Plaza to a pulp last year, just because he didn't deliver his bags to his room fast enough. The poor guy almost died! They kept the episode out of the papers, but a friend of mine is a desk clerk there, and he told me all about it."

"But that was an isolated incident," I said. "Maybe he was just—"

"Having a bad day?" she scoffed. "Not a chance, Vance. Hedda Hopper's written tons of blind items about Corona's uncontrollable anger. She calls him 'the Crooner,' but it's obvious who she's talking about. She says he's always causing trouble in Las Vegas when he plays the Flamingo. As soon as his last show is over, he throws down about ten shots of bourbon, lights up a cigar, sticks a gun in his pocket, and hits the blackjack table. And the house knows he'd better win, because if he doesn't, he goes berserk and threatens to shoot the dealer."

"Maybe he's just suffering from a neurotic fear of failure," I quipped.

"Or a psychotic urge to kill," she replied, in total seriousness.

I gave her a puzzled look. "So, what are you saying? Now you think *Corona* murdered Virginia?"

"No, I still think Hogarth did it. But Tony the Tiger's running a close second."

I was about to bring up the subject of Sabrina Stanhope when my phone started ringing.

"That must be Dan!" I whooped. I jumped to my feet and darted into the hall before she could object. "Stay there or be square," I called over my shoulder. "I'll be right back."

Chapter 17

I THREW MYSELF DOWN ON THE COUCH, tucked my icy feet under my bottom, reached for the ringing phone, and snatched the receiver up to my ear. "Hellohhhhh," I cooed, breathing directly into the mouthpiece, doing my best to sound sexy but probably sounding like a hoot owl with a head cold.

"Hi, babe," said Dan. "You sound terrible. Are you drunk again, sick, or just tired? I hope you haven't caught the flu from Lenny."

(See, I told you!)

"I'm not drunk or sick," I said (although I was probably a bit of both), "but I *am* pretty tired. I didn't get much sleep last night."

"Really? That surprises me. The state you were in, I figured you'd be down for the count." I couldn't see Dan's expression, of course, but I had a strong suspicion he was grinning.

Struck with an overwhelming desire to feast my eyes (and lips) on his gorgeous face, I said, "On second thought, I *am* feeling a little feverish, Doctor. I think you'd better hurry over here and take my temperature right now. I'm hot all over and I might need a thorough examination." I was shocked by my provocative response. All of a sudden I was sounding like Abby.

Dan let out a deep, slow, sensual moan. "Don't tempt me,

babe. You have no idea how much I'd rather be with you than where I am. Can't do it, though. I'm working on a big case, and I can't leave my station."

"What? You're still at the station? I thought you were going to be out tracking some Mafia goons."

"I didn't mean station *house*, Paige," he said, chuckling. Then he lowered his voice and confided, "I'm doing double-duty surveillance tonight, and I've stationed myself in a certain place where I can keep an eye on some underworld hotshots. I'll be here for another few hours at least."

"Oh," I said, embarrassed that—after my brief but bold career at *Daring Detective* (not to mention my brief but bold romance with Detective Street)—I wasn't an expert in police jargon. "So, where are you?" I asked, growing curious about his location and concerned about his safety.

Dan laughed out loud. "You think I'm crazy enough to tell *you* that? Next thing I know, you'll be rushing uptown in a trench coat, wig, and sunglasses to take over the investigation."

"Hardeeharhar." My ego was sagging, but my curiosity was climbing the rafters. *So, he's uptown, not down,* I noted, *stationed in 'a certain place' where mobsters tend to congregate.* I screwed my ear tight to the phone, listening for more clues to his mysterious whereabouts.

There was a lot of noise in the background: people talking and laughing; faint scraping, knocking, tinkling, and whirring sounds. I could hear glasses clinking and fingers snapping. Was he in a bar? Music was playing in the distance. A jazzy saxophone riff. Was it live or coming from a jukebox?

"You can't fool me, Dan Street," I said, acting mad, pretending that I'd flown into a jealous tizzy. "I hear people laughing and music swinging. You're not working on a case! You're carousing in a nightclub!"

Dan laughed again. "The two aren't mutually exclusive, you know," he said, inadvertently answering my unspoken questions. "But I can assure you there's no carousing going on. Not on my part, anyway."

"That's what they all say," I grumbled, continuing my petulant charade, still straining my ears for acoustical clues. The band was in full force now, and a strong male voice was belting out the lyrics to a popular song I'd heard before but couldn't name.

"Cut it out, Paige," Dan said, getting annoyed. "You have no reason to be upset. I'm *working*, not playing—and you know it."

"Well, couldn't you knock off early and—"

"No, I couldn't." His breathing was heavy and his voice was stern. "I have a job to do, and I'm not leaving here until it's done."

The vocalist began singing the song's familiar chorus, and a portion of the audience chimed in.

"Will I see you tomorrow?" I asked.

Dan was an avid interrogator, but he didn't like being questioned himself. "Can't say," he grunted. "It depends on how things go here tonight. And how much your lousy mood improves."

The singer and the musicians brought the song to an explosive, drum-rolling, cymbal-crashing finish, and the audience broke out in wild applause.

"I'm sorry I doubted you, Dan," I said, eager to make amends. "Please forgive me. I'm not myself. I've been out of sorts all day. Chalk it up to loneliness, exhaustion, and a hangover that just won't quit."

"Forget about it, babe," he said, granting me an immediate pardon. (Dan can be very understanding—sometimes.) "I miss you, too. And I'm itching to take your temperature."

"Then I'll see you tomorrow night?"

"Come hell or high water. It'll be late, though. Look for me around midnight."

Not until after we'd hung up did it dawn on me that the song the band had been playing was "Love on the Rocks," and the man who'd been singing it was Tony Corona.

"ABBY!" I CRIED, LEAPING BACK ACROSS THE hall and into her kitchen like a demented kangaroo. "The most incredible thing just happened! I was talking to Dan on the phone, and listening to the music in the background, and Tony Corona was singing 'Love on the Rocks'!"

She looked up from her place at the table and stared at me as if I'd lost my marbles. "What's so incredible about that? That song is number two on the charts, right under "Rock Around the Clock." They play it on the radio all the time."

"It wasn't on the radio, it was live!"

"You mean a live *broadcast*," she said, convinced that I was confused and making a fuss over nothing.

"No!" I shrieked, flailing my arms in the air for emphasis. "I mean a live performance—in person!"

"Oh?" She raised one eyebrow and curled her lips in a big fat smirk. "Tony Corona was singing his hot new hit in your boyfriend's living room?"

By this point I really *was* losing my marbles. "Okay, let's start over again," I said, heaving a big sigh and flopping down in the same chair I'd been sitting in before. "I'll take it from the top, but you have to shut your mouth and listen. No interruptions."

Abby kept on smirking, but—wonder of wonders!—she didn't say a word.

"Dan's working tonight," I began, "and he called me from a place he wouldn't identify, where he's spying on some mobsters. All I could find out from our conversation was that the place is uptown. I kept him on the phone as long as I could, though, listening hard to the background noise, trying to figure out where he is. I'm pretty sure he's in a big nightclub or someplace like that, because I heard people laughing, chatting, and ordering drinks, and music playing, and a man singing, and an audience cheering and clapping. The song being sung was "Love on the Rocks," and the singer was none other than Tony Corona. Live and in person. I'm certain of it." I sat back and smugly crossed my arms over my chest. "So, what do you think about that, Pat?"

She was still smirking. "Am I allowed to speak now?"

"Please do," I urged, eager to get her reaction to this incredible, mind-blowing coincidence.

"Dan's at the Copa," she said.

And that was all she said.

"What?" I screeched. "The Copacabana? Are you kidding me? How the hell do you know that?" The last of my marbles dropped out of my head and rolled across the floor.

"I read it in the papers." Her tone and demeanor were dispassionate, but she looked pleased with herself nonetheless.

"They said Dan was going to be at the Copa tonight?" I sputtered. (Look, I *know* that was a really dumb response, but give me a break, okay? It's hard to hit the mark when all your shooters are gone.)

"No, silly! They said *Corona* was going to be there. He's headlining for two weeks. Two shows a night, three on the weekends. He opened last Saturday."

"Oh," I said, staring down at the tabletop in shame. How could I—Manhattan's champion news-sniffer and column-clipper—have missed this all-important announcement?

"And kingpin Frank Costello owns the joint, you know," Abby continued, "so it's crawling with gangsters. You dig what I'm saying? All the pieces of the puzzle fit." Her smirk changed into a smile. "Dan is on stakeout at the Copa."

I knew Abby was right. And if I had used my brain for just two of the ten minutes preceding her revelation, I would have put the pieces of the puzzle together myself. Though I hadn't been aware that Corona was playing the Copa, I *had* known—from firsthand experience—that Mafia boss Frank Costello was the secret owner of the famous nightclub (a little nugget I'd dug up while working on my first murder story). And since Dan had told me, just last night, that he needed to "track down and question some of Frank Costello's boys" . . . well, you get the picture. I could have—in fact, *should* have—put two and two together.

"I'm such an idiot," I said.

"No, just a nitwit," she teased.

"It's good you saw the promos in the papers."

"Glad to be of service." With an exaggerated air of authority, she rose from her chair, tossed her ponytail over the opposite shoulder, and propped one hand on her jutting hip. "So, what's next on the agenda, Brenda? I'm assuming you've got a plan."

"Well, no, not really. I guess I need to—"

"Get your mojo working!" she jumped in, finishing my sentence for me. "You can't catch a murderer by sitting around like a blob in my kitchen! You know what I think?" she said, eyes beaming like oncoming headlights. "I think we should get all dolled up and go to the Copa tonight. We can get there before the second show ends. Then we can sneak backstage, corner Corona in his dressing room, pretend we're big fans, and ask him a lot of probing personal questions. Stuff like that probably happens to him all the time, so he won't have a clue what we're up to."

"*We?*" I croaked, shuddering my shoulders and shaking

my head. "Forget about it, Abby! I will not—under any circumstances—let you get involved in this mess. It's too dangerous." I lit another cigarette and spewed the smoke out in an obstinate huff. "Besides, I can't possibly go to the Copa tonight. *Dan's* there. And he would spot me for sure. And if he finds out that I'm working on another unsolved murder case, he'll murder *me*."

"Okay, then we'll go tomorrow night."

There was that word again.

"*We* are not going anywhere. I'm working this case alone. I promised Sabrina."

"Oh, come on, Paige! You need me. You know you do. We're a team, you dig? We're Ozzie and Harriet, Martin and Lewis, Lucy and Ethel. We're peanut butter and jelly!"

She was using the term *we* again, but I was beginning to like the sound of it. Playing detective was a lonely game, and Abby could be very good company (when she wasn't being a pain in the butt). She had been a big help to me in past investigations, and—by clueing me in that Corona was playing the Copa—she was *already* helping me with this one. And I had to admit that descending on Corona in his dressing room would be a heck of a lot easier and safer than trying to ambush him in his private suite at the Plaza.

"Okay, okay!" I caved in. "We'll join forces and hit the Copa tomorrow night. Seems like a pretty good plan. Except for one thing: We can't go on our own. They won't let us in without a male escort."

"No problem," she said. "I'll make Jimmy go with us. After tonight, he owes me one."

"Do you have something for me to wear?"

"Does a cat have whiskers?" Abby was a fiend for fashion, and she loathed my mail-order wardrobe, and she had closets—actually a whole *room*—full of fabulous clothes and costumes. She had dressed me up for previous uptown sleuthing excursions, and I could tell from the wicked gleam in her eye that she couldn't wait to do it again.

"Hold on a second, Ab," I said, suddenly realizing our pretty good plan had a pretty big hole in it. "There's one more problem. How the hell are we going to get reservations? The Copacabana on a Friday night? It's next to impossible. And with Tony Corona on the bill, you *know* they're all booked up."

"Booked, shmooked," she said, sounding an awful lot like Lenny's mother. "There are ways to get around these things."

"Oh, yeah? Exactly what do you propose we do?"

"Don't worry, Murray. I'll think of something."

Chapter 18

I STUBBED OUT MY CIGARETTE AND LOOKED AT my watch. It was almost midnight. (Time also flies when you're *not* having fun.) "It's getting late, Ab," I said, yawning between syllables. "I'm so tired I can't see straight. Let's continue this dialogue over coffee in the morning, okay?"

She scowled. "You can't leave now! We're just getting started. Have you forgotten about Sabrina?"

"Huh?" I didn't get what she was driving at.

"You have to brief me on Sabrina," she insisted. "She's the queen bee in this hive of hornets, and—other than the fact that she's a high-society madam who manages a stable of high-priced call girls—you haven't told me a damn thing about her!"

"That can wait until tomorrow," I said, rising to my feet and picking up the lavender list from the table. "I'm too tired to—"

"Sit down, Paige!" Abby leapt out of her chair and snatched the list out of my hand. "Sabrina gave you plenty of information about Melody and Brigitte and Candy in these notes," she said, unfolding the list and flapping it in front of my face, "but do you see anything here about *her*? She didn't write a goddamn word about herself."

"But that's because she—"

"Oh, hush! I'm not an idiot. I *know* why she didn't want to put anything about herself in writing. What I *don't* know is all the stuff she told you but didn't write down. I'm not a mind reader, you know! And if you don't sit tight and give me all the dope right now, I'm gonna go nuts wondering about it all night. I'm talkin' insane, Duane."

"Can't you just—"

"No! I can't! I need you to give me the lowdown on Sabrina this very minute! You know how I am."

Abby was right. I *did* know how she was—which meant I knew enough to sit down and start dishing out the details before she worked herself up into one of her snit fits (a sure to be noisy and unseemly process that would delay my bedtime indefinitely).

"Oh, all right!" I snapped, giving in and flopping back down in my chair. "Have it your way." (As if there could ever be any other way.) "But you'd better make me some coffee, or I'll fall asleep at the wheel."

"Good idea," she chirped, twirling over to the kitchen counter. "I'll brew some java while you tell me about Sabrina.

"I can tell you only what she told me," I grumbled, "and as soon as I'm finished, I'm going home to bed!"

"So who's stopping you?"

Groan.

"Sabrina was born into an affluent family," I began, talking fast, hoping to wrap the story up as quickly as possible. "She was raised by governesses and educated in Switzerland. She was a debutante, a pampered beauty, a social butterfly who dated lots of wealthy young men. And now—according to Sabrina—many of those young men are rich, powerful, and influential *older* men, and some of them are her clients. I'd say Sam Hogarth and Oliver Rice Harrington belong to that fraternity."

"Well, that's pretty damn interesting," Abby said, pausing, blinking, obviously savoring the scandalous possibilities. "But it's not the whole story, Rory. What I want to know is *how* it happened. I mean, how and why did Sabrina become a madam to begin with?"

"I don't know."

"What?" she said, turning the flame on under the percolator. "Didn't you ask her about it?"

"No, it wasn't my place."

"What?" she said again, only this time it was more of a screech. She spun around, stared me in the eye, propped her hands on her hips, and cried, "It wasn't your *place*?! How could you be such a boob, Paige? Don't you have any chutzpah? The woman runs a whorehouse, for Pete's sake, and you're worried about your stupid *place*?"

"It's an escort service, not a whorehouse."

"Oh, excuse me!" she said, sarcasm seeping out of every pore. "The last time I checked, call girls and whores were the same thing. And prostitution, by any other name, was still a crime."

"Yes, but I don't believe it *should* be," I said, thinking of all the desperate young women who peddled their flesh because that was the only thing of value that they had.

"Don't change the subject!" Abby blustered. "We're talking about *you* now. You and your fearful, self-conscious ways."

She was starting to tick me off. "I'm not fearful, I'm cautious," I said, keeping my voice low and my emotions under control (for once). "There's a big difference between the two. And I'm not self-conscious, either; I'm self-aware. Also modest, polite, and reserved—which is more than I can say for *some* people."

"Oh, stuff it, Paige! That's a crock, and you know it. You're as modest and reserved as Milton Berle with a lampshade on his head." She took two cups out of the cabinet and plopped them down on the counter. "You know what? This is a really stupid argument, and I refuse to take part in it." (She had, apparently, forgotten that she was the one who *started* it.) "All I want to know is how you could spend a whole afternoon talking to the madam of a brothel—excuse me, *escort service*—without asking her how she got into the racket."

I was two seconds away from blowing my top. (Okay, one second.) "For God's sake, Abby!" I bellowed, blood rushing to my head. "What the hell do you want from me? I was sitting in an impressive Gramercy Park apartment, having lunch with a total stranger, talking about the brutal murder of a beautiful young woman! I was in shock that I was there, appalled and intrigued by the sinister circumstances, and madly scratching in the dirt for information—so focused on the hideous death of Virginia Pratt that I could hardly breathe. And you're telling me . . . what? That I should have ignored that little problem? That I should have—first and foremost—found out why my snooty, short-tempered hostess had given up a life of leisure to become a madam?!"

Unaffected by my tirade, Abby calmly replied, "I never said you should ignore anything. I simply felt it would be useful to have more clues to Sabrina's character. She could be the murderer, you know."

Aaargh!

"I'm very well aware of that," I said, inhaling deeply, trying to cool myself down from a boil to a simmer. "That's why I'm going back to question the queen in the morning. I'm going to storm her big white castle, fight off the two knights in armor standing guard at her door, charge up to her private turret, and force her to tell the true tale of her secret passage from maidenhood to madamhood."

Abby rolled her eyes. "What the hell are you dithering about? Castles! Knights! Turrets! Secret passages! I think you're going bats."

Frankly, I thought so, too. "Sorry, Ab," I said. "I was just trying to describe the odd building Sabrina lives in, but I got a little carried away."

She shrugged it off and charged ahead. "Are you really going to see her tomorrow?"

"Yes," I said, coming to a firm decision. "First thing in the morning. But don't think for one minute that you're going with—"

"I'm going with you," she said.

"No, you're not."

"Yes, I am."

"No, you're not."

"Yes, I am!" She stomped one foot on the floor, then filled the two cups on the counter with coffee and brought them over to the table. "We're a team, remember? Burns and Allen. Abbott and Costello. And as your partner, I have a right to meet and interrogate the notorious Miss Stanhope myself."

"That's impossible," I said, with Charlton Heston–like conviction. "I swore to Sabrina I wouldn't tell anybody about her involvement, so I could *never* show up at her apartment with you at my side. She'd know I broke my promise, and she wouldn't trust me anymore, and then she wouldn't provide me with any new information. And she wouldn't divulge any of her personal sex secrets to you, either," I added, tossing a bucket of ice water on Abby's eternal flame, "so you can kiss *those* burning questions good-bye."

That cooled her off, thank goodness. "I get your drift," she said, spooning sugar into her coffee and staring off into the distance like a Gypsy telling her own fortune. "I have to be slow and sneaky and stay deep undercover."

"Right," I said, heaving a huge, but silent, sigh of relief. "The deeper, the better."

Chapter 19

IN SPITE OF MY FATIGUE, SLEEP DIDN'T COME soon. I thrashed around in my bed for a good two hours before Morpheus finally scooped me up in his arms, breathed a warm, seductive promise of peace into my ear, and then swept me off to dreamland.

But Morpheus is a liar and a cheat. Did you know that?

My slumber was anything but peaceful. *Hostile* was more like it. And my dreams were so horrible, I woke up howling. (Believe me, if you had been dreaming that you were tied up and naked, with your nose and mouth packed tight with huge wads of turpentine-soaked cotton, you'd have woken up howling, too.) I got out of bed at seven and went straight into the shower, hoping a blast of hot water would drive the demons out of my skull and bring me back to the land of the living.

It worked—sort of. I wasn't exactly *alive,* but at least I was walking and talking (mostly to myself, since I was the only one there—but also to Virginia, who, I hoped, could hear my heart-felt pledge to see her vicious killer locked up for life).

After slathering on some makeup and getting dressed in a dark green pencil skirt and pale yellow sweater set, I staggered downstairs to look for my shoes. After finding them on the floor in the living room, I straightened my stocking seams and slipped on the dreaded high heels. Then I stuck the fresh pack of Pall Malls and the five one-dollar bills Abby had loaned me last night in my purse, put on my camel hair jacket and red wool beret, dashed down the stairs to the street, and headed for the subway.

I wanted to get to Sabrina's early. Hopefully *before* she got out of bed. That way, I might get to talk to her maid, Charlotte, for a few minutes in private—i.e., without Sabrina's supervision. And since Sabrina never went to bed before three in the morning and probably slept at least until ten, I figured I had a pretty good chance to accomplish this goal.

It was the middle of the morning rush, so the uptown express was packed tighter than a tin of sardines. (Yes, I know that's an overused analogy, but it really is the perfect description.) I stood mashed between two men who wore gray flannel suits, overcoats, and fedoras, and who smelled of cigarettes, coffee, and English Leather. Their big briefcases kept bashing me in the knees.

I squeezed off the train at 14th Street and trudged up the crowded stairs to the street. It felt good to be out in the open air, even though I had a ten-block walk ahead of me and my feet hurt so much I wanted to crawl the distance instead. I looked around for a crosstown bus, but the only one I saw was going in the wrong direction. Wishing I could stop at Chock Full for coffee and a roll, but not wanting to take the time, I hunched my shoulders, bowed my head against the morning chill, and marched onward like a migrating penguin to Gramercy Park.

Even though I'd seen it before, the gargoyle-and-cherub-trimmed façade of Sabrina's weird white building still came as a surprise. It was so completely out of place. It belonged in a different country *and* a different century. And I couldn't get over the two knights in shining armor positioned on either side of the walkway leading to the building's entrance. The first time I'd seen the twin statues, I found them forbidding, but now they just looked silly. As I passed between them, I gave them a hearty "Hello, boys!" but they didn't seem to notice.

Luckily, the uniformed fellow who opened the front door for me was the same doorman I'd met before. "Good morning, sir," I said, entering the marble lobby and giving him a friendly smile. "Remember me? I was here to see Miss Stanhope the day before yesterday."

"Yes, miss," he said, straightening the sleeves of his maroon and gold jacket and standing at attention. I half expected him to salute.

"Well, I'm here to see her again," I said, "only this time it's a surprise visit."

"Surprise, miss?"

"Yes, today is Miss Stanhope's birthday, and I'm going to treat her to a special breakfast in bed. She says I make the best pancakes in the world, so I thought a hot, syrupy stack of flapjacks would be the perfect gift." (Why this ridiculous story sprang to my lips, I'll never, ever know.) "I want it to be a big surprise, though, so you'll be doing me a big favor if you let me go upstairs without calling to announce my arrival."

"But I can't do that, miss," he said. "I'm supposed to—"

"Oh, no need to worry about that," I cut in, dismissing his concerns with a quick wave of my hand. "Miss Stanhope's maid, Charlotte, knows all about my secret plan, and she'll be standing at the door to meet me. Sabrina's still sleeping, and we don't want the phone or the doorbell to wake her."

"Charlotte knows you're coming?" he asked. The look in his eye suggested he knew and trusted the beautiful, dark-skinned domestic.

"Yes, of course," I said, "and she told me to give you this for your trouble." I eased one of Abby's dollar bills out of my purse and tucked it into his palm.

Problem solved. The doorman led me straight to the elevator and directed the operator to take me up to the eighth floor.

BY SOME INCREDIBLE COINCIDENCE, CHARLOTTE was standing or walking near the door to Sabrina's apartment, because the minute I gave it one little knock, she peeked through the peephole and then pulled the door open.

"Mrs. Turner?" she said, bewildered, smoothing a few stray hairs back into her twist and tying her blue robe tighter around her narrow waist. "I'm surprised to see you here. Miss Stanhope is still sleeping. I'm quite sure she isn't expecting you."

"You're right," I said. "She isn't."

"Then may I ask why you've come?"

"I came to see you," I said, trying to make my voice sound soft and firm at the same time. "I know this is highly unusual, Charlotte, and I certainly don't want to disturb you in any way, but I need to speak to you in private, and I thought now would be a good time."

She gave me a puzzled look, but didn't say anything.

"May I come in for a few minutes?" I asked. "It's cold outside, and I've had quite a long walk, and my new shoes are threatening to kill me if I don't sit down."

Charlotte glanced at my red suede stilettos and smiled knowingly.

"This won't take long," I pleaded. "I just want to relax for a second and ask you a couple of questions while I massage my crippled feet." To prove my urgent discomfort, I wrinkled my face up in pain and took a lurching, very wobbly step forward.

(Hey, don't look at me like that, okay? I wasn't putting on an act or being deceitful in any way! I swear! All I was doing was demonstrating my distress—which was, I can assure you, almost one hundred percent real.)

Charlotte opened the door all the way and motioned me inside. "We can talk in the kitchen," she said, holding the top of her velvet robe closed and gracefully leading the way down the hall. "Would you like some coffee?"

"Oh, that would be heavenly," I said, wondering what I should do first—massage my feet or kiss hers.

The large kitchen was well designed, beautifully decorated, and spotlessly clean. The modern appliances were sparkling white (nary a plaid refrigerator in sight), and the glass-paned wood cabinets, white tile walls, black marble countertop, and black-and-white tile floor were gleaming in the light from two floor-to-ceiling windows. A round oak table, topped with a vase of fresh flowers and surrounded by four cane-bottomed chairs, was positioned between the two windows. Charlotte indicated that I should take a seat at the table.

I dropped into the closest chair, pried off my shoes, and sighed noisily. "Whoever decided that American women have to wear three-inch heels to be stylish should be shot in the head. Or at least in the feet."

Charlotte smiled and stepped over to the stove. "I don't have that problem," she said, taking a china cup and saucer out of the cabinet and filling the cup with hot coffee. "When you're six feet tall, as I am, you're practically forbidden to wear high heels. Nobody likes to be towered over—especially by a Negro woman." She carried the coffee, a linen napkin, and a silver spoon to the table and put them down in front of me, next to the silver cream pitcher and sugar bowl. Then she retreated midway into the kitchen and came to a statuesque standstill near the end of the counter.

I shrugged off my jacket, folded it over the back of my chair, and put my purse and beret on another chair. "Won't you join me?" I asked, wishing she would stop acting like a servant and sit down.

"No, thank you, Mrs. Turner. I've already had my breakfast."

She may have been telling the truth, but it certainly wasn't the *whole* truth. I could tell from her strained posture and cautious attitude that Charlotte was afraid to sit at the table with me. She thought she'd be overstepping her bounds (the bounds imposed on her by our racially segregated society), and she was too proud and polite to take such a bold step.

"Please call me Paige," I urged, trying to break down the social barriers between us and set her mind at ease. "Perhaps you haven't heard, but we're fellow employees now, Charlotte. I'm working for Sabrina, too! And in light of this fact I think we can—and should—dispense with the stupid formalities."

She smiled again, but this time it was a broader smile, with all her beautiful white teeth showing. "Well, if you're sure. . . . I guess another cup of coffee won't hurt me." She glided over to the stove, filled the plain white mug sitting on the counter near the percolator, then returned to the table and sat down.

"Cigarette?" I asked, snatching Abby's pack of Pall Malls out of my purse, opening it, and holding it forward.

"Thank you, Paige." She took one and lit it. Then, tilting her head back and exhaling a blossoming cloud of smoke toward the ceiling, she inquired, "What did you want to talk to me about? You said you have some questions for me."

"Yes, I do, but I thought we could chat a little bit first, get to know each other."

"I don't have that much time. Miss Stanhope will be getting up and wanting her breakfast soon."

"Okay, then I'll try to make this quick. Do you know why I'm working for Sabrina? Has she told you what she hired me to do?"

"Yes." A veil of deep sorrow fell over her face. "She wants you to find out who murdered Melody."

With this one answer, Charlotte divulged much of what I

needed to know: that Sabrina had confided in Charlotte about the murder, that she had told Charlotte about me, and that Charlotte had been on a first-name basis with Melody—all of which confirmed that the mysterious maid was privy to some of the most private details of her employer's professional life.

"Did you know Melody well?" I asked.

"As well as I know any of Sabrina's girls," she said, abruptly (and, I thought, purposely) revealing that she was *also* on a first-name basis with her boss. (I wanted to discuss this point further, but thought it best not to interrupt the flow of the conversation.) "Melody was very discreet," Charlotte went on, "and she kept to herself a bit more than the others, but anybody with any sense could see that she was a lovely, hardworking, well-meaning young woman who didn't deserve to die."

I nodded in mournful agreement and took a sip of my coffee. "Do you have any insights or suspicions that could help me identify her killer?"

"None whatsoever."

"Do you know why Melody became a call girl?"

"No, I don't. I'm quite friendly with all of the girls, but I don't pry into their private lives. That's the way Sabrina wants it. She insists that we keep our personal and family histories secret, locked in the past, where they belong. We don't even know each other's real names. Sabrina knows everything about all of us, of course, but she doesn't share that information with anybody."

I wasn't surprised to learn that Charlotte wasn't her real name (I *told* you it was an alias, didn't I?), but I *was* caught off balance to hear her talking as though she were one of Sabrina's call girls.

"What are you trying to tell me, Charlotte? Are you a prostitute, too?"

"Not anymore," she said, looking me straight in the eye.

"But you used to be?"

"Yes." Her gaze remained steady and intense.

"Did you work for Sabrina?"

"I wasn't that lucky," she said. "I worked for the meanest, most brutal pimp in Harlem. It's a miracle I survived. If Sabrina hadn't saved me, I'd have been planted in the dirt long before Melody."

"You were *saved* by Sabrina?" I blurted, crazy for more information. "What happened? How did you meet her? What did she do?"

Charlotte paused, took another puff on her cigarette, and stared out the window for a few silent seconds. Then she turned and looked me in the eye again. "I shouldn't be talking about this," she murmured. "Sabrina says it's not good for me to brood about the past. I have to focus all my thoughts and energy on the future. And if I reveal any more facts about my former life, I'll be breaking Sabrina's rule of secrecy."

Dear God in heaven, don't let her clam up on me now!

"But I really need your help, Charlotte," I pleaded, pulling out all the emotional stops. "I've been working on this case nonstop since the day I came here for lunch, and I'm getting nowhere! I've interviewed one of the major suspects, and Brigitte and Candy have answered all my questions, and I'm *still* floundering around in the dark. I can't see where I'm going, and I don't know which road to take next."

"But how can *I* help you?" she wanted to know. "What does my past, or my relationship with Sabrina, have to do with Melody's murder?"

"I don't know," I said. "Maybe those particulars are significant, and maybe they aren't. The point is, I have to gather all the details I possibly can, to understand the big picture. And the tiniest scrap of information could turn out to be the most important clue." I took another sip of my coffee, staring intently at her over the rim of my cup.

"Well, okay, then," Charlotte gave in. "I'll tell you whatever I can. I liked and respected Melody very much, and I'm praying that you'll catch her killer, and—in spite of Sabrina's strict secrecy demands—I believe she'd want me to help you in your investigation."

"Good!" I exclaimed, jumping to seal the bargain before she could change her mind. "Then let's start with—"

A loud *bzzzzzzz* cut the tail off my sentence.

"That's Sabrina," Charlotte said, quickly crushing her cigarette in the ashtray and getting up from the table. "She wants me to fix her breakfast now."

Chapter 20

"WANT SOME EGGS?" CHARLOTTE ASKED, TAK-
ing a carton out of the refrigerator and placing it on the counter
near the stove. "Sabrina likes them poached, on toast. How
about you?"

"I'd love some!" I croaked, stomach growling. "And
poached would be fine. But what about Sabrina? Will she be upset if she finds me in her kitchen?"

"No, she always has breakfast in her room. And after that it
takes her at least an hour to bathe and dress. You can stay if
you'd like, and have something to eat while we continue our
conversation."

Was this my lucky day, or what?

"I'll tell Sabrina that you're here, of course," Charlotte went
on, "and that I'm trying to help you in your investigation. Do
you want to talk to her, too? If so, I'll ask if she can see you after breakfast.

"Thanks, Charlotte!" I said, grinning like Bucky Beaver in
the Ipana toothpaste ads. "I *do* want to talk to Sabrina. And I'm
so famished I could eat a horse, though poached eggs would be
preferable."

"Coming right up," she said, moving around the kitchen, setting a pot of water on the burner to boil, putting two slices of
bread in the toaster.

Food questions settled, my hunger for clues returned. "When and where did you and Sabrina meet?" I asked, hoping Charlotte could cook and talk at the same time.

"It was about seven years ago, when we were both in the hospital," she said, setting a place mat, napkin, and silverware on the serving cart near the kitchen door. "I had been beaten up by my pimp, and she had been beaten up by her husband. We arrived in the emergency room at the same time. I had several broken ribs and a broken arm; she had a dislocated shoulder and a fractured leg. After they patched us up, they put us in the same room for a few days. The ward was full, and Sabrina graciously agreed to share her semiprivate accommodations with a colored woman."

"Is that how she 'saved' you?" I asked.

"That was just *one* of the ways." Charlotte cracked four eggs and slipped them gently into the simmering water. "She also took me with her when we left the hospital, saving me from Sonny 'The Blade' Marino, the gangster who swore he'd slash my throat if I didn't obey my pimp and earn my keep." The toast popped up, and she put each piece on a porcelain plate trimmed with pink and gold roses. "I owe Sabrina my life."

"Did you become a call girl for her after you left the hospital?"

"No. She wasn't a madam then. She was just a woman on the run from a husband who liked to beat her up for fun. She has the scars to prove it, not to mention a permanent limp." Charlotte filled two glasses with fresh-squeezed orange juice, placing one on the serving cart for Sabrina and one on the table for me.

"So where did you go? Where did you live?"

"We hid out at the Gramercy Park Hotel for a few weeks while our broken bones healed and Sabrina got her affairs in order. That's when I began masquerading as her maid. The hotel wouldn't admit Negro guests, but they *did* accept the Negro servants of their white guests. While we were staying at the hotel, Sabrina noticed that an apartment in this building was available for rent. She looked at it, liked it, and signed the lease the same day. We've been here ever since." Scooping the eggs out of the water one by one, Charlotte drained them and placed two on each piece of toast.

"So you're not really a maid?" I asked. "You're just masquerading as one?"

"No, I really *am* one now. By choice. I like cooking and cleaning and making things nice for Sabrina. She takes good care of me, and I take good care of her. I'm happier than I've ever been in my life. Not only has Sabrina given me a beautiful room of my own, three square meals a day, a closet full of nice clothes, and a very good salary, but she has also tutored me in math, reading, manners, grammar, and diction. I'm a brand-new person. I could get a decent job most anywhere now. I won't have to sell my body to any man ever again."

Grinning widely, Charlotte put a plate of eggs in front of me, plus a small cup of fresh strawberries and some extra toast, butter, and jam. Thanking her profusely, I watched as she arranged identical dishes on the serving cart, along with a carafe of hot coffee. "I'll be back in a few minutes," she said, nimbly maneuvering the laden cart through the swinging kitchen door and gliding swanlike down the hall.

I HAD CONSUMED EVERY CRUMB OF MY BREAKfast by the time Charlotte returned. (I'm such a pig sometimes.) As it turned out, though, it was a good thing I had eaten so fast.

"Sabrina wants to see you now," Charlotte said. "Without delay."

"But, why?" I asked, reluctant to leave the cozy kitchen and venture into the lioness's den. "Doesn't she want to bathe and dress first?"

"Apparently not. She told me to bring you to her room right away."

Uh-oh.

"Is she annoyed that I'm here?"

"I don't think so. Why would she be? I think she's just eager to hear what you've learned about the murder."

"Well, in that case. . . ." I stood up and stuck my feet in my shoes.

"Come," Charlotte said, heading for the door and gesturing for me to follow. "I'll show you the way."

She led me back to the foyer, then across a large, beautifully furnished living room, then down a dimly lit corridor to the partially open door of Sabrina's bedroom. Opening the door wide enough for both of us to enter, Charlotte stepped over the threshold and signaled for me to do the same. "Paige is here, Sabrina," she said, no longer addressing her patron, or colleague, or bene- factor, or friend as "mum." (I had the feeling that title was reserved for use in front of strangers ... or anyone who might disapprove of their cozy interracial relationship.)

"Good morning, Paige," Sabrina said. "Come in and sit down."

There were only two chairs in the big lavender bedroom, and Sabrina was sitting in one of them, so I walked over and parked myself in the other.

"You can get dressed now, Charlotte," Sabrina said, smiling. "I'll buzz you if we need anything."

Charlotte nodded and left the inner sanctum, closing the door behind her.

Sabrina's smile vanished instantly. "I hope you don't mind that I'm not dressed and haven't finished my breakfast," she said, voice saturated with scorn. "You can't expect me to be presenta- ble, since you didn't have the courtesy to let me know you were coming. If you had informed me of your plans, I could have greeted you in a more acceptable manner." Even sitting behind a serving cart littered with dirty dishes, wearing a purple bathrobe and a pair of fuzzy slippers, she managed to maintain her snooty disposition.

"I don't mind," I said, refusing to apologize for my unan- nounced appearance. (I was, after all, just doing the job she had hired me to do.) "You keep insisting that time is of the essence, Sabrina—that I need to find Melody's murderer immediately— so I thought I'd better get the day off to an early start."

Her expression softened for a moment while she took a sip of coffee and ate her last strawberry. "Well, I'm glad for that, at least," she said when she finished chewing and swallowing. "But I still don't understand why you're *here*. Shouldn't you be out *investigating* someone or something?"

I was annoyed by her sarcastic tone, but anxious to get past it and move on. "Don't worry," I said. "I'll be interrogating two of the major suspects today, so I won't be wasting any of your time or money. And my little chat with Charlotte this morning was very informative. She understands how important the seem- ingly insignificant background details can be."

"Yes, she told me about your conversation, and about all

the things she told you, and—though I don't fault her for her honesty or her eagerness to help you find the murderer—I *do* wish she hadn't revealed quite so much about our past lives. Those stale details have absolutely nothing to do with Melody's life or death, and will in no way help you catch her killer."

"Maybe not, but at least they'll help me comprehend the situation. And you'd be surprised how often simple comprehension leads to the solution of a complicated crime."

Sabrina tilted her head and stared at me for a few moments. And then suddenly, out of the blue, she reversed her position on the subject. "So, is there anything else you'd like to know?" she asked. "Far be it from me to obstruct your precious comprehension."

Her tone was still disrespectful, but—in the interest of collecting more clues—I chose to ignore it. "I'd like to know why you became a madam," I replied, striking while the iron was hot. "Whatever induced you to start your own escort service?"

"Money, of course," she said. "I ran out, and I needed more."

"But what about your family? I thought they were very wealthy. Couldn't they have given you what you needed?"

"Oh, sure, they *could* have—but they never *would* have. When I ran off and got married, they disowned me—totally and forever—making it clear that I wouldn't be welcome under their roof, or even in their *neighborhood,* again. Luckily, I had some money of my own—a personal savings account, a few stocks and bonds, a nice inheritance from my grandmother— but it wasn't enough to last forever."

"But why did your family cut you off so completely?"

"They didn't approve of my choice in husbands."

"Why not? Who did you marry?"

"The gardener," she said, with a cryptic smile.

I wasn't prepared for that one. "Who?" I asked again, eyes blinking in surprise.

"The gardener on the grounds of the family estate in Connecticut. A gorgeous, hotheaded Puerto Rican named Ramón. He was the sexiest man I ever met, and I was the richest girl he ever screwed. I wanted him for his strong, tan, energetic body, and he wanted me for my ... well, let's just say my beauty played a secondary role to my bank account. I didn't know that at the time, of course, but it probably wouldn't have made a difference. I was accustomed to buying whatever I wanted."

"So you defied your parents and ran away to get married?"

"Right. It was the bravest thing I'd ever done, and by far the stupidest. I've been suffering the consequences ever since." She stood up, pushed the breakfast cart to one side, then limped over and sat down at her dressing table. Scowling at herself in the mirror, she snatched a pearl-handled brush off the table and began yanking it through her ash blonde hair.

"Consequences?" I asked, urging her to elaborate. I knew part of the story already, but I wanted to hear her tell it in her own words.

Sabrina's eyes met mine in the mirror. "The repercussions were severe. Just three days after we were married, I discovered that my husband not only believed he had a *right* to beat his wife, but that it was his favorite form of entertainment. I spent half my honeymoon—and eight hideous months after that—holed up in the Carlyle Hotel bridal suite, then our Park Avenue apartment, waiting for various cuts and bruises to heal. As soon as one black eye got better, he'd give me another one. I was ashamed to show my face in public."

"Why didn't you leave him?"

"I was too stupid and confused—and too proud to let my family know that they'd been right about Ramón all along. I kept hoping that things would get better, that he'd wake up and realize what a good life we could have together."

"But that didn't happen."

"Not by a long shot." She put down the hairbrush and began cleansing her face with cold cream. "Things got worse, not better. Ramón started drinking too much and gambling too much and staying out all night. He'd come home in the morning, slap me around for a while, and then force me to have sex with him. After that, he'd pass out and sleep for the rest of the day. He didn't even *try* to get a job."

"So you were paying all the bills," I said, gazing into the mirror, watching her wipe the cold cream off with a tissue.

"Yes, and Ramón racked up a *lot* of them." She looked more embarrassed than angry, and she wasn't acting snooty anymore. "So when I finally came to my senses and left him—which was the day Charlotte and I were released from the hospital—there wasn't much money left. I had enough to rent a suite at the Gramercy Park Hotel for a few weeks and to put a deposit on this apartment, but I knew my life of leisure was over for good. I had to go to work, or start a business, or find *some* way to make a living, and I had to do it *fast*."

"So that's when you started the escort service?"

"Right," she said, wadding the gooey tissue up in a ball and tossing it in the wastebasket.

"And it was successful right away?"

"Beyond my highest expectations."

"But what gave you the idea, and how did you know what to do? How did you get the operation up and running so quickly?"

Sabrina powdered her face and applied a little rouge to her cheeks. "I got the idea from Charlotte. Her hair-raising tales about the way prostitutes are treated by their pimps and johns led me to imagine a different kind of sex service—where the girls would be managed by a considerate, fair-minded woman and dealt with as professionals; an agency that would screen all potential clients and accept only the best. It was a can't-fail concept, I thought, which would be as beneficial to others as it would be to me.

"And it required virtually no capital outlay," Sabrina went on. "I put a HELP WANTED ad in the paper, offering 'after-hours employment for attractive young ladies in the city's most elite escort agency,' then sat back and waited for the phone to ring. Which it did—off the hook. Within a week I had signed up sixteen beautiful, polite, and articulate young women who—for reasons too numerous and diverse to discuss—were willing to perform sexual favors for discreet, well-mannered gentlemen in exchange for money.

"Then, after Charlotte filled me in on the rules, regulations, and going rates in the trade, *I* got on the phone and called all my male acquaintances from my debutante and socialite days— men I knew to be respectable, successful, rich, and horny. I told them about my new venture, described all my high-class and high-*priced* call girls, then began arranging the supply to meet the demand. By the end of my first month in business, my clients were as happy as clams, my girls had earned more income than they ever thought possible, and Charlotte and I were comfortably settled on Gramercy Park East."

"You make it sound so easy," I said, marveling at Sabrina's

vision, ingenuity, and fortitude. Prostitution was a filthy business, but her enterprise seemed almost clean.

"It was a simple two-step," she said, smiling at her reflection in the mirror. "Charlotte showed me the ropes, and I pulled the strings."

Chapter 21

SABRINA'S REVELATIONS WERE INTRIGUING, TO say the least, and they gave me a deeper understanding of her character as well as the overall situation. But I had to admit that her confessions probably wouldn't—as Sabrina had so fiercely contended—help me identify the killer of Virginia Pratt. If I was ever going to reach that goal, I realized, I'd have to get tough and press for the hard answers.

"I've asked you about this before, Sabrina," I said, "and so far you've refused to respond. But now I'm demanding a full disclosure. Why did Virgi—I mean, Melody—become a call girl?"

Sabrina stood up from her dressing table, crossed her arms over her chest, and turned to face me head-on. "You won't give up, will you? It's not enough that you've dredged up the most painful secrets of my past, and also Charlotte's, but now you won't rest until Melody's saddest and most closely guarded secret is exposed! I've told you repeatedly it has nothing to do with her murder! Why can't you leave this one alone? Why can't you just accept the fact that I've told you the truth?"

"Because secrets have a way of *hiding* the truth—maybe even from you."

My words must have touched a nerve or exhumed another distressing memory, because the next thing I knew, Sabrina lunged across the room, threw herself facedown on her big, unmade bed, and started crying.

I was shocked to the core. This was a side of Sabrina I had never seen—and had never expected to see. "What's wrong?" I yelped, jumping to my feet and darting to the side of the bed. "What's the matter? Why are you so upset? Was it something I said?" I felt confused, concerned, and responsible. Had I pushed the poor woman to the breaking point?

Sabrina didn't say anything. She just buried her face deep in her pillow, smudging rouge on the lavender pillowcase and muffling her heartrending sobs in the mound of feathers.

I didn't know what to do, but I felt I had to do *something*. "Please don't cry," I said, sitting down on the side of her bed. I leaned forward and gave her an awkward pat on the back. "I'm so sorry, Sabrina. I didn't mean to—"

"No, *I'm* the one who's sorry," she said, suddenly raising herself on her forearms, turning her crying jag off like a light. Her eyes were still red and wet, but her shoulders had stopped shaking. "You don't have to apologize, Paige. It's not your fault. You're just doing your job, and I'm acting like a crazy woman. I've got to pull myself together." Putting her weight on one elbow, she drew her knees up to her chest, swung her legs over the edge of the bed, and slowly pushed herself up to a sitting position.

We sat in silence for a few seconds, not looking at each other, slumped side by side on the edge of the bed like two strangers on a park bench. I waited for her to say something, but she didn't, so I finally asked, "What happened just now, Sabrina? What got you so upset?"

"It wasn't any one thing," she said, sighing heavily. "It's the whole goddamn bloody mess. I'm devastated about what happened to Melody, and it's all my fault. I fixed her up with a homicidal maniac! Can you imagine how that makes me feel? She was like a daughter to me. She trusted me. I was supposed to protect her, and I failed. Miserably." A final tear slithered down her cheek, and Sabrina swiped it off with the sleeve of her robe. "And now you want me to betray her trust again," she went on. "You want me to tell you why she joined my escort service, when I swore to her I would *never* reveal that secret to another living soul."

"But things were different when you made that promise," I said. "And if you could talk to Melody *now,* I believe she'd release you from that vow. In fact, I think she'd *want* you to give a full account to anybody who's trying to bring her killer to justice."

Sabrina turned and gave me a grave but compliant look. "I know you're right, Paige. I've known it all along. And I was planning to tell you everything, anyway. I was just trying to put it off as long as possible. I guess I needed to have a mental breakdown first."

I smiled. "A perfectly normal reaction, it seems to me." I felt I was finally meeting the real Sabrina—a classy woman with a big heart. A shady lady with shiny morals. A woman I could actually like.

AFTER A SHORT BREATHER, SABRINA STOPPED putting me off. "This won't be easy," she said, standing up and returning to the lavender-and-white-striped armchair she'd been sitting in before. She resumed her seat and pulled her robe tight over her knees. "And it's a long, complicated story, Paige, so you might as well come sit over here and be comfortable."

I took her advice and moved from the bed back to my chair.

"I'll tell it straight from beginning to end," she murmured, "as succinctly and quickly as I can. These are painful memories for me, and I don't want to dwell on them. So I'd appreciate it if you could just sit still, listen carefully, and refrain from interrupting me. Think you can do that?" Her tone was genial, not snippy.

"My lips are sealed," I said, smiling.

Sabrina nodded, and rested her head against the back of her chair. "Melody came to me to apply for an escort position two and a half years ago," she said, gazing ahead and upward as if watching a movie from the first row. "She had just turned eighteen. She was the most beautiful applicant I'd ever interviewed, but so young and inexperienced, I was reluctant to hire her. I gave in, though, after she broke down in tears and told me why she needed the money.

"Melody had a twin brother who was severely retarded. She was a perfect child, but he was defective in every way. The parents were so ashamed of the boy that they kept him hidden away in a back bedroom with a nurse, never spending any time with him, or taking him outside, or even discussing him with their friends and neighbors. Melody loved her brother very much, though, and spent as much time with him as her parents would allow—which was a lot, since they went to their country club every night of the week and left both children in the nurse's care.

"Melody played with her brother and took naps with him when they were young, and later, as they grew older, she sang to him, and tried to teach him how to eat and speak and dress himself. He never made much progress, but Melody refused to give up hope. She dreamed of becoming a famous singer when she grew up so she could earn enough to support them both. She wanted to buy a beautiful house for them to live in together, far away from their parents' rejection and repression.

"But one day, during her senior year in high school, Melody came home after school and discovered that her brother was gone. Her parents had packed him up and shipped him off to a New York State mental institution without ever telling her of their plans. Melody became hysterical and begged them to bring her twin back home to Vermont, but they wouldn't listen to her plea, or even tell her where in New York he'd been sent. They had washed their hands of him. They wanted him out of their lives for good.

"Melody was desolate. She felt like half a person without her twin, and she vowed they would be reunited someday, no matter how long it took her to find him. Therefore, shortly after her graduation, she convinced her parents to let her move to Manhattan, where she took a room in a women's boarding-house, went to work at her uncle's accounting firm, and—without the knowledge of anyone in her family—launched an all-out search for her brother.

"Six weeks of sleepless nights and countless phone calls later, she found him. He had been committed to the Willow-brook State School on Staten Island under his real name. Melody went to see her brother the very next day, and was hor-rified to discover that Willowbrook was more of a prison than a school—a penitentiary for the mentally retarded. The enormous stone-walled facility was cold, overcrowded, and deplorably filthy, and many of the residents showed signs of physical abuse. Disease—most commonly hepatitis—was rampant.

"Melody wanted to take her brother home with her that day,

but the school authorities refused to release him. They said the parents would have to give their permission in person, or in a witnessed and notarized letter sent by certified mail. And such an occurrence was highly unlikely, they insisted, since her brother had been legally committed to the institution for the rest of his natural life.

"Melody didn't know where to turn. She knew her parents would be furious if they learned of her desire to take her brother out of Willowbrook, and she couldn't ask her uncle for help, for fear he would inform her parents of her intentions. She also knew she couldn't take care of her brother by herself. He didn't remember who she was, and during the seven months he'd been institutionalized, he had regressed to a near feral state.

"In desperation, Melody concluded that the only way she could save her brother's life was by making a lot of money. If she had enough money, she reasoned, she could bribe the Willowbrook officials to release her brother to her, and then she could put him in a private establishment—a place with clean, decent living conditions and humane, round-the-clock supervision and health care. A nice place close to the city, where she could visit him every week.

"First she tried earning the money by singing, but after two weekends working for pennies at one of the Village cafés, Melody realized it could take her a lifetime to raise the kind of cash she needed. That's when she came to me." Sabrina paused for a moment, sat up straighter in her chair, raked her fingers through her hair, and went on. "She had seen my ad in the paper, and even after I explained to her what working for an escort agency really meant, she begged me to take her on.

"At first I flatly refused. She was a *virgin,* for God's sake! But after she broke down in hysterics, and told me why she had to have the money, and swore she'd become a prostitute for somebody else if I didn't hire her . . . well, I was forced to rethink the matter. I couldn't, in good conscience, let her fall into the hands of a pimp like Charlotte's. I agreed to handle her on one condition: that she let me start her off slow and easy—with a certain client who couldn't afford to pay top dollar but who I knew would be a gentle lover and teacher. She accepted my terms, we sealed the bargain with a cup of tea, and then I advanced her enough money to pull her brother out of Willowbrook and put him in a reputable private facility in Brooklyn.

"After several weeks, when she was fully qualified and prepared, I began arranging dates for Melody with my wealthiest clients. And they were so entranced with her youth and beauty that she quickly became their favorite. Her services were requested so often and so regularly that she managed to pay back her advance within the year. And soon after that—as a result of her ongoing earnings as a call girl—she was able to assume complete responsibility for her brother's monthly maintenance and expenses.

"In order to keep her brother's whereabouts and her means of supporting him concealed from their parents, Melody continued working at her uncle's accounting firm during the day. And late at night, when she got home from her appointments and could grab a little time for herself, she worked on her music. She still hoped to become a successful singer and songwriter, and looked forward to the day she could rely on her musical rather than her sexual skills to support herself and her twin.

"And I believe with all my heart that she would have reached that goal," Sabrina said, collapsing against the back of her chair and drawing her sad tale to its tragic conclusion, "if she had lived long enough."

Chapter 22

SABRINA WAS EXHAUSTED. HER PAINSTAKING narration of Virginia's short, unhappy life had taken its toll. I could see that she wanted me to leave. She wanted to take a hot bath, wash away the past, put on a clean dress and a fresh face, and focus her remaining energy on the day ahead.

But I wasn't ready to give up.

"What will become of Melody's brother now?" I asked. "Will he be sent back to Willowbrook?"

"Over my dead body. I'll pay all his expenses and watch over him from now on. It's the least I can do. I'll have to keep his location—actually his *existence*—under wraps, though, or outside parties might intervene. That's why I didn't want you to know about him, Paige, for fear you wouldn't keep the secret. Please swear to me you'll never breathe a word of this to anybody."

"I swear," I said without hesitation, pledging my solemn allegiance to Melody as well as Sabrina.

As I made that wholehearted promise, I realized that—at some point during the emotionally charged morning—my relationship with Sabrina had undergone a complete transformation. We were confidantes now, not combatants. In sync instead of at odds. She wasn't acting aloof and secretive anymore because she had no more secrets to keep. And I didn't doubt her motives anymore because I finally understood them. In short, we had come to trust each other.

"Do you think I should talk to Melody's uncle?" I asked. "His office is on 23rd Street, not too far from here. Maybe he knows something that could lead us to the killer."

"Don't waste your time. The man knew nothing about Melody's real life, so it's safe to conclude he knows nothing about her death. Also, if you start making inquiries about his niece, you'll alert him to the fact that there's more to her murder than meets the eye. And then he'll alarm Melody's parents, which could lead to more grief and trouble for all concerned, including Melody's brother. Better steer clear of the uncle, Paige. Let sleeping dogs lie."

"You're right," I said, in firm agreement. "I need to concentrate my full attention on our prime suspects—the three clients on your list. Which brings me to my next question: Have any of them called you since we last spoke?"

"Yes!" she said, perking up and leaning forward in her chair. "I meant to tell you before, but I got lost in the past and forgot. Sam Hogarth called me last night! He wanted to schedule an appointment with Melody."

"Oh, my gosh!" I said, pulse pounding. "What did you tell him?"

"I said she had gone out of town for a couple of weeks."

"How did he react?"

"Calmly. He just asked when she was expected to return."

"That's it? You didn't discuss anything else?"

"I asked him if he wanted me to set him up with another girl, but he said no, he'd wait for Melody to come back."

"Did he sound sincere? I mean, do you think he really doesn't know that Melody is dead?"

Sabrina shrugged and shook her head. "I couldn't tell, Paige. I listened to his voice very carefully, trying to determine his mood and motives, but I couldn't make out a thing. He sounded the way he always does—cordial but businesslike."

"Like a politician," I said, remembering the way Hogarth had shuffled me out of his office, smiling all the while.

"Exactly," Sabrina agreed. "Hard to read. He *did* make the phone call, though. Do you think that means anything?"

"It means something, all right, but the question is *what?* If he was actually calling to make a date with Melody, it means he doesn't know she's dead, which means he's definitely not the murderer. But if he was calling just to make it *look* like he doesn't know she's dead, it means he probably *is* the murderer. So there's your answer in a nutshell: District Attorney Sam Hogarth is either the murderer, or he's not. Any more questions?"

Sabrina groaned. She looked like I felt—confused and over-whelmed. "What a mess," she said, rubbing her swollen eyes with her fingertips. "Will you ever be able to sort it all out?"

"God willing," I said, though I had serious doubts He'd want to get involved.

"I know you went to see Candy at Saks yesterday," Sabrina continued. "Was she able to help you at all?"

"Not really. They gave her such a short break we didn't have much time to talk. I'll try to see her again tonight or tomorrow. Meanwhile, you had dinner with her last night, right?"

"Yes, she came here for her monthly review. Charlotte made beef Wellington."

"Monthly review?"

"I have each of my girls come to dinner once a month. It gives me the opportunity to study their appearance and inquire about their health, and it gives them a chance to talk about their personal lives and voice any grievances they might have with their clients."

"Did you discuss the murder with Jocelyn . . . er, Candy? (I still hadn't gotten used to the two-name game.)

"At length," she said. "We shared our pain and relived our fondest memories of Melody. It was very therapeutic."

"Did she say who she thought the murderer was?"

"She wouldn't speculate." Sabrina gave me a tired, burned-out look and said, "Like the rest of my girls, she's in shock and can't imagine who could have done such a horrible thing."

A siren went off in my head, then shrieked its way to my tongue. "That's not what she told me! She said she was convinced the killer was either Hogarth or Corona. She even used their first names. 'It was either Sam or Tony,' she said. 'I'd stake my life on it.' Then she claimed they were both 'devils in disguise.' Why would she say this to me and not to you?"

Sabrina was visibly stunned and upset. "I haven't the slightest idea," she said. "I've always insisted that my girls give me an immediate report if they have any problems with their clients. It's one of my strictest rules. It's the only way I can monitor the

customers and keep the girls safe. I set Candy up with both Hogarth and Corona a few times in the past—before Melody joined
the agency—but she never had a bad word to say about either of
them. On the contrary, she said she liked them both a lot. Believe
me, if Candy had ever complained about their behavior or given
me any reason to believe that they were 'devils in disguise,' I
would *never* have introduced them to Melody. In fact, I would
have dropped them from my client list altogether!"

My pulse was pounding again. Had I finally dug up a mean-
ingful clue? "What about the present?" I asked. "Have you fixed
Candy up with Hogarth or Corona recently?"

"No. After they met Melody, they always asked for her."

"Was Candy bothered by this? Do you think she was jealous
of Melody?"

"If she was, she never gave any indication. I was under the
impression that they were good friends. Candy confided in me
more than once that she liked Melody better than any of the other
girls. She said it again just last night."

"Does Candy always tell you the truth?"

"I trusted her completely—until now. She told you one thing
and me another, so she's obviously lying to somebody. But *why*?
What could she possibly have to gain? She *knew* that you and I
would talk about this, so she also knew her lie would be exposed."

"That's a reasonable assumption," I said, "assuming that
Candy was in a reasonable state of mind. But maybe she wasn't.
She could have been freaked out about something and not
thinking logically. Or maybe something happened between my
talk with her at Saks and your talk with her at dinner to change
her mind about the two suspects' guilt and discourage her from
mentioning them to you."

Maybe she was threatened in some way, I said to myself. (I
didn't want to frighten Sabrina.) "The point is," I continued,
"we can't leap to any conclusions about Candy. This matter re-
quires a thorough examination. So, I'm going to do my best to
see and question her again tonight. What's her schedule like?
Have you set up any dates for her?"

"Just one—dinner and dancing with her regular Friday night
client. They meet every week like clockwork."

"What time does she usually get home?"

"Pretty late. Around two, two thirty in the morning. And she
takes a swim after that, so—"

"Swim?"

"The Barbizon has a pool," Sabrina said, "and Candy swims a few laps every night when she gets home. She says it washes away her sins."

"That's good to know," I said. "I'll take my bathing suit."

ABOUT HALF AN HOUR LATER—AFTER ADVISING Sabrina of my investigative plans for the rest of the day and night—I left her luxurious lavender bedroom and made my way back to the entrance hall. Not surprisingly, Charlotte was waiting for me at the door. She had my jacket, beret, and purse in her hands. I thanked her for the delicious breakfast and edifying conversation, then slipped out of the apartment and down the hall to the elevator.

When I landed in the lobby, I checked my watch. It was eleven fifteen. I had just enough time to get uptown to my bank, which was near my office (or what *used* to be my office), before lunchtime, when all the local employees would rush in to cash their paychecks. With any luck, I could withdraw a few bucks from my savings account before Mike and Mario—or, worse, Pomeroy!—pranced in. I owed Abby eight dollars, counting the four I still had in my purse, and I figured I'd need about fifteen more to get through the night and the rest of the weekend. Drinks at the Copa were expensive.

I had all the time and luck a down-on-her-luck, out-of-work crime writer could reasonably ask for. I caught an uptown train immediately and arrived at the Lexington and 42nd Street station at eleven thirty-five. My bank was just around the corner, and not yet crowded, so I was able to walk right up to a teller's window without waiting in line. I made out my check, collected ten singles and a fiver, and—footsteps echoing against the green marble walls and ultrahigh ceiling—fled the stately financial establishment before the noontime stampede began.

The good news was: I never laid eyes on any of my lousy ex-coworkers. The bad news was: All I had left in the bank was a lousy thirteen dollars.

Chapter 23

THE MAIN OFFICES OF HARRINGTON HOUSE Publishers were located at Madison and 45th, a short walk from my bank (which was another lucky break for me, since my feet hurt so much, I was considering having them amputated).

I had been in the sleek, modern Harrington House headquarters once before—when I was first hired at *Daring Detective* and had to fill out some forms for the accountants—but I had never met Oliver Rice Harrington in person, or set foot in his penthouse office. I wondered if the voluptuous redhead sitting behind the large reception desk in the company's outer lobby would allow me to reach those heights now.

"Hi," I said, stepping up to the desk and giving the plump, middle-aged woman my friendliest, toothiest smile. (I was trying to imitate Dinah Shore, but I probably looked more like Bugs Bunny.)

"Oh, hi!" she replied, quickly covering her open copy of *Confidential* magazine with a manila file folder. "Can I help you?"

"I'm here to see Mr. Harrington," I said, still smiling but trying to be assertive as well. "My name is Paige Turner, and I'm a staff writer for *Daring Detective* magazine. It's a Harrington House publication."

Her false eyelashes began to flutter. "Yes, I know!" she said.

"I can get free copies of anything the company publishes, and I grab that one as soon as it comes in. It's so scary and gory! You probably think I'm some kind of weirdo, but I really *love* to read stories about murder." She stretched her bright orange lips in an enormous smile and flapped her thick black lashes even faster. "So what are you writing about now, honey? That girl that was killed on Monday night? The one that was tied up naked and smothered with turpentine? Gawd, that was awful! I get chills all over my body just thinking about it." Her large breasts were heaving, and her heavily rouged cheeks flushed even rosier. She wasn't chewing gum, but she should have been. Then the caricature would have been complete.

"I'm not covering that story," I said, disregarding her avid questions and pointedly looking at my watch. "I came to see Mr. Harrington about a different matter. He may be expecting me, and I need to catch him before he goes out to lunch. Is he in?"

"I don't know, honey. He never tells *me* what he's up to. You'll have to talk to his personal secretary about that kinda stuff. Want me to call her for you?" She raised one eyebrow and reached for the phone.

"No!" I snapped. "I'd rather talk to her in person. Can you direct me to her office?"

"Sure, honey. She works upstairs with Mr. Harrington, on the top floor. She sits out front and her name is Frieda." She nodded toward the wall of elevators across the way and went back to reading her magazine.

As I approached the elevators, one of them whisked open and released a stream of passengers. They poured into the lobby and surged toward the exit, all dressed for the crisp fall weather, and all in a hurry to have a nice lunch at Schrafft's, or grab a hot dog and a Coke at Grand Central, or cash their Friday paychecks. A drugstore blonde in a bright green coat and a fake fur-trimmed hat waved to the red-haired receptionist and cried, "See ya later, Cora! I'll meet ya for a beer after work."

I stepped into the empty car and pushed the button for the penthouse. On my slow but steady rise to the top, I mapped out a plan of attack. Knowing I'd never get past Harrington's secretary without an appointment, I decided I should cause a disturbance of some kind—kick up a fuss until I got my way. *You've got to be strong and forceful!* I told myself. *You've got to march right in and* demand *to see him. You have a right to speak to*

*your boss if you want to! Even if he isn't your boss anymore! If
you're too nice and polite, his secretary will just turn you away.
Be firm, Paige. Be tough!*

By the time the elevator reached the top floor, I was primed
for action. And when the door to the penthouse slid open, I
charged through it with my dukes up (Rocky Marciano in a tight
skirt and high heels). Forging my way across the thick gray carpet
to the large ebony desk parked in the center of the plush reception area, I sucked in a deep breath and threw my first punch.

"I want to see Mr. Harrington," I said to the small gray-haired
lady sitting behind the desk, "and I want to see him *now!*"
To illustrate my point, I bonked my fist down on her large,
blue-leather-rimmed blotter.

She gasped and froze straight as a stick in her chair. "Do you
have an appointment?" she whimpered, gaping up at me as if I
were the Bride of Frankenstein—or a female incarnation of The
Thing.

"No, Frieda, I *don't* have an appointment!" (I stomped my
foot on the floor when I said that, but the carpet was so thick, it
barely made a sound.) "I don't need one! Mr. Harrington will
want to see me anyway—I guarantee it! So let's stop wasting
time, okay? Just pick up the damn phone and tell him Paige
Turner is here."

Frieda was shocked by my language and behavior—and, to
tell you the truth, so was I. I had never spoken so rudely—or so
crudely—to an older woman in my entire life. Feeling contrite
and ashamed of my deplorable conduct, I made a mental note
to apologize to the poor soul on my way out. Then I put on an
even more furious scowl, planted both hands on my hips, and
stared daggers at her until she got on the intercom and told
Harrington—in a very shaky voice—that I was there, demanding
to see him.

I didn't know how Harrington was going to react to my unexpected arrival, of course, but I had a hunch he'd consent to
see me—either in the capacity of a curious boss, or an irate ex-
boss, or a philandering murderer who was hoping to avoid detection by conning and misleading the most determined crime
reporter in the city. (In case you're wondering, that means *me*.)

My hunch was dead right.

"Mr. Harrington will see you now," Frieda said, anxiously
fingering her white lace collar and giving me a worried look.

She hung up the phone, stood up, and took a few steps toward an archway in the rear of the reception area. "Please follow me, I'll show you the way." As she led me through the arch and down a long corridor lined with framed book covers, magazine covers, and newspaper front-page tear sheets, she kept glancing nervously over her shoulder, as if she thought I might spring forward and bite her on the back.

HARRINGTON'S OFFICE WAS HUGE—AND SO WAS the man himself. When he stood up and walked around his desk toward me, I guessed his height at about six foot two and his weight at two eighty or more. He reminded me of Raymond Burr, the actor who played the villain in Alfred Hitchcock's latest movie, *Rear Window*. He wore a dark gray suit, white shirt, maroon tie, and classic wire-rimmed glasses. He had thick, wavy salt-and-pepper hair—heavy on the salt—and a barrel-chested baritone that was loud enough to curl your toes. (I know this for a fact, because the minute I entered his office, he started yelling at me—and my toes did, indeed, curl.)

"What's the meaning of this intrusion, Mrs. Turner?" he bellowed, marching up so close to me that I almost fell over backward. "You've got a lot of nerve barging in this way! Haven't you ever heard of making an appointment? You scared my secretary half to death. I never would have told her to let you in if I thought she could handle the situation and kick you out."

"Kick me out?" I screeched, flying into a genuine rage. "Kick me out?!" I repeated, for emphasis. "You kicked me out of the whole darn company yesterday! Wasn't that enough for you?"

Harrington cocked his head and gave me a puzzled look. "What are you talking about?"

"I'm talking about the fact that you *fired* me, goddamn it! You threw me out of *Daring Detective* on my rear. You took away my hard-won career and my major source of income in an instant. With one little snap of your fingers. And when I asked Mr. Crockett why, all he could tell me was that you and your sniveling cousin, Brandon Pomeroy, wanted me out. *Sayonara*. Bye-bye. Gone for good. Was my termination so meaningless to you that you've already forgotten all about it?"

He didn't say anything. He just pushed his glasses higher on his nose, stared intently at me for several burning seconds, then turned and started walking back to his desk.

I didn't know what to make of his stern silence. Was he surprised to learn that I'd been fired and wondering why it had happened, or was he shrewdly avoiding the subject in order to keep his homicidal motives hidden?

There was only one way to find out.

"You know what I think?" I sputtered, shooting my words, like arrows, into his broad, retreating back. "I think there's something fishy going on here!"

I regretted the silly word choice immediately. *Fishy?* I berated myself. *Jeez! Couldn't I have said* sinister *instead? Or* evil? *Why do I always have to sound like Betty instead of Veronica? Am I just a wretched, aging replica of Nancy Drew?* (Please don't answer that.)

Harrington stopped short in his tracks, turned his huge body around, and gave me a menacing smile. "Something fishy? What makes you say that, Mrs. Turner? Are you so sure of yourself that you don't believe an employer could have a *legitimate* reason for letting you go?"

That wasn't the response I'd been hoping for. But once the comment was made, I felt compelled to defend myself. "Yes, I *am* sure of myself," I declared. "I'm an excellent crime writer and a diligent employee, and you know it as well as I do. Every time one of *my* stories is put on the cover, *DD* sells thirty percent better."

Harrington hit me with another creepy smile. "And you think you're the only one responsible for that?" He walked around his desk and sat down in his chair without offering me a seat. "What about the editorial director, art director, printer, distributor, and sales staff? What about the newsdealers? And the readers? Shouldn't they at least receive honorable mention?"

The conversation was *not* going the way I wanted it to. "Yes, of course," I said, trying to think of a way to move on to more urgent topics—such as the murder of Virginia Pratt. "But you can't deny the fact that the issues that featured my last few stories hit new sales highs. And that the only discernible difference between those sales and the sales of other issues was my exclusive, on-the-street, behind-the-scenes reporting." I took a deep breath, then delivered what I hoped would be the zinger. "And you definitely can't deny that the Virginia Pratt murder story should have been assigned to me instead of Mike Never-Leave-the-Office-Except-for-Lunch Davidson!"

I stopped talking and focused all my attention on Harrington's face, studying his reaction like a hawk, trying to pick up clues to his character if not his crimes.

He drew his dark, bushy eyebrows together so tightly they almost met in the middle of his face. Then he narrowed his eyes and glared at me through the slits, ruthless lips smiling all the while. "These matters are of no concern to me, Mrs. Turner," he said, keeping his voice down to a low, tense, intimidating growl. "Brandon Pomeroy and Harvey Crockett are in charge of the *Daring Detective* operation, and I fully support any decision they choose to make."

"*They?*" I squawked. "This wasn't a joint decision! Mr. Crockett didn't fire me, Pomeroy did. And Pomeroy was acting alone when he gave the Virginia Pratt assignment to Mike instead of me."

"Stop whining, Mrs. Turner," Harrington said, shifting his bulk from one side of his high-backed leather chair to the other. "I can't be bothered with petty personal problems such as yours. I have more important business to conduct. Perhaps you haven't noticed, but I have an international empire to run."

"Well, excuse me for breathing," I said, steam shooting out of my ears and nostrils. "I guess my paltry little life is as meaningless to you as Virgina Pratt's was."

I shouldn't have said that.

Harrington bolted out of his chair and lumbered toward me—big eyes bulging out of their sockets, giant hands clenched into fists. "Get out!" he roared, bearing down on me like a rampaging bull. "Get out of my office right now!"

I decided to take his advice.

Chapter 24

I FLEW OUT OF HARRINGTON'S OFFICE AND down the hall to the penthouse lobby, admonishing myself all the way. *Nice going, Paige! If you weren't actually fired before, you definitely will be now! And if Harrington murdered Virginia, you're bound to be his next victim!* There was no getting around it, I had the judgment of a rock and the brains of a bird.

After a quick stop at Frieda's desk to offer my apologies (which she timidly and most kindly accepted), I darted into an open elevator, rode down to the ground floor, and exited the building as fast as I could. Scrambling down Madison toward the subway, I came across a Thom McAn shoe store and zipped inside. Plopping down in the first empty chair I came to, I kicked off my stilettos and moaned with relief. It was the first time I'd sat down since I left Sabrina's.

A skinny young salesman with a buzz cut and a bad case of acne approached me and asked, "Is there something special you'd like to see?"

"Anything without heels," I said, flexing my arches and wiggling my toes.

"We have some nice ballerina flats on sale."

"How much?"

"Two ninety-nine. They come in black, white, red, blue, and pink."

"Red," I said, wanting my shoes to match my beret. "Six and a half narrow."

Twelve minutes later, I was back on the pavement, headed for the downtown IND. I was three inches shorter and three dollars poorer, but at least I could walk without plotting suicide.

It was 2:05 PM. Still early in the afternoon, but it felt like midnight to me. I was drained, depressed, and downhearted. I wanted to go home, get into bed, and pull the covers over my head. I wanted to hide out from all the gardeners, gangsters, pimps, parents, bosses, politicians, millionaires, and murderers in the world—for the rest of my pitiful, insignificant, and sure-to-be-brief existence.

But first, I wanted to have a drink and a late lunch with Abby.

I hopped on a train at 42nd Street and hopped off at West 4th. (It's easy to hop when you're wearing ballerina slippers.) A short walk down Sixth Avenue, a right turn on Bleecker, and a block over to Cornelia brought me to my first destination: Zito's bakery. I stepped inside the tiny store and bought a fresh-baked loaf of Italian bread, then continued toward my apartment, stopping at Faicco's deli for a wedge of cheddar, a small salami, and a couple cans of tomato juice, and at Angelo's for two limes and a green pepper.

I carried the sacks of groceries and the shopping bag with my stilettos upstairs, straining my ears for sounds of life in Abby's apartment. But all was quiet. And her door was locked. And she didn't answer her doorbell. Heart sinking like a lead balloon, I set my bags on the floor of the landing and started fishing in my purse for my keys. I felt so tired and lonely, I wasn't even hungry anymore. I decided I really would go straight to bed and pull the covers over my head.

But just as I found my keys and leaned over to open the door to my apartment, the door from the street burst open, and Abby catapulted into the stairwell. *Hallelujah!* I shouted in silence, fresh energy surging into my veins. "Oh, hi," I said out loud. "Where have you been?"

Abby bounced up the stairs with a mile-wide grin on her face. "Hey, babe," she said, opening the door to her apartment. "Come on in. I've got something to tell you." She charged inside, tore off her jacket, and tossed it on the loveseat. Then she flounced into the kitchen, took a bottle of vodka out of the cabinet, and set it down on the counter. "Want a drink?" There was a mischievous gleam in her eye. "I know it's early, but what the hell? You only live once."

I picked up my bags and carried them inside. "I bought some limes and tomato juice. Want to make Bloody Marys?"

"Great!" she said, cranking open a tray of ice. "What else have you got there? Anything to eat? I'm famished!"

"Bread, cheese, salami, green pepper." I put the grocery bags down on the table and removed the contents. Then I took off my jacket and beret and put them on the loveseat. Catching a glimpse of the painting propped on the easel in Abby's living room–cum–art studio, I went over for a closer look. A bosomy blonde in a skimpy pink bikini was tied spread-eagle to the large wheel of a covered wagon, and several bare-chested Indians with feathers in their hair and tomahawks in their hands were doing a war dance around her.

"Your new painting's really far-out," I said, returning to the kitchen to help get things ready. "I didn't know pioneer women wore bikinis."

Abby laughed. "In *Men's Wild Adventure* magazine, *all* the women wear bikinis—unless they're going swimming, of course, in which case they just wear seaweed or lily pads."

I snickered and said, "What's the cover line for this one? Wait, don't tell me. It's 'Busty Blonde Gets a Hatchet Haircut!' Am I right?"

"Close," she teased. "It's 'Scalped Blondes Have More Fun!'"

We giggled while we prepared our lunch. Except for the tomato juice, everything I brought needed slicing. After stirring our drinks and assembling assorted slices of food on two plates, we sat down to eat.

"Here's blood in your eye," Abby said, raising her glass in a toast, then taking a big gulp of her Bloody Mary.

I did the same, and we were quiet for a while after that. (It's not polite to talk with your mouth full.)

"SO, WHAT HAVE YOU BEEN UP TO?" I ASKED, AS soon as we finished our feast. "You said you had something to tell me."

"Yeah, I do," Abby murmured, "but you're not gonna be very happy about it, so I think we'd better have another drink first."

She took our glasses over to the counter and plunked in a few more ice cubes.

"Oh, no!" I said, stomach churning. "Why won't I be happy? What have you done now?"

She measured out the vodka and poured in the tomato juice. "Nothing really bad, babe. And it was for your own good. But you're still not gonna like it." She squeezed a segment of lime into each glass, then added more than a few drops of Tabasco and brought them over to the table. "Stir it with your finger," she said, setting one of the drinks in front of me. "All the hot stuff's on top."

Too upset to listen, I grabbed the glass and guzzled down a third of the fiery cocktail. It didn't even faze me. My brain and tongue were already ablaze. "Stop stalling!" I screeched. "What the hell happened? What are you afraid to tell me?"

Abby sat down and lit a cigarette. Then she propped her feet up on an empty chair, blew a perfect smoke ring in my direction, and announced with an air of defiance, "I went to see Sabrina this afternoon."

"What?" I thought my skull would explode. "Are you crazy? How could you do that to me? I told you it would be disastrous if you met Sabrina! Whatever made you—"

"Oh, hush, Paige," she said, untying her ponytail and shaking her shiny black mane down her back. "You always make such a *tsimmis*." (For those not familiar with Yiddish, that means stew, fuss, mess.)

"But there was no reason for you to go there!" I shrieked, making another *tsimmis*. "I spent the whole morning with Sabrina, and she answered every single one of my questions, and now I *know* she didn't kill Virginia. You hear what I'm saying? She's not a suspect anymore, and that's all there is to it!"

"Well, now that I've met the woman, I agree with you. But I needed to see for myself."

"But how did you know where to go? I never gave you her address."

"No, but you told me she lived on Gramercy Park, and you gave me a very vivid description of her building. How many white castles with gargoyles and cherubs and knights in shining armor could there be? The minute I stepped onto the sidewalk surrounding the park, I spotted the right place."

I took another swig of my drink. And then another. "So what

did you do then?" I whimpered, wondering if she'd destroyed my credibility with Sabrina altogether. "Burst into her apartment and tell her that Paige Turner sent you? Claim that I had appointed you my deputy?"

Abby rolled her eyes. "No way, Doris Day. I wouldn't dream of such a thing! You said Sabrina had sworn you to secrecy, so I was careful not to jeopardize your pact with her. I told her I heard about her operation from a friend of a friend of a friend who used to be one of her girls. Trust me, babe, your name was never spoken."

I found that heartening but hard to believe.

"So what did you say after that? What reason did you give for suddenly appearing at her apartment and sniffing around like a demented beagle?"

"I told her I was broke and wanted to join her escort service."

"What?"

"You heard me. I said I wanted to become one of her call girls."

Aaargh!

"Well, that's just great," I spluttered. "My best friend wants to be a whore."

"Oh, shut up, Paige! You know it's not like that. I went there for one reason, and one reason only: to protect you."

"Protect me?" I cried, incredulous. "That's a laugh and a half. I fail to understand how pretending you want to be a call girl—if, indeed, you *were* pretending—could afford me any protection at all. What the hell were you thinking?"

Abby shot me a furious look and blew another smoke ring. "Can't you figure that out for yourself, Miss Marple? For a crime writer, you're not too swift. My motives were simple and pure, you dig? I thought I'd talk to Sabrina for a while, and study her behavior up close, and then—if I came away from the interview convinced that she was capable of murder—I'd do whatever I could to pry you out of her evil clutches."

"Pry?" I questioned. "Evil clutches?" I scoffed. "Aren't you being a bit melodramatic? You make it sound as though I'd been brainwashed or something."

"Well, it was possible, you know!" Abby said, pouting. "Sabrina *was* in control of your actions to a degree. And she *could* have been feeding you false clues, steering you to pin the murder on somebody else. And the way I saw it, you weren't anywhere *near* as suspicious of her as you should have been. I mean, what if she *did* lead you to identify and incriminate an innocent man? Wouldn't she then have to kill *you* to make sure the truth never came out? Sorry, Paige, but I was really wigged out about this. I thought you weren't watching your back, so I decided to watch it for you."

"Well, that was very sweet of you," I said, with just the slightest hint of sarcasm, "but I wasn't born yesterday, you know. I was supicious of Sabrina's motives from the outset, and—though I admit to being more focused on her list of primary suspects than I was on her—I never once lost sight of her possible involvement in the crime.

"That's all changed now, though," I added, giving Abby a potent Bette Davis gaze. "After my emotional heart-to-heart with Sabrina this morning, I'm convinced she would have killed herself before lifting a finger against Virginia."

Abby nodded and smiled. "I'm with you, Lulu. Sabrina and I never discussed the murder or even mentioned Virginia's name, but I could tell from the way she treated me during our interview, and by the kind of questions she asked, that she's a real mensch. Sure, she was sizing me up—trying to judge how good a prostitute I'd be—but she was also concerned about me as a person. My welfare actually mattered to her. I could see it in her eyes. I tell you, Paige, if I ever *do* decide to become a call girl, Sabrina's the madam for me!"

"So, when do you start?" I asked, only half kidding.

"Tonight," Abby said, not kidding at all.

Chapter 25

"OKAY, WHAT THE HELL'S GOING ON, AB?" I SAT rigidly in my chair, struggling to keep my voice down and my emotions under control. "You're just playing games with me, right? You haven't actually signed on with Sabrina, have you?"

"Not yet," Abby admitted. "She insisted that I think things over before making my final decision. I'm supposed to call her tonight and tell her if I'm ready to take the plunge."

"And what, may I ask, do you plan to say to her?" My voice was low, but my tone was scathing.

"Nothing," Abby said, smiling.

"Huh?"

"Nothing at all," she repeated, eyes gleaming.

"What do you mean?" I pleaded, wondering if I'd live long enough to hear the whole story. "C'mon, Abby! Come clean! Are you going to call Sabrina or not?"

"Nope," she said, still smiling. "*I'm* not going to call her, *you* are."

If there had been any bedcovers nearby, I'd have pulled them over my head and nailed them in place. "I can't take this anymore," I said, too tired to shriek or screech. "Stop winding me up. I'm not a toy. Just tell me what's going on in your twisted and perverted little mind."

"Oh, all right!" Abby scowled and smashed her cigarette in

the ashtray. "You're no fun anymore, you know that? I was just fooling around a little—trying to lighten things up and have a few laughs. And where's the harm in that? A little silliness never hurt anybody, you dig? It might even help us put things in perspective! But noooo, that's totally impossible now, thanks to you, because you're so sensitive and serious and impatient and boring, a girl can't even—"

"Abby!"

"All right, already!" she snapped, raising her hands in surrender. Then she took a sip of her drink, twirled a lock of ink-black hair around her index finger, and said, "Okay, here's the skinny, Minnie. There's a reason you need to call Sabrina, and it's a good one. Remember I said I would get Jimmy to take us to the Copa tonight? Well, he can't go. He's got a poetry gig at the Vanguard. I called around for a substitute, but all my backup boyfriends are busy, so now we're up the creek without a male escort.

"And that's not all," she continued. "I also called a girlfriend of mine—a model who works the coat check at the Copa—and she told me the club is booked so tight tonight not even an ant could sneak inside. She said Corona has so many bodyguards standing around backstage his own mother couldn't get anywhere near him."

Kerplunk. Our scheme to ambush Tony Corona in his dressing room hit the water and sank like a stone.

"Well, that's that," I said, shoulders slumping in defeat. "It was a foolish idea to begin with, I guess. I should have known it wouldn't work out." My head was hanging so low it almost touched the table. "Now I'll have to revert to my original plan and try to corner Corona at his hotel. It'll be tough to crash his suite at the Plaza, and a heck of a lot more dangerous, but what other choice do I—"

"Hold the phone, Joan!" Abby broke in. "Did you lose your faith along with your sense of humor? I told you I'd dream up a scheme to get us into the Copa, didn't I? Where's your confidence, babe?" She arched one eyebrow to the hilt, stuck her chin out, and said, "What would you say if I told you I know a way we can catch Corona's show tonight, be treated to a free dinner and a slew of champagne cocktails, and then be invited—that's right, *invited*—backstage to his dressing room?"

"I'd say you're playing poker with half a deck."

Abby stretched her scarlet lips from one earlobe to the other.

"Then you'd lose the game, Mame. Because all you have to do to make this happen is call Sabrina."

IT TOOK A WHILE FOR ABBY TO EXPLAIN HER crazy plan to me, and even longer for me to accept it. After I thought it over, however, and realized how snugly the pieces of the puzzle fit into place, I came to the conclusion that Abby's scheme was not only feasible—it was perfect. So, without further delay, I picked up the phone and dialed Sabrina.

First I told her the truth about Abby: that the bold and beautiful brunette who had suddenly appeared at her apartment earlier today was my best friend and next-door neighbor—*not* a potential prostitute—and that she was helping me search for Virginia's killer. Then, seeing that my broken secrecy pledge didn't upset Sabrina nearly as much as I thought it would (it seemed we'd both become more trusting and forgiving since our chummy morning chat), I went on to outline the way that she could help us get in to see Corona at the Copa.

At first she flatly refused. It was too dangerous, she said, and she'd never forgive herself if something awful happened to me or Abby as a result of her actions. But after I spoke to Sabrina awhile—pointing out that trying to hunt down a murderer was *always* dangerous, regardless of the methods used, and that the crowded Copacabana was probably the safest possible setting for such a venture—she agreed to set our scheme in motion.

She said that as soon as she hung up with me, she'd call Tony (he'd been a client for so long she always used his first name). And once she got him on the line (she knew he'd take her call—he always did), she would tell him about the two gorgeous, shapely, incredibly sexy young women who had just that day joined her escort service. Then she'd offer him first dibs, saying she would send the two young ladies to the Copa this evening and—if he'd arrange for them to be admitted at the door and seated at a good table for dinner and the eight o'clock show—they'd be pleased to meet him in his dressing room afterward, where he could look them over and choose the one he wants for the night.

(I would have been happy to forgo the dinner and the show, but Abby wouldn't hear of it. "All work and no play makes Paige a dull detective," she insisted.)

I gave Sabrina Abby's number and told her to call us back when she got off the phone with Corona. Then, while we waited to learn whether or not Corona would take the bait, I guzzled the rest of my Bloody Mary, lit up a cigarette, and filled Abby in on the earlier details of my day—my heart-to-heart talks with Charlotte and Sabrina and my explosive confrontation with Oliver Rice Harrington.

"I *told* you not to bother with him," Abby snorted. "Harrington's not the murderer. You just got yourself fired—*really* fired—for nothing."

"I'm sure you're right about my job," I said, "but you could be dead wrong about Harrington. He's a very brutal man, Ab. He's a cold-hearted cutthroat, a ruthless tycoon, a merciless bastard who probably commits some form of murder every day. Look at how easily—not to mention guiltlessly—he killed my career!"

"That's not the same as killing a person."

"Oh, no? Well, you should have seen the way he reacted when I mentioned Virginia Pratt! He went insane, Jane. He was breathing fire! I swear, if he had gotten his hands on me, he would have killed me, too. He would have hauled me up under his arm, lugged me across the room, plowed my head through the glass of the penthouse window, and then chucked me— screaming and flailing—over the ledge." (Okay, that was a pretty rash and gruesome conclusion, but what can I say? I was in a rash and gruesome mood.)

The phone rang, and we both shot to attention. I sucked in a lungful of smoke, snatched up the receiver, and croaked, "Yes?"

"It's a go," Sabrina said. "Tony wants to meet you and Abby tonight after the eight o'clock show, just as we discussed."

"Good," I said, giving Abby the thumbs-up.

"You should arrive at the Copa at seven sharp," Sabrina continued. "Tell the man at the door your names are Gina and Cherry—those are the names I gave Tony. You can decide for yourselves who's who, but make sure you remember the names and use them whenever you introduce yourselves to someone or speak to each other. Gina and Cherry. The doorman will be expecting you and the maître d' will show you to your table.

"He'll probably seat you up front, near the band and the dance floor, so that Tony can watch you while you're watching him perform. He likes to observe the effect he has on women. It turns him on. So, bat your lashes a lot and try to look as if you're about to swoon. And show plenty of leg and cleavage. He likes to examine the merchandise closely before making a purchase."

Ugh.

"Order your dinner as soon as you're seated," Sabrina went on, "and eat it as fast as you can, because once the show starts, you *must* give Tony your full attention. If you don't, he'll get miffed, and he might change his mind about seeing you after the show."

"Sounds like you've been through this before."

"A couple of times, with a couple of different girls. One of them ate a stalk of celery during his opening number, and he had her kicked out at intermission."

"Nice guy," I grunted, mulling over this new information. "Did Melody ever annoy him in any way?"

"Not to my knowledge. She was aware that Tony has a quick temper, so she was always on her best behavior. And as long as she was properly respectful of him, he treated her with the utmost respect in return. At least that's what she told me."

I took a drag on my cigarette and exhaled loudly. "I wonder if she was properly respectful last Monday night."

"Good question," Sabrina said, her voice turning to stone.

"Did Corona say anything to you about Melody?" I asked. My pulse had quickened to a staccato beat. "Did he try to schedule a new date with her?"

"No," Sabrina said, sighing heavily. "Her name never came up."

Chapter 26:

"OOF!" I GASPED, AS ABBY FASTENED THE LAST hook on the back of the excruciatingly tight, waist-length, strapless push-up bra she was making me wear. "Undo this torture device immediately! I can't breathe! My ribs are all crunched together, and my breasts are rammed so high they're blocking my nasal passages."

"Stop whining, Paige! Sabrina said we have to show a lot of cleavage, and this is the only way you can swing it."

"Who cares about *my* cleavage? In that puny excuse for a dress you've got on, you'll be showing more than enough for both of us." (I wasn't exaggerating, you should know. The scoop neck of her purple satin sheath was cut so low her own scoops were boldly bobbing in the breeze.) "And if you think I'm going to wear anything that revealing," I added, "you've got another think coming. It's cold out, Ab! I want something warm and cozy and—

"Mmmmph!" I grunted, as she pulled a skintight, sleeveless, and, for all intents and purposes, chestless black cocktail dress down over my head and roughly zipped it up the back.

"There!" she said. "Now turn around and let me see."

"Are you kidding? The skirt is so tight I can't move."

"Shut up, or I'll cut a slit up the side."

I groaned and turned around. "Forget about it, Abby. I'm not going anywhere in this skimpy thing. It's nothing but a long swimsuit. Only Esther Williams would wear this dress! I feel like a goddamn mermaid, and I'm *walking* like one, too." To prove the truth of my words, I took a few baby steps forward, waving my arms for balance and advancing about an inch.

"Stop clowning, Paige!" she squawked. "It's getting late. We have to be at the Copa in one hour, and I haven't even put your makeup on yet." She frowned intently, shoved my hair back off my face, and began rubbing pancake foundation into my skin so hard it hurt.

"Ow!" I complained. "*Now* who's being serious and impatient? You're no fun anymore, you know that? I was just fooling around a little—trying to lighten things up and have a few laughs. A little silliness never hurt anybody, you dig?"

If Abby noticed that I was mocking her and throwing her own words back at her verbatim, she kept it to herself. She just finished applying my makeup—pink rouge, red lipstick, icky blue eyeshadow, etc.—vigorously and without comment. Then, after pinning my hair up in a taut little bun, she yanked a curly blonde wig down over my head and mashed it in place.

"Ugh! Do I *have* to wear this mop?" I asked, even though I already knew the answer to that question. "It's so uncomfortable! It feels like my cranium's been carpeted."

"Would you rather have it shot full of holes?" Abby said, with a sniff. "If Tony the Tiger is the murderer, and if he recognizes you from any of your past newspaper photos tonight, your skull will be a bloody breezeway by tomorrow."

"I get the picture," I said, wishing that I didn't. The image was a bit too graphic for my taste.

"Besides, you look really cute like this!" Abby bubbled, fluffing the short blonde curls and arranging them around my face. "You don't look like yourself at all. You look just like Janet Leigh!"

"Harpo Marx is more like it," I grumbled.

"Oh, hush. You're such a kvetch." Abby finished styling my fake hair and sprayed it with something smelly and sticky. Then she took a pair of sky-high black patent pumps out of her closet and insisted that I put them on.

"But I don't want to!" I whined. "My feet hurt. I'm going to wear my new ballerina slippers."

"Oh, no, you're not," she said. "You have to look really sexy tonight—like a hot, high-class call girl—*not* like a gawky, flat-footed preteen. Put those heels on, and come downstairs right now. We've gotta go, Flo!"

Abby was having fun. You could tell by the way she bounced down the steps, slipped into her fur-trimmed purple satin coat (it came with the dress), and then twirled over to the door like an Arthur Murray ballroom dance student.

I was in perfect misery. You could tell by the way I dragged myself down to the kitchen, shoved my cold, naked arms into the sleeves of Abby's gray chinchilla jacket, trailed my former friend down the stairwell to the street, and then shivered, lurched, and wriggled—like a bare-breasted, fin-shackled mermaid out of water—toward the uptown IND.

THE COPA WAS AT 10 EAST 60TH STREET, JUST a few steps off Fifth Avenue. When Abby and I turned the corner and headed for the entrance, we saw that the entire block was crammed with long, shiny limousines, honking taxicabs, and town cars discharging prosperous-looking men in tuxedos and bow ties, and beautiful women in jewels and furs. Scads of shouting newspaper photographers were engaged in fierce combat for position and the chance to pop another batch of blinding flashbulbs.

Tony Corona was packing them in.

"Follow me!" Abby whooped, happily pushing her way into the fray. I tucked my chin to my chest and stayed as close behind her as I could, hoping nobody would poke their elbow in my eye or—worse—take my picture. (When you're on a dangerous undercover hunt for a killer—and trying to keep your mission hidden from your overly protective, short-tempered detective boyfriend—photographic exposure in the press can be hazardous to your health. Wig or no wig.)

Jostling and shoving and yelling "Hot stuff!" at the top of her lungs, Abby thrust her way up to the entrance of the club with me wobbling right behind, huddled as close to her hindquarters as a kid riding piggyback.

"Hi, handsome!" she hollered at the doorman. "I'm Gina, and this is Cherry!" She leaned to one side, forcing me to show my face (which was surely beet red from embarrassment).

"You're expecting us, right? We're Mr. Corona's guests for dinner and the show."

The doorman didn't say a word. He just arched one skinny black eyebrow, nodded his ham-sized head, pulled the door open a few inches, and shooed us inside.

I was shocked at how quickly we'd been allowed to enter. Abby and I were now sauntering—*without* male companions—across the luxurious, potted palm–lined lobby toward the glittering, welcoming gates of the most famous nightclub in the world, while scores of Manhattan's most fashionable, celebrated, and properly escorted wives, girlfriends, actresses, models, and socialites were still being screened for admittance.

It's cool to be a cookie with connections, I mused to myself, *but being a call girl with a well-connected madam takes the cake.*

AFTER BEING SEATED AT A FRONT-ROW TABLE (as Sabrina had predicted), and immediately ordering our dinner and drinks (as Sabrina had advised), I turned and swept my gaze around the glitzy interior of the club. The decor was classy and Cuban, with white tablecloths, red velvet chairs, and glistening mirrored walls. There was an elevated bandstand, a small hardwood dance floor, a lofty, wraparound mezzanine, and several enormous floor-to-ceiling columns shaped as palm trees. Their trunks were pure white and their leaves were bright gold.

The band was playing a rumba, and the tables were filling up fast. Several couples ventured onto the floor to dance. "Hey, bobba ree bop!" Abby shouted to me above the music. Torn between watching the dancers and checking out the people who were quickly filling up the tables around us, she was twisting her head in all directions at once. "This is the living end!" she cried. "The air's so thick with excitement you could slice it like a turkey."

"Right," I said, feeling far more nervous than excited. I had been to the Copacabana once before—when I was working on my very first *Daring Detective* story—and it had been a crazy, dangerous, hair-raising experience. I hoped tonight's expedition wouldn't turn out the same way.

"Hey, look upstairs!" Abby squealed, gaping toward the

mezzanine in sheer delight. "It's Gordon MacRae! Yummmm. He's so handsome, it's shameful. And what a sexy voice he's got! Whenever he sings, my ovaries melt. He's probably making the rounds tonight, showing up at the hottest nightspots to promote his new movie, *Oklahoma!* . . . Oooh! Wow! Guess who's sitting over there!" she sputtered, eyes shifting toward a different spot in the balcony. "It's Kirk Douglas! And he's sitting next to Lana Turner! Holy smoke! Aren't they both married to somebody else? I wonder if they're having an affair!" She couldn't have been more elated if James Dean had suddenly come back to life and sat down at our table.

"Cool it, Ab—er, Gina!" I hissed. "Get a grip on yourself. You're acting like a starstruck bobby-soxer instead of a wicked woman of the world. And you'd better calm yourself down right now, kiddo, because a lot of famous people will be here tonight. And since they'll all be sitting in the mezzanine—which, according to the gossip columnists, is reserved for VIPs—you need to keep your starry eyes fixed on the dance floor. Especially after the show begins," I cautioned. "We can't afford to offend our generous and demanding host."

"I get your drift," Abby said, wrenching her gaze away from the upper level and happily focusing it on one of the two champagne cocktails our waiter had just placed in front of us. "Here's to life, liberty, and the pursuit of justice!" she warbled, holding her glass up for a toast.

"Cheers," I said, clinking her cocktail for good luck, trying to suppress my nagging fear that we were headed for a nasty night.

ABOUT FORTY-FIVE MINUTES LATER—AFTER we'd devoured our Waldorf salads, broiled lobster tails, lyonnaise potatoes, and chocolate éclairs (well, we had to keep up our strength!)—the bandleader brought a torrid tango to a heart-throbbing climax and then signaled for a drumroll. The spotlights mounted in the golden leaves of the palm trees closest to the dance floor began to flash and spin, prompting the lingering hoofers to return to their seats.

It was showtime.

Suddenly, without any introduction or fanfare, eight gorgeous young women wearing silver dresses and silver flowers in

their hair pranced onto the dance floor. These were the celebrated Copa girls—the uniformly tall, slinky, and ultrabuxom
beauties often referred to in the gossip columns as "Manhattan's choicest" (which I thought made them sound more like
meat than showgirls, but maybe that was the point).

The band struck up a snappy cha-cha and the girls began to
dance—four in front, four in back—swaying their hips to the
music and shaking their shoulders to the beat. Their dresses
were strapless, and even more revealing than Abby's and mine,
so every little shimmy caused a turbulent undulation of exposed
flesh. All of the men in the audience were mesmerized. Some of
the women, too.

I, on the other hand, was in agony. I had to pee so bad I
thought I would pop. Knowing Corona would be making his entrance soon, and that I couldn't possibly last through his entire
performance without relieving myself, I decided I'd better make
a run for the bathroom while I had the chance.

Jumping to my feet, but crouching as low as I could to avoid
obstructing the audience's view, I leaned over and announced
my intentions directly into Abby's ear:

"Gotta go to the loo, Sue. Be back in a few."

She was having such a good time, she barely noticed my
rhyme. Or, for that matter, my frantic departure.

Chapter 27

THE LADIES' ROOM WAS EMPTY—AND IN VERY short order, so was my bladder. (Word to the wise: If you're in a crowded nightclub and you want to pee in private, hit the john during showtime.) I wasn't alone in the elegant lavatory for long, however. As soon as I stepped out of the stall and over to one of the pearl white porcelain sinks to wash my hands, a tiny Negro woman in a black dress and a starched white apron appeared out of nowhere with a white linen hand towel draped over her skinny arm. She smiled and handed the towel to me at the exact moment I needed it.

I thanked her profusely and gave her a dollar, an expansive gesture that—since I'd splurged on a pair of shoes that afternoon, and bought a bunch of stuff for lunch, and repaid the eight bucks Abby had loaned me over the last couple of days—left me with three singles, three quarters, one dime, one nickel, and two pennies. Not that I was counting.

As I left the lavatory and entered the plush, gray-carpeted lounge, the door to the room burst open, and a woman in a turquoise taffeta cocktail dress burst in. Her green eyes were flashing with fury, and her light brown pageboy was flying out of control. She rushed straight over to me, grabbed me by the shoulders, and stared intently at my face.

"So it really *is* you!" she spluttered. "I thought it was, but with the blonde wig I wasn't so sure. What the hell are you do-ing here? Are you following me or something?"

I almost wet my pants (again). It was Jocelyn Fritz, other-wise known as Candy, and she was *not* happy to see me.

"Following you?" I rasped, keeping my voice down to a near whisper. (I didn't want to alarm the little woman hiding in the washroom.) "Why on earth would I be following you? I didn't even know you were here."

"Does Sabrina know?" Now she looked frightened as well as furious.

"That you're here?" I said. "I don't think so. She knew I was coming, so I'm sure she would have mentioned it if she thought you were, too."

Jocelyn heaved a harsh sigh, released her grip on my shoul-ders, then spun around and sat down on one of the posh pink-and-gray-striped chairs in front of the glass-topped makeup counter. She propped her elbows on the counter and dropped her head in her hands, covering her face with her fingers.

"Are you okay?" I probed, quickly sitting down next to her. "You seem really upset. What's the matter?"

She raised her head and gave me a guarded look. "I can't tell you," she said. "You'd just make trouble for me, and God knows I'm in enough of that already."

"Trouble?" I croaked. "What kind of trouble?"

"Forget about it. It's none of your business."

"Does it have anything to do with Melody's murder?"

She didn't answer.

"Because if it does, then it *is* my business, and I need you to tell me exactly what's going on." I peered deep into her anxious eyes and gave her my sternest Susan Hayward scowl.

Jocelyn turned away from me and looked at herself in the mirror. Then she sat up straight, poked her nose in the air, and patted her pageboy back into place. "Nice try, Sherlock," she said, "but it won't work. You'd better back off. I've told you too much already."

Backing off was not a specialty of mine. "You must be refer-ring to what you said about Sam Hogarth and Tony Corona," I pressed on. "You were really serious when you called them 'de-vils in disguise.' I've been wondering why you used those par-ticular words, and why you never voiced them to Sabrina."

She whipped around to face me again. "So, did you tell her

what I said?" Her distress was palpable. Likewise, her annoyance.

"Of course I did!" Jocelyn was starting to tick me off. "Your statement was relevant to the murder, you know! And Sabrina and I are desperately trying to identify the monster who killed Melody. Remember her? The poor girl who was stripped naked, tied up, and exterminated last Monday night? She used to be your best friend . . . or so you said. And if that was the case, why would you want to keep your suspicions about her death secret from Sabrina?"

I had hit a nerve. Jocelyn's shoulders slumped and her chin fell to her chest. She was silent for a few moments, then said, "Melody *was* my best friend. We were as different as night and day, but I loved and respected her more than you can imagine. And I didn't mean to hamper your investigation in any way. I swear."

"Then what the hell's going on? What are you trying to hide?"

Her shoulders slumped even lower. "My own guilt," she mumbled, suddenly looking very guilty indeed.

"Oh, my god!" I gasped, heart banging against my breastbone. "Are you saying that you had something to do with the murder?"

Jocelyn groaned, threw her hands up, and snapped, "Good lord, no! I'm saying nothing of the kind! I may be a devious, dishonest, money-grubbing whore, but I'm no killer."

"Then what else *are* you guilty of?" I pressured, praying for a straight answer. Getting information out of Jocelyn was like pulling molars from the mouth of a mastodon.

"If I tell you, do you promise not to tell Sabrina?"

"Yes," I said, crossing my fingers behind my back, "but only if it has nothing to do with the murder, and if it won't hurt Sabrina's well-being or livelihood in any way."

"Take my word for it, Paige, what Sabrina doesn't know won't hurt her. The only person who stands to get hurt is me."

"Okay, then, shoot," I said, offering her a cigarette and lighting one myself, hoping the nicotine would loosen her tongue and my nerves. "I'm all ears." (My failure to show Jocelyn any sympathy at this point was a result of severe time restrictions, you should know. No lie! If I didn't get back to my table before Corona came out on stage, there'd be the devil to pay—whether he was in disguise or not.)

Jocelyn took a deep drag on her cigarette, blew out a great *whoosh* of smoke and said, "Look, I'm not proud to admit it, but here's the story: I really *am* a devious, dishonest, money-grubbing whore. I've been servicing Sam Hogarth and Tony Corona on the sly for almost two years. When Melody joined the agency and took over the wealthiest clients, I lost a few perks and a fair amount of income. To make up for it, I gave Sam and Tony my home phone number and told them they could bypass the agency and dial me direct; that I would charge them a lot less than Sabrina charged for Melody."

"Oh, so *that's* it," I said, not totally surprised. "And I take it they both accepted your offer."

"In an instant. As filthy rich as they are, they both jumped at the chance to save a few bucks. And they're still jumping. Sam calls me at least once a week for a lunchtime quickie, and Tony's so oversexed he hooks up with me every day or so when he's in town. I'm making a hell of a lot more money than I was before."

"And you're sure Sabrina doesn't know?"

"She doesn't have a clue. She thinks I haven't set eyes on either one of them since they started dating Melody. That's why I couldn't reveal my true feelings about Sam and Tony to her. I knew she'd wonder how I came to develop such strong suspicions, and then it would be just a matter of time before she figured out what I was up to. And I couldn't afford to let that happen. If Sabrina ever realizes that I've been seeing her top two clients on the sneak and beating her out of her cut, she'll kick me out of the agency for good."

I was thoroughly disgusted by Jocelyn's confession. "Oh, now I get it," I said, voice dripping with contempt. "You want to keep screwing Sabrina no matter what, right? The almighty dollar is more important to you than helping to solve your best friend's murder."

"No, that's not the way it is!" Jocelyn cried, eyes begging me to understand. "I told *you* my true thoughts, didn't I? I knew Sabrina had hired you to look for the killer, and I really wanted to help you in your search. And I *did* help! I gave you the dope on Sam and Tony even though I was putting myself at risk. Don't I at least get a good grade for that?"

D minus, I said to myself, feeling anything but forgiving. If Jocelyn had told Sabrina how she felt about Hogarth and

Corona *before* the murder, Sabrina would have crossed them both off her client list, and Melody might still be alive. I wanted to castigate Jocelyn for her greedy and thoughtless behavior, but I didn't have the heart—or the time—for such a sad and futile confrontation.

"If you really want to help me," I hurried on, "you'll tell me why you called Hogarth and Corona devils in disguise, and how you came to the conclusion that one of them killed Melody."

She blew another plume of smoke in my direction. "Look, I don't have any proof of anything, okay? All I have are my opinions. And as far as I'm concerned, both of these creeps are homicidal hypocrites. Tony's a talented charmer with a vile temper and strong Mafia connections, and Sam's a heartless pervert posing as a devoted public servant. I believe either one of them is capable of murder."

"But *why* do you believe that? Are your opinions based on pure conjecture or something real?"

"Hey, you can tell a lot about a man by the way he acts in the sack," she declared, "and Tony and Sam are both brutal in the bedroom. Neither one has ever really injured me, or anything like that, but they'd like to. I can feel it. Sam enjoys pretending he's a rapist—ripping my clothes off and taking me against my will—and Tony likes to spank me and tie me up. Sometimes he uses handcuffs." She grimaced and smashed her cigarette in one of the crystal ashtrays on the makeup counter. "The point is, neither one of them ever wants any tenderness or affection. They just want sex. Hard, rough, unfriendly sex."

"Did they treat Melody the same way?"

"Who knows? Melody wouldn't discuss her johns with me or anybody—not even Sabrina. The subject of sex always embarrassed her."

"Did Hogarth or Corona ever say anything to you about Melody?"

"Tony never did. And neither did Sam . . . until tonight."

A jolt of electricity shot up my spine. "You spoke to Hogarth tonight?"

"I spoke to him *and* Tony tonight. Tony called earlier to tell me he'd reserved a table for me and my date for the eight o'clock show, as I'd requested, and then I had a little chat with Sam just a few minutes ago at the bar. I spotted him when I was chasing you to the ladies' room."

"What?" I screeched. "You mean Hogarth is here at the Copa right now?" Blood was rushing to my head so fast I thought it would explode.

"Yeah, crazy, huh? What are the chances of both suspects being here, under the same roof with you and me, at the same time? Tony is probably onstage already, singing his evil little heart out, and Sam must have left his lawyer cronies at the bar and joined his wife upstairs. Tony reserved a table for them in the mezzanine, with all the other celebrities and criminals. "

A dark memory stirred in the depths of my brain, and then dug its way out to the light. I recalled sitting on the couch in the waiting room of the district attorney's office, eavesdropping while his blushing receptionist yakked and flirted on the phone. She was saying something about her boss and his wife, and Friday night, and the Copacabana at eight o'clock sharp. She must, I realized with a start, have been talking to Tony Corona.

Aaargh. The signal had been blinking all along, but I'd been too dim to pay attention.

"Did you know that Hogarth was going to be here tonight?"

"Not on your life," Jocelyn insisted. "If I had known, I would've made my date take me someplace else. I don't mind watching Tony perform, prancing around like he's God's greatest gift to women. After all, he's a really good singer. But it makes me sick to my stomach to see Sam pulling the wool over everybody's eyes, strutting around in public like a fine, upstanding law enforcer when he's a vicious rapist at heart. He's got the morals of a goat, but everybody treats him like a god."

I wanted to know more about Jocelyn's involvement with Hogarth and Corona—and about Hogarth's and Corona's involvement with each other—but the clock was ticking too fast. I had to stick to the big questions.

"What did Hogarth say about Melody?" I urged, breathless to get back to my prime concern. "How did her name come up?"

"I brought it up myself, just to get a reaction. I asked him if he missed Melody as much as I did."

"What a nervy question!" I said. "How did he answer it?"

"He didn't. Not with words. But if looks could kill, I'd be deader than a goddamn doornail."

"That's it? He just gave you a dirty look? That's all that happened?"

"No. After he knifed me with his steely stare, he winked and smirked and said, 'Who's Melody?' He looked so smug and cocky I wanted to spit in his face."

"I hope you didn't."

"No, I thought better of it."

"So, what *did* you do?" I implored. "What happened next?" I sucked down one last blast of smoke and stubbed out my cigarette.

"Well, first I answered his arrogant question," she said, looking pretty arrogant herself. "I said that Melody was Virginia Pratt, and he damn well knew it! Then I leaned real close and whispered in his ear that if he wasn't careful, a few other people would know it, too."

"Oh, my God, Jocelyn! You threatened him? Are you completely out of your mind? You shouldn't have done that!"

"I know, I know!" Her haughty expression warped into a grimace of fear. "Why do you think I'm so upset? I can't imagine what got into me. I saw red, and completely lost my cool. I wanted to wipe that ugly smirk off Sam's face and bring him to his knees. I wanted to shock him into thinking I knew something about the murder, then watch to see if he would do or say something incriminating."

"And did he?" I croaked. (I'm ashamed to say my curiosity outweighed my concern.)

"No, not really, but—"

The door to the ladies' lounge flew open, and three very silly, very drunk young ladies tottered in. Giggling, weaving, and hanging on to each other like muddle-headed monkeys in a strong wind, they made their way across the room and disappeared in the recesses of the lavatory. Their whoops and shrieks echoed loudly against the white-tiled walls.

Through the still-open lounge door I could hear a man singing. It was Tony Corona, of course, and he was wrapping his killer voice around the lyrics to the popular old standard "Fools Rush In." Realizing that I'd missed my demanding host's big entrance and had to get back to the table fast, I gave Jocelyn a hasty excuse, made a mad dash for the door, and—charging through it like a witless fool—rushed in where angels fear to tread.

Chapter 28

FROM THE MOMENT HE SAW ME APPEAR IN THE crowd and start working my way to the front, Corona glowered at me and sang louder. His angular, clean-shaven face turned hard, and his lean, muscular body grew tight with tension. Standing poised in the spotlight in his sleek black tuxedo, he looked like a panther preparing to pounce. Then—when I finally made it to the table and sat down next to Abby—he *did* pounce. He snatched the microphone off its stand and bounded over to us, aiming the words of his song, like bullets, at the target of my blushing face.

"So open up your heart and let this fool rush in," he bellowed, making the final line of the ballad sound more like a fierce command than the tender appeal the lyricist had surely intended. Then he shot me another creepy sneer, strutted back to the center of the dance floor, and—as the spotlights began to spin and the band brought the song to a climactic close—took an angry bow.

The audience went wild. (Either Corona's forceful voice and tough demeanor turned them on, or they got a kick out of watching me squirm.) The men whistled, the women squealed, and everybody clapped like crazy. Some people jumped to their feet and shouted, "Bravo!" I, on the other hand, sat quiet as a mouse in my chair, ducking the swirling spotlights and staring down at the white tablecloth, wishing I could crawl under it.

"Where the hell *were* you?" Abby cried, shouting in my ear to be heard over the crowd. "You missed Corona's entrance and most of his opening number! How could you do that? Don't you remember what Sabrina said about—"

"Hush!" I shouted back at her. "Something happened in the ladies' room and I couldn't leave. I'll tell you about it later."

She gave me a snotty look and then signaled our waiter to bring us two more champagne cocktails.

While Corona was taking a few more bows and basking in the glow of his standing ovation, I snuck a quick peek at the mezzanine to see if Manhattan's deceitful district attorney was really there.

He was.

Sitting tall and proud at a choice table near the railing with his beautiful and elegantly dressed young wife, Sam Hogarth looked as if he were posing for an official courthouse photo—or, more precisely, a presidential portrait destined to hang on a wall in the White House. His wavy gray hair gleamed silver in the revolving lights, and his wide, toothy grin was so dazzling the glare hurt my eyes. I turned away to avoid serious ocular damage.

When the applause died down, Corona fired me another disapproving frown, then spun around and snapped his fingers at the band. They played the intro to one of his more current hits, "Hearts on Fire," and—without a nod or a word to the audience or me (thank God)—he launched into the song.

I couldn't put it off any longer. It was time to pay the piper. Knowing tonight might be the only chance I'd ever get to interview Corona, I had to do whatever I could to get back in his good graces. I hiked up my skirt, crossed my legs in plain sight, leaned low over the table, and—following Sabrina's direction—showed Corona as much cleavage as was humanly possible (for me, I mean). Then I took a deep breath, batted my lashes like an idiot, and gave the cruel crooner my undivided attention for the rest of the show. I didn't once avert my eyes, or smoke a cigarette, or say a word to Abby. And at the end of every song I whooped and shimmied and clapped till I thought my hands would fall off.

I was dying to drink my cocktail, but I didn't dare. Partly because of Sabrina's caution, but mostly because I was so repulsed by Corona and the sinister circumstances (and by my own sickeningly subservient behavior), I felt another sip of Copa champagne would make me puke.

WHEN THE ORDEAL WAS FINALLY OVER—WHEN Corona had left the stage, and the band had stopped playing, and the spotlights had stopped spinning, and the audience had stopped applauding—a huge gorilla in a tuxedo appeared at our table and introduced himself as Little Pete, Tony Corona's main man.

"Tony wants youse to come back to his dressin' room now," he said, running his hairy hand down the front of his white pleated shirt, which was stretched so tight across his bulging belly I thought the onyx studs would pop off, blast through the air, and land like bits of shrapnel in my wig. "C'mon, I'll show youse the way."

Abby was on her feet in a flash. She couldn't wait to go backstage and meet Corona in person. (If you haven't already noticed, Abby goes crazy for celebrities. All celebrities. Even lechers and murder suspects.) I, on the other hand, was dragging my tail. As eager as I was to conduct a close study of Corona, I wasn't cheered by the knowledge that he'd be conducting an even closer study of me.

Trailing Little Pete and Abby through a door tucked in an alcove near the bandstand, I straightened the girdle-like skirt of my dress and tried to strut instead of stagger. Ha! It was so crowded backstage, all I (or anybody else) could do was dodge, swerve, and waddle forward like a duck (or a mermaid in high heels). The narrow hall outside the dressing rooms was packed with beefy bodyguards in tuxedos, big-breasted Copa girls in various states of undress, restless musicians taking a cigarette break, and swanky VIPs waiting for an audience with the pope—I mean, Corona.

As Little Pete led us down the hall and up to the front of the line of people outside Corona's dressing room, I spotted a couple of familiar faces. Comedian George Gobel was there, looking cute in his red bow tie and bristly buzz cut, and just a few feet up the line, in a yellow chiffon dress and a sable stole, stood Ann Sothern, the smart, wisecracking star of the *Private Secretary* TV series (which, due to its amusing focus on the plight of single working women, was one of my favorites).

Abby recognized the two stars before I did. She was right in front of me, so I saw her head snap in their direction as we wad-dled by, but—wonder of wonders!—she didn't squeal, or stop dead in her tracks, or even ask them for their autographs. She was calm, cool, and collected, which was a heck of a lot more than I could say for myself. If the lurch in my walk, and the sweat under my wig, and the sick feeling in the pit of my stomach were any indication, I was—even without the second champagne cocktail—about to throw up.

Little Pete knocked on the door of Corona's dressing room, then opened it and stuck his head inside. "I got the dames here, boss," I heard him say. "You wanna see 'em now?"

"Yeah," Corona answered, in a loud, spiteful tone that was audible to everyone in the near vicinity. "Bring 'em in. Then get me another bottle of bourbon from the bar. This one's dead."

Little Pete opened the door wider and—ignoring the impa-tient groans and glares of those at the front of the line—ushered us inside. (Moses couldn't hold a candle to Abby and me. High-priced call girls—even fake ones—can part the waters in a New York minute.)

Corona was slouching indolently in a leather swivel chair on the far side of the small dressing room. His head was lolling against the backrest and one leg was flung wide over an arm of the chair. His jacket was lying in a heap on the makeup table, and his untied black bow tie was hanging down the front of his open-collared dress shirt. His dark brown hair was damp and di-sheveled, his smile was cold and crooked, and as he watched me and Abby enter his dimly lit lair, his big brown eyes turned small and mean. He didn't stand up, or say hello, or offer us a seat on the black leather couch against the wall.

"Anything else, boss?" Little Pete asked, heaving his huge body forward, nabbing the empty bourbon bottle off the makeup table, and then huffing his way back to the door.

"A pack of weeds and a bucket of ice," Corona said, still squinting at Abby and me, sizing us up as if we were horses (or slaves) on the auction block. "And two more glasses," he added as an afterthought.

"You got it," Little Pete grunted, turning to leave.

"Hold on a minute," Corona said. "What's the scene out in the hall? Anybody waiting to see me?"

"Sure, boss. Lotsa people, like always."

"Any big shots?"

"Nah, just Georgie Gobel and some TV actress. The rest ain't nothin' to honk about."

"What about Hogarth?"

"He's still up in the mezz with the wife. They're havin' dinner. Said he'd see ya later."

"Then you can tell everybody else to scram," Corona grumbled, swinging his leg off the arm of the chair, leaning forward, and raking his fingers through his hair. "I'm not in the mood for visitors and ass-kissers. Tell 'em I'm not feelin' too good and I gotta rest up for the next show."

"Okay, boss." Little Pete nodded and reached for the doorknob.

"One more thing," Corona said, looking toward the ceiling and rubbing the back of his neck. "Did that dick come back tonight? The rat who's been sittin' lookout at the bar all week? He thinks he's undercover, but he's not. The bartender made him right off. Said his name is Street and he's a hotshot in Homicide."

Little Pete let out a booming laugh. "Yeah, I know the rat you mean. Buys one rye and ginger and don't even drink it. What a tip-off. Don't he know any better'n that?"

Corona didn't laugh or even smile. He jumped to his feet and started pacing, like a caged animal, around the tiny room. "So what's the story?" he growled. "Is Street out there again tonight? Because if he is, I want you to get rid of him. Once and for all. I'm sick of looking at his ugly mug."

"No, boss, he ain't here yet. He usually don't show up till after the second show."

"Well, if he does come in, lemme know right away." Corona continued his feverish pacing, not looking at Abby or me, but brushing so close to us I could feel the heat coming off his body.

"Sure thing," Little Pete said. "You want that bottle of bourbon now?"

Corona came to a sudden standstill, ripped off his loosened bow tie, and tossed it on top of his rumpled jacket. "Yeah," he said, unbuttoning his shirt all the way down to his black satin cummerbund, "and don't forget the ice."

Chapter 29

I DIDN'T THROW UP, BUT I ALMOST PASSED OUT. A hurricane was howling in my head. Corona and his boys knew all about Dan! And about his stakeout at the Copa! And that meant the city's most powerful crime boss and the secret owner of the Copa, Frank Costello, knew all about Dan, too! And since Costello was now under investigation in the city's big crackdown on organized crime, there was a damn good chance that Dan's identity and recent surveillance activities had also been brought to the attention of District Attorney Sam Hogarth.

Oh, my God! What the holy hell is going on? Could it be that—?

My screaming thoughts were interrupted by Corona's silky yet surly voice. "Glad to see you could make it," he scoffed, walking up to me and screwing his mouth into an ugly sneer. "Which one are you? Gina or Cherry?" He was standing so close I could see every detail engraved on the gold St. Christopher medal visible through the gap in his wide-open shirt.

"Cherry," I said, without hesitation. (My near-virginal state had prompted Abby to pin that alias on me, and—though I hadn't appreciated her derisive snorts and giggles at the time— I was now grateful for the name. At least I could remember it.)

"Cherry, huh?" Corona said, changing his sneer to a lusty smirk. "Does that mean you've still got a cherry to pop? Because if you do, you've come to the right place, honey. Poppin' cherries is my favorite sport."

I knew this was my cue to start flirting with the man—to make nice and bat my lashes and shower him with suggestive come-ons—but I couldn't bring myself to do it. I was consumed with worry about Dan. He was in danger, and I had to do something about it! I needed to drop the nauseating call girl act and get back to playing detective—*now*.

"I hate the name Cherry!" I snapped, face flaming. "It has nothing to do with me or my precious maidenhead. Sabrina just wants me to use it because she thinks it sounds sexy. I wanted to take the name Melody, but Sabrina said it belonged to another girl . . . a girl who was—"

Before I could say the word *murdered,* Abby shoved me aside and planted her own cleavage in front of Corona. "What about *my* name, Tony?" she said to him, pouting and striking a voluptuous pose. "Doesn't it turn you on? I borrowed it from Gina Lollobrigida. She and I have a lot in common, you see. We're both busty brunettes, and we both just luuuuuvvv to ride Italian stallions." Abby was pulling out all the stops, doing her best to distract Corona from my ill-advised (okay, incredibly stupid) outburst.

It worked.

Corona's eyes grew wide as quarters, and his lean, hard face (think Frank Sinatra with a touch of Victor Mature) turned a little pink around the edges. He stopped breathing and started panting. "I hear what you're sayin', doll," he snorted, "and I like what I see. But I want to see more. Step out in the middle of the floor and turn around real slow, so I can get a better look."

"Whatever you say, Tony," Abby murmured, smiling like the girl in the Colgate toothpaste ads. Then she took a deep breath, puffed up her nearly naked breasts, and—writhing her shoulders and hips like a professional stripper—did as she was told. (Look, I understood what she was doing, okay? She was making a sexual spectacle of herself so Corona would get all hot and bothered, and forget about my uncooperative conduct, and let us both stick around long enough to observe his behavior and fish for clues to the murder. But here's what I *didn't* understand: Did she really have to have so much fun doing it?)

As Abby was making her third or fourth slow, sensual (and annoyingly cheerful) turn around the floor, there was a loud

knock on the door. "I got the booze, boss," Little Pete called
out, opening the door about an inch. "You want I should bring it
in now?"

"Yeah," Corona said, motioning for Abby to stop twirling
and move out of the way. "Come in and put it on the table. You
got the other stuff, too?"

"Sure thing, boss." Grasping an ice bucket in one hand and a
bottle of bourbon in the other, Little Pete lumbered across the
room and set down the items as directed. A waiter carrying a
tray topped with three glasses and a pack of Chesterfields followed close behind him. After everything was deposited on the
makeup table, they both returned to the door. "That all, boss?"
Little Pete asked. "Got what you need?"

"Yeah, scram. Shut the door on your way out."

The waiter left the room in a hurry, but Little Pete hung
back, belly hovering like a blimp in the doorway. "Street just
came in, boss," he said in a lowered voice. "He parked his ass at
the bar. Want me to do somethin' about it?"

"Sure," Corona snarled. "I want the bastard put down. I want
his goddamn head on a platter. But I gotta talk to Frank first. Is
he here?"

"Yeah," Little Pete said. "At his reg'lar table up in the
mezz."

"Okay, I'll catch him later, after the girls leave." The anxious
look on Corona's face suggested our departure would be sooner
rather than later—which was just hunky-dory with me.

Little Pete nodded, huffed his way into the hall, and closed
the door tightly behind him. Corona sloshed some bourbon in a
glass, threw his head back, and slugged it down straight. He
didn't offer Abby and me a drink or a cigarette or a seat on the
black leather couch. We stood side by side in silence, not looking at each other, waiting for further instructions.

"So you like to ride Italian stallions," Corona said to Abby,
remembering the ice cubes and plunking a few in his glass. He
covered the cubes with bourbon, then poured half the liquid
down his throat. "That's good," he said between swallows, "because I'm always hot to trot. Come to my hotel later, and we'll
saddle up."

"I'll be there, Tony," Abby said, simpering like a fool. "Which
hotel and what time?"

"The Plaza," he said, absently fingering his large gold St.

Christopher medal and the curly chest hairs around it. "Suite 814. Be there at three thirty."

"AM or PM?" she chirped.

"If you're a good little cowgirl, we'll do both." His words were teasing, but his tone was deadly. Looking tense and preoccupied, he sat back down in his swivel chair and—slowly twisting from side to side—took another slug of his drink. "Now giddyap and get outta here," he said, wiping his sweaty forehead on his shirtsleeve. "I've got some business to take care of."

ABBY AND I FLED THE STAR'S DRESSING ROOM and dashed back into the main arena. The band was playing a mambo, and the dance floor was full. Both the main level and the mezzanine were packed to the rafters, and people (mostly men) were standing three-deep at the bar. I madly searched the crowd for Dan, but he was nowhere to be seen.

"Quick! Come over here!" I shouted to Abby, grabbing her by the arm and pulling her to the shadows behind one of the huge palm tree columns. Only one thought was racing through my mind: I had to warn Dan of the impending peril immediately! But before I could do that, I realized, I had to slow down for a second, talk it over with Abby, and come up with a sensible plan of action.

(Stop snickering! So what if all my previous plans and actions had fallen far short of sensible? I still had to try, didn't I?)

"Hey, you're bruising my arm!" Abby squawked, wrenching herself free from my viselike grasp. "What's your freaking problem?"

I couldn't believe she asked me that question. "My *problem*," I said, gritting my teeth, "is that Dan's life is in danger! Weren't you listening in there? Corona knows he's a homicide detective, and he told Little Pete to get rid of him—to put him down!"

"Oh, cool it, Paige! Tony didn't mean it that way. He just meant for Little Pete to kick Dan out of the club."

"You don't know that!" I shrieked, ticked off that she was still calling Corona by his first name. Hadn't she cozied up to him enough? "Corona got really upset when he heard that Dan was here," I went on, "and he said he was going to talk to Frank about it!"

"So?"

Aaaargh!

"So he was talking about Frank Costello!" I cried. "The crime lord who owns the Copa. Don't you get what that means? It means he's going to talk to Costello about having Dan rubbed out!"

Abby cocked her head and gave some thought to the things I'd said—but she still wasn't convinced. "Gee, I don't know, Paige. Sounds like a stretch to me. You could be overreacting, you know."

"Yes, but what if I'm *not?*" I paused to let the full weight of my words sink in. "Don't you see, Ab? I can't just float around, waiting to find out what's going to happen. Costello's here tonight. And he probably has a couple of hit men with him! Dan could be killed at any minute. I've got to warn him before it's too late!"

She propped one hand on her hip and rolled her eyes at the ceiling. "And how do you plan to do that, Nat? Make a person-to-person phone call? Dispatch a carrier pigeon? Send him a singing telegram?"

"Stop it! This isn't a joking matter. I've got to find Dan at the bar *right now* and give him the lowdown."

"And how are you going to explain the wig, my friend? Or that skimpy dress you're wearing? If Dan sees you like this, he's going to kill *you.*"

"Who cares?" I cried. "Dan's life is more important to me than my own!" (That sounds really sappy, I know, but what do you want from me? A woman who's wildly in love is *supposed* to be sappy.)

Abby shrugged and rolled her eyes again. "Have it your way, Doris Day," she said. "It's your funeral."

I stuck my head out from behind the big white-and-gold palm tree and searched the bar area for Dan. This time I spied him at once. He was sitting at the end of the bar, his back to the counter, smoking a cigarette, and gazing at the crowd. He looked very relaxed and handsome in his dark gray suit and royal blue tie. I ducked back behind the palm tree, pulse racing out of control.

"Dan's at the bar, Abby! I saw him! He's sitting at the end closest to the entrance. So here's what I want you to do. Walk straight through the club and out into the lobby and over to the checkroom to get our coats. Turn your face away when you walk past the bar. Don't walk too fast, or too slow, or wiggle your hips, or wink at any guys, or draw attention to yourself in any way. Just get our coats and wait for me in the lobby near the exit. Think you can handle that?"

She gave me a dirty look. "I guess so, Mommy, but I'm too scared to be alone. Can't I stay with you and hold your hand?" Her phony little girl voice set my nerves on edge.

"Please stop it, Ab. You know I have to do this as quickly and inconspicuously as possible. There's no telling who'll be watching. So just pick up our coats and wait for me at the door, okay? I'll be there as soon as I can."

"Oh, all right!" she said, petulantly stomping one foot on the floor. "You're no fun anymore, you know that?"

"Yeah, that's what I've heard. Now pull yourself together and trot on out to the lobby like a good little cowgirl. Go ahead. Giddyap. Go!"

Chapter 30

"HELLO, STRANGER," I SAID, SAUNTERING UP TO Dan at the bar. "Got a light?" I raised the cigarette I had ready in my hand to my lips and leaned close to him, cupping my fingers around my mouth and lowering my voice to a whisper. "Don't be shocked, Dan," I said, eyes begging him not to explode. "Pretend you don't know me. Pretend I'm a prostitute making a pitch. It's a matter of life and death!" I was doing my best to act cool, but I was so fearful and self-conscious—and my heart was beating so hard and so fast—I thought I would turn into a blob of quivering jelly on the spot.

Dan, on the other hand, grew stony-faced and rigid as a post. He didn't say a single word to me, but his intense emotions—astonishment, dismay, concern, outrage, and anger—were clearly visible in his jet-black eyes. Teeth clenched so tight you could see the hard knots of his jaw muscles, he took his Zippo out of his pocket, flipped it open, and lit my cigarette.

"Thanks, handsome!" I said, turning up the volume, throwing my shoulders back and my hips forward, putting on a big show for the bartender and any snoopy boozers (or mobsters) who might be tuning in. "Hey, you know what, big boy? You're my kind of guy. A real gent. Want to buy a thirsty girl a drink?" I was smiling and posturing and flapping my lashes like crazy—playing my phony call girl role to the hilt—hoping that Dan would get the message and play along with me.

Sharp, insightful detective that he was, he did.

"Sure, babe," he said, giving me a sexy wink and an arrogant, exaggerated once-over. (I knew he was appalled by the blonde wig and the indecent way I was dressed, but—to his credit and my profound relief—he didn't let his disapproval show.) "What'll you have, sweetheart?" he said, putting on a show of his own, playing the part of a potential john to perfection. "Name your poison."

"I'll have a *screw*driver," I said, loudly emphasizing the first part of the word. "Won't you have one with me?" I giggled my head off for a few seconds, then draped my arm around his neck, cuddled up to his side and started whispering in his ear again, trying to give all onlookers the impression that I was offering him my body for the night and quoting my price. "They're on to you, Dan," I hissed. "Corona knows who you are and why you're here. He's going to talk to Costello about having you bumped off. Maybe tonight! You've got to get out of here. Now!"

Dan yanked his head away from mine and stared deep into my eyes for a few tense, probing seconds. Then he grabbed me around the waist and pulled me so tight to his chest that my feet left the floor. "Message received," he said, breathing his words directly into my ear. "Thanks for the tip. Now hold on to your wig, Blondie. It's time for act two."

He let go of my waist and my feet dropped back to the carpet. Then he stood up from the bar stool, grabbed my shoulder with one hand, shoved me out to arm's length and—looking so forceful and hot I thought my flesh would melt right off my bones—whipped out his badge.

"You're under arrest," he said to me, speaking loud enough for everyone at the bar to hear. Then he turned toward the excited eavesdroppers and—holding his badge high in the air for them to see—made the following announcement: "I'm an officer of the NYPD. This woman just offered me sex for money. I have placed her under arrest for solicitation, and I'm taking her into custody now. You are all witnesses to this fact."

Dan stuck his badge back in his pocket and—still gripping me by the shoulder—plucked the burning cigarette out of my hand and dropped it in his drink. "Don't give me any trouble, sister," he bellowed, "or I'll clap on the cuffs." Then he lowered his angry grip to my elbow and led me—breathless, stunned, and limp as a rag doll—out to the lobby.

ABBY WAS WAITING AT THE DOOR WITH OUR coats. When she saw that Dan was with me, her face lit up like the sun. She didn't say anything, but her relief was dangerously conspicuous. She gave a little whoop and started to run toward us.

"Hold it right there, miss!" Dan shouted across the lobby, sticking his hand up like a stop sign, then quickly retrieving his hat and coat from the checkroom. "I'm an officer of the law, and this woman is under arrest. I'm taking her to the station house now. Please clear the exit and vacate the premises immediately!"

Abby caught on quick. She spun around and sprang through the door like a virgin on the run from the Cossacks.

"Hang your head and don't look back," Dan said to me, putting on his hat and flinging his trench coat around my shoulders. He grabbed hold of my arm again and propelled me across the lobby floor. "Just keep your mouth shut and keep walking."

I followed his orders, and within several suspenseful seconds we were out on the sidewalk, sweeping past the doorman and the photographers and the new herd of people clamoring for admittance, heading for Fifth Avenue in a big fat hurry. We met up with Abby at the corner.

"Keep walking," Dan said to both of us, still gripping my arm so hard it hurt. (Did he think I would try to escape?) "My car's right down the street."

Abby fell into step with us, and we made it to the car without incident. Once we were seated inside and zooming down Fifth, however, all hell broke lose.

"Whooooeee!" Abby squealed at the top of her lungs. "What a gas that was! Scary and sexy at the same time! I never had so much fun in my whole freaking life! Let's go back and do it again!" She was bouncing up and down on the back seat like a teenybopper at a Pat Boone concert.

"For Christ's sake, Abby!" I shrieked, feeling as though my brain would burst. "How can you say such things?!" I spun around to glare at her over the backrest of the front seat. "Don't you realize the danger we were in?" I cried." Dan could have been killed, and—"

"We *all* could have been killed!" Dan roared, pounding his fist on the steering wheel and stomping on the gas pedal. He was speeding downtown in a fury, honking the horn repeatedly, screeching and swerving through traffic like a madman. (Did he think we were being followed?) "You're both criminally insane!" he howled. "I ought to arrest you for real and lock you up for life!" The undercover car we were in had no siren, otherwise it would have been howling, too.

Cowed by Dan's ferocious anger and wild speed, I turned around to face the windshield, holding on to the edge of my seat like a drowning woman clinging to a life raft. Now I was just as afraid of being killed in an automobile accident—or at the hands of my menacing, out-of-control boyfriend—as I was of being silenced by a sadistic murderer.

The lights of the city streaked by as Dan rocketed south— past the RCA Building and Rockefeller Center and the New York Public Library—giving us a whiplash tour of midtown Manhattan. Racing through more than a few red lights, and still honking to clear a path through the traffic, he kept his jaw clenched tight and his demon eyes fixed on the road ahead. Careening past the Empire State Building, Dan hooked a hard right on 34th Street, tore past Macy's, then swung left on Seventh Avenue, whizzing by the enormous stone structure of Pennsylvania Station—with its marble columns and colossal stone eagles—like a cab driver out of hell. I wished I could jump out of the car and hop a train to New Jersey.

When we reached the Village, we were all still in one piece. (Physically, I mean. I had lost my sanity somewhere along the way, but I don't think it showed.) Dan hung a left on Bleecker, shot down the narrow street, and brought the car to a screeching halt at the curb across from our building.

"Get out," he said, still staring straight ahead with his jaw in knots. It was an order, not a suggestion.

I couldn't move. My body was locked in position and my fingers were frozen—clawlike—to the edge of the seat.

Abby, on the other hand, hopped out of the car and flounced gaily across the street. "Good night, all!" she shouted, turning to wave at us through the car window. "Jimmy's here!" She gestured toward the shadowy figure sitting on the stoop, then—tucking my (or, rather, her) chinchilla jacket under one arm and grinning like a darn fool—reached out and pulled the bearded Birmingham to his feet. Otto was hanging on to Jimmy's arm for dear life. (I knew how the little dog felt.) "We're going upstairs now, okay?" Abby called out. "I'll catch you later!" She blew me a kiss and unlocked the front door. Then the Three Musketeers disappeared in the stairwell.

Dan and I sat in silence for what seemed like an eternity but was probably just a millisecond. Finally, he spoke. "I said get out," he growled. "Go upstairs and lock yourself in. Don't open the door to anybody."

"Aren't you coming with me?" I was in a real panic now. Dan looked so mad I felt that if he left, he'd never come back.

"No. I have some unfinished business to attend to." His profile was set in stone, but in the yellowish light from the street lamp, I could see that a vein in his temple was throbbing.

"But you've got to let me explain!" I cried.

"What's to explain?" He turned and aimed his merciless black gaze at me. "The writing's on the goddamn wall. You broke your promise to me again. You're working on another unsolved murder story, and you're in a shitload of danger because of it. That's all I need to know."

"No, it's not!" I screamed, kicking my foot against the dashboard. (I was a little upset myself.) "There's a lot more you need to know, Dan, and I have to tell you about it now! Please come upstairs with me and listen to what I have to say. It's a long and complicated story, but it's really, really important! A lot of lives and reputations are at stake."

"You should have thought of that before."

"Before what?"

"Before you lied to me and made a complete mess of everything."

"What?" Now I was hurt as well as angry. (I mean, is that any way for a boyfriend to talk after you've just saved his life?)

"You heard me," Dan said. "Your lying has compromised my current murder investigation and put both of us in grave danger."

"Murder investigation?" I shrieked. (I'd been doing a lot of that lately.) "You said you were investigating the mob war!"

"And so I am!" he raged, spitting his furious words in my face. "The mob war *and* the hideous murder of a young woman that resulted from it."

My heart came to a sudden standstill. Was he talking about—?

"Don't look so shocked, Paige," he sputtered. "Do you really think you're the only person in the whole damn city who's been trying to find out who killed Virginia Pratt?"

I was speechless—or, to put it more precisely, struck dumb. My mouth was hanging open, but no sound was coming out of it.

"Go upstairs," Dan said, leaning across me and opening the passenger door from the inside. "Right this minute! Lock your doors and windows and don't go anywhere or do anything until you hear from me. I mean it, Paige!" he yelled, practically shoving me out onto the sidewalk. "I've got to leave now. Go upstairs and stay there!"

"Okay," I said, standing on the pavement in shock as Dan jerked the car door closed. Then I pulled his trench coat tighter around my shivering shoulders and slunk across the street like an anxious alley cat. As I opened the door to my building and ducked into the stairwell, I heard Dan peel away from the curb and blast down Bleecker, burning rubber all the way.

Chapter 31

HAVE YOU EVER HAD THE FEELING THAT YOU'VE just been shot out of a cannon? That you're hurtling through the air like a big metal ball—or a curled-up clown with orange hair and a red nose? Then you know exactly how I felt as I crashed into my apartment, dropped my purse and Dan's coat onto the living room chair, kicked Abby's stilettos into a corner, and fell—with a heavy thud—into a fetus-shaped lump on the couch. And you also understand why I was trembling in fear, and sick with worry, and blubbering in so much confusion and self-pity that my bright red nose was dribbling all over my favorite Woolworth's throw pillow.

Where had Dan zoomed off to? Would he be safe? Would I ever see him again? How on earth had he discovered that I was investigating another homicide? And how did he know it was the Virginia Pratt murder? And why was Dan involved in the case at all? The papers had said Detective Sergeant Casey O'Connor at the Midtown North Precinct was in charge. Dan was in Midtown South. And the two precincts were so competitive that they practically never joined forces. Something really strange was going on here!

Head swirling and pulse pounding, I bolted to an upright position, yanked off my clown wig, pulled a Kleenex from the box on the table near the phone, and blew my nose. I didn't have time for a nervous breakdown! A potent mixture of curiosity and dread was surging through my system like an electrical current. All I could think about was digging up some answers to my many burning questions—and finding Melody's murderer before he murdered Dan.

I was dying to talk to Jocelyn (aka Candy) again, but knowing she wouldn't be home from her date for hours, I quickly ditched that idea. I figured Melody's other good friend, Ethel (aka Brigitte), wouldn't be home, either, but in a frenzy to take some kind of positive action, I decided to call her anyway. Jumping over to the bookcase and snatching Sabrina's lavender list out of its hiding place in *The Maltese Falcon,* I returned to the couch, found Ethel's number, and dialed it.

To my surprise, she answered.

"Hello, Ethel?" I said. "Ethel Maguire?"

"Yes, who's this?"

"Paige Turner. I hope I didn't wake you or your husband up. I'm sorry to call so late, but I—"

"That's okay," she broke in. "My husband's sleeping soundly, and I just got home."

"Were you out with a client?"

"I was *with* a client," she sniffed, "but we didn't go *out.*" I could tell from her tone that she found my question inane. "Look, I wasn't asleep, Paige, but I *am* pretty tired. Is there something you need to talk to me about?"

"Just one thing," I said. "I happened to run into Candy tonight, and she admitted that she's been seeing two of Melody's regular clients—Sam Hogarth and Tony Corona—on her own, without Sabrina's knowledge. Did you know anything about that?"

"No!" Ethel exclaimed, with an audible intake of air. "I can't believe she would do something like that."

"Well, she did. She said she did it for the money."

"But Sabrina has been so good to us! How could Candy deceive her that way? It's the same as *stealing.*"

"That's true, Ethel, but weren't you ever tempted to—?"

"Never!" she exclaimed. "I'd rather starve than steal from Sabrina. She's dearer to me than my own mother. I would never hurt her in any way." Her words were a bit effusive, I thought, but I believed them just the same.

"Well, then, did Sabrina ever fix you up with Hogarth or

Corona or any other of Melody's clients? Either before or after she was killed?"

"I met with Oliver Rice Harrington a few times," she said. "Next to Melody, he liked me best. I liked him, too. He's a real gentleman. Very nice and considerate."

Ha! Either my ex-boss has a split personality, or there are two Oliver Rice Harringtons in this town.

"Have you seen him since the murder?"

"No. I asked Sabrina about him, but she said he hasn't called to make any new appointments." Ethel stopped talking for a second, then added, as an afterthought, "But the man I was with tonight used to date Melody, too. Actually, he dates *all* the girls."

I almost swallowed my tongue. "What did you say?" I gasped. "Who are you talking about? What's his name?"

"Umm . . . er . . . I can't tell you," she stammered, voice suddenly turning wary. "He's the one john Sabrina doesn't want me to discuss with you, and I forgot. I'm sorry, Paige. I made a big mistake. I shouldn't have mentioned him at all."

"But why?!" I screeched. "Why is this guy such a well-kept secret? Why didn't Sabrina tell me about him herself? And why can't you tell me his name?"

"I'm sorry," she said again. "You'll have to ask Sabrina those questions."

I SAID GOOD-BYE, BUT I DIDN'T HANG UP THE receiver. I quickly clicked the button with my finger, got a new line, and dialed Sabrina.

"It's Paige," I croaked, as soon as she answered. "I just got back from the Copa."

"That was fast," she said. "It's not even midnight. What happened? Did Tony give you the boot?"

"No, he just dismissed the class early." Deciding to save my questions about Ethel's mystery date for later, I gave Sabrina a full report on the tumultuous events at the nightclub—beginning with Jocelyn's surprise appearance and confession in the ladies' lounge, and ending with Dan's and Abby's and my hasty exit from the premises.

"What a nerve-racking night," she said when I finished.

"That's a placid way to put it," I mumbled. "What do you make of the whole mess?"

She sighed. "I'm so disappointed in Candy, I could cry."

"You really had no idea?"

"None whatsoever. In fact, I thought Candy was one of my most trustworthy girls. A real straight talker. I knew she loved money—she was very honest about *that*, at least—but I chalked it up to good business sense. I even entertained the notion that if she failed to reach her goal of marrying a millionaire, I might make her my partner someday."

"Well, at least she came forward when the chips were down."

"But it was far too late!" Sabrina cried. "If she had revealed her feelings about Sam and Tony to me earlier, I would have dropped them both as clients before the murder. And then poor Melody . . . might still be . . . alive." I couldn't see Sabrina's face, but I knew her thin mouth was contorted and her soft gray eyes were brimming with tears.

"I know, Sabrina," I said. "It's a sad twist in a terrible tragedy." I paused for a moment to let her compose herself, then collected my thoughts and went on. "But all we can do now is try not to make the same mistake again. We've got to do everything in our power to see that the killer is caught before he kills somebody else. That's why you have to give me the name of another client, Sabrina. The one you chose not to tell me about. The one who dates *all* the girls. The one you fixed Melody up with in the past . . . and sent Brigitte to meet with tonight."

Sabrina remained silent, but I could hear the wheels spinning in her sly, secret-keeping brain.

"Oh, come on, Sabrina!" I cried. "Haven't you screwed with me long enough? You're withholding crucial information! You're purposely impeding my progress in the case. What the hell is going on? If I didn't know better, I'd think you had something to do with the murder yourself."

"Don't be ridiculous," she huffed. "I resent the implication."

"And I resent the fact that you're keeping a major suspect secret from me! Who is this man, and why are you protecting him? I want his name, and I want it *right now*!"

"Okay!" she hissed. "I'll tell you who he is. But he is *not* a major suspect. He's not even a minor one! You have to trust me on this, Paige. Promise me you'll guard his identity as carefully as I have."

"I'm not promising anything. Not until I have all the facts."

"Oh, all right!" she said, with a loud groan of surrender. "The client's name is Casey O'Connor."

I almost choked. "You mean Detective Sergeant Casey O'Connor? The top detective in the Midtown North Precinct? The one who's in charge of Melody's murder investigation?"

"The one and only," she said. "*Now* do you understand why I didn't tell you about him?"

"No, I don't!" I screeched. "I don't understand it at all. O'Connor's personal connection to both the case *and* the victim seems awfully suspicious to me! What makes you so damn sure he's not the killer?"

"O'Connor is a raving sex maniac," Sabrina replied, "but he's not the murderer. The night Melody was killed, he was holed up in the Waldorf Astoria with three of my other girls—Mitzi, Gabriella, and DeeDee. They swore to me that O'Connor was with them all night—from early that evening until late the next morning—and they have the signed room service receipts to prove it. Also, the manager of the Waldorf, a personal friend of mine, confirmed their report."

"But why didn't you tell me about this?" One decibel louder and I would have shattered her eardrum. "It's important information! It could have helped me in my investigation, given me a better grasp of the situation. Why the hell did you keep me in the dark?"

"It was necessary," Sabrina said. "I had to protect O'Connor so he would continue protecting me." She took a deep breath and went on. "When I first started the agency, he was in Vice, not Homicide. And he had informers all over his precinct—especially in the posh restaurants, nightclubs, and hotels where my wealthiest clients liked to meet with my girls. Within weeks of my going into business, O'Connor was tipped off that there was a ritzy new escort service in town.

"Next thing I knew he showed up at my door, flashed his badge in Charlotte's face, muscled his way into my apartment, and demanded to speak with me. Shaking in terror, Charlotte showed him to my study, where he proceeded to stomp around in all his ugly, pudgy, red-faced glory, threatening to have me, Charlotte, and all of my girls arrested, and to close down my agency for good. There would be a huge scandal, he promised, and we'd all be sent to prison. . . . *Unless*, he was quick to add, I chose to play the game his way."

"And what way was that?" I had a pretty good idea how the game was played, but I wanted to hear the rules.

"It was a simple trade agreement," she said. "You scratch my back, and I'll scratch yours. He said he would protect me and my girls and my agency from the authorities if I gave him free, unlimited access to the merchandise—*all* of the merchandise—whenever and wherever he wanted it. He was a very virile man, he said. He needed a lot of sex and a lot of variety, and if I would take care of his needs, he would take care of mine."

"So you shook hands and became friends."

"There was nothing friendly about it," she grumbled. "I totally despise the man, and he thinks I'm a pompous bitch. We've each kept up our end of the bargain, though, and we've both benefited from it."

"But what about Virginia?" I wailed, squirming in outrage. "O'Connor must have seen her murdered body! He had to know that she was Melody! And he couldn't possibly conduct an honest and thorough investigation without disclosing his relations with the victim—and his deal with you."

"Precisely," Sabrina said. "O'Connor was in the hot seat. He couldn't break the case without breaking himself. So he took— as you would expect—the corrupt way out. He kept everything he knew about Melody under wraps and launched a phony, totally superficial investigation into the death of Virginia Pratt. He even kept her picture out of the paper, so nobody would recognize her and put the two names together. On the one hand, this worked in my favor. It saved me and my girls from exposure and prosecution. On the other hand, it meant Melody's murder would probably never be solved."

"And this was acceptable to you?" I felt sick to my stomach again. So sad and angry that I wanted to scream.

"Of course not!" Sabrina said. "I called *you*, didn't I?"

"Yes, but you didn't give me the dirty details. You didn't tell me you were in collusion with—"

"Whatever you may think of me," Sabrina cut in, "I was— and still am—horrified and disgusted by the whole situation. I hate O'Connor for who he is, and I hate myself for collaborating with him. Believe me, Paige, if I could have found any other way to save my business and secure my girls, I would have taken that route. But there really was no other way. And now

I'm stuck—in bed, so to speak—with O'Connor, and I have to keep our connection secret."

"Meanwhile, Melody's murderer goes free," I said in my most cynical and disapproving tone.

"But it won't be for long!" Sabrina protested. "With *you* on the case, who needs O'Connor? We're getting really close now, Paige. With my leads and your legwork, we're going to nail the bastard soon."

"Not if Dan has anything to say about it."

"What do you mean?"

"I mean Dan's on the case now, too," I said. "I'm not sure how it happened, or how much he knows, but I'm certain he's participating in the investigation. He's aware that I've been conducting a search for Virginia's killer, and he's *very* upset about it. He thinks the murder is related to the mob war that's going on in the city, and that I'm in danger because of it. He ordered me to stay home and keep my doors locked."

Sabrina was quiet for a second or two, then asked, "Has Dan discovered that Virginia was a call girl?"

"I don't know. He didn't say anything about that."

"Did he mention me or my agency?"

"No, he didn't. But if he hasn't found out about you yet, he will soon."

"Why do you say that?"

"Because the next time I see him, I'm going to tell him myself."

Chapter 32

IT TOOK ME A WHILE TO CONVINCE SABRINA that telling Dan the whole truth was the right (actually, the only) way to go. Understandably, she didn't want to cause harm to her girls, or lose her entire income, or be sent to jail, or be unable to continue her support of Charlotte and of Melody's retarded twin brother. After I explained the seriousness of the situation more thoroughly, though, and promised to speak to Dan and the other authorities on her behalf, she started to come around. And then—when it finally sank in that the Mafia really could be involved in Melody's murder and that my life, as well as Dan's, might really be at risk—she gave in.

"I've been such a fool," she said, choking back tears. "I thought I could see to it that Melody's killer was brought to justice without sacrificing myself or anybody else. I should have known that would be impossible. I'm so sorry I dragged you into this, Paige."

"You didn't drag me anywhere," I sadly admitted. "I jumped in with both feet and started running around like a beheaded chicken. I just wish we'd had enough sense to tell Dan the truth from the start. He probably would have caught the murderer by now . . . and I would still have a job." *Not to mention a boyfriend,* I whimpered to myself.

"It's all my fault," Sabrina said. "I should have let you bring

Dan into the case that very first day. He would have conducted an honest investigation. I should have given you permission to write the story, too. At least I would have known that the coverage would be fair."

When I heard the word *story*, I perked up considerably. "It's not too late, you know. I can still write the story, whether I'm working for *Daring Detective* or not. Once the scandal breaks, every newspaper and magazine in the city—maybe even the whole country—will fight for the rights to an exclusive inside report."

"Then I want you to write it, Paige. I trust you, and I know you'll treat me and my girls—especially Melody—with respect."

"You can count on it," I promised, feeling a heady resurgence of journalistic energy and purpose. "And you can bet I'll treat O'Connor, Corona, Hogarth, and Harrington with respect as well—all the respect they deserve." My voice was oozing with sarcasm.

"Don't be too hard on Harrington, Paige. I've known him a long time, and he's been very good to me and my girls. I don't believe he's the murderer. I put his name on the list only because he was a regular client of Melody's and called for a date the night she was killed."

"Reason enough, if you ask me. And you'd be amazed at how often the most innocent-looking suspects commit the most atrocious crimes. It would be a mistake for either one of us to jump to conclusions about Harrington."

"I guess you're right," she said, sighing heavily. "Please be careful, Paige. These are very powerful men. And it's possible they *all* have connections to organized crime. And since Hogarth and Harrington both know who you are, and what you do for a living, you could already be at the top of some savage Mafioso's hit list."

"Don't worry about me," I said, pretending a tad (okay, a lot) more courage than I felt. "I'll be careful. And once Dan knows all the facts and recruits the rest of his department in a wider, more intense investigation, I'll be off the case and in safe hands. In the meantime," I added, feeling a serious surge of adrenaline (and a stupid gush of Brenda Starr bravado), "I've got a story to write."

THE INSTANT I CLICKED OFF THE LINE WITH Sabrina, I dialed Jocelyn's number at the Barbizon. I knew she wouldn't be there—Sabrina had said she usually didn't get home from her regular Friday night date until two or three in the morning—but I simply had to do *something*! I was desperate for more information—about O'Connor, Hogarth, Corona, and what went on at the Copa after I left—and Jocelyn was the only one who could provide it. I must've let her phone ring a thousand times.

By the time I hung up, I was feeling a bit more composed (i.e., less like a runaway train and more like a ticking time bomb). I was still crazy with worry about Dan, and dying to know how he got involved in the Virginia Pratt case, and struggling to think of a way to ensure his safety, but I was also determined to keep my emotions and actions under tight control—to stay locked in my apartment until I heard from him, just as he'd told me to do.

I rose from the couch and headed into the kitchen, grabbing my cigarettes out of my purse and a Dr. Pepper out of the fridge. Then I darted upstairs to my bedroom. Setting the soda and ciggies on my dresser, I wriggled out of Abby's tight black dress and somehow freed myself from her horrid push-up bra. After peeling off my girdle and stockings, I put on a normal bra, a fuzzy white sweater, a pair of black capris, and my new ballerina flats.

It was almost one o'clock in the morning. I could have skipped the clothes and gone straight to bed, but with my tangled thoughts and jangled nerves, I knew I wouldn't be able to sleep. And if Dan came back, I reasoned, I should be decently dressed and fully alert and perfectly prepared to tell him everything I knew about the murder.

Plus, I wanted to get a head start on my story.

Giving my wig-matted hair a quick brush-out, I snatched the soda pop and cigarettes off the dresser and took them into the tiny spare bedroom I had turned into an office. I switched on the gooseneck lamp, sat down at my battered wood desk, and tuned my little white plastic radio to a popular all-night station (The Platters were singing "Only You"). Then I rolled two pieces of paper and a carbon into my baby blue Royal and began typing like a madwoman, making notes on everything that had happened to me since Wednesday morning (just two and a half days ago!), when I first read the reports of Virginia's death and received the fateful phone call from Sabrina inviting me to lunch.

One empty Dr. Pepper bottle and an ashtray full of burned-out L&M filter tips later, I had produced a seventeen-page list of notes for my story—plus a carbon copy for Dan, which I figured he could use as a reference in his soon-to-be expanded investigation. I had also typed up a quick prologue to the based-on-fact "novel" I was determined to write about the murder, and—hurrying to get the details down while they were still fresh in my mind—written a few pages of chapter One. (To say that I was charged up would be like calling Jerry Lewis perky.)

It was three-fifteen in the morning. Nat "King" Cole was singing "When I Fall in Love" on the radio, and I was still aching to talk to Jocelyn, who, I figured, would be home from her date by now. Seizing my cigarettes and the carbon copy of my story notes, I turned off the lamp and the radio, bounded out of my office, and headed downstairs for the phone. Tossing the notes on the kitchen table as I scurried by, I leapt into the living room, scanned the lavender list for Jocelyn's home number, snatched up the receiver, and dialed it.

There was no answer.

I clicked the button and dialed again.

Still no answer.

I slammed down the phone and darted to the living room window. Prying a peephole in the blinds, I peered down into the street, searching (and praying) for some sign of Dan. Both the sidewalks and the street were totally deserted. And as far as I could tell in the dim light from the streetlamp, all the parked cars were empty. Where was he? Was he okay? Would he come back tonight? Would he *ever* come back? Was he sleeping like a log in his Murray Hill apartment or—God help me!—floating like a log in the East River?

I whisked back to the phone and dialed Dan's home number. No answer. I called him at the station house after that, but the officer manning the desk said he hadn't been there all night and hadn't called in to report his whereabouts. Skin crawling and nerves jumping, I got a new line and tried Jocelyn again. Even after eleven rings she didn't pick up. Why didn't she answer? Where the hell could she be?

The suspense was killing me. Literally. And as much as I truly wanted to follow Dan's directions and stay locked inside my apartment, I couldn't stand it for another second. Grabbing my jacket and red beret out of the closet and putting them on, I snatched my purse off the living room chair, burst out into the hall, and scrambled down the stairway to the street.

The sky was black, the air was cold, and the vacant street was dead quiet. Running as fast as I could toward Sixth Avenue, all I could hear were the loud huffs of my steamy breath and the scrapes and scuffs of my ballerina slipper soles against the pavement.

When I reached the corner of Bleecker and Sixth, however, I detected another sound. It was the rumbling engine of the Checker taxicab that was speeding uptown in my direction. Knowing the subway trains would be few and far between this time of night (I mean, morning), I pounced out into the avenue and flagged the cab down. Then I hopped inside, gave the driver an address, and told him to step on it.

Sixteen minutes later, we reached my destination: 140 East 63rd Street. I gave the driver two dollars (the meter fare plus a thirty cent tip), jumped out of the taxi onto the sidewalk, and lunged like a beheaded chicken into the lobby of the Barbizon Hotel for Women.

Chapter 33

THE SMALL, DIM, ART DECO LOBBY HAD A
sickly, greenish cast. Whether it was because of the early morning gloom or the faded colors of the walls and aging furniture, I couldn't tell. Luckily, a garish orange Tiffany lamp was
glowing at the reception desk, or I might not have been able to
find it.

The man sitting behind the desk was large, bald, and dressed
in a rumpled brown suit that looked as old as the furniture. He
was also sound asleep. His head was lolling against the back of
his chair, and his mouth was hanging wide open. He was snoring
loudly.

"Excuse me," I said, knocking my knuckles on the ornate
wooden desk to rouse him. "I'm here to see one of your residents. Can you help me?"

The man started, snorted, and shot up straight in his chair.
Rubbing his doughy, pink face with his nail-bitten fingers, he
shook himself awake and aimed his unseeing gaze in my direction. "*Umph!* Wha—? What did you say?"

"I'm here to see one of your residents," I repeated. "Jocelyn
Fritz. Is she in?"

"Fritz . . .? Uh, yeah," he mumbled, clearing his throat and
turning to look at the clock on the wall behind him. "She came
in a while ago. But it's kinda late to be gettin' visitors now, ya

know." He swiped his hand over his hairless noggin and eyed me suspiciously. "Is she expectin' you?"

"No, but she'll be glad to see me. Would you be kind enough to ring her suite and tell her Paige Turner is here?"

"Huh? Oh, yeah . . . sure," he said, picking up the phone and dialing three numbers. While he was waiting for Jocelyn to answer, he gave me another distrustful look. "Paige Turner, huh? That a trick name or somethin'?"

"It's my nom de plume," I said, just to be tricky (and to practice my fake French accent).

"That's funny," he grunted, giving me a puzzled look and hanging up the phone. "Miss Fritz don't answer. And I know she's there. Came in 'bout a hour ago." He looked at the clock again and scratched his pink scalp. "Or maybe she's still takin' a swim."

"That's it!" I said, feeling a warm rush of relief. "She swims every night before she goes to bed! I should have thought of that before." I straightened my beret and gave him a sympathetic smile. "I'm sorry I woke you up, sir. Which way is the pool?"

He yawned and pointed to an open doorway on the far side of the lobby. "Down that hall and follow the signs."

I COULD HAVE FOUND MY WAY WITHOUT THE signs. All I had to do was follow my nose toward the smell of chlorine. The lighting was poor, but I managed to dash down the hall and cut through a small gym full of exercise equipment without difficulty. Then I came to an entry marked POOL, clanked the heavy door open, and slipped inside.

The elegance of the spacious, windowless pool room took me by surprise. All visible surfaces—the walls, the floors, the numerous floor-to-ceiling pillars spaced evenly around the large rectangular pool—were inlaid with glistening, multicolored mosaics. And at the base of every pillar, in huge green and blue ceramic planters, sat an assortment of tall, lush, thriving palms. Golden light from the overhead fixtures and wall sconces twinkled across the gently rippling water, creating the effect of a set for a Hollywood movie starring—who else?—Esther Williams.

But it was too quiet to be a movie set, and there wasn't a single swimmer in sight.

"Hello?" I called out, voice echoing against the tiles. "Is anybody here?" When nobody answered or appeared, I hollered again. "Hello, Jocelyn? Are you here? Come out, come out, wherever you are!" I made a beeline for the changing room at the far end of the pool, thinking she must have finished washing away her sins and begun toweling herself dry.

Jocelyn wasn't there, but her clothes were. The turquoise cocktail dress I'd seen her wearing at the Copa—plus the lacy undergarments and mink coat I hadn't seen—were draped across the long wooden bench under the shelves of white terry cloth robes and towels. Her silver stilettos were sitting side by side on the floor. "Jocelyn?" I called again, opening the door to the adjoining bathroom and sticking my head inside. Maybe she was taking a shower.

But she wasn't there, either. Nobody was. It was as quiet as a tomb, and all the toilet and shower stalls were empty. Heart pounding like a kettledrum, I closed the door to the bathroom and stole back through the changing room, slinking past Jocelyn's discarded clothes with every cell in my body on alert. Something was terribly wrong. I could feel it.

And as soon as I stepped back into the pool room, I could see it.

Jocelyn's nude body was floating, faceup, on the right side of the pool—so close to the large arrangement of potted palms near the entrance that it had been hidden from my sight when I first came in. Her eyes were wide open and bulging, her gaping mouth was full of water, and her long, thin limbs were limp and ghostly pale. You didn't have to be a doctor to know that she was dead.

Stifling a scream, I ran to the edge of the pool where she drifted, in silky silence, like a strip of seaweed hugging the shore. I knelt on the ledge beside her and, though I knew it was pointless, checked for signs of life. She wasn't breathing, and she had no pulse at her neck or wrists. To affirm the cause of death, I looked her over more carefully. There were no visible wounds, bruises, scrapes, or scratches on her body; no finger marks around her throat. There was no blood in the water. She had obviously drowned—whether by accident, suicide, or murder, I wasn't sure.

I had a pretty good idea, though.

I wanted to pull Jocelyn's poor corpse out of the water and

cover her nakedness in a soft terry cloth robe, but I knew enough not to disturb the evidence. Holding back tears, I rose to my knees and scanned the area for signs of a struggle. There were no indications that a physical bout had occurred. Several big puddles of water were around the pool's wide brim, but they could have been caused by anything—or anyone. Jocelyn herself could have splashed the water onto the ledge just by jumping or diving or kicking her feet while swimming.

I was about to stand up and run out to the lobby to call the police when a sudden glint of gold caught my eye. It flashed up from the bottom of the pool, just a few feet away from the corpse. I moved closer to the flash and leaned over the water, peering down through its depth, trying to pinpoint the source of the gleam. In the pool's underwater lighting, I spied the object quickly. It was small and round and shiny—a button? a quarter? a subway token?—and it lay still as a stone on the blue tiled floor.

Without thinking, I pulled off my beret, jacket, and shoes, and tossed them, with my purse, in a pile near the potted palms. Then I stuck my bare feet in the water and—too crazed and hurried to take off my clothes—lowered myself all the way into the pool. My feet didn't come anywhere close to the bottom. Taking a deep breath and holding it, I bent forward at the waist, plunged my face into the water, and dived—headfirst and eyes open—toward the glittering prize.

When my fingers found the object and snatched it up from the floor, I grasped it tight in my fist, turned myself aright, kicked off from the bottom, and shot back toward the surface in a stream of exhaled bubbles. Breaking through to the air and taking a big gulp of it, I paddled over to the side of the pool and hoisted myself to a sitting position on the ledge. Then— gasping, coughing, spitting, and dripping, slumped in a big puddle of my own making—I slowly opened my fist and looked down at the item in my palm.

It was a gold St. Christopher medal. The very same one I'd seen dangling from Tony Corona's neck just a few hours ago. I could prove it, too. His name was engraved—like a signed confession—on the back.

NEITHER DAN NOR O'CONNOR RESPONDED TO the desk clerk's frantic call to the police. Several cops in uniform and a team from the medical examiner's office were the first to arrive, and just a couple of seconds after that, Detective Sergeant Dominick Mudd from the 19th Precinct swaggered into the Barbizon lobby and took charge of the investigation.

Great, I thought. *Just what we need—another daring detective mucking up the case.* Pulling my jacket tighter around my soggy sweater and shivering shoulders, I sat hunched in a wet armchair in the middle of the lobby, wondering how I should deal with the distressing new developments.

After a quick word with the desk clerk, Mudd dispatched four of his men and the ME's team to the pool room. Then he strode over to me and stood—legs apart—right in front of my chair. In his dark suit, white shirt, tan trench coat, and gray fedora, he looked just like every other dick in the city. Except for the scar. Etched across the entire right side of his face, it was long, wide, and jagged—like a Z. I wondered if he'd had a run-in with Zorro.

"You're the dame that discovered the body," he said.

It was a statement, not a question, so I didn't bother to answer.

"I want to talk to you after I inspect the scene," he added, "so don't leave the premises. Stay here in the lobby until I get back. Give your name, address, and phone number to Officer Murphy while you're waiting."

"Yes, sir," I said, suppressing the urge to salute.

Mudd hurried away, and I gave Murphy the required information. Then I got up and moved to a dry chair. Opening my purse and checking to see that the St. Christopher medal was still there—safe in the zippered side pocket where I'd stashed it—I took out my comb and pulled it through my soggy hair. *What the hell am I supposed to do now? What should I say to Mudd when he comes back? How can I handle his questions?*

I felt strongly that I shouldn't tell him the truth. It would take too long to relate the whole story, and even longer to explain all the ramifications. And how would he react to the information? Was he honest or corrupt? Did he have secret mob connections? Close ties with the DA? Would he arrest Corona or protect him? And what would he do to Sabrina?

No, the truth was too risky. I couldn't give it away to a stranger with a Z on his face. I had to save it for Dan. My best bet, I decided, was to stay as close to the truth as I could without revealing the link between Jocelyn's death and Virginia's, or disclosing any significant facts.

By the time Mudd returned, I had my story down pat. When he asked me how I knew the victim, I told him I'd met her at Saks (which was true). I said she was a hat designer (also true), and that she made the most stylish berets in the city (which, as far as I knew, could have been true), and that we'd become such good friends, she designed this special red one just for me. (This statement was totally false, of course, but when I picked up my crimson cap and angled it on my cold, damp head, I almost believed it myself.)

When Mudd asked me why I had such a weird name and what I did for a living, I told him the truth, but when he wanted to know why I'd come to see Jocelyn at such an "ungodly" hour (his word, not mine), I lied through my teeth. I said I'd had a big fight with my boyfriend and was desperate for company. (Actually, when I think about it now, that wasn't such a big lie after all!)

After Mudd informed me that Jocelyn's death appeared to be murder, our Q&A session turned fierce. Mudd probed, poked, and prodded me to the hilt, and I gave him a song and dance worthy of Ann Miller. When he asked if I had any idea who killed Jocelyn, I hugged my purse (and the precious evidence it carried) close to my side and said, "None whatsoever." To his query about how I got so wet, I replied that while leaning over the edge of the pool to take Jocelyn's pulse, I had slipped and fallen in.

At this point Mudd gave me a skeptical smirk. "You expect me to believe that?" he jeered.

"Well, yes," I said, taken aback. "Why wouldn't you?"

"Because you're the one who found the body."

"So . . . ?"

"So the one who discovers the corpse often turns out to be the killer."

Uh-oh.

"You could have jumped into the pool on purpose," he said, still smirking. "It could have been you that held the victim's head underwater until she died." He stuck a cigarette between his lips, lit it, and went on. "Maybe you were crazy jealous of her. Maybe *she* was the reason you had a big fight with your boyfriend."

"My boyfriend never even met her!" I declared, realizing— as I spoke—that I didn't know if he had or not.

Mudd took a quick puff on his cigarette and flicked some ashes on the carpet. "The desk clerk says that, besides himself, you and the victim were the only people here on the ground floor at the time of the murder. He says Miss Fritz came in about three and went straight to the pool for a swim like she always did, and that nobody else entered or left the hotel until an hour later, when *you* showed up."

"What a crock!" I sputtered, on the verge of blowing my stack. "The desk clerk can't possibly be sure of that. He was sound asleep when I came in! A full-grown elephant could have tromped through the lobby and gone for a dip without him knowing it."

"Be that as it may," Mudd grunted, "you're still a prime suspect in this case."

Great.

"And I've got a lot more questions to ask you."

Swell.

"And if you know what's good for you, you'll give me straight answers."

I was too weary to put up a fight. "I'll be happy to answer your questions, Detective Mudd," I said, "but does it have to be now? It's been a very long, hideous night, and I'm exhausted. I had a blowup with my boyfriend, and found one of my dearest friends dead, and fell into a swimming pool, and now I can't think straight. I need to go home and get some sleep."

He looked at his watch and nodded. "Monday morning, then," he replied, being far more accommodating than I'd thought possible. (Maybe he was weary, too.) "Come to the station for further questioning. Nine o'clock sharp."

"Thank you, Detective. I'll be there on time. May I have your permission to leave now?"

"You can leave the hotel," he said, scar twitching, "but don't leave town."

Chapter 34

THANKS TO THE PROTECTIVE (AND SURPRIS-
ingly polite) public policy of the NYPD, Officer Murphy drove
me home. It was eight o'clock Saturday morning. The sky was
bright, the traffic was light, and the Italian merchants of Bleecker
Street had begun opening the doors to their food shops, eager to
rake in their weekend windfalls. When I got out of the squad car
and headed into my building, the aroma of fresh-baked bread
wafting from Zito's bakery made my mouth water. Normally, I
would have rushed to buy a loaf while it was still warm, but today I was too tired. I had barely enough energy to climb the
stairs to my apartment and let myself in.

The second I stepped through the door, however, and caught
sight of the large, manly figure lounging in my living room, my
energy returned with a vengeance. It was Dan! And he was all
in one piece! One great big, gallant, gorgeous, glorious piece.
Sitting on the couch in his shirtsleeves, with his long, strong
legs stretched out in front of him, he was casually smoking a
cigarette and reading Sabrina's lavender list.

"Thank God you're here!" I cried, ripping off my jacket and
beret and tossing them, with my purse, on a kitchen chair. "I've
been so worried about you!" I bounded into the living room,
leapt over Dan's outstretched legs, and plopped down on the
couch beside him. "How long have you been here?" My tail was

wagging out of control, but I managed to stop myself from licking his face.

"Long enough to read this list and all your notes about the Pratt murder," he said, sitting up straight and putting the stack of pages on the telephone table. "I see you've been a very busy girl." He took a drag on his Camel and gave me a crooked smile. I couldn't tell if it was hostile or friendly.

"Are you still mad at me?" I asked, sucking in a deep breath and holding it.

"I haven't decided yet."

I let out a tortured sigh. "When do you think you'll reach your verdict?"

"When you stop deceiving me and tell me everything you know."

"I've wanted to do that all along, Dan. I swear!"

"Then why didn't you?" he snapped, aiming his jet black gaze right between my eyes.

"Because I gave Sabrina my word!" I croaked. "She said if the police found out that Virginia was a prostitute, they wouldn't even *try* to catch her killer. She said they'd close up her whole operation, and arrest her and all her girls, and then Charlotte and Melody's twin brother would be. . . . Oh, what's the use?" I cried, nerves tied up in knots. "You don't know who or what I'm talking about. And the story's so long and crazy and complicated you can't possibly understand." My hands were flapping around like birds, and I was on the verge of tears.

Dan loosened his tie, opened his shirt collar, and rolled up his sleeves. "You underestimate me, Paige," he said. "You always have. And this time it's particularly insulting. I understand a lot more than you think I do. And I did even before I read your notes."

"Really?" I said, perking up and paying attention, busting to learn how much he knew, and how and when he'd come to know it. "I'm glad to hear that, Dan. I really am! It'll make it so much easier for us to talk about the case together. Look, I have a good idea. Why don't you tell me everything you know, and I'll fill in the blanks?"

Dan laughed out loud. "Nice carrot, Paige, but I'm not hungry. It's time for *you* to do the talking." (Was it my imagination, or had he suddenly slipped into a good mood?)

"But I don't know where to begin," I whined, trying to get my thoughts together. (I swear to God I wasn't stalling. There was so much to explain, and I was so tired and discombobulated, I really *didn't* know where to begin.)

"Well, for starters you can tell me where you were all night," Dan growled, turning angry again. (That was the shortest good mood in history.) "I brought you home from the Copa around twelve, and you promised to stay here—with the doors locked—until I got in touch with you. That was eight goddamn hours ago. Why the hell didn't you stay put, and where the hell have you been?"

"First of all, I *did* stay home for a long time, just like you told me to. I wrote up my notes and I made a few phone calls and I—"

"Who did you speak to?"

"A woman named Sabrina Stanhope," I said. "She's in my notes. She runs an elite call girl service and she's the one who—"

"I know all about her," Dan cut in. "Who else did you call?"

"Ethel Maguire, otherwise known as Brigitte. She's one of Sabrina's girls, and—"

"Anybody else?" he asked, too impatient to let me finish a sentence.

"You," I said. "I called you at home and at the station, but you were nowhere to be found, so—"

"Is that it? Nobody else?"

"I tried to call Jocelyn a few times, but she didn't answer. That's why I—"

"Jocelyn Fritz?" he asked. "The one who goes by the name of Candy?"

"That's right," I said. "She was at the Copa last night, and she told me that she'd been seeing two of Sabrina's major clients—Tony Corona and Sam Hogarth—without Sabrina's knowledge. She said they were both devils in disguise, and she was certain one of them had killed Virginia."

"Go on," Dan urged.

"So when she didn't answer her phone at three in the morning, I got worried about her. And that's when I left the apartment and grabbed a cab to the Barbizon Hotel for Women, where she lived."

"Lived?" Dan said. "Past tense?" Years of tricky interrogations had made him a good listener.

"Right," I said, with a sorrowful sigh. "When I got there, I found her drowned in the hotel swimming pool. It was horrible, Dan . . . not a pretty sight." Fighting back the memory of Jocelyn's poor deluged face, I steadied my shuddering shoulders, took a deep breath, and went on. "She was killed shortly before I found her. I know this because the hotel desk clerk said she came home around three, and I got there at a few minutes to four."

"Are you sure?"

"Yes, and that's where I've been for the last four hours," I hastened to add. "At the Barbizon Hotel discovering the body of another murdered call girl, and then sitting like a lump in the lobby, where I was detained for questioning by Detective Sergeant Dominick Mudd of the 19th Precinct."

"The one with the X on his face?"

"No, it was a Z. I guess Y was busy."

Dan cracked a little smile, but quickly turned it back into a scowl. "What questions did Mudd ask, and how did you answer them? I hope you didn't tell him the truth."

I almost dropped my teeth. Dan had never *wanted* me to be dishonest before, and now here he was hoping I'd kept the truth hidden—from the police, no less! I considered making a joke about it, but decided not to run the risk of upsetting him further.

"Don't worry," I soothed. "I didn't say anything that would interfere with our investigation." (Notice how I slipped the word *our* in there?) "I told him Jocelyn was a good friend of mine— that I'd rushed uptown to see her in the middle of the night because I had a big fight with my boyfriend and needed somebody to talk to."

"Good," he said, with a nod of approval.

"Good for you, maybe," I said, "but not so good for me. Now *I'm* the prime suspect in Jocelyn's murder. Mudd thinks she was fooling around with my boyfriend and I killed her out of jealousy. I have to go in for further questioning, and he told me not to leave town."

"What a mess," Dan said, slumping forward and shaking his head. "This case gets more complicated with every second. I'm beginning to wonder if we'll ever get all the facts untangled."

"Of course we will!" I exclaimed, happily repeating the word *we*. "If we put our heads together, we'll solve this puzzle in no time. The clues are surfacing fast now, Dan. In fact, I found a really important piece of evidence at the Barbizon pool! I've been aching to tell you about it ever since I came in. It's one hundred percent conclusive, and it proves that Jocelyn was killed by Tony Corona!"

Dan sat up straight and shot me a disbelieving look. "That's impossible," he said, shaking his head again.

"No, it's true!" I yelped, jumping up off the couch and retrieving my purse from the kitchen. "Look at this!" Returning to the living room, I took the gold St. Christopher medal out of my bag and wiggled it, like a fishing lure, in front of Dan's nose. "I found it on the bottom of the pool, just a few feet away from the corpse. It belongs to Tony Corona. I saw it around his neck at the Copa, and if that's not enough to convince you, his name is engraved on the back!" I was so proud of myself, I thought I would pop.

Dan took the medal out of my hand and looked it over carefully. "Did you dive into the water to get this?"

"Uh, yes . . ." I said, surprised by his question—not to mention his tepid reaction to my outstanding skills of detection.

"That explains it, then," he said.

"Explains what?"

"Why you look so clammy and smell of chlorine."

Aaaaaaaaarrrrrrrrgh!

"Is that all you have to say?" I screeched. "That I look bad and smell funny? Jesus, Dan! The least you could do is admit that I'm a good swimmer! And a darn good detective. And would it kill you to acknowledge the fact that I have—quickly, bravely, and *single-handedly*—nailed Jocelyn's murderer?"

"That's just it, Paige. You haven't."

"Haven't what?"

"Nailed Jocelyn's murderer."

"What are you talking about? You've got the proof right there in your hand! We've got him dead to rights, Dan. Tony Corona killed Jocelyn Fritz, and that's all there is to it!"

"He didn't do it, Paige." Dan's tone was stern, but his gaze was sympathetic.

"Have you lost your mind? That medal puts Corona smack-dab at the scene of the crime. It's enough to convict him!"

Dan squared his shoulders and said, "Corona was nowhere near the Barbizon at the time Jocelyn was killed."

"That can't be true!" I cried, the wind whooshing out of my sails. "How do you know that? Are you sure?"

"Positive," he said, "because at the time of Jocelyn's death, Tony Corona was with me, at the Midtown North station, being booked for the murder of Virginia Pratt."

Chapter 35

HAVE YOU EVER BEEN STRUCK BY LIGHTNING? Well, neither have I, but I'm sure it's a shocking experience. Almost as shocking as having your credibility, stability, and self-confidence shattered—in one blow—by the man you love and trust most in the world.

(Okay, okay! So maybe I'm laying it on with a trowel here, but I'm the one telling this story, and I think I'm entitled to express my emotions. No matter how stupid they happen to be. And besides, when Dan revealed that he'd arrested Tony Corona for Virginia's murder, I really *did* feel as though I'd been struck by lightning—or something equally electrifying.)

"Holy moly!!!" I shrieked, bones rattling, hair standing on end. "Corona killed Virginia? And you already booked the bastard? I don't freaking believe it!" I threw both hands up and stamped one foot on the floor. "What was his motive? How the hell did you figure it out? Have you got enough proof?" Curiosity was burning a hole in my brain (and inflaming my vocabulary).

"Simmer down, Paige," Dan said, standing up, putting his arm around my waist, and guiding me into the kitchen. "I think you're flipping out. You'd better compose yourself and make us some coffee. Then we can sit down at the table and compare notes, discuss the case like two calm, sensitive, and mature adults."

I probably deserved Dan's patronizing little speech, but I

still found it annoying. How did he come off acting so calm and sensitive when just minutes ago he'd been bombarding me with impatient questions and telling me I looked clammy and smelled chlorinated? (I mean, how sensitive was *that?*) I thought the coffee was a good idea, though, so I filled the pot with water, spooned a ton of Chase and Sanborn into the filtered basket, and put the trusty device on the stove to perk. Then I sat down across the table from Dan and lit up one of his Camels.

"Please proceed, Detective Street," I said, batting my lashes and beaming a fake angelic smile in his direction. "I find your work simply fascinating. Tell me, how did you ever get involved in this compelling case, and what led you to conclude that Mister Corona killed Miss Pratt?" I was doing my best Loretta Young (i.e., acting so sensitive and self-composed it was silly).

Dan groaned and gave me a warning look. "Knock it off, Paige. It's been a long night, and I'm not in the mood for any more drama. If you want to hear my side of the story, you'd better behave yourself and just listen."

"Okay, shoot," I said, immediately dropping my charade and craning my neck over the table. "I'm a giant ear. Tell me everything."

Dan raked his fingers through his wavy hair, leaned back in his chair, stretched out his legs, and propped his folded arms behind his head. "The chief brought me into the case at the start," he began, looking so languid and seductive I thought I would die. "He said he had reason to believe the detective in charge wouldn't conduct a proper investigation, and he asked me to undertake a behind-the-scenes, one-man search for Virginia's murderer. He thought her death had something to do with the mob war raging through the city right now, and—since I was already investigating the conflict and a couple of related rubouts—he figured I would be in contact with some underworld informers.

"And he was right," Dan continued, "on both counts. I do have a few Mafia pigeons, and one of them is very close to the top. It turned out he knew a lot about the murder, and after I plied him with a pile of cash and promises, he gave me the inside dope. He told me that Virginia had been a high-priced prostitute known as Melody, that she had worked for a high-class madam named Sabrina Stanhope, and that mob boss Frank Costello himself had ordered her hit after learning that she was keeping company with District Attorney Sam Hogarth as well as with his own protégé, Tony Corona."

"Protégé? Are you saying that—?"

"Right. Corona owes his whole career to Costello. The top Mafioso made him a star. Now hush, Paige, and let me finish."

Aaaargh!

"It all boils down to this," Dan went on. "When the DA recently put the crunch on Costello—dragging him into court, threatening him on TV, closing down his gambling operations, and so forth—Costello got teed off and swore to get even. He wanted to have the DA assassinated, but decided against it because the cops and the feds would know he was responsible and would come down even harder on his case. So when Corona told him that he and Hogarth were sleeping with the same expensive call girl, and that Hogarth was so infatuated he had given her a mink jacket and some diamond jewelry, Costello came up with an alternate plan: He would have Melody killed and her nude body dumped in the park, along with her ID and the presents Sam Hogarth had given her. That way, he figured— incorrectly, as it turned out—the police would discover that Melody was a hooker, trace the fur and diamonds back to Hogarth, and then accuse the district attorney of murder.

"Costello didn't care if Hogarth was ever convicted of the crime or not. He just wanted to destroy the DA's reputation, career, and political future, and he knew the sex scandal alone would take care of that. He also knew he could make Corona take care of Melody's murder for him just by calling in a few favors. So the hit was arranged, and Corona did the dirty deed. And—thanks to the inept and corrupt detective in charge of the case—the DA wasn't exposed. Instead," Dan added, looking like a cat with a mouthful of canary feathers, "the country's favorite crooner is singing sob songs in the slammer."

I couldn't hold my tongue one second longer. "But how can that be?" I spluttered. "You can't book a man for murder based on the word of a Mafia stoolie! You've got to have solid evidence—and a heck of a lot of it!"

Dan chuckled and sat up straighter. "I was coming to that part, Paige, but since you're too impatient to sit still and listen, I think you'd better get up and pour me a cup of coffee—use up some of that nervous energy."

If he hadn't given me a really sexy smile when he said that, I would have had a hissy fit and refused to move. As it was, though, I stabbed out my cigarette, jumped out of my chair, hopped over to the stove, filled two mugs with coffee, and brought them back to the table in a flash.

I couldn't wait to hear the rest of Dan's story.

And I hoped to earn another sexy smile.

BY THE TIME THE COFFEEPOT WAS EMPTY, both of my goals had been realized. Dan had smiled at me twice during the course of his detailed account, and when he concluded his lengthy monologue, I knew every single step leading up to his sudden—but completely lawful—arrest of Tony Corona for the murder of Virginia Pratt.

I would repeat Dan's report for you word for word, but that would take too many pages and tax my wretched memory beyond its capacity. I hope, therefore, that you'll be satisfied with the following summary.

As soon as Dan got the scoop from his stoolie, he went looking for proof that the story was true. He didn't bother searching for evidence of Costello's involvement because he knew he'd never find any. So he focused all his energy and effort on proving Corona's guilt. He hung out at the Copa at night—watching Corona and his entourage in action, listening in on private conversations at the bar and in the men's room—and he spent the rest of his time digging for evidence at the Plaza Hotel.

Dan spoke with the maid responsible for cleaning Corona's suite and learned that the day after the murder a sheet was missing from the suspect's bed. And as she was replacing it with a new one, the maid remembered, a faint but distinct odor of turpentine had wafted up from the mattress. She never mentioned the odor or the missing sheet to her supervisor for fear she'd be blamed for both, but when Dan asked her to give him the replacement sheet for evidence, she readily complied. And when this sheet was compared with the one Virginia's body had been wrapped in, it proved to be the same size and have the same label, stitching, and thread count as the original. Traces of turpentine were detected in both examples.

Dan discovered more incriminating evidence in Corona's suite, which he entered one evening after Corona and his henchmen left for the Copa. In a cabinet under the bathroom sink he found a length of rope, a roll of adhesive tape, a box of cotton, and a small can of turpentine. Astounded that Corona had held on to these damning indications of his guilt—that he hadn't even attempted to hide them!—Dan confiscated the items and had the lab compare them with the rope, tape, and turpentine-soaked cotton used to bind, gag, and asphyxiate Virginia. Each test showed a perfect match.

Dan could have arrested Corona at this point. He had plenty of proof. He was afraid, though, that it wouldn't hold up in court; that the defense would argue the evidence had been planted; and that—due to the all-too-neat and convenient stash of incriminating articles under the sink—the jury would believe the claim. So, to nip this possible scenario in the bud, Dan continued searching for something more conclusive—an irrefutable verification of the facts.

And this he got, in very short order, from Corona's frightened, loose-lipped chauffeur. Thinking the driver might have had something to do with transporting Virginia's corpse from the Plaza to Central Park, Dan cornered him in the garage of the hotel, grilled him about the night of the murder, and accused him of being an accomplice in the crime. The hapless chauffeur broke down in tears and started shaking uncontrollably, saying he'd been forced to do what he did, and that he'd be killed if he told anybody what happened. But after Dan convinced him that he'd probably be killed anyway, and then promised him a new identity and a new life in Arizona in exchange for the truth, he admitted that he'd helped Corona and his strong-arm man, Little Pete, dispose of the body.

He said they had wrapped the dead girl and her belongings in a sheet, hidden the bundle under a pile of linens in a hotel laundry cart, and then wheeled the cart into a service elevator and taken it down to the garage. He said Little Pete lifted the bundle into the trunk of the limousine and then went with him to unload the body in Central Park. Corona went back upstairs.

Dan found plenty of evidence to substantiate the chauffeur's story—several rope fibers and a splotch of turpentine in the bottom of the linen cart, numerous long blonde hairs and a diamond stud earring in the trunk of the limousine—and decided that, combined with the chauffeur's testimony and the evidence he'd already collected, it was more than enough to convict Corona.

So while Abby and I were drinking champagne and watching Corona perform at the Copa, Dan was taking the terrified chauffeur into custody, making sure he would be kept safe and comfortable until he could testify at the trial and then begin his new life in Phoenix.

And while Abby and I were doing our dumb Gina and Cherry act in Corona's dressing room, Dan was checking his hat and coat and taking a seat at the Copa bar, waiting for the right moment to make his move.

And then later that night (which was just *last* night, if you can believe it!)—after I had rescued Dan from certain death with my clever prostitute impression and he had driven Abby and me home in a heedless, fire-breathing fury—Detective Sergeant Dan Street made a hasty (and, if you ask me, heroic) return to the Copacabana and arrested the club's (maybe the whole galaxy's) star entertainer for murder.

Chapter 36

"GREAT WORK, DAN," I SAID, WHEN HE FIN-
ished his arresting tale. "You are, without a doubt, the world's
best dick. I'm so proud of you! And I can't wait to tell Sabrina
that Virginia's killer has been caught. She'll be so grateful."

"Does she know about Jocelyn?"

"Not yet. I haven't had a chance to talk to her. I'll call her as
soon as you leave. Meanwhile, we've still got our work cut out
for us. It's one murder down and one to go."

"Yeah," he said, with a hefty sigh. "But the next one won't
be so easy to crack."

"It may be easier than you think."

Dan gave me a quizzical look. "Why do you say that?"

"Because I know who did it, that's why." I straightened my
shoulders and puffed out my chest in pride.

"Oh, really?" He didn't snicker, but he might as well have.

"Yes, really!" I snapped.

"Then suppose you tell me who it is." Here came that sexy
smile again.

"I will, if you promise not to laugh at me," I said. "I'm not in
the mood to be ridiculed."

Dan's smile vanished, and a look of pure sincerity took its
place. "Don't worry, Paige, I won't laugh. Murder's not a laughing matter . . . and neither are you."

That was all I needed to hear. "Okay, I'll tell you," I said, "even though you'll think I'm nuts. I'm convinced—*way* beyond the shadow of a doubt—that Jocelyn Fritz was killed by District Attorney Sam Hogarth."

He didn't laugh, but he didn't applaud my sleuthing genius, either. He just raised one eyebrow and said, "Twenty minutes ago you would have sent Tony Corona to the electric chair for the same crime."

"I know that, Dan!" I croaked, getting snippy again. "But this time is different! This time I'm *right!*" I banged my fist on the tabletop for emphasis. (Okay, so your baby brother does the same thing when he's cranky—but does that make me a petulant child? Don't answer that!)

"Simmer down, babe," Dan said, leaning forward and looking me straight in the eye. "You don't have to be so defensive. I didn't say you were wrong about Hogarth. In fact, I'm sort of inclined to agree with you."

"What?" If the man yanked one more squirming bunny out of his hat, I'd faint dead away on the spot. "You're kidding me, right?"

"I'm not kidding you *or* laughing at you," Dan soothed. "As much as I hate to admit it, the district attorney *does* seem to be a likely suspect. *I'm* not at all sure that he's guilty, but I would like to know why *you* are."

I felt as though I'd just been crowned Miss Manhattan: rhinestone tiara, velvet cape, armful of roses, and all. Eager to walk down the runway and share my brilliant deductions with Dan and the rest of my worshipful fans, I held my head high, took a deep breath, and declared, "It's because of Corona's St. Christopher medal!"

"Come again?" Dan said. I had surprised *him* for a change.

"The medal!" I exclaimed, trying, but failing, to curb my excitement. "Hogarth swiped it from Corona's dressing room at the Copa, and then planted it in the Barbizon pool after he drowned Jocelyn. I'm certain of it!"

"What makes you say that? Don't you think you're—"

"Jumping to conclusions? No way, Doris Day! Hogarth wanted Jocelyn dead, and he wanted the murder pinned on Corona, so he decided to kill both birds with one stone."

Dan was skeptical but intrigued. "Why did he want Jocelyn dead?"

"Because she threatened him, that's why! She told me all about it in the ladies' lounge last night. She said she spoke to Hogarth at the bar, and when she brought up the subject of Melody's murder, he smirked and pretended not to know who she was talking about. And this made Jocelyn hopping mad. Melody had been her best friend, and she couldn't let Hogarth's smirking denial go unchallenged. She lost her head and threatened to expose him."

"And this all happened at the Copa last night?"

"Right."

"I didn't know Hogarth was there. I didn't see him at the bar."

"By the time you came in, he was up in the mezzanine, having dinner with his wife."

"How do you know he went to Corona's dressing room?"

"When Abby and I were there, Corona asked Little Pete if Hogarth was waiting in the hall to see him. Little Pete told him the DA was having dinner upstairs and would come down to see him later."

Dan's face was flaming, and his eyes were shooting sparks across the table. I thought he was furious that Hogarth had been chummy with Corona. I thought he was going to start ranting about strange bedfellows, and shared hookers, and power-mad politicians and mobsters, and the deceitfulness of our degenerate DA, and the vile corruption in our city's criminal justice system—but he didn't. All he said was, "What the hell were you and Abby doing in Corona's dressing room?"

Uh-oh. Dan wasn't going to like this part of the movie.

"Well, um, er," I stammered, looking for a way to bypass the sexual aspects of the dressing room scene. (The last thing I needed at that point was to make Dan jealous.) I quickly realized, however, that it would be impossible to avoid the sex angle without lying, so I gave up and took the next best way out:

I put the blame on Abby.

"The whole thing was Abby's idea!" I blustered. (Well, it was the truth, you know!) "She thought the easiest and fastest way for us to observe and question Corona in person would be to masquerade as call girls. So we spoke to Sabrina, told her our plan, and asked her to arrange it. Sabrina then called Corona, told him two new girls had just joined her agency, gave him first choice of the fresh recruits, and offered to send us to the Copa for his inspection. Corona took the bait and invited us to dinner and the eight o'clock show, and to his dressing room afterward.

"And it was darn lucky for you that we went!" I barreled on, talking as fast as I could, not giving Dan a chance to express his disapproval. "Otherwise, I wouldn't have heard Corona tell Little Pete to get rid of you! I wouldn't have heard him say that he wanted you 'put down,' and that he wanted your head on a platter, and that he was going to talk to Costello about it that very night! And I wouldn't have raced like the wind out of that dressing room to find you at the bar and warn you that your life was in immediate danger!"

Dan's jealous scowl melted into something soft and kind of swoony. It wasn't a smile, exactly; it was more like an honest, open, goofy look of love. "I'm sorry, Paige," he said. "I should have thanked you for that before. You did a very brave and daring thing, and I'm lucky to have such a clever, quick-thinking girlfriend."

My heart did a double cartwheel. "You're pretty fast on your feet yourself, babe," I replied. "Pretending to arrest me was downright inspired."

Dan grinned and gave me a sexy wink. "So you liked that, did you?"

"It was very exciting," I admitted.

Chuckling and rolling his sleeves up another notch, he shoved his chair back from the table and stood up. "Then I think I'll arrest you again," he said. "Right now."

The next thing I knew, he scooped me up in his arms and carried me over to the couch. And the next thing I knew after that, he grabbed a fistful of my clammy hair, pulled my head away from his shoulder, and lowered his hot, luscious, demanding mouth onto mine. Then he pressed me all the way down into the seat cushion and climbed on top of me, burying the length of my body in his writhing warmth, covering my face and neck with ravenous kisses, breathing hotly in my ear, driving me out of my mind, making me cry out for more. . . .

What can I say? I was dying for it. Who gave a flying fig about marriage? I wanted Dan to make love to me, and I wanted it *now*. This very instant. Diaphragm or no diaphragm. "Take me, baby!" I begged. "I want you so much I can't stand it. Please take me now!"

(A word to all sex-crazed girlfriends: Be careful what you

beg for. If you get it, you might feel screwed. If you *don't* get it, you'll feel like a dope.)

Dan pushed himself away from me, swung around to a sitting position, rubbed his face in his hands, and dropped his chin to his chest. He was panting like a racehorse.

"I'm sorry, Paige," he groaned, chest heaving. "I can't go through with it."

"What's wrong?" I gasped. (I was panting a bit myself.) "Is it the chlorine? I'll run upstairs and take a shower if you—"

"No! It's nothing like that!"

"Then what is it? I don't turn you on anymore?" I sat up and hugged my knees to my chest. "Maybe I should put the blonde wig back on." I was kidding, but just barely.

Dan smiled and put his arm around my shoulders. "You turn me on as much as ever, Paige," he said, holding me tight. "Even more, if you want to know the truth."

"Under the circumstances, I find that a weensy bit hard to believe." I wasn't kidding at all now. I was dead serious and teetering on the verge of a king-size crying jag.

"But it's true, babe," Dan said. "I love you and want you more than ever."

"Then what's the problem? I don't understand."

"It's not the right time."

Aaargh!

"Right time?!" I screeched. "I'm so hot I'm *screaming* for it, and you say it's not the right time? What time would be good for you? Greenwich time? Mountain time? Alaska time? Suppertime?"

Dan sniggered and shook his head. "Where's your patience, Paige? We've already waited so long, I didn't think it would hurt us to wait a few weeks longer."

"A few weeks? What for? What possible difference could a few weeks make?" I was getting more confused by the second.

"It would give us some time to get our ducks in a row," Dan said.

"Ducks? What ducks? I don't know any ducks."

Dan laughed, and pulled me closer. "Look, what I meant was a lot could happen in a few weeks' time. A promise could be made. A license could be issued. Blood could be sent to the lab for testing. A ring could be found. A killer could be caught. A date for the execution could be set . . ."

I almost wet my pants. Was Dan saying what I thought he was saying? Afraid of jumping to conclusions—especially *this* conclusion—I peered deep into his laughing black eyes and asked, "What's on your mind, Detective, murder or marriage?"

"Both," he said—which, to my way of thinking, was the perfect answer.

Chapter 37

RENEWING OUR RESOLVE TO SAVE THE MAIN
event for our wedding night, Dan and I decided to celebrate our
engagement by indulging in another sensual experience we'd
never shared before—a home-cooked breakfast. Dan went
downstairs to buy the essentials—bread, eggs, bacon, juice—
and I ran (okay, *floated*) upstairs to shower and change my
clothes. Chlorinated capris and a matted Angora sweater just
didn't seem festive enough for our first feast together as husband and wife. (Okay, okay! What I meant was *future* husband
and wife. You don't have to be so persnickety about it!)

By the time Dan got back to the apartment with the food, I
was back downstairs in the kitchen, playing the happy little
homemaker, looking very wifely in my clean black capris,
fuzzy pink sweater, and ruffled blue-and-white-checked apron.
I set the table with my best china (okay, two of my four
melamine plates), put up another pot of coffee, and hoisted my
almost-never-used, two-ton cast-iron skillet out of the cabinet
and lugged it over to the stove. (And I thought hauling around
the office Coffeemaster was hard!)

While Dan unpacked the groceries and poured the orange
juice, I heated the skillet and cooked the bacon. While Dan sat
at the table sipping juice and smoking a cigarette, I fried four
sunny-side up eggs in the bacon grease and sliced, toasted, and

buttered the bread. Then I poured us some more coffee, dished up the food, and brought everything to the table.

"To us!" I said, sitting down and holding my juice glass up for a toast.

Dan grinned and clinked his glass against mine. "And to many more conjugal breakfasts like this!" He shot me a cocky smile, downed the rest of his juice, then dunked a piece of toast into one of his egg yolks and started eating. "And now that we're going to be married," he said between mouthfuls, "I want you to think about quitting your job."

I almost choked on my first bite of bacon. "Jesus, Dan!" I cried. "We've been engaged for less than an hour and already you've got me chained to the stove and giving up my career?! What's next? A baby every year?" I was only half teasing. Maybe this whole marriage thing wasn't such a good idea. . . .

Dan laughed and shoveled an entire egg white into his mouth. He chewed it up, swallowed, and said, "I didn't mean it that way, Paige, and you know it. Yes, I *do* want you to leave your dangerous job at *Daring Detective*, but I'm not asking you to give up your writing career. I'm just saying you don't have to work nine-to-five anymore. I can support us both. Besides, things have been so lousy for you at *DD* lately, I thought you'd *want* to quit."

"I couldn't quit under any circumstances," I said.

Dan's face fell into a deep, dark frown. "Why not?"

"Because I don't work there anymore."

"You mean you already quit?" His frown flipped into a mile-wide grin.

"No, I think I was fired."

"What? . . . When? . . . Why?" His eyes were in shock, but his grin was still firmly in place.

"It happened Thursday afternoon," I said. "Pomeroy had a holy hemorrhage over the fact that I sent Lenny home early on deadline day. He said I was insolent and insubordinate, and he told Mr. Crockett that he and Harrington both wanted me terminated immediately. Since Harrington was involved in the decision, Crockett had no choice but to let me go."

"I don't believe it," Dan said, shaking his head. He wasn't grinning anymore. "You're the best damn reporter that magazine ever had, and Harrington's never shown any concern about your conduct before."

I finished the piece of bacon and took a sip of coffee. "It's not *my* conduct he's concerned about. It's his own."

"His connections with Sabrina and Melody, you mean."

"Right. I'm sure that's the real reason Harrington wanted me fired—so I wouldn't write a story about Melody's murder for *DD* and, during my investigation, uncover the truth about his sex life. His marriage probably couldn't stand the strain of such a scandal. And divorce can be very expensive, you know."

"Tell me about it," Dan grunted, referring to his own costly trek through divorce court. (His promiscuous ex-wife had secured a good settlement by seducing the judge.) Wolfing down another yolk-dipped piece of toast and following it with a slug of coffee, Dan asked, "Was Harrington sleeping with Jocelyn, too?"

"Not according to Sabrina. She fixed Brigitte up with him a few times a couple of years ago, but after Melody joined the agency and Harrington started dating her, he wouldn't settle for anybody else."

"So you don't think he's a suspect?"

"No," I said, in my firmest tone. "Sam Hogarth killed Jocelyn. I *know* it. We've got to concentrate all our skills and energy on proving his guilt. Anything else would be a waste of time."

"I wish I was as convinced as you are."

"You will be—just as soon as you start digging up the evidence."

"But that will be next to impossible, Paige. Just think about it. This is the Manhattan district attorney we're talking about! The most powerful prosecutor in the city. He's rich, smart, politically connected, and *very* well protected. The commissioner will never put me on Hogarth's tail. He'll never put *any* detective on his tail."

"No, but he'll put you on Jocelyn's murder case once you tell him it's connected to the Virginia Pratt case. He'll see right away that you're a better man for the job than Mudd." I forked a gooey piece of egg into my mouth and chewed it slowly. "And you don't have to mention Hogarth to the commissioner at all," I said when I'd swallowed. "You can investigate him on your own and in secret—the same way you did Corona."

"Yeah, sure. I can do that. But it won't make any difference. I still won't be able to get the goods on Hogarth. He's as insulated as Frank Costello. Nobody can touch him." Dan finished off his last egg and the rest of the bacon. "And what proof could I find, anyway? Lipstick on his collar? A smear of chlorine in his clothes? Believe me, everything Hogarth was wearing last night is already at the cleaners. And that St. Christopher medal you're so proud of? It doesn't prove a thing. You didn't actually *see* Hogarth snitch it from Corona's dressing room, and you're the only person alive who knows it was found at the scene of the crime.

"I've got news for you, babe," he added. "It would be a hell of a lot easier to pin this murder on *you* than on Hogarth.

"Well, that's not very comforting!" I said, shuddering.

"No, but it's the truth," he gloomily replied.

"But what if Sabrina comes forward and tells the press about Hogarth's relationship with Jocelyn?" I sputtered. "Wouldn't that point to the DA's guilt?"

"Pointing isn't proving. And besides, didn't you say that Hogarth and Jocelyn were seeing each other on the sneak? Sabrina didn't even know about their arrangement until you filled her in. So how could she go to the papers with an undocumented story like that? It's nothing but hearsay, and no respectable crime reporter would risk his career and reputation—not to mention his all-important relations with the DA's office!—to print it.

"I hate to say this, Paige," Dan concluded, "but if Hogarth is the one who killed Jocelyn, there's a damn good chance he's going to get away with it."

I couldn't finish my breakfast. One more bite would have made me throw up. "But that's unthinkable!" I cried, jumping up from the table and pacing from one end of the kitchen to the other. "We can't let it happen, Dan! We can't just back away and let the bastard go free! There's got to be something we can do!"

Dan stood up and stepped into the middle of the room, blocking me in my tracks. He grabbed hold of my shoulders and squeezed them hard. "Listen to me very carefully," he said, staring into my eyes like an ultrastrict father (or husband). "There is nothing *you* can do. Nothing whatsoever. Do you hear what I'm saying? You are through with this investigation as of now! You're going to lock yourself in this apartment and stay here until I come back."

"But when will that be?" I whimpered.

"I don't know. First, I'm going to the commissioner's office, to get him to pull Mudd off the case and put me on. At least that way you won't have to go in for questioning Monday morning. Then I'll go over to the Barbizon, talk to Jocelyn's neighbors, check out her apartment and the pool. Since Hogarth gave Melody expensive presents, maybe he gave some to Jocelyn, too. Maybe I'll get lucky and find something traceable."

"I saw a mink coat in the changing room at the pool. It was lying on a bench with the rest of her clothes."

"Mudd probably took that into evidence last night. I'll look into it."

I groaned, twisted my shoulders out of Dan's grasp, and started pacing again. "God, Dan! I can't just sit here like a chunk of cheese! I'll go out of my mind. I've got to do something! Isn't there some way I can help?"

"The best way you can help is by staying home and staying safe," he insisted, rolling his sleeves down, buttoning his collar, and tightening his tie. He walked into the living room, took his leather shoulder holster off the back of the chair, and buckled it on. "You can call Sabrina," he said, throwing me a bone. "Tell her about Corona's arrest and Jocelyn's murder; see if she's heard anything." He put on his suit jacket and anchored his hat at a sexy angle on his head.

I was too tired and muddle-headed to protest. "Okay," I said, heaving a loud sigh of defeat. "Be careful . . . and don't forget your coat." I opened the closet and took out his trench coat. Then I walked over to the door and held the garment open while Dan shoved his arms into the sleeves.

Adjusting the coat around his shoulders and turning to face me, he said, "Hey, babe, I could get used to this—you slaving over breakfast and then sending me off to work like a good little wife." He gave me a big wink to make sure I knew he was kidding.

"The engagement's off," I bluffed. "Find yourself another cook and coat-check girl. I've got better things to do with my—"

I was going to say *time,* but he didn't give me enough time. He threw his arms around me, pulled me tight to his chest, and gave me a kiss so deep and long and hard I knew I'd feel its effects forever.

WHEN DAN LEFT, HE TOOK ALL MY ENERGY with him. I was completely spent—so worn-out it was an effort to move. (Well, I'd had a pretty tough day and night, you know! And I hadn't slept in over twenty-eight hours.) I managed to clear the dirty dishes off the table and stack them in the sink, but I didn't have the strength to wash them. I wanted to pour the bacon grease from the cast-iron skillet into the empty coffee can, but I couldn't even lift the damn thing off the stove.

Thinking a few lungfuls of fresh air would clear my head and jump-start my engine, I opened the kitchen door, stepped onto the rusty balcony overlooking the weed-choked rear court-yard, and inhaled deeply. Big mistake. The putrid smell wafting up from the fish store under my apartment made me gag. I stag-gered back into the kitchen and slammed the door, hoping to keep the odor from seeping inside. Then I turned and headed, like a zombie, up the stairs to my bedroom, praying I would make it to the mattress before I passed out.

Halfway up the stairs I remembered Sabrina. I needed to call her. I needed to give her the good news about Corona . . . and the horrible news about Jocelyn. I needed to know if she'd heard anything from Hogarth or Harrington or any cops or de-tectives working the two murders. Forcing my weary legs to wobble back down the stairs and stumble into the living room, I collapsed on the couch and picked up the phone.

I was in the process of dialing Sabrina's private number when my consciousness turned into a cloud and drifted away. The phone fell out of my hand, and my head fell onto a pillow, and every cell in my dead-tired body fell asleep.

Chapter 38

DAN AND I WERE HONEYMOONING IN HAWAII. The sand was hot, the surf was warm, and we were making love on a deserted beach just like Burt Lancaster and Deborah Kerr in that sizzling seaside sex scene in *From Here to Eternity*. Only we weren't wearing bathing suits. And we weren't trying to curb our passion because now we were married and it was full steam ahead. So we were locked in a torrid embrace at the water's edge, exulting in each other's naked flesh, rolling around in the sun and the sand as waves of ecstasy crashed over us, and . . . well, you get the picture. We were having a pretty swell time.

So swell, in fact, that I was aware of nothing else in the whole wide, wonderful world but the sunny, surging pleasure of it all. I didn't realize that Bleecker Street was teeming with loud, laughing, late Saturday afternoon shoppers, or that Luigi was having a big sale on littleneck clams and trout, or that Faicco's deli had finally received its long-awaited shipment of Sicilian salami. I didn't know that every machine in the Laundromat across the street was in use, or that rowdy NYU students were lining up at John's Pizzeria for their first meal of the day.

And I had no idea that someone wearing a black knit cap and a brown leather jacket had sneaked through the courtyard behind my building, climbed the metal stairs to my balcony, entered my apartment through the back door, and crept—gun in hand—into the living room, where I was sleeping. It wasn't until the intruder jabbed me in the ribs and ordered me to wake up that I opened my eyes and saw that I wasn't in Hawaii anymore—and that the man hovering over me wasn't Dan.

"Good afternoon, Mrs. Turner," the man said, standing next to the couch and staring down at my supine body with a hideous grin on his face. He was aiming a small handgun with a big silencer at the center of my chest. "Have a nice nap?"

I didn't recognize him at first. With the tight black cap pulled down past his cheeks and over his eyebrows, and his features twisted in an ugly smirk, he looked like an evil, earless version of Batman. But when he yanked off the cap and threw it on the floor—thereby revealing his thick crop of wavy silver-gray hair—I came to the sudden but not shocking realization that the grinning gunman was Sam Hogarth.

I'll never know how I did it, but I managed to keep my panic-stricken scream to myself. "And a good afternoon to you, Mister District Attorney," I said, fighting to keep my tone light, struggling to hide the fact that my insides were convulsing in terror. (I didn't want to give him the satisfaction of watching me squirm.) Rising up on my elbows, I forced myself to smile and said, "To what do I owe this unexpected pleasure?" I hoped my lips weren't trembling.

"You think you're pretty cool, don't you?" he snorted, blue eyes blazing. "You think you're God's gift to Manhattan—a fearless female crime reporter with the DA's balls on a fucking string. Ha! I bet you don't feel so fearless now! And I doubt if you'll look so cool when I put a bullet between your breasts."

He was getting turned on. I could see it in his greedy eyes and in the way he was standing (legs apart, pelvis thrust forward). Remembering what Jocelyn had said about Hogarth—that he was a closet rapist; that he liked to rip off her clothes and take her against her will—I grew doubly alarmed. Was he planning to rape me as well as murder me?

"I don't understand," I said, slowly, carefully, cagily (and, I'm surprised to say, successfully) inching myself up to a sitting position. "What's going on here? How did you get into my apartment?" I hugged my arms to my waist and slumped forward, hoping to make my breasts a less interesting and accessible target.

"I'm the DA, honey," he crowed. "This city belongs to me. I can open any door I want." He took a ring of master keys out of his pocket and proudly jangled them in front of my face. "I didn't need a key today, though, since you were kind enough to leave your back door open."

Great. I must have forgotten to lock the door after going onto the balcony for a breath of fishy air. I was the biggest idiot who ever walked the earth. If Hogarth didn't shoot me soon, I was going to grab his gun and do it myself.

"Okay, that explains *how* you got in," I said, "but it doesn't explain *why* you wanted to get in. So will you please tell me why you're here and why you're pointing that ugly gun at me?"

"Don't play games with me, doll," he said. "You know exactly why I'm here."

"No, I don't!" I cried, sensing that the time for acting cool was over. I dropped my daring detective routine and let my scaredy-cat emotions out of their cage. "I really don't know what's going on! Please tell me what's wrong," I begged. "What have I done? If you're going to kill me, couldn't you at least do me the favor of explaining why?" If I could get him to start talking, I reasoned, maybe he wouldn't start shooting.

Hogarth's grin grew even wider. "So the notorious Paige Turner isn't as smart or brave as people think she is," he said, gloating, grunting, glaring at me in triumph. He stepped away from the couch, and lowered the gun to his side. "You want to know why you're going to die, pussy? Then I'll tell you. It's because you're a devious, conniving slut, that's why! You wormed your way into my office under false pretenses, and you asked a lot of disrespectful questions, and you wouldn't stop prying into matters that didn't concern you. I had your number from the start. Then, when Candy admitted she told you about our secret sex arrangement, and that you would back her up if she decided to go to the papers with the story, I knew both of you had to die."

"But I never said I would talk to the press! When did Candy tell you that?"

"At approximately three fifteen this morning," he said, still grinning. "Right before I drowned her."

"*You* drowned her?" I sputtered, acting as astonished and confused as Lucy always does when she's caught with her bloomers down. "I thought Tony Corona killed her! I found his St. Christopher medal at the scene and I—"

"Yeah, that was a pretty slick trick," Hogarth said, eyes glistening with pride. "I should get a medal for that one."

His ego was showing, and it was time for me to stroke it. "You mean *you* dropped the medal in the pool?" I fawned, batting my lashes, acting impressed, hoping to keep him talking forever. "That really *was* a slick trick! Incredibly clever. But how did you get it off Corona's neck?"

"Ha! That was the easy part. The stupid bastard took it off for me. While I was talking to Tony in his dressing room last night, he was pacing around, nervously pulling on the chain, and the clasp broke. He yanked the medal off and slapped it down on the makeup table. I stuck it in my pocket on the way out."

"You are one smooth operator," I wheedled, buttering his ego on both sides. "A man of true ingenuity! I never, ever would have guessed that you—"

"Oh, can the crap!" Hogarth snapped. "You think you can fool me with your phony flappy-eyed performance? When are you going to get the fucking message? I'm the goddamn district attorney, dollface. I have a lot more connections and inside informers than you or your stupid boyfriend will ever have! And according to Detective Dominick Mudd of the Nineteenth Precinct, you never even mentioned Corona's name when he questioned you at the Barbizon. So you were either lying to him, or you're lying to me."

"I was lying to him!" I croaked, telling the God's honest truth. "You've got to believe me! I thought Corona killed Melody *and* Candy."

"Maybe you did, and maybe you didn't," he sneered, "but that hardly matters now, does it, pussy? Detective Casey O'Connor of Midtown North tells me your big bad boyfriend arrested Tony Corona for Melody's murder last night, and that he brought him into the station for booking around three this morning—which we both know was the approximate time of Candy's death. So you knew damn well—even *before* I admitted it to you—that I killed Candy. And I knew that you knew. And that's why I'm here, you stupid bitch—and that's why you're going to die. Your hotshot boyfriend will be next."

"But killing us won't keep the truth from coming out!" I cried, even though I knew it probably would. (I hadn't even had a chance to tell Sabrina and Abby the whole story!) "Dan and I aren't the only ones who know what you did," I blustered on, "and if we're found dead, you'll be convicted of three murders instead of one!" (I didn't believe a word I said, but I'll defend to the death my right to say it.)

"Not a chance, dollface," Hogarth declared. "I'll never be convicted, or even accused, of a goddamn thing. All three murders will be laid at Frank Costello's door. I'll make sure of that. There's a big mob war going on, in case you haven't heard. And with Tony Corona under indictment for a related homicide, it'll be a cinch to link three more killings to Costello's murder squad."

"You're out of your mind!" I screeched. "Dan's with the police commissioner right now, planning a full-scale investigation into your connections with Sabrina Stanhope and Melody and Candy. And my boss, Oliver Rice Harrington, is standing by to print the facts in all his newspapers and magazines! If you kill me or Dan, you'll go straight to the chair."

Oh, who was I trying to kid? The goddamn district attorney, that's who. I was up against Goliath without a stone or a sling. I might as well paint a bull's-eye on my bosom and lie back down on the couch.

Hogarth had the same idea. "Shut up!" he said, leering at me and aiming his gun at my chest. "I'm sick of listening to your whiny voice. And I've heard enough of your absurd and boring lies. I'm in the mood for something more stimulating. So take off all your clothes, sweetheart, and lie down on your back. I want to see you helpless and naked before I shoot you to smithereens."

Chapter 39

THE JIG WAS UP. I HAD TWO CHOICES. I COULD strip down and try to lure Hogarth into raping me instead of killing me. Or I could shriek like a banshee, fly off the couch in a fury, kick him in the groin, and then hurl myself through the living room window—hopefully *before* he plugged me full of holes. In my freaked-out, stressed-out, burned-out condition, however, neither option was viable. I couldn't move. I couldn't even breathe. All I could do was squeeze my eyes shut and pray for a miracle . . . or, at the very least, a speedy death.

Since my eyes were closed so tightly, I didn't see what happened next. And since the sounds I heard were so odd and unexpected, they didn't quite penetrate my addled consciousness. I was braced for the silenced thwack of a bullet hitting flesh and bone (*my* flesh and bone), but what I heard was something entirely different. It was a crazy scraping, skritch-scratching sound that took off from the rear of the kitchen, charged into the living room, and then changed into a ferocious growl.

My eyes flew open and searched for the source of the growl, which I located on the floor at Hogarth's feet. But when I caught my first glimpse of the savage, long-nosed, short-haired growler, I thought I was dreaming again.

It was Otto! Jimmy's brave and beloved little dachshund, Otto! The dog had dashed through the open kitchen door, scrambled into the living room, and seized one of Hogarth's pants cuffs in his teeth. And now—judging from his fierce and tenacious gnashing, snarling, gnawing, and twisting—Otto was determined to keep his jaws clenched on that cuff forever. Hogarth was kicking and cursing and trying to shake the little dog loose, but his frantic efforts were having no effect at all. Otto was relentless.

And Hogarth was so distracted, he was no longer pointing the gun at me!

I felt a sweet spurt of relief—but it didn't last more than a split second. Before I could gasp or even blink, Hogarth spun around, straightened his arm down toward the floor, and aimed the gun at Otto.

"Nooooooo!" I wailed, jumping off the couch and lunging forward, hoping to knock Hogarth off balance and make him miss his mark. But before I could reach him, the gun went off. And a horrible, gut-wrenching howl pierced the air. And a series of pitiful whimpers filled my ears. And my legs buckled, and my soul crumbled, and I fell to the floor in a heartbroken heap. And then I just lay there, coiled in the fetal position, sobbing uncontrollably and praying that Hogarth would kill me immediately—spare me the agony of seeing my poor little canine savior suffer and die.

Only half of my prayer was answered. Fortunately, it was the latter half. As I was lying there waiting to meet my maker, a cold, wet nose nuzzled my neck! And a warm, wet tongue licked my face! And before I knew what was happening, Otto was snuggling up next to me on the floor, curling his completely intact little sausage-shaped body into the curve of my stomach and snuffling contentedly.

It took me a few seconds to realize that the horrible howls and whimpers of pain had come from Hogarth, not Otto (thank God). But it wasn't until I sat up and looked around, and saw all the blood in the middle of the rug, that I understood the cause of his tortured cries. Hogarth had—most effectively and deservedly (and, for me, quite conveniently)—shot himself in the foot!

I would have laughed out loud at the crazy, felicitous justice of it all, but I didn't dare. Hogarth was still standing strong (on one leg, to be sure, but with the gun still gripped in his steady hand, one leg was one too many). Braced against the bookcase for balance and holding his mangled, bloodied foot up off the floor, the homicidal DA had stopped whimpering. Now he was actually grinning again. Eyes gleaming and teeth flashing, he raised his arm out straight, pointed the silenced pistol at my face, and said, "Bye-bye, Paige Turner. It's been a pleasure doing business with—"

Hogarth never finished his sentence or fired the gun. He got his skull cracked open instead—by a very handsome, bearded beatnik poet (and dog owner) swinging a two-ton cast-iron skillet dripping with bacon grease. One solid *whomp* and Hogarth went down, crashing to the floor like a huge duffel bag full of dirt. His gun skidded under the couch and his face landed squarely in a puddle of blood flecked with bits of bone and shoe leather. He wasn't grinning anymore.

Jimmy dropped the skillet on the floor and hurried over to Otto and me. "Are you all right?" he croaked, sinking into a squat, scooping Otto up in the crook of one arm and hugging him close to his chest. He flung his other arm around my shoulders and gave me a wild-eyed look. "What happened? Who *is* that creep? Did he hurt you?" He kept shifting his eyes back and forth from Otto to me, making certain we were both unharmed.

I was about to assure Jimmy that I was okay when Abby plowed through the back door and stomped into the kitchen. "Hey, Birmingham!" she squawked, spotting the top of his head above the telephone table and marching across the linoleum. "What the hell happened to you? You were out in the courtyard for ages! How long does it take for a dog to poop? And why are you—?"

The bloody scene on the living room floor stunned Abby into silence. She stopped dead in her tracks and took it all in, a look of sheer horror deforming her beautiful face. Then, when she saw that Jimmy and Otto and I were all okay—clinging to each other in a shaky huddle on the edge of the rug—she let out a yelp and leapt forward, arms spread wide enough to embrace all three of us at once.

But as her leading foot came down to the floor, it landed in a splotch of bacon grease and slipped right out from under her. She came flying toward us like an awkward angel—or, more precisely, a giant albino bat on the wing. She fell smack in the middle of our huddle and floundered around for a couple of seconds, but quickly sprang up—giggling and unhurt—into a kneeling position. Then she wrapped her wings around us, pulled us into a tight, cozy circle, and released a joyful sigh. And then Otto (who shall now and forevermore be known as Otto the Wonder Wienie Dog) poked his little head up through the center of the circle and licked all of our faces until they were shiny with slobber.

I was in Heaven—and by some incredible miracle (okay, *several* incredible miracles), I didn't have to die to get there.

HOGARTH WASN'T DEAD EITHER, BUT HE WAS pretty close to it. He never regained consciousness while we were waiting for the police and the medics to arrive. Then, when they came and saw who he was and the terrible shape he was in, he was whisked away on a stretcher and rushed to the nearest hospital in a scream of sirens.

I wasn't sorry to see him go.

I *was* sorry, however, to see Detective Sergeant Nick Flannagan of the Sixth Precinct come strutting into my apartment, brandishing his ego along with his badge. Abby and I had had dealings with Detective Flannagan a few months before, when he was trying to pin a gruesome murder on a perfectly innocent gay friend of ours, and my feelings about the man were not favorable.

He didn't like me, either.

I had wanted to get in touch with Dan before calling the local station (the last thing in the world we needed was yet another homicide detective from yet another police precinct getting involved in this crazy, mixed-up case!). But Hogarth needed immediate medical attention, and I had to call for an ambulance right away—which meant I also had to report the name of the injured party, and the fact that he had been hurt during an attempted murder. Hence, the unwelcome appearance of Detective Nick Flannagan.

"Good evening, Mrs. Turner," he said, swaggering over to me, screwing his boyish, clean-shaven face into a nasty smirk. "We meet again. Tell me, have you developed a homicide habit, or do you just get a kick out of stirring up trouble?"

"Neither," I said. "I'm a justice junkie. I like to see *real* criminals punished for their actual crimes."

"Oh, yeah?" he scoffed. "And your idea of a *real* criminal is the Manhattan district attorney?" The expression on his face made it clear he thought I should be strapped in a straitjacket straightaway.

"You bet your sweet badge!" I seethed. "Sam Hogarth murdered an assistant hat designer and high-priced call girl named Jocelyn Fritz this morning, and he tried to murder me this afternoon. And if Otto the Wonder Wienie Dog hadn't foiled his attempt, and if the poet laureate of Greenwich Village, Jimmy Birmingham, hadn't brained him with an iron skillet, our illustrious district attorney would be out on the streets tonight, lurking in the shadows, aiming to put a bullet—or two, or three—in my fiancé Detective Dan Street's back!"

To say that I was upset would be like calling Daffy Duck a tad touchy.

Flannagan didn't believe me, of course. I could see the wheels turning in his narrow little mind as he stared daggers at Jimmy, jumping to the warped conclusion that the bearded bohemian was to blame. (Flannagan was, I knew from experience, intolerant of all nonconformists.) Looking for a way to substantiate his biased belief, he sat Jimmy, Abby, and me (and Otto, who was sticking to me like glue) down at the kitchen table and grilled us for hours.

Okay, it was probably for just forty minutes or so. But the interrogation would have lasted much longer if Dan hadn't heard the district attorney's name and my Bleecker Street address broadcast over the police radio and sped down to the Village in a panic to see if I was all right.

"Paige!" he hollered, running up the stairs. "Paige!" he cried, bursting through my front door like a tiger through a ring of fire. "Are you—?" Dan came up short when he saw Flannagan standing near the door, positioned like a prison guard between the ME's evidence-gathering team in the living room and my team of saviors and supporters at the kitchen table. But when his eyes landed on me and he saw that I was alive and uninjured, he bounded across the floor, grabbed me up in his arms, lifted me out of my chair, and hugged me so hard all the air was expelled from my lungs in one thunderous *whoosh*.

Having slid off my lap when Dan hoisted me to my feet, Otto hit the floor barking. And when he saw the way Dan was squeezing me, he started growling again. And then, when Dan pulled my head back and clamped his mouth down over mine, Otto clamped his teeth onto Dan's pants cuff and—snarling and gnashing just as doggedly as he had before—gave a rousing reenactment of the scene in which he saved my life.

I was elated. I laughed and clapped so hard they probably heard me in the Hamptons. Otto's encore performance was, I thought, a fitting denouement to the drama of the last four days, and I was doggone glad to see the final curtain fall.

Epilogue

THE ENSUING EVENTS OF THAT MURDEROUS BUT miraculous Saturday night are kind of blurry in my mind. Except for a piece of bacon that morning, and a catnap that afternoon, I hadn't eaten or slept in eons. And considering the fact that I had gotten engaged to the love of my life that morning and my life had been nearly obliterated that very afternoon—well, I think you can understand why my body and brain were running on empty.

I wasn't *totally* oblivious, though, so I was able to take note of the major stuff that happened that evening. And for those of you who are still interested, here's a brief report.

I remember Dan telling Flannagan that he (Dan) had been put in charge of the case and that his (Flannagan's) services were no longer needed, and I have a pretty sharp recollection of Flannagan spewing out a stream of curses and leaving my apartment in a huff. (I found that part rather amusing.)

I recall that Dan made sure the ME's team collected, tagged, and bagged all the important evidence—the silenced pistol, Hogarth's knit cap, the greasy skillet, etc.—even though it was an attempted rather than actual murder scene and Hogarth was the perpetrator rather than the victim. (Dan was leaving nothing to chance.)

I saw that several samples of blood, bone, and shoe leather were collected before my gory Woolworth's area rug was rolled up and removed, and then I watched while the bullet was pried out of the floor. (Luckily, it hadn't blasted all the way through Luigi's ceiling. Otherwise, the fish odor would have had a direct duct to my living room.)

After all the work was done, and all the officers and evidence collectors were gone, Dan left to "take care of business" at the hospital and the station house. Telling Abby and Jimmy to take good care of me, he gave me a parting soul kiss and said he'd be back later.

As soon as he split, I walked across the bare wood floor to the couch and picked up the phone. I couldn't put it off any longer—I had to call Sabrina. Although I was busting to tell her that Dan had arrested Corona for the murder of Virginia, I really did *not* want to tell her that Jocelyn had been killed. (I can't bear to be the bearer of bad news.) I finally faced the music, though, and dialed her private number.

Our conversation was short and bittersweet. She already knew about Corona's arrest (Detective O'Connor had leaked the news to Sabrina as well as to Hogarth), and she had learned about Jocelyn's death from the manager of the Barbizon, whom she contacted after all her phone calls to Jocelyn had gone unanswered. She had tried to call me, too, she said, but my line had been busy for hours. (I knew this was true, since my receiver was off the hook from the moment I fell asleep and dropped it on the floor, until a few dreadful decades later, when I snatched it up to call for an ambulance.)

Sabrina didn't know whether Jocelyn had drowned by accident or been murdered, but she wasn't surprised when I gave her the lowdown. And she wasn't shocked that the DA had done the dirty deed. She *was* shocked, however, that Hogarth had tried to kill me, and she felt so sad and guilty about it that I thought she'd never stop apologizing. When I told her how Hogarth had suffered for his sins, however, she felt a lot better. And when I described in detail how Otto and Jimmy had saved my life, she was euphoric. She was going to send Jimmy a cash reward, she said, and Otto a ten-year supply of dog biscuits.

When my phone call with Sabrina ended, the celebration began. And that's when my brain and body *really* went on the blink. I have a fuzzy recollection of drinking glass after glass of Chianti, eating slice after slice of pepperoni pizza, smoking a jillion cigarettes, laughing my head off over nothing in particular, crying my eyes out over the tragic deaths of Virginia and Jocelyn, and rejoicing in the knowledge that Hogarth and Corona were, in one way or another, going to pay for their atrocious crimes.

I was also raving on and on about Dan's and my engagement, clinking glasses with Abby and Jimmy in a never-ending series of silly toasts, and stroking Otto's soft, warm, brave little back till it was almost bald.

Sometime around midnight (I think), Dan came back. He had a glass of wine and tried to join in the festivities, but he looked exhausted. Taking their cue from Dan's tired eyes and sagging shoulders, Abby and Jimmy said good night and went across the hall. They would have taken Otto with them, but I had grown so attached to his sweet, protective presence, I wouldn't let him go. I begged them to let Otto spend the night with me, and they cheerfully agreed.

As soon as they left, Dan guided me upstairs and helped me get undressed. (Well, I was sort of tipsy, you know! And it's hard to take off your sweater when you're cradling a dachshund in your arms and won't, even for a minute, put him down.) Then, after Dan got Otto and me into the bed and tucked us in, he went back downstairs and slept on the couch, in his clothes. I guess he thought one guard dog wasn't enough.

WHEN OTTO AND I GOT UP IN THE MORNING, Dan was already gone. He'd left a note on the kitchen table saying he was going to his own apartment to shower and change, then heading uptown to pick up his daughter, Katy, for our ritual Sunday lunch and afternoon movie. He said I should meet him and Katy at Schrafft's at the usual time. I gave Otto a bowl of water and a leftover piece of pizza, and ran upstairs to get ready.

I was happy as a clam (or any other merry mollusk). I'd had a good night's sleep and I felt almost sane. Corona was in jail, Hogarth was in the hospital, and I was engaged to be married! I took a long, hot shower, washed and dried my hair, slathered on some makeup, and put on my favorite slim gray skirt and pale blue sweater (Sears Roebuck, of course). I even put on a string of pearls (cultured, not real) and a dressy pair of black suede pumps (Thom McAn, $7.99). In spite of my low-cost attire, I thought I looked like a million bucks.

When I went next door to return Otto, Abby was sitting at

her kitchen table in her red negligee, long black hair fanned out over her shoulders, drinking coffee, and smoking a Pall Mall. Jimmy was still sleeping upstairs. "Hey, babe," she said when I stepped inside. "You're looking pretty slick this morning. Pearls and pumps, no less. Just like a married lady."

I let out a goofy giggle, walked over to the stove to pour myself a cup of coffee, then sat down at the table with her. I had thought Abby was happy for me, but when I took a good look at her face, I saw I was mistaken. She had a sulk the size of Kentucky on her kisser.

"What's the matter?" I asked. "Is something wrong?"

"Oh, nothing much," she said with an overly dramatic sigh. "I'm just losing my best friend, that's all. She's getting married and moving away, you dig? I'll probably never see her again." If her lips had been any poutier, they'd have been drooping down over her chin.

"That's nuts!" I said, hurrying to reassure her. "I may be getting married, but I'm not moving away. No way, Doris Day! I *like* it here." I really hadn't given this matter much thought before, but now that I was, I felt a very strong desire to stay put. "Dan will move in with me!" I declared, hoping my words would turn out to be true. "I couldn't live anywhere else but here. And we could fix the place up a lot—carpet the living room, buy a real couch, plant a garden in the courtyard. The apartment's small, but it's fine for two people . . . even three," I added, thinking ahead, imagining how I could turn my office into a neat little nursery.

"Absolutely not, Dot!" Abby cried, pounding her fist like a gavel on the tabletop. "That's a big fat no, Flo! I refuse to live next door to a screaming baby! I think you and Dan better move to Levittown." It was obvious that she was joking. Her sulk had turned into a smile so wide you could slide a ruler through it sideways.

Crisis over, we laughed and chatted together for a while, drinking coffee, smoking cigarettes, feeling good about the future. Then it was time for me to go. "Gotta split, Ab," I said, standing up and walking to the door. "I'm meeting Dan and Katy uptown for lunch."

"Later, gator," she chirped, tying her hair up in a pony and waving bye-bye with the tail.

The minute I got back to my place the phone started ringing.

Thinking it was Dan calling to make sure I got his note and would be leaving on time, I picked up the receiver and cooed, "Don't worry, baby cakes. I'm on my way. I'll be there in twenty minutes."

"No rush," Mr. Crockett said. "Tomorrow morning will be soon enough."

"Huh?" I was a tad confused.

"Tomorrow is Monday," Crockett grunted. "Be in the office at the usual time. Sort the mail, clip the papers, make the coffee."

I finally got the message. "You mean I haven't been fired? I've still got a job?"

"Right. Harrington wants you to come back to work. And he wants to see you in his office tomorrow at eleven."

I was too stunned to speak. What was this all about? Did Harrington want to apologize for the way he kicked me out before, or did he just want to do it again?

"So?" Crockett asked.

"So what?" I replied.

"So are you coming in?"

"Uh, yeah, I guess so," I mumbled, knowing I wanted to keep my job, but also knowing that Dan wouldn't want me to.

"Good. See ya tomorrow."

Click.

I stood there for a few seconds, holding the dead receiver to my ear like a dope, trying to figure out how I should deal with this new development. Then, realizing I couldn't make an informed decision until I spoke with Crockett and Harrington again, I gave up trying. I slammed down the phone, put on my jacket and beret, stuffed my ciggies in my purse, and took off for Schrafft's.

THE POPULAR BUT DIGNIFIED RESTAURANT WAS packed, as it always was on Sunday. All the seats at the long wood and marble counter near the entrance were occupied— mostly by middle-aged women in furs and hats, their purses and white gloves nestled securely in their laps. They were sipping martinis or manhattans or hot tea, and savoring their creamed chicken on toast or lobster pie or tomato surprise. A couple of men were sitting at the counter, too, but in their dark suits and fedoras, and with their platters of steak and potatoes, they looked out of place.

I made my way through the crowd to the doorway of the dining room, hung my jacket and beret on the nearby coatrack, and looked around for Dan and Katy. They were sitting at a table for four in the corner, lost in an intimate but animated conversation, looking very happy to be together. I felt like an intruder as I walked toward them, but the minute they saw me approaching, both of their faces lit up.

"Hi, Paige!" Katy said, as Dan jumped to his feet and pulled out a chair for me. "You look so pretty today."

"Thanks!" I said. "I appreciate the compliment, but if anybody looks pretty, it's you." I wasn't just being polite. With her pale blonde hair, perfectly proportioned features, porcelain complexion, and bright blue eyes, Katy is a portrait painter's dream. She's fifteen years young, fresh as a flower, and so poised she makes other girls her age seem gawky and rude—which is a flat miracle when you consider the fact that her beautiful mother is a bitch and a tramp. (Hey, don't blame me! Those are *Dan's* words, not mine. I've never even met the woman, so I certainly wouldn't presume to categorize *or* condemn her behavior—no matter how bitchy and trampy it is.)

Dan sat back down and put his hand on my arm. "I was just telling my daughter about us," he said, with an earnest wink. "She knows that I've asked you to be my wife. And she's very happy about it, aren't you, Katy?" He turned and put his other hand on her arm, encouraging her to speak.

I held my breath and crossed my fingers. Had Katy given Dan her honest opinion? Did she *really* approve of our engagement? Was she truly okay with the thought of me being her stepmother, or was she just trying to please her dad?

"Are you kidding?" she said, beaming at me across the table. "I'm crazy about the idea! I like you so much, Paige, and it's fun when we're all three together, and I love seeing my father so happy. He was sad for a long, long time, and I knew that he was lonely, and I was always worried about him. Now I won't have to worry anymore!"

So, I ask you, who was the most parental person at our table? (I'll give you one guess.)

"You can't imagine how glad I am to hear that, Katy," I said, stretching my free arm across the table and putting my hand on hers. "I love your father, and I love you, and I think our collective future is going to be great."

"Cool!" she said, giving me and Dan a cheerful nod, then gently removing her arm and hand from our grasp. She picked up her menu and scanned it. "I'm starving! I want a bacon, avocado, and tomato sandwich on cheese bread, and a hot fudge sundae for dessert." Her bright blue eyes were twinkling in anticipation.

I placed the same order (well, it sounded really good), and Dan ordered—yep!—a platter of steak and potatoes. And then we relaxed and proceeded to have a wonderful time—laughing, chatting, eating, telling jokes—enjoying each other's company to the hilt. We could have posed for a Norman Rockwell illustration.

After lunch we went to see the new movie *Oklahoma!,* starring Gordon MacRae and Shirley Jones. It was a fabulous, wide-screen, Technicolor production, with gorgeous scenery and great Rodgers and Hammerstein music. Katy loved it. I probably would have loved it, too, if every time MacRae came on screen I hadn't been reminded of the previous Friday night at the Copa, when Abby spotted him sitting with the other celebrities up in the mezzanine, and we were all waiting for a Mafia-connected murderer to come out and sing to us.

WHEN THE MOVIE WAS OVER, DAN TOOK KATY back to the Upper East Side, where she lived with her mother, then went to the station house to tackle the pressing paperwork on the Hogarth and Corona cases. I took the subway home. I was sorry that I wouldn't be spending the evening with Dan, but I was glad to have the free time to write up the final notes for my story. Since I was going back to work in the morning, I needed all the free time I could get.

I had wanted to tell Dan that Crockett had called—that I hadn't been fired and was still a staff writer at *Daring Detective*—but I couldn't see discussing it in front of Katy. It would have disturbed the peace and spoiled our lovely afternoon. And I knew Dan didn't want that to happen any more than I did. I would tell him tomorrow, I decided, after I felt out the scene at the office, and met with Harrington, and had a better idea of what I wanted to do.

As soon as I got home, I changed my clothes and washed my face. Then I sat down at the typewriter and added all the details about Corona's arrest, Jocelyn's murder, and my own near demise to my story notes. When I was finished, the document numbered thirty-six pages. I was almost out of paper, and my typewriter ribbon had faded to gray. It had been a busy few days.

Too tired and ill equipped to do any more writing, I went downstairs and called Sabrina. I wanted to see how she and Charlotte were doing. I also wanted to know if she'd heard any further talk about the murders, or received any phone calls or unannounced visits from reporters or police. She hadn't. O'Connor and I were the only ones who'd contacted her about the crimes. She said that she and Charlotte were both thrilled that Melody's and Candy's killers had been caught, but were still shaken by Hogarth's attempt to murder me, and very concerned about how the soon-to-erupt scandal would affect their own lives.

I told Sabrina that Dan and I would do our best to keep her name out of the papers, but we couldn't promise anything. She understood completely. Having already come to terms with the fact that Virginia and Jocelyn would be exposed as prostitutes, she knew her call girl enterprise was likely to be exposed as well. She had, therefore, called an emergency meeting with the rest of her girls to tell them that she was—for personal reasons—disbanding the agency. She gave each one a check for a thousand dollars and urged them to find legal occupations. Ethel Maguire (aka Brigitte) would have no trouble making the transition, she said, since she would be graduating from nursing school soon.

In the event that she was arrested and sent to jail, Sabrina had arranged with the landlord for Charlotte to stay on in her apartment as maid and caretaker. And she had set aside enough money for Charlotte to pay both the rent and Virginia's brother's bills for up to a year. After that, she said, she'd be bankrupt.

Sabrina was still hoping, however, that she wouldn't be imprisoned for so long, and that she'd be able to set up and finance the new business she wanted to launch: the Stanhope Modeling Agency. Some of her girls would make wonderful models, she thought, and she'd already spoken to some of her wealthy clients about investing in her perfectly legitimate new enterprise. She didn't know a whole lot about the modeling business

yet, she laughingly admitted, but how much different from her
previous profession could it be?

I GOT TO THE OFFICE EARLY THE NEXT MORN-
ing, and the place was a complete mess. The Coffeemaster had
an inch-thick layer of muck on the bottom, and all the cups
were dirty. The contents of the cream pitcher had curdled, and
sugar was scattered all over the table and the floor. Lenny's
drawing table was heaped with so many unfinished layouts and
boards, I figured he hadn't been in to work since the day I sent
him home sick, and my desk was piled halfway to the ceiling
with unclipped newspapers, unopened mail, unsorted deliver-
ies, unedited manuscripts, and uncorrected page proofs.

Ugh. Maybe I didn't want my job back after all.

The first thing I did was check out the morning papers. The
main headline on every front page of every edition was TONY
CORONA ARRESTED FOR MURDER!, or words to the same effect.
Virginia was named in some of the headlines and all of the stories, of course, but the reporters had—for obvious reasons—
focused ninety-nine percent of their attention and copy on the
accused killer rather than the murder victim. A world-famous
singer and movie star would sell a hell of a lot more newspapers
than a lowly secretary for an accounting firm (or even a high-
priced hooker—a fact not mentioned in any of the articles).

Each paper had a brief write-up about the death of a young
Saks Fifth Avenue hat designer named Jocelyn Fritz, who
drowned in the pool at the Barbizon Hotel for Women, but none
of the accounts mentioned murder. It was also reported that
Manhattan District Attorney Sam Hogarth had been admitted to
the hospital late Saturday afternoon with severe head and foot
injuries. He was in critical condition. The cause of his injuries
had yet to be determined, but some newswriters suggested they
might have been mob-inflicted, in retaliation for the DA's
courageous crusade against organized crime.

So much for accurate journalism. If the full truth about Hogarth and Corona was ever going to be reported, I realized, the
reporter would have to be me.

I slapped all the papers closed and carried them into Mr.
Crockett's office. I wanted to put them out of my sight. As I was
returning to the main workroom, Mr. Crockett came through the

front door and gave me—wonder of wonders!—a hearty hello. He was clearly glad to see me. Knowing that now was the best time to talk to him—while he was weak from a debilitating caffeine deficiency—I walked right up to him and asked why Harrington had changed his mind about firing me, and why he wanted to see me in his office.

"Harrington didn't fire you," he said. "Pomeroy did it without his knowledge."

"You mean Pomeroy lied?"

"Right. Scummy thing to do. I wanted to fire *him*, but Harrington said no. Family reasons. And blood is thicker than whatever, so we're stuck with the bastard."

Figures. "So why does Harrington want me to come to his office?

"Don't know. You gotta go see for yourself." He hung up his hat and coat. "But make the coffee first, okay?"

As I carried the Coffeemaster into the hall and headed for the ladies' room to wash it, Lenny burst out of the stairwell, huffing and puffing like a marathon runner at the finish line. He was thinner and more red-faced than usual, but he'd made it up nine flights of stairs, so I knew he'd made a full recovery. I walked over, patted him on the back, and, while I was waiting for him to catch his breath, gave him a quick rundown of recent office events.

He was shocked that I'd been fired, relieved that I'd been re-hired, and very upset that his illness had caused me so much trouble. I told him not to worry about it—that I'd been glad to have the time off, and that our crabby bosses and lazy coworkers had been at such a loss without us, we'd probably be treated with kid gloves from now on. Or for a couple of hours at least.

As if to prove my words, Mike and Mario stepped out of the elevator and walked toward us—faint but detectable smiles slipping across their faces. They were surprised to see me, but not sorry. You could tell by the way they each nodded and said, "Good morning, Paige," without a single snicker, rude comment, or lousy joke about my name. They even gave Lenny a civil hello.

OLIVER RICE HARRINGTON GAVE ME AN EQUALLY civil welcome when I arrived at his office later that morning.

"Thank you for coming," he said, ushering me inside and guiding me to the guest chair closest to his desk. He offered me a cigarette, lit it, then sat down and extended his "sincere" apologies for the "inappropriate" actions of his "headstrong" cousin Pomeroy, and for the "unseemly" way in which I was "terminated," and for the "unpleasantness" of our last "visit," for which he took full responsibility, asking me to forget it ever happened. (I knew I wouldn't, but I said I would.)

After that, he raked his fingers through his salt-and-pepper hair, adjusted his wire-rimmed glasses on his prominent nose, and got down to business.

"I asked you here to discuss a matter of some importance to us both, Mrs. Turner," he said, eyes fastened on mine. "I know that you're working on a story about the murders of Virginia Pratt and Jocelyn Fritz, and I want to purchase exclusive rights to that story for my newspapers and magazines, *Daring Detective* included. And after your report has been featured in the selected Harrington News publications, I want you to turn the story into a full-length crime novel for Harrington House Books. I am, of course, prepared to pay a large sum for your efforts, with a twenty-five percent advance due the day you sign the contracts."

I was agog. I took a deep drag on my cigarette and exhaled slowly, through my nose, hoping the sting of the rising smoke would scare my eyeballs back into their sockets.

"So what do you say, Mrs. Turner? Does my proposal interest you?"

"Well, uh . . . sure," I said, doing my best to act blasé. "But I can't give you a commitment right now. I have to talk things over with my fiancé first."

"Ah, yes," he said, "the indefatigable Detective Dan Street. You must consult with him, of course. And congratulations on your engagement."

Harrington was starting to spook me out. "How do you know so much about me?" I asked. "Are you having me tailed or something?"

He chuckled and leaned back in his chair. "I run a successful *news* empire, Mrs. Turner. There isn't much that escapes my notice."

I decided to test the validity of his statement. "Are you aware that District Attorney Sam Hogarth murdered Jocelyn Fritz?"

"I've heard rumors to that effect."

"And that he also tried to murder me?"

"Yes . . ."

"And are you willing to publish all the dirty details about the DA's many crimes—including the fact that he had a hot and heavy relationship with *your* favorite call girl?"

A storm cloud fell over his face, but he remained calm and in control. "I was getting to that point, Mrs. Turner," he said, "and these are my terms: I *expect* you to write the truth about Hogarth and Melody, but I want you to keep *my* name out of it."

"Oh, so that's it," I sneered. "You're trying to buy me off. I should have known your offer was too good to be true. Tell me, Mr. Harrington," I said, in the most scathing tone I could summon, "are there any other special clauses in your contract I should know about?"

"Just one," he said. "Somebody else I want you to protect."

"And who, pray tell, is that?"

"Sabrina Stanhope."

SO THERE I SAT, IN A CUSHY LEATHER CHAIR IN the luxurious penthouse office of the most powerful media mogul in the country (maybe even the whole world), wondering what crazy quirk of fate had determined that said mogul should want to defend the same high-class madam that *I* had pledged to protect. (Well, it was a pretty bizarre situation, don't you think?) It took me a good half hour to gather my wits, ask the right questions, extract the true answers, and get to the mind-boggling bottom of things.

And here's what it all boiled down to: Harrington had known Sabrina during her debutante days. He was twelve years her senior—too old for her, he knew—but that hadn't stopped him from admiring her beauty and style. He took her out on a few dates, hoping she would find his maturity, keen mind, and vast wealth attractive, but she'd been more interested in the young, dark, and dangerous type. They remained friends for a while, but lost touch after he married and started his family.

Harrington didn't hear from Sabrina again until many years later, when she called to tell him about her new call girl enterprise. He'd been shocked to learn that she'd become a madam, but after she told him about her abusive husband, and the physical, emotional, and financial damage she'd suffered at his hands, he understood her motivation. And he approved of the "respectable" way she was running her business. And since he was a man with a healthy sexual appetite, a frigid wife, and a huge discretionary income, he soon signed on as a client.

Shortly after that, Sabrina introduced him to Melody. And he became so enamored with the beautiful young call girl that he started phoning Sabrina two or three times a week to schedule appointments with her. And as a result of those regular phone conversations, Harrington and Sabrina became friends again. At first they just talked about old times, but then they began having intimate chats about their personal and business lives—sharing confidences, offering and asking for advice, listening to each other's problems.

"And now I feel like a brother to Sabrina," Harrington concluded. "A very close and concerned older brother. And I don't want to see her get hurt by the sex-and-murder scandal that's about to rock the city. She doesn't deserve it. She's worked very hard to protect me and her other clients from the press and police, and I want to return the favor."

"But if you're so close to Sabrina, why didn't you call her after Melody was murdered?" I asked. "She was suffering a lot, and scared to death the killer might go after her other girls. She could have used some comforting and encouraging words from you, but you didn't call even once!"

"I was too devastated to speak with anybody," Harrington said, his massive shoulders falling into a slump. "Melody's death hit me really hard. I was so upset that I told my family I thought I was getting sick, and then I locked myself in my study for days, swilling bourbon, eating nothing, sleeping on the couch. It was a childish and cowardly thing to do, but I couldn't help myself. I didn't leave my study until late Friday morning, when I finally sobered up and dragged myself back to the office. That was the day you burst in and accused me of firing you."

"Right," I said, looking down at my lap, suddenly feeling ashamed of my brash behavior. "I'm sorry I made such a fuss."

"Don't be. You had a right to be angry and hurt. Pomeroy treated you very unfairly. He thought he was helping *me*, of course, but still . . . that's no excuse."

"How was hurting me supposed to help you?"

Harrington gave me a sad look. "I'm not proud of that part

of the story, Mrs. Turner, but here's what happened. Pomeroy
came to my home last Wednesday morning to ask me for a loan,
but found me drunk and sobbing in my study. I had learned
about Melody's murder on Tuesday—the day before the news
hit the papers—so I was in the depths of depression. Pomeroy
asked me what was wrong, and—too weak and stupid and inebriated to know what I was doing—I blubbered out a full confession.

"And *that*," he went on, "is why Pomeroy gave the Virginia
Pratt assignment to Mike Davidson instead of you. He knew that
you would conduct a thorough, relentless search for the truth,
and he was afraid that you'd uncover my infidelities in the process. He had you fired for the same reason. He wanted to derail
any thoughts you might have about investigating the story on
your own in order to save me and my family—and, by extension,
his family—from the ruination of a raging sex scandal. I didn't
know about any of this at the time, of course. I was too busy wal-
lowing in pain and self-pity and booze. As soon as I found out
about it, though, I told Crockett to give you your job back."

"Thanks a lot," I said.

If Harrington noticed my sarcastic tone, he didn't let on. He
just pushed his glasses higher on his nose, raised his bushy eyebrows, and said, "Now about that contract, Mrs. Turner. May I
have my lawyers draw up a draft for your approval?"

I sat quietly for a few seconds, giving the matter further
thought, coming to the realization that I was already in accord
with Harrington's terms. He had had nothing to do with the
murders of Virginia and Jocelyn, so I saw no earthly reason to
expose his private affairs to the public. And as for his brotherly
resolve to protect Sabrina . . . well, given the fact that I was determined to protect her myself, I certainly couldn't find fault
with that.

"Okay," I finally agreed. "Give me a buzz when it's ready."

ABBY THREW A SURPRISE ENGAGEMENT PARTY
for Dan and me that night. Well, it wasn't exactly a surprise,
since she called us both at work to tell us to be at her place at
seven, and it wasn't exactly a party, since Jimmy, Otto, Lenny,
Dan, and I were her only guests. What it was, actually, was an
engagement dinner—with an enormous turkey cooked by Abby,

and about a thousand potato pancakes cooked by Lenny's mother. (Lenny carried them across town in a suitcase.)

Oh, yeah, there was some champagne, too. Quite a few bottles, as I recall.

Abby had strung colorful Christmas lights all around her studio and decorated her kitchen table with a dark blue madras bedspread and a small vase of yellow mums. We dined by candlelight, listening to the hi-fi sounds of Thelonious Monk and the Modern Jazz Quartet. Everything was swell. With Otto curled up on my lap, and Dan's arm resting on the back of my chair, and my best friends gathered so closely around me, I would have been content to sit at that table forever.

Abby cleared the dishes and served the dessert and coffee (she wouldn't let me lift a finger!). Then, motioning for us to quiet down, she stood up and said, "It's time for another sweet treat, you dig? While I spent the day basting the bird, our soulful hero, Jimmy 'The Bard' Birmingham, was writing a poem for this engaging occasion. And he's going to read it for you now, kids, so listen up!"

Abby sat down and Jimmy stood up. Fingering his beard and looking slightly embarrassed, he took a crumpled piece of paper out of his hip pocket and began to read.

> *Slam pan man*
> *Doin what you can*
> *Hip hound*
> *A cool hot dog*
> *Blowin his tune*
> *Rockin and sockin*
> *With the mood*
> *Mother of toils*
> *Who told us so much*
> *How high to climb*
> *How low to fall*
> *All been written*
> *All been said*
> *Wrongfully repeated*
> *Often misread*
> *Happy endings inside my head*
> *A day anew*
> *A lot too few*

Umm . . . well, what can I say? There seemed to be a message in there somewhere, but I couldn't figure out what it was. But who cared what the words meant, anyway? They were written by Jimmy Birmingham! The grooviest poet in Greenwich Village! The original slam pan man! The man who, along with his cool hot dog, had snatched me from the jaws of death! It was the best poem I ever heard in my whole darn life, and if I live to be a hundred (which is beginning to seem like a distinct possibility), I will never hear another one like it. (Unless Jimmy writes a sequel tomorrow—which is also a distinct possibility.)

After the poem, the chocolate cake, the coffee, and several additional rounds of champagne, Abby put a stack of 45s on the record player and tried to get everybody up to dance. Lenny, Jimmy, and Otto joined her on the floor—cavorting to the beat of Chuck Berry's hot new single about a car named Maybellene—but Dan and I remained seated at the table, smooching, nuzzling, sighing, and making plans for the future.

We decided to get married in two weeks on the coast of Maine, in the small fishing village where Dan's parents lived. We would take Katy with us, of course, but after the brief ceremony in the office of the local justice of the peace, she would spend the rest of the weekend with her grandparents in their cozy cottage on the bay. The weather would be cold and wet this time of year, but Dan and I would be warm and happy— making love by the fire in the Marrytime Suite at the Moby Dick Inn.

We wouldn't be able to go on our honeymoon right away (I had a big story to write and Dan had two complex murder cases to wrap up, don't ya know), but we were looking forward to the spring, when we would squander the advance from my Harrington House contract on a fabulous two-week holiday in—where else?—Hawaii. (I wanted to see how my dream would come out.)

As we sat cuddling at the table, sipping champagne and watching our goofy friends rock around the clock with Bill Haley and The Comets, I finally screwed up the courage to tell Dan that I had decided to keep my job at *Daring Detective*. I thought he was going to flip out and start yelling at me—maybe even (gasp!) threaten to break off our engagement—but I was wrong. He just gave me a sexy wink and said, "Look, I'll be moving in with you soon, Paige, and I intend to keep a *very* close eye on you and keep you out of trouble. So if you want to hold on to your job, it's fine with me. Just promise me one thing. No more unsolved murder stories, okay? No more dangerous investigations. No more chasing killers and meddling in police business. No more telling lies and keeping secrets."

That sounded like *six* things to me, but I was in no mood to argue. "Don't worry, babe," I said. "I learned my lesson this time. I really like my life—especially now that I'll be spending it with you—and I won't risk it again. I promise you my sidewalk sleuthing days are over. For good."

I meant it then, and I still mean it now. I'm going to stay in the office and stay out of danger—even if it kills me. I'm going to make coffee and clip newspapers and write in-house stories only. And no matter what happens—no matter how curious or fixated on a breaking murder story I become—I am never, ever, ever going to play detective again.

Honest.

About the Author

Amanda Matetsky has been an editor of many magazines in the entertainment field and a volunteer tutor and fundraiser for Literacy Volunteers of America. Her first novel, *The Perfect Body*, won the NJRW Golden Leaf Award for Best First Book. Amanda lives in Middletown, New Jersey, with her husband, Harry, and their two cats, Homer and Phoebe, in a house full of old movie posters, original comic strip art, and books—lots of books. You can visit the author online at www.amandamatetsky.com.

Cozy up with Berkley Prime Crime

SUSAN WITTIG ALBERT
*Don't miss the nationally bestselling
series featuring herbalist China Bayles.*

LAURA CHILDS
*The Tea Shop Mysteries are the
toast of Charleston, South Carolina.*

KATE KINGSBURY
*The Pennyfoot Hotel Mystery
series is a teatime delight.*

**For the armchair
detective in you.**

penguin.com

M6G020